Ash Street

Ash Street

Lee Thomas

Published by
Sinister Grin Press
Austin, TX
www.sinistergrinpress.com

November 2012

Cover Art by Kyushik Shin
www.shinybrush.com

Cover Design by Shane McKenzie
Type and Interior Design by Brian Cartwright

Acknowledgements

For their talent and inspiration, I'd like to thank the Heart of Texas Horror Group: Nate Southard, Wrath James White, Joe McKinney, Rhodi Hawk, Shane McKenzie, Hank Schwaeble, Bev Vincent, Boyd Harris, Ed Kurtz, and Megan Zimmerman.

Similarly I'd like to recognize the VCFA Circle of Death (in no particular order)—Donald, Jennifer, Phillip, Courtney, Mathieu, Kali, Mike, Ian, Timmy, Shawn, Christine, Jacqueline, Greg, Hollie, Mandy, John, Catherine, and Jane—because… damn… these are some talented folks.

Many thanks to Shane and Travis of Sinister Grin Press for taking on *Ash Street*, and putting it in your hands.

Finally, thanks to my ever-enduring partner, John Perry, for the whole bottle and then a drop.

Dedicated to Peter Straub

ASH STREET

"Grief fills the room up of my absent child, lies in his bed, walks up and down with me, puts on his pretty looks, repeats his words."

—*King John*. William Shakespeare.

"No one ever told me that grief felt so like fear."

—C. S. Lewis

My name is Alan Means, and I don't sleep well…

The Fire

The little girl ran up the stairs and the old man followed, splashing gasoline as he climbed. The house was dark, and the girl's clothes, a red blouse and blue jeans, appeared as fluid smudges against the gloom; her brown hair, a drape woven from the shadows, was visible only in its motion. The man's chest ached. He clutched the plastic gas can—one of four he'd brought to the property—in fingers knotted with arthritis. The heavy container pulled at his arm, causing his shoulder to grind painfully in the socket. The man rocked his arm back and cast another spray of the flammable liquid on the staircase. A cramp pinched behind his ribs, and he stopped to grasp the banister. Setting the gas can on the edge of a stair he bent over to rest his joints and catch his breath. A tide of gasoline vapor soured the air he was struggling to breathe. Ahead, the little girl continued to climb until she reached the landing above, and then she peered down on him, a concerned mask floating in the gloom. The man took three deep breaths and the cramp in his chest faded to a dull ache.

"I don't think I can make it," he said.

"You have to try," the little girl replied. "You just have to."

"Why are we doing this?" he asked, suddenly unable to recall the sequence of events that had brought him to this miserable house.

"You know why," she said. "You know what they did."

Yes, he thought. *That's right. This is where they lived.*

The gas fumes insisted on his attention, blocking out the odors of dust and garbage. For a moment he swooned and nearly lost his grip on the banister, but he steadied himself. *Only a few stairs left,* he thought.

Once the lightheadedness passed, he gripped the handle of the gas can tightly and with the other hand he pulled himself upward. Only a little ways to go.

Those terrible people had lived here. Those monsters. It had to burn. The house shouldn't have been allowed to stand this long.

"Hurry," the little girl whined. "You have to hurry."

"I'm trying," he said before gasping for his next breath.

"You promised," she said

"I promised."

Ash Street

The little girl reached out her hand, but the old man didn't take it. He was afraid that if he released his grip on the banister, he would crumple and roll down the stairs. Instead he swung the gas can again, splashed the upstairs hallway. The girl backed away from the droplets. He hoisted himself with a final aching pull and reached the landing. Again, he paused to catch his breath.

"We have to hurry," the girl insisted.

"I'm trying, honey," he said. "I really am."

"It's almost done."

"I know."

A scratching sound from below made the little girl gasp. She backed against the wall and clutched herself as if very cold. The noise came again; this time louder. Closer.

"They're coming," the girl said in a hushed and frightened tone.

The old man turned to look down the stairs. There was nothing below but shadows and ghosts of moonlight swimming through murky windows. The scratching came again like fingernails being dragged over the dusty wooden floor at the foot of the staircase, and he should have seen its maker in the light creeping through the windows beside the front door, but he saw nothing.

The oddity of the situation frightened him as much as the noise itself. He backed to the wall and the gas can fell from his weakened fingers. It hit the boards with a *thump* but didn't tip.

A cramp came up in his chest. It felt like a fist had clamped one of the muscles on his right side mercilessly. The right side? That was good, wasn't it? Not the heart?

"Hurry," the girl said. "Please."

"Just a moment, honey," he said, trying to sound amused so the little girl wouldn't worry about him. He closed his eyes against the pain and stretched his arm over his head hoping to relieve a bit of the cramp's tension. He took two deep breaths and the worst of the pain subsided.

From the lowest step came a frantic scratching like a dog trying to dig its way through the floorboards. The girl shrieked and raced down the hall away from him. The darkness engulfed her in seconds, leaving the old man alone on the landing, squinting after her into the gloom. His heart tripped like a metronome suddenly advanced to double time.

"Don't run off," he called. "Don't leave me here."

The scrabbling on the steps grew louder. Whatever made that terrible sound was climbing toward him.

The old man reached for the gas can and struggled to wrap his aching fingers around the molded plastic handle. He tugged but couldn't get the thing off the floor. His shoulder, his fingers, his chest, his hips—everything hurt so badly. He could hardly breathe. The girl would be so disappointed if he failed, but his body refused the task.

He straightened up and the cramp returned. Infuriated by his weakness, the old man kicked out and knocked the gas can on its side. He heard the liquid *glugging* out onto the floor. The reek of petroleum stung his nostrils, and he backed away.

The scratching on the stairs grew louder. He put his hands over his ears to block out the frightening racket and stumbled backward down the hall. Working his way deeper into the darkness, the gloom hardened around him, grew tangible, creating resistance for his complaining muscles.

What am I doing here? he asked himself again. *It's late. I should be home in bed, or at least sitting in my chair with a glass of brandy. I don't belong here. No one belongs here. This is a place for dead things. This was* their *place.* On the tail of these thoughts came another: *It belonged to them, and it has to burn.*

He took a hand from his ear and discovered the scratching sound had ceased. Quickly, he shoved his hand in his pocket, and his fingertips tapped the top of his lighter. It had been a gift from his daughter. She'd given it to him, even though she hated his cigars.

Thinking of his daughter, the old man grimaced bitterly. He hadn't been very good to his family over the years. Maybe this could make up for some of his neglect.

He unfolded his clenching fingers as best he could and managed to work the lighter free of his pocket. With great effort he pulled the lighter's cap back. Then he positioned his thumb on the roller.

"Oh hell," he muttered.

"What's wrong?"

The little girl stood at his side. He didn't know where she'd come from. The last time he'd seen her she had run into the darkness on the other side of the landing. How had she managed to make it around to join him?

"Hurry," she whined.

"We won't be able to get out," he said. "We have to go downstairs before we light it."

"There isn't time," the girl told him.

Her little hand shot out and snatched the lighter from his crippled fingers. Then she was running to the center of the landing, back to the head of the stairs. A tear of flame leapt from the silver lighter, casting yellow light on her pretty young face.

"Don't," he called. "Honey, we'll be trapped."

"Thank you, grandpa," the little girl said.

She dropped the lighter to the gasoline soaked floor. The liquid ignited with a thundering flare, and the house went from dark to brilliantly lit. A trail of flames raced down the staircase and blossomed across the ground floor. A blast of heat sent the old man back several more steps as he stared with dread at the landing.

The little girl—his granddaughter, his Dory—stood in a pool of fire. Flames rose to her shoulders, but they didn't ignite her clothes or her skin. Smoke from the burning boards swept up around her, billowing like a charcoal sheet at her back. Against this backdrop, her lovely face changed. It hardened. The features drew sharp with displeasure, rather than pain.

"Dory!" he called.

"You should have been watching me," the little girl shouted over the sounds of the fire. "You should have been watching!"

"I know," he cried.

"You let them take me. You let them bring me here."

"Dory," he called pathetically, unable to conjure any sufficient words of apology. "Dory, please."

But the little girl was gone. She'd been gone for three years now.

His mind spun with the realization. The disease that ate his mind had gotten the better of him again. Another goddamn "incident." Suddenly he couldn't remember where he was or why he'd come here, but he smelled gasoline and saw flames, and the disorienting fear that accompanied his all-too-frequent spells hardened in his veins.

What have I done?

The old man fell to his knees as a wave of blazing air crashed over him. He tried to regain his footing, but the effort was just too much. His aching shoulder gave out, and he fell to the boards. The old man rolled onto his back, telling himself he needed a second, just one second, to allow his strength to return. Smoke ran like a foul river along the ceiling. The boards on his back were already baking hot as the fire rose from below. The cramp in his chest tightened. His eyes filled with tears. The salty liquid pooled then spilled out to run in rivulets toward his ears. He sobbed and gasped for breath until the air turned so hot it seared his throat and lungs.

The old man died moments before the fire came through the floor for him.

Part 1
The Scarlet Letter

1

Police Detective Stuart Lancaster looked forward to breakfast on Friday mornings. He woke thirty minutes earlier than usual, left the box of granola in the cupboard, and drove into town for eggs and sausage at Teddy's. The eggs were scrambled, buttery and light. The sausage was of the plump and savory variety the British called bangers, and Teddy's was the only place in Barnard that served them. Though certainly part of his regimen, Stuart considered these breakfasts a daring break in his routine. Dr. Flynn had warned him about cholesterol, hence the usual morning fare of orange juice, wheat toast, and cereal, but at forty-nine, Stuart's health was sterling, and he'd said farewell to his share of vices over the years. He'd be damned if he was giving up his Friday breakfasts.

Except for the sausage, Teddy's was unexceptional. The walls were painted an off-white that had yellowed over the years. Three neatly spaced ceiling fans spun, sluggishly moving around air scented liberally by coffee, frying potatoes, old tobacco and the grease from a thousand hamburgers. The original owner had been named Teddy, naturally, and he'd been a television buff. Eight by ten glossies of former celebrities, some familiar and some Stuart had never been able to identify checkered the wall behind the counter and ran in columns down the narrow strips between the windows. Stuart sat in a booth by a window, newspaper open, coffee steaming in a white porcelain mug. Morning light showered his left side, bathing a cracked and chipped Formica tabletop the color of watermelon meat. There, in his favorite booth, he drank his coffee in the company of Barney Miller, Maude, Jim Rockford, and Mike Brady. They smiled out at him from the wall on the other side of the table.

Teddy's daughter, Monica, had taken over the restaurant eighteen years ago after a massive coronary had sent Teddy face down in the fryer. Monica hadn't changed a thing, except the prices.

A screen door creaked and Stuart looked up from his paper to see his buddy, Harlan, Teague step into the restaurant. The man was short, barely five-foot-six with a round body and a rounder head. Teague looked like someone had yanked the top two tiers off of a snowman, slapped legs and arms on, and then dressed the whole thing up to look like an unimaginative banker vacationing in Cabo. Today, Teague's shirt was olive drab, and the sleeves stretched over his biceps like they were giving birth to his arms. Even at a distance, Stuart could see there was something different about the man. His hair was shorter, and he seemed to be growing a beard.

"Stuart," Harlan said, strutting toward the booth. "Got room for me?"

"Maybe if you dropped fifty pounds."

Harlan flipped Stuart off and said, "Drop this, asshole."

"Pull up a seat."

"What's the news?" Harlan asked, nodding at the paper. He slipped behind the table, his chest cutting against its edge.

"Same old. Car bombs. Celebrity DUIs and some conservative senator got himself filmed with a male prostitute, doing not-so-conservative things."

"Saw that on YouTube. They only broadcast the first few minutes. Apparently, Senator Jones was a naughty talker. I guess the rest of it went hardcore, and we'll have to wait for the DVD."

"What a wonderful world."

"Believe it." Harlan smiled, and Stuart noticed something else had changed about his friend's appearance.

Years ago, Harlan had lost a couple of teeth in a bar fight. Some drunk bubba with fists as big as softballs had sucker punched Harlan, knocking out a molar and bicuspid on his upper jaw. Harlan had managed to recover from the blow in seconds and return a few of his own. The bubba ended up at Barnard General for four days, and still walked around with his eyes half-lidded. Though he could easily afford it, Harlan hadn't bothered getting the teeth replaced, preferring to call the gap a trophy of battle. Now, the gap was gone, replaced by shiny white bridgework.

"When did you get your teeth fixed?" Stuart asked.

"Been to the mouth guy a few times over the last month," Harlan said. "Got tired of chewing on the left side."

"A haircut, too," Stuart noted.

"Yeah, I'm all kinds of pretty these days," Harlan replied. He turned in the booth, his belly pushing the table toward Stuart. Harlan waved at Margaret, their usual waitress, and pointed at Stuart's coffee cup.

"Right there," Margaret called.

"You got plans tomorrow night?" Harlan asked.

"Nothing important."

"Good. Gretta's out. She's doing this dance recital thing with her students. I snuck some steaks into the freezer, and I'm thinking they need a grillin'. All of her vegetarian crap is shrinking my dick."

"Sounds good." After momentary consideration, Stuart added, "The steak part."

They sat quietly until Harlan's coffee arrived. Margaret, a woman with wheat-colored hair, set it down in front of him and topped off Stuart's mug from a pot.

"The usual?" she asked.

"Why change a good thing?" Stuart replied.

Ash Street

"Hey," Harlan said, pressing forward against the table. Over his shoulder, Mike Brady grinned. "I heard they found a body in that torch-job over on Ash Street."

"Yeah," Stuart said. He drank some coffee and leaned back in the booth. That was a sad business. "The old guy's daughter said he'd been losing it lately. Early onset Alzheimer's. He'd been going through some delusional periods. Can't imagine what was going on in his head."

"You knew him didn't you?"

"Not well," Stuart said.

He'd met Alan Means a few times. The first time he'd encountered the poor old guy, Means had been bawling his eyes out. His granddaughter had been one of the first victims of Selma Baxter and Derek Thomason: a couple of lunatics who'd used the house on Ash Street as their personal torture chamber. Means had been beside himself, all but ranting. Apparently, he'd been babysitting when Dory Addison had been snatched from the front yard of her parent's home. Stuart saw Means sporadically during the investigation, but their interactions were limited, shaded and defined by Stuart's professional detachment. They met again under circumstances far more personal to Stuart.

His wife, Clarissa, had been Baxter and Thomason's tenth victim. The department shrink had suggested Stuart join a grief management group to discuss what had happened to her, and his superior Captain Gann had made it an unofficial order.

He'd become reacquainted with Alan Means in a gray-walled room at the Barnard Community Health Center, in a counseling group run by a woman named Hannah Bolger. Even then he'd carried on only the most superficial conversations with Alan. The older man had lost his granddaughter. Stuart had lost his wife. They shared tragedy and nothing else. It wasn't the kind of thing you built a lasting friendship from, at least Stuart didn't.

"Well, you have to be glad the place is gone."

"It's just a house," Stuart replied. But that was a lie.

It wasn't just a house any more than Columbine was just a school or Jonestown was just a compound. Terrible things had happened under that roof. Over the course of eighteen months Selma Baxter and Derek Thomason had lured eleven victims to the basement of that place, brutalized and humiliated them sometimes for days before they had gotten bored and ended the torment with murder. Stuart had worked the case for over a year, then had been pulled off of it a month before it broke: the day after being summoned to the morgue to identify his wife's remains.

"I heard the city was going to raze the thing in a few weeks anyhow," Harlan said.

"Heard that, too."

The city council had gotten fed up with the serial killer fanatics visiting the site and trying to break in for bits of grisly memorabilia. Stuart was disgusted by the whole circus. The two killers had been treated like movie stars. Already, a made-for-tv movie had aired and another film was in production. Barnard's city council wanted the property demolished and after a long legal battle with the property's owner, had finally managed to settle on an amount. In a couple of weeks the financial matters would have been closed, and the bulldozers were scheduled to arrive before the ink dried on the contracts.

"You don't want to talk about this do you?" Harlan said. "You're turning frog-colored."

Margaret appeared. She set plates of food shimmering with grease in front of them. Stuart's stomach kicked happily from the smell. Despite the welcoming scent of his breakfast, Stuart's mind was elsewhere, in a less pleasant place.

"Sometimes you're not as far from a thing as you thought you were." Stuart rubbed the back of his neck with his palm. "These days, I've stopped wondering why Clarissa isn't there when I wake up in the middle of the night, but I'll see something or hear something, and like a flash I'm just getting the news again."

"Two years isn't so long," Harlan said. "But it's also long enough. I know you're getting out there and dating a bit, but you're not really taking it seriously. You should find someone before you get too old to fuck."

"We can't all be as charming as you," Stuart said, toasting his round friend with a forkful of eggs. "Besides, you're older than I am."

"I'm atypically handsome," Harlan said, his voice deadpan. "And rich. You are neither atypically handsome nor rich. The clock's ticking for you, buddy."

"Are you going to eat breakfast or do you just want to make me feel like shit all morning?"

"Got both covered. I'm multi-tasking."

Stuart chuckled, and when Harlan smirked at him, the recent addition of teeth again struck him. Stuart figured it was a mid-life crisis thing; everyone went through it. Stuart seemed to be going through a phase himself, dating a variety of women, some half his age, though as he often said, "Dating was really too strong a word for it." There was certainly no harm in Harlan doing a bit of personal renovation before the roof fell in.

The chat they shared over breakfast was similar to a hundred other chats they'd had. Harlan spoke in reverence about his girlfriend, Gretta, whom he'd lived with for just over five years. He spoke with disdain over politics and sports because he was a democrat and his Astros were having a crap season. Food and coffee vanished, the latter frequently replenished by Margaret's pot.

The call came as Stuart dropped a twenty on the table to pay the check.

Ash Street

It was his week to buy. Harlan was discussing a television program Stuart hadn't seen when the cell phone interrupted the conversation.

He took the call and slid out of the booth. His partner, David Ballard, was calling from the scene of a homicide. It was nasty. *Get your ass up here.*

"You got work?" Harlan asked.

"Got a dead guy," Stuart said.

"Nice way to start the weekend."

"I'll call you later."

Barnard, Texas had a year-round population of one hundred and fifty thousand people, give or take, and when university classes were in full swing, the number of souls increased by ten percent. Tracing the city limits on a map would result in a shape very much like an anvil; bordered by a lake scooping out the west side of the town and a forest, primarily cedar, scooping out the east. New housing and retail construction—void of both style and soul—rapidly filled the flared northern area, and long-established residential neighborhoods the "heart of Barnard" covered the southeastern quadrant, running from the business district in the center of town down to Carter Park and the Guingol River. Stuart's house was there. His family had lived in Barnard for generations, though he'd not followed in the family business—his father had sold the butcher shop when Stuart was eighteen and moved to Florida. Where once there had been fishing shacks and functional cottages, mansions now surrounded the lake, providing marvelous views of the water and the hill country beyond to the owners, while simultaneously denying them to casual passersby. Like its neighbor to the south, Austin, Barnard had benefited from the tech explosion of the last three decades, and served as home to nearly thirty software companies, component manufacturers, video game design firms, and information storage businesses. In the evenings hipsters and high-tech hippies joined college students on Brown Street, where fancy watering holes and trendy restaurants had sprung up next to landmark establishments like Bob's Chile Bowl, "Where you go to get your tongue blistered;" Miriam's Pies, "Nothin' but good in here;" and Crazy Fran's Beer Hall.

Stuart drove through the Beresford District where the wealthy residents kept their palaces and continued up into the hills. He tried to not think about the house on Ash Street and the miseries, both abstract and intimate, the place called to mind. Baxter and Thomason were off the streets. They would remain in prison for the rest of their natural lives with zero chance of parole, and now, thanks to Alan Means and fifty bucks worth of gasoline, the house was gone.

After ten minutes Stuart arrived at a familiar wrought iron gate, gaping open, and he drove through it toward a sprawling multi-leveled house. Stuart hadn't immediately recognized the address the dispatcher had recited, but he'd been here before—two-and-a-half years ago; the news hadn't been good then either.

The architectural style was what folks called Texas Tuscan. Boxy wings surrounded a peaked turret. The tiled roof alone cost more than Stuart's whole house. Thick vegetation landscaped the sides of the yard, providing privacy for the owners. Stuart parked behind one of the police cruisers in the drive and pulled off his sunglasses, dropping them on the driver's seat before he closed the door of his car.

Two uniformed officers, McNeal and Ingram, greeted Stuart casually. McNeal took a final puff from a cigarette and knocked the cherry off to be crushed under his shoe. The officer should have known better than to be smoking at a crime scene, and Stuart considered pointing this out, but a buried craving leapt out and knotted in Stuart's stomach, distracting him.

He'd smoked his last cigarette the night of Clarissa's funeral, swearing he'd never touch one again. Clarissa had been on him to quit for years, but he'd only accommodated the request once she was dead. He looked at this abstinence as a form of deathbed promise, and it was this thinking that had kept him away from cigarettes for nearly two years, but right now the urge to bum a butt off of McNeal hit him hard.

"Detective Lancaster," said McNeal.

"What have we got?"

McNeal, with his burly build and square head, looked like a golem in street blues. He straightened his shoulders as if being called to attention. Ingram was also tall, but his face was smooth and tanned and looked like it belonged in a fashion magazine. Ingram stepped to the far side of the doorway, allowing McNeal to take the stage.

"Ingram and I were first on the scene," the officer said. "The wife called it in at eight-twenty-two. Arriving at the scene we found a Caucasian male, approximately fifty years old, lying face down in the kitchen. Cause of death appears to be multiple stab wounds. The wife has identified the victim as Pudge Taylor, the home's owner."

Stuart nodded. The name wasn't a surprise so much as a confirmation. He knew the Taylor's, shared a similar painful history with them. Pudge Taylor came from oil money, and the man counted the mayor of Barnard and the governor of the state among his buddies. Taylor had three children. Two boys and a girl named Ella. Ella had been eighteen when she'd met Derek Thomason at a party. Nineteen hadn't been in the cards for her. She'd been Thomason and Baxter's eighth victim.

Multiple lacerations and contusions.

Multiple stab wounds to the thighs and sternum (pre- and post-mortem).

Sexual assault: vaginal, anal

Cause of death: gunshot (shotgun) to the head.

Neither Pudge nor his wife, Colleen, had attended Hannah Bolger's grief-counseling group, but Stuart knew them well enough from his investigation.

"Does the wife have an alibi?"

"Yes, sir," McNeal said. "Colleen Taylor attended a seven a.m. Pilates class at the Aloe Ranch Day Spa. It checks out. When she came home, she found the victim and called it in."

David Ballard appeared in the doorway behind McNeal, emerging from the darkness of the house like smoke. Ballard was another detective with the BPD and Stuart's partner. They had worked together for twelve years and despite sharing duties and similar interests, they were not close friends. Ballard's history included two ex-wives, both of whom detested the man they'd married; a number of departmental reprimands for cultural insensitivity and sexual harassment, which led to Ballard's officially mandated therapy sessions and an ongoing regimen of mood stabilizers. The guy was okay, and these days he certainly behaved himself, but Stuart and Ballard's personalities simply didn't click.

"The victim's getting cold," Ballard said before turning around and fading back into the gloom.

Stuart thanked McNeal and Ingram and walked into the mansion's foyer, which was as cold as an icebox. Though he'd spent little time in the Taylor's home during the investigation of their daughter's murder, he remembered the place well—from the gleaming travertine marble floors to the wrought iron chandelier. The walls were a burnt yellow with dirty orange blotches—a faux finish job to make the place look tastefully weathered. Stuart stepped into the living room and noted the place seemed to have no doors. In their places, stone arches separated the rooms, and Stuart was reminded of caves or catacombs; the chill in the air only added to this impression. Someone had sprayed the place down with air freshener recently. The floral odor rode on an underlying chemical scent. Ballard passed beneath an archway to enter a sprawling dining room and Stuart followed.

They continued walking until they reached the kitchen. Half a dozen of his colleagues worked the scene. Ballard loomed over an island at its center with a slate tile surface. His head cocked to the left, indicating Pudge Taylor's corpse.

The man lived up to his name. Stuart remembered Pudge being an imposing figure, but the last couple of years had seen the man swell from stout to just plain fat. Lying face down on the tile amid a considerable pool of blood, he resembled a professional wrestler down for the count, except Pudge was naked and his lower back was covered with a nest of puckered wounds and coagulating blood. His belly bulged from beneath him as if it had tried to ooze away once its master was killed. Trails of blood ran down the man's buttocks and the back of his legs. The soles of his feet carried a thick stain of the stuff. Stuart checked the floor on the far side of the island and saw a number of red footprints, like dance step templates, stomped in a small circular pattern amid freckles and blotches of scarlet. Pudge's face rested in this chaotic design. One glassy blue eye was turned upward so Stuart could see the emptiness behind it. Though disturbed by the dead man's stare, Stuart would not allow himself to look away immediately, because Stuart saw a question there, and it was the question he always encountered in the eyes of the murdered: *Can you help me?*

I'll try, Stuart thought.

It was a mental game he'd played with himself since he'd started on the force. Of course, in those early and ridiculously naïve days his answer had been invariably positive and emphatic. *Yes, I will help you. I will find your killer and they will be punished for what they did to you. I can do that.* But over the years he'd learned to temper these promises to the dead.

Stuart stepped back and took in the rest of the room as he began piecing together a likely scenario. The blood expert would be along to document, photograph, and report on her findings, suggesting the likely movements of both the victim and his killer once the red let loose, but Stuart didn't think it would take an expert to put this one together.

Pudge had been at the refrigerator. He woke up and came downstairs for breakfast or maybe just a cup of coffee. He went to the fridge, and the rest was pain, confusion, and fear.

"What have you got?" Stuart asked.

Ballard looked away from the body and fixed his cool green eyes on Stuart. Then he shrugged. "Not much. The victim's wife said nothing seems to be missing."

"Could still be a robbery gone wrong," Stuart noted aloud. "The intruder could have run into Pudge before he got to work."

"True enough."

Stuart walked around the side of the island, away from the body. He stopped at the far corner and examined the bloody footprints.

Pudge Taylor had been panicked. (*Who wouldn't be after having a knife slid into them?*) The prints on the floor, all seeming to come from the same pair of enormous bare feet, were smeared and seemingly directionless. Pudge hadn't known what to do or where to go, but considering the placement of the body, he'd finally decided to try an escape. Stuart peered over the edge of the counter and looked at the dead man's profile.

"There might have been two perps," Stuart said.

"Yeah?" Ballard replied blandly as if bored with the whole scene.

"Taylor was initially assaulted at the refrigerator," Stuart continued, voicing the scenario playing out in his head. "The guy came up behind him and got in a couple of jabs. Taylor panicked, tried to figure out what was happening. Finally, he tried to get away from the guy, and he made it halfway across the kitchen, but then he stopped and turned around, heading back toward the refrigerator. That's why his head is down here with the footprints. He was going for the door and saw a second intruder, someone that scared him more than the one he was fleeing."

"Makes sense," Ballard agreed. "What doesn't make sense is why we only have one set of footprints in that mess, and those belong to the victim. There are over a dozen holes in Taylor's back, and he didn't get all of them before he decided to run. So how was the perp able to inflict multiple wounds on a moving target and avoid stepping in the guy's blood?"

Good question, Stuart thought. "Where's the widow?"

Colleen Taylor sat hunched in a chair, face in hands and hair draping forward over her fingers. The sheer white curtains behind her had been drawn and morning light played against them, creating a screen of glare at her back. Stuart approached her and took up a position beside a pumpkin-colored chaise lounge. Ballard walked to the woman's side and stood over her like a guard. When Colleen looked up, her eyes were red and swollen from crying. She had a round and well-featured face, though her pageboy hairstyle looked a bit dowdy. Thick at the hips and thighs and small breasted, she was a pleasant looking woman, if not the glossy trophy bride Stuart expected of an oil heir's wife.

His first thought upon seeing Colleen was: *She murdered her husband.* This consideration had nothing to do with the evidence, the woman's posture or demeanor; Stuart couldn't even put it down to a gut feeling. It was simply another mental callisthenic he performed to stay sharp. In truth, he didn't believe Colleen Taylor had anything to do with her husband's death, not yet anyway, but being Pudge's wife made her a suspect and statistically speaking a good one. The idea of her guilt helped balance Stuart's overwhelming empathy for the woman. He'd been in her position before, and it had been like swallowing glass.

"Mrs. Taylor," Stuart said.

"Mr. Lancaster," Colleen Taylor said.

"Detective Lancaster," Stuart corrected softly. "I know this is a difficult time, but we'd like you to tell us what happened."

Colleen sniffed and produced a wad of tissue. She scrubbed it across her irritated nose. "I already told…" Another sniff.

"We understand," Ballard said, his voice dry and cold. "But we need to hear it in your own words, and we'll need to get a formal statement."

Stuart winced at his partner's mechanical tone. Not so much as a hint of sympathy or concern flavored his words, and Stuart attributed this to his partner's medications. The pills had doused a number of fires raging in Ballard's head, and Stuart had to commend his partner's commitment to improving himself, but the cold voice struck a discordant note with Stuart.

After Clarissa's murder, Stuart had sat on the other side of this interaction, and it had given him a perspective no training class ever could. Though he knew it was important to gather information fast so leads didn't grow cold, he couldn't help but feel his friends on the force had been intruding on his grief, badgering him when he should have been thinking about his wife, and he'd felt a pronounced distance from his fellow officers following those interrogations.

"Please, Mrs. Taylor, it's very important," Stuart said.

She regarded him with large brown eyes melting beneath a sheen of tears. After nodding, she repeated the story Stuart had already heard from Officer McNeal. There was no detail, no embellishment. Colleen Taylor woke up, drove to her friend Rachel Cobb's house to pick the woman up. Together they went to an early Pilates class. She dropped Cobb off, returned straight home, and found her husband dead on the kitchen floor.

"Do you have a housekeeper?" Ballard asked when the widow had finished. "A gardener? Anyone who has access to the house?"

"Of course."

"We'll need a list of names and their contact information."

"Pudge," Colleen said softly, shaking her head.

"Mrs. Taylor," Stuart began.

"Colleen," the woman corrected.

"Colleen, then, do you know of anyone who might want to see harm come to you or your husband?"

"No."

"He was a wealthy man with some powerful connections, are you certain he never mentioned any…?"

"No," Colleen snapped.

The response took Stuart off guard. Naturally the widow was grieving and lashing out, but it was that very thing that sent alarms off in his head. Colleen's husband had been brutally murdered, wouldn't she be trying to make sense of the whole thing? Pointing fingers. Identifying some target for her pain? Stuart had done so blindly after Clarissa's body had been found on the side of the highway. He'd blamed everyone: his colleagues on the police force, for not having caught the sadistic killers; the media who'd turned a series of inhuman crimes into entertainment television; Clarissa's brother, Phil, for not calling to let Stuart know his sister had never made it to his apartment; and of course, more than anyone else Stuart had blamed himself. But Colleen Taylor made no accusations, whether they be legitimate or inspired by anguish. It seemed odd, seemed wrong.

"Do you have any firearms in the house?" Ballard asked the widow.

"Of course," Colleen replied.

"What do you mean 'of course?'" Stuart asked.

"This is Texas," she replied. "Pudge kept at least a dozen different guns around the place, but I don't understand the question. Was my husband shot as well?"

"No ma'am," Ballard replied. "It's a standard question. We'll want an inventory of those to make sure the perpetrator didn't take them. Now, do you keep the house locked?"

"We didn't used to," Colleen said. She looked across the room, and her chin dipped as if nodding to someone. Stuart turned but saw nothing in the archway or the room beyond. "But after Ella—after Baxter and Thomason—we got in the habit of keeping the door locked. I hated it. I don't think a place is much worth living in if you have to lock it up."

"What about security?" Stuart asked. "Do you have a monitoring system? Cameras?"

"I'd think if I did, we'd be watching those tapes right now instead of sitting here," Colleen said. "Pudge wouldn't hear of cameras or anything of the sort. We talked about it once, and he threw a fit, saying he wasn't about to be spied on in his own home. Pudge liked his privacy. He was adamant about it. Once, he bought one of those computers with the camera built in, and he kept the lens covered with a post-it note because he didn't know who might be watching." The corner of Colleen's mouth notched up into a pained sneer and she shook her head. "We have the alarm system, but I turn it off when I get up in the mornings."

"And your husband didn't say anything to you recently about trouble with his businesses, employees, or anyone he might have had a disagreement with? Anything at all?"

"No."

"You're certain?" Stuart pressed.

"Do you find repetition effective?" Colleen asked, "Or do you just find it as annoying as I do?"

"Mrs. Taylor, we're…"

"I know what you're trying to do," she blurted, rising from the chair to face Stuart. "I know. I *know*. But my husband is dead and all I want to do is cry because there isn't anything I can do about it *except* cry, and I'm tired. Most of my family is gone. My husband is gone. And I'm tired. Tired. Tired. You have to know how that feels, Detective Lancaster. *You* have to."

Stuart took a step back, conscious of Ballard's eyes on him. The distraught woman was begging them for time to mourn, asking for nothing but basic courtesy. He understood completely, but that didn't change the job or his responsibility.

"Mrs. Taylor, I do understand how you feel," he said. "Now if you'd please sit down; we have a few more questions."

2

Michael Addison walked out of school during his lunch period. The still air was desert-hot and dry, and he wanted an ice-cold bottle of cola or a Red Bull. Any other Friday and he would have had to endure another three and a half hours in class before the final bell rang. Today would be worse.

Today was his grandfather's funeral, and he'd gladly trade out of that event for another ten hours in class. Another hundred.

He scratched at his shoulder. The cut there was healed well enough, but it itched liked a curse, and it *was* a curse, he knew. Further, he knew he deserved it.

Walking along the white concrete path toward the student parking lot, Michael tried to clear his mind. He still blamed himself for what had happened to his grandfather and yes, he knew his grandfather had been full on brainsick before he'd gone gasoline shopping and lit up the place on Ash Street. His grandfather had Alzheimer's and hadn't been able to think straight for a long time.

One night a little over four months ago, Michael had woken in the middle of the night. A noise from the living room downstairs had startled him, and he'd climbed out of bed to see what was going on. Sneaking to the top of the stairs, he'd heard his grandfather calling, "Dory," at the top of his lungs. "Dory, that's quite enough. You come inside. You come inside, right now!" Michael's mom had appeared a minute later and told him to go back to bed before hurrying downstairs to tend to her father. The fact that his grandfather's mental expiration date was fast approaching was no surprise, but Mike still felt responsible for what had happened to his granddad. Mike should have never gone into that house, and more importantly, he never should have told his granddad what he'd seen there.

Of course, he'd felt responsible for what had happened to Dory, too.

He still did.

Three years now and he couldn't shake the awful feeling. The little girl who liked playing UNO and reading stories with unicorns in them and eating mint chocolate chip ice cream, the little girl who called her older brother "Mik-Mik," had been taken from the front yard, as Mik-Mik sat up in his room, playing a video game—immersed in the shocking gloom of a fictional world, while his sister was taken away in the real one. Yeah, his grandfather had insisted on watching Dory. The old guy had made a big production about it over lunch that day, assuring Michael's mom that he wouldn't let the girl out of his sight.

But Dory had slipped out when Grandpa Alan fell asleep on the sofa. It shouldn't have mattered. She was ten years old, more than old enough to play unsupervised in her own front yard.

Abducted. Murdered. *Fuck.*

Michael shook his head and crossed the parking lot. For months after his kid sister's death, a thick emotional paste made of equal parts anger, grief, and fear had filled his veins, occasionally clotting painfully in his heart. He'd come out of that period convinced that life wasn't simply unfair; it was fucking cruel. Unfair suggested indifference, but life wasn't indifferent, it was a calculating villain, always watching, always testing, always waiting to strike in some new and completely vicious way.

And then there'd been all of the sympathy, poured out on MySpace and Facebook and delivered every other second via email. He'd hated the attention and had wished people would leave him alone, so he'd suspended his accounts to the online sites, and that only caused another wave of panicked emails as if removing himself from the web were a form of suicide, demanding comment and further condolence.

"Mike," someone called behind him.

It was a girl's voice, and he knew it would be Gwen Clermont before he turned around. Gwen was the only girl at school that ever talked to him, and the only one he could imagine who would chase him across the parking lot. He heard her shoes slapping the pavement and slowly eased around to see her stumble, nearly falling flat on her face when the toe of her Skecher dipped into a pothole. She did a quick dance forward and managed to avoid a nasty fall. Mike was glad she hadn't hurt herself, but that didn't mean he was happy to see her.

"Mike," she said again, her cheeks flushed from the run.

Up until about two weeks ago, Gwen had been one of his best friends. She was laid back and fun and could hold her own with an Xbox controller. Her hair was a rich shimmering red, like the skin of a polished apple. Her pale face hung above a thin neck, and both were framed by the crimson sheet of her hair. Gwen was ghost-white. It was genetic and not some goth statement like Holly Muldowney or Wendy Paulson tried to pull off. In the age of manufactured golden tans, Gwen's pallor was exotic.

"Hey," he said, coolly.

"Yeah, yeah, I know, you're not talking to me," Gwen said. "I get it, but I wanted to let you know how sorry I am about your granddad."

"You already told me that."

"I know, but you weren't listening."

"Whatever," he said.

Gwen's eyes grew soft with concern.

Suddenly, a cold steel door slammed shut in his mind. It happened more and more frequently these days. He couldn't take any more pity. It was as rank as the guilt he fed himself. Three years, ever since Dory was killed, he'd walked around under sympathetic stares. Strangers used to walk up to him to express their deepest condolences as if they too had lost a little sister, but they didn't even know Dory. Their sadness for him was hollow and meaningless, and it was exhausting. After so long, he'd finally thought the plastic concern had been shelved, but then his grandfather had gone and burned down a house, had torched himself in the process, and the sad fucking eyes were on him again. Mike couldn't even remember what normal felt like anymore.

"Look Mike, we're sorry. How many times are we supposed to say it?"

"You've said it enough."

"Evan and I feel like shit."

"Join the club."

Gwen's expression changed into one of annoyance. She shook her head, sending waves through her red hair, and gazed at the pavement, turned away. Then she rethought her exit and said, "You can blame us all you want, but we didn't make you go in that house. I tried talking you out of it, but you wouldn't listen. I know you're freaked, but we're still your friends, so whenever you get past this shit give us a call."

Mike turned away and continued toward his car.

He drove down the eastside. His house was only a mile from school, but the direct route meant crossing Ash Street where it intersected with Dowling and that was too close. Instead, he swung wide, skirting the neighborhood with its grim history and traveled another mile out of his way.

We didn't make you go in that house.

That was true enough. In fact, the whole thing had been brought up as casually as ordering a pizza or renting a DVD. Evan had suggested they sneak into the place before it was torn down, not even thinking about what had happened there, what terrible things were done to Mike's sister Dory and ten other people under that roof. Evan was like that. He got an idea, and it jazzed him, and all other switches in his brain shut down until the idea was explored or put to rest. To Evan, it was a morbid goof, just checking out the scene of a well-known crime before bulldozers leveled the place.

And Mike had agreed to go, even though Gwen had argued against it. For some reason the plan had struck Mike as a reasonable thing to do, and at the time he hadn't known why. Three weeks later, he still didn't understand why he'd endorsed such a sick idea.

At home, he grabbed a soda from the fridge and ran upstairs. He set the can of cola on his desk and turned on his computer. Once the screen lit up, he crossed to his closet and pulled the new black suit his mother had bought him at Macy's from the clothing bar and laid it on the bed. (He'd had too many black suits for a kid his age.) The thing looked like a deflated headless corpse. Mike stared at the suit, unnerved by the effect. Fingers of static ran over his neck and he turned away. He crossed the room to sit in front of the monitor on his desk.

Once seated and motionless the atmosphere of the room settled around him, and he became uneasy. It smelled wrong, electric-scented like the air before a thunderstorm, and his skin prickled while the hairs on the nape of his neck danced. For no reason at all, he was suddenly agitated, feeling anger and sadness in equal measure.

Jabbing keys and swatting the buttons on his mouse, he checked email, but it was mostly spam, and that made him angrier because he hated the digital pimps who sent him this shit. Why should he have to endure their pathetic pitches for affordable insurance, porn sites, and pills to make his dick bigger? He hated these assholes, but they seemed to be all that was left to him since he'd all but told his two best friends to go fuck themselves, and he only communicated with his gaming buddies when they were playing online. Checking the subject headings, he found a note from his mother, reminding him about the funeral. (As if it was a minor errand he could forget.) She'd been like that since his parent's had split, always emailing or texting him reminders of things he had to do. He erased the bulk of the emails. Again, the scent of ozone tickled his nostrils and Mike leaned forward to check the cables on his computer, wondering if Dexter, the family cat, had chewed through a wire.

He traced the cords and shook his head, wondering why he suddenly felt like crying. What the hell was going on? His emotions, always buried deep and controlled, now flared.

"You should have been watching me," a soft, high voice said at his back.

It startled Mike. He released the cords and spun around to find his sister, Dory, sitting on the edge of the bed. His breath rushed out of him and his head began to spin. Pressing back and away from her, he ground his side into the edge of the desk.

Dory's skin appeared gray, sickly. Her red shirt was shredded, and long tears ran over the thighs of her jeans. Terrible wounds showed through these gashes. Mike closed his eyes, hoping to blink the horrible apparition away, but Dory was still there when his lids lifted. She sat motionlessly like a perverse doll created in his sister's image, propped on his bed, awaiting play. The bottoms of her small bare feet faced him. An A had been cut into the left sole. The edges of the wound were ragged, and he thought he could see bone through the deepest of them.

"Fuck," he groaned, leaning away from the specter of his sister, frightened and repulsed.

"You should have been watching," Dory repeated. Her jaw moved up and down like a puppet's, lips barely contorting to the shape of the words she spoke.

The static in the room increased and Mike heard tiny crackles snap in the air.

"Do you know what they did to me?" she asked.

Mike couldn't speak. He leaned as far away from the girl as he could pressing painfully into the desk, trying to will his legs to lift him from the chair and carry him out of the room, but his muscles wouldn't respond.

"I'll show you, Mik-Mik," Dory said with pointed petulance. "One day, I'll show you what they did to me. You should have been watching."

Then, the little girl slid off of the bed. She glared at Mike and took a step toward him.

"I'll show you," she cried, her voice rising high and sharp. The little girl whirled away and raced for the door. "I'll show you, Mik-Mik."

The final word pierced the air like a spear tip, then vanished into a clatter of static.

Sweat dripped into Mike's eye. The stinging salty drop shocked him out of his frozen state, and he convulsed as if the visitation were a foul substance he could shake from his skin. He leaped from the chair and crashed back against the desk, eyes scanning the room, expecting another specter to charge at him from another part of the room.

"Shit," he said with a breathy hiss. "No way. No way."

The static charge of the air faded, but the cold remained. Mike stood against his desk, shivering. His head grew light, and he thought he might faint, but he leaned back on his palms and breathed deeply until the dizziness passed.

"No way," Mike said, unable to stop trembling.

He sat in the pew of the Lily Funeral Home with his mother at his side and listened to a friend of his grandfather's deliver a eulogy. The weathered old man, short and darkly tanned with a sweep of snow-white hair, threw occasional looks at the shiny chestnut coffin, eyeing the box with uncertainty as he spoke. Mike's eyes flitted from one face in the small assembly to another. His gaze ran over the red curtain on the left side of the room, reminding him of Gwen's hair. The shadows, the nooks, the corners of the room, these drew his attention. He fully expected to find Dory in one of those dark places, glaring out at him with furious accusation.

You should have been watching.

His mother sobbed quietly and wiped her eye with a tissue. His father grasped her hand in a gesture Mike found hypocritical. They weren't together anymore. His father had moved to Dallas over a year ago and rarely took the time to visit. Mike didn't even know why his parents had separated; they'd never bothered to tell him a thing about it, except they felt it would be better for them to "spend some time apart." They hadn't gotten a divorce, not yet anyway, and Mike didn't know if they were going to, but it struck him as kind of pathetic for his dad to show up and play hero.

Mike looked away and tried to listen to the old man by the coffin as he spoke, but he felt distant from the ceremony. This was the final event in his grandfather's existence. Everything else would be memory, but he couldn't access sadness for the man, not after what he'd seen only an hour ago in his bedroom. Focus on anything was impossible. He kept darting his eyes from side to side.

A large woman with a tight helmet of steel gray hair caught his attention, and she nodded solemnly at Mike. Crying had reddened her eyes and pale lines down her cheeks showed the path of her tears. Mike recognized the woman and offered a tentative nod in return.

Her name was Hannah something-or-other, and Mike thought she was okay. She'd visited the house several times after Dory was killed. Hannah was the moderator of a grief-counseling group his parents and grandfather had attended after Dory's death. The group had formed specifically for the loved ones of victims of the Baxter-Thomason murders. The freaks had killed Hannah's husband. Mike's parents had tried to get him to attend the meetings, but he'd refused, preferring to deal with Dory's death in his own way rather than sharing his misery with a bunch of strangers. Even his parents had stopped attending after a couple of months, they'd had other problems, but his grandfather had continued with the group until the formal meetings disbanded eight months ago. Mike had always thought his grandfather had crushed on Hannah, but the old guy never said anything; it was just something Mike'd felt when listening to the man talk about her.

Movement at the corner of his eye drew Mike's gaze to the aisle. For a heart quickening moment he saw Dory walking down the aisle toward him, but the image of his sister faded into that of another little girl, who grasped the hand of a man Mike knew was a business acquaintance of his mother's.

The funeral service seemed to drag on forever, but Mike didn't mind; the service could go on all day and night, and he'd be just fine with it. Though, he'd dreaded coming to this event, he now found comfort among the handful of people in the funeral home's chapel. He knew that once it broke up, they'd all gather at his aunt's house for the repast. There too, he would be surrounded by people, but then he would have to drive home, and his mother would resume her normal routine, which rarely included Mike. Maybe she'd be clingy tonight, insisting they share a meal or a game or a night in front of the television. Maybe his mother would revert to the overprotective shadow she'd become in the months after Dory's death, but it wouldn't last. Sooner or later, he would have to be alone, and the idea made the acid in his stomach churn.

3

Rosemary Memorial Hospital stood empty and silent on the outskirts of a sad city in northern Louisiana called Marchand. Unlike the university hospital closer to the city center with its state of the art facilities and cutting edge equipment, Rosemary Memorial had been considered a dinosaur of a medical institution even before it closed in 1982. Standing four stories tall in a field of hip-high, brown grass, the building's blocky unimaginative design more resembled that of a warehouse than a place of healing, and the residents of Marchand were convinced the decrepit structure housed more than insects and foraging rats. Witnesses claimed to have seen a ghostly woman walking through one of the wards or peering sadly through a second-floor window. They spoke of floating lights and the screams of the dying, though these last two points of interest had emerged from the building's mythology in recent years (mostly in tourist brochures and on the city's website). Tales of the mysterious specter, supposedly that of a young nurse, had been consistent and dated back to the mid-1950s, and it was because of these stories that four people descended on the property just before sunset. Two men and two women unloaded digital recording equipment, high-intensity lamps, and a dozen spools of cord from two black SUVs. The doors of the vehicle bore the words *The Haunt Club*, stenciled in jagged, stylized letters.

One of The Club was named Melanie Bell. She looked younger than her thirty-one years; her petite build and large eyes made her seem as if she had yet to experience the final growth spurt of youth. She kept her dark hair short and easy to care for because she had little patience for vanity, even though she appeared on television at least once a week.

After setting up their cameras and running cords to the generator outside, they tested the video images feeding to their laptop. Once again, Melanie found herself in a gloomy room, bathed in the glow of LCD light. Water-stained plaster peeled from the walls around her. On the six-foot table she'd brought to the site sat the expensive laptop, its screen divided into quadrants, each playing a different video feed. A number of other smaller electronic pieces littered the table, but those were for proximate investigation, not distance surveillance.

Her three colleagues stood behind her. All together they were known as the "Para-Troopers," paranormal investigators who'd managed to catch the eye of a cable television producer and had gone on to star in a weekly program said producer had whimsically titled "The Haunt Club."

Ash Street

Melanie wasn't fond of the show's producer, Kee Ulrich. She knew he didn't take their work seriously—of course neither did most of their audience—but the steady paycheck was welcome, even if it meant smiling at Kee, a hipster bobble-head with too-white teeth and overly-bronzed skin.

Maybe she was foolish, but she wanted to believe in the work. Of course, she understood that most reported hauntings were nothing more than the wishful thinking of grieving loved ones or the imaginings of "true believers" who saw spirits in every darkened hallway and the corners of every empty room, but she couldn't shake the belief that the natural order, defined by human beings over thousands of years of observation, constituted only a small piece of the universe. Sometimes she worried that her fascination with spirits was nothing more than a fear of mortality, ghosts representing an existence beyond skin and bone, but rationally, the idea fascinated her.

Melanie had seen a ghost once, or at least, she thought she had. When she was eight years old her father had taken her and the rest of the family on a road trip to Wisconsin to bury her Grandpa Abe. The house in Madison was small, cramped, and always seemed to be hotter than an oven. The first night, after sitting with her crying grandmother, and eating a dinner of cold rubbery chicken, and going grocery shopping with her parents (because there was no food in the terribly hot little house), and brushing her teeth and climbing onto the uncomfortable sofa in the living room, she'd seen a pale shape from the corner of her eye. Startled and fascinated in equal measure, she'd cringed back into the covers, only to throw them off a moment later and give chase to the shape. It was Grandpa Abe, she knew, though she'd never gotten a good look at the man's spirit. One moment it was there in the foyer, lit only by some internal glow, and then it was gone.

She'd spent the next half an hour looking through the house for him, whispering his name and hoping to see him again. In many ways, she'd spent her whole life on the same search. It was what brought her to places like Rosemary Memorial Hospital.

"The setting works," her co-host Mack said of the deserted hospital. "It's got the right vibe and will read full-on freaky. We do a handful of night-vision shots—me and Mel stumbling around in the dark—and then the obligatory what-the-fuck moment when Reg kicks a piece of rubble or an old beer can. It'll play."

Melanie didn't respond, but rather kept her eyes on the laptop screen. Not long ago, Mack Durham had been her assistant. Before the Shiver Channel had picked up the Para-Troopers and built a program around them, Mack had been in charge of hauling equipment and filing research, but Mack looked pretty, too pretty for most men—just right for television. When Melanie had questioned her producer about promoting Mack to what was essentially a co-starring role,

Kee Ulrich had spouted off about the "chick demographic," and the "gay base," and the errand boy became a star—at least as much of a star as the limited cable audience allowed. It took Mack all of two episodes to become as insufferable as Kee. Whatever sincerity he'd once had for the work soon drowned under a deluge of ratings stats and focus-group feedback. Mack didn't care what they found during an investigation, or if they found anything at all, because he was going to sell the idea they'd found *something* to his minor legion of late night fans regardless.

"I can feel a presence," Yvonne whispered. Melanie didn't even need to turn around to know Yvonne was hugging herself tightly and gazing at the ceiling with an expression of disturbed wonder as she uttered the words. It was Yvonne's way. Of all of them, Yvonne was the "true believer," a woman convinced that ghosts moved among the living, that death was merely a release from the confines of life and not the period at the end of it. "It's so very *full* here."

"Something's full," Mack said. "What about the basement? This place has got to have a wicked belly—hallways and rooms and water and shit dripping from the walls. The bitch would read like a motherfucker."

"The morgue's down there," Reg Corak, the audio-visual expert and fourth member of the team, muttered.

"Awesome," Mack announced. "The morgue. So fucking perfect. All we have to do is get a shot of the word on the door, you know one of those little plaques and the audience will do all the work for us."

"It may not have a plaque," Reg said.

"It will before we finish filming the episode," Mack replied.

Melanie shook her head. Finally she turned from the monitor and faced her crew.

"No one has seen anything in the basement," she said. "The sightings are always here on the second floor. A woman's shape. A nurse. The stories say she used to work here, and she was so dedicated to her patients she continues to visit their beds."

"Or an angel of death, returning to the scene of her crimes, making sure no one leaves the hospital alive," Mack suggested, enthusiastically.

"We are not changing the story," Melanie insisted. "Jesus, all we need is one townie blogging about it and any credibility we had gets torched."

"But it's a better story," Mack said. "It's got a built-in creep factor."

"So do you," Melanie said, "but that doesn't make you interesting."

"Ha-ha," Mack said.

Melanie checked her other colleagues to gauge their reaction. She didn't need to worry about Yvonne. Yvonne was in it for the ghosts, not the money and certainly not the exposure. It was Reg who worried her, and her mistrust of the man did little but make her feel guilty. He'd been her boyfriend for nearly six years, and she loved him completely, but more and more he was slipping to the dark side. The television experience hasn't gone to his head, the way it had Mack's, but Reg had become progressively more savvy about the business, and had taken to letting questionable content slide. She'd once been confident he would support her in all of the big arguments, now she couldn't be so sure.

"We can't change the story," Reg finally said. "It might make for a good show, but Melanie is right: long term it'll screw us. The second floor is good. Those empty beds in the ward give us more than enough creep, and it keeps in line with the established mythology. That's not to say we can't do a series of establishing shots, including one of the morgue, to play at the opening of the show."

"That works," Melanie said. "Thank you."

Reg smiled and nodded his head, and then quickly looked away, busying himself with a handheld video camera.

"I'm still running it by Kee," Mack put in, refusing to give up.

"Yes, run to daddy," Melanie said.

"Kee knows the business."

"Which is why he's producing reality crap for a miniscule cable channel?"

Reg sniggered and scratched the back of his neck. Mack shot him a furious glare.

"Whipped much?" Mack asked.

A shadow of embarrassment stained Reg's cheeks. He didn't look away from the accusation, but it seemed to have deflated him some.

"Ignore the diva," Melanie said.

"I'm fine," Reg replied, resting his hand on her shoulder.

She reached up and squeezed his hand, grateful he had joined her in this strange career. He was calm and pragmatic and ever present in her life, following her through marathons of work, sometimes spanning eighteen-hour days, and then together at home, eating microwaved meals accompanied by bottles of inexpensive wine, watching recorded television programs from the sofa before heading off to bed. She considered Reg the romantic equivalent of a comfortable shirt—perhaps not the most attractive or exotic fashion with his thickly-built body and receding hairline, but always snug and present and available. Before Reg, she'd experienced the complicated puzzles of illogical passion, which snagged and trapped and further entwined her emotions the more she struggled. These razor-wire romances had left her drained and cautious. Reg had come along like a salve, soothing and promising no further damage.

After another quick squeeze, she released his hand and turned back to the monitors. The video quality was so high and the lighting so stark, the laptop resembled a partitioned window more than an electronic display. On the screen, she saw rows of gray beds, clothed in tattered, moth-gnawed mattresses. One of the beds, the fourth one from the bottom right of her screen, harbored a nest of mice. She'd noticed it while scouting the room for camera placement. The mother mouse was mottled, white and brown, and she'd been lying on her side, while her young, seven or eight similarly marked mice, pushed in for an available teat. At first, it had looked like they were devouring their mother, chewing at her belly with enthusiasm.

"We got something," Mack said.

Melanie's eyes hadn't left the monitors. She didn't see anything, so her co-host's assertion startled her. Mack reached over her shoulder as Yvonne and Reg moved in at her back. He jabbed at a small device on the tabletop. It was the temperature read out from the thermometer in the ward. The numbers on it eased down from seventy-eight degrees to seventy-five in just under five seconds.

"That's impossible," Melanie said.

"I told you I felt something," Yvonne whispered dreamily. "This place is full of lost souls, crying for release."

"We've never seen a reading like this," Melanie noted, her heart beginning to pound heavily in her chest. Seventy-three degrees. Seventy-one.

"What should we do?" Reg asked.

"You should be filming, dumb ass," Mack snapped.

Reg didn't respond. He picked up the handheld and aimed it at the laptop.

"We're getting strange signature readings," Mack told the camera. "We're heading into the ward."

"Let's wait," Melanie said. She focused on the screen directly in front of her. The anticipation turned hard and painful in her chest. "We have to see it on the screen. If we go running in there, it'll never show."

"Sixty-nine degrees," Mack said. "We can't ignore this."

"It could be a draft," Reg noted.

"It's eighty degrees outside," Melanie pointed out. "A draft couldn't account for this kind of temperature fluctuation."

"Do you feel that?" Yvonne asked. "It's like everywhere."

Melanie paused wondering what her friend was talking about, because she felt nothing, except the excitement of the moment. It hadn't turned cold. No static crackled the air, no scent of ozone. She assumed Yvonne was just being Yvonne, snatching random signs from the void.

"Sixty-five degrees," Mack said. "We need to get in there."

"No," Melanie said. She took her eyes off of the thermal readout and looked at the screen, all but begging it to show her something besides two rows of ancient, miserable beds. Nothing. "Reg, where did you put the thermometer?"

"Mack handled it while I was wiring up the generator."

"Mack?"

"It's right here," he said, pointing to the center of the laptop's screen. The area he indicated wasn't captured by any of the cameras. "On the wall by that back doorway, the one that led into the hall with the showers."

Melanie thought about the placement, trying to remember if there was anything in that area that might account for this sudden drop in temperature, but it was just a door, leading to one more grim hallway. She checked the camera angles in the other windows, but couldn't see the thermometer on any of them.

"Fifty-nine degrees," Reg noted.

"Come on," Mack said. He pulled away from Melanie's shoulder and began an anxious jig in the middle of the room. "Whatever is happening, it's happening now. We have to get in there."

"We lost the temperature feed," Reg said.

Melanie checked the device on the table and the readout was blank. "Damn it," she said.

"Come on," Mack insisted.

Melanie regarded the laptop one last time as if seeking its approval, and found herself disappointed that the ephemeral shape of a concerned nurse wasn't floating across the floor to tend to her long-dead patients.

She pushed herself out of the chair and nearly knocked Yvonne on her ass. Melanie shot out her hand to stabilize her friend and offered a quickly muttered apology. Then she ran across the room and hit the door, sending it back on its hinges.

"That's what I'm talking about," Mack said, immediately following her into the hall.

Before nightfall, they'd set up a string of lights in the corridors. The bulbs glowed harshly, exposing every crack and hole in the old plaster walls. Doors stood open. The rooms beyond were out of the light's reach, making the darkness inside black as velvet cloth.

Melanie raced past the openings. Her skin shriveled at the base of her neck and sweat crept onto her brow. Anything could jump out of that gloom. Squatters, felons, any manner of miscreant could launch himself from one of those black places and be on her before she even registered his presence. A childlike thrill coursed through her. Adrenaline poured into her veins and saturated her muscles. This was the rush. Even if she weren't so intent on proving that flesh was a single vehicle for the human soul, she'd want to do this work for the sheer buzz these moments of fear brought her.

Mack caught up to her and then slid by. His shoulder brushed a wall, sending up a cloud of old plaster. The impact didn't slow him as he tore ahead to reach the door of the ward.

Always has to be the star, Melanie thought. *He always has to be first on the scene, first to make a proclamation, first to expose the anomalies that had been mistaken for spirit visitations.* Mack's unapologetic vanity could be amusing, but often enough it was just annoying. She knew he recorded and timed each episode of *The Haunt Club* to make sure he'd received equal, if not greater, screen time than she did. It was all so pathetic.

Mack disappeared into the ward and the door slowly swung shut. Melanie reached it before it hit the jamb and pushed it open. She could hear Yvonne and Reg in the hall behind her. Yvonne would be clambering forward like a woman lost in a dream, her palm in constant contact with the crumbling plaster wall to assure herself that her surroundings were real. Reg would move more cautiously, exercising only as much haste as was necessary to keep them all in frame. He would have his camera running, capturing the moments leading up to the discovery; if a discovery was to be found.

Stepping into the ward, Melanie had expected some tactile confirmation of the temperature reading she'd witnessed on the display in the observation chamber—a blast of cold air, or at least a breeze. She knew that temperature fluctuations in these situations were often isolated, and a cold spot could occupy the narrowest of spaces, but she'd been hopeful. The room was as warm as the corridor, though. She took in the ward with its narrow, shabby mattresses and metal-framed beds. All of the windows on this side of the building were intact, which was a mystery unto itself. The front windows had been smashed out by rocks and bricks and garbage, as were those on the east side of the building, but here on the west side, vandals had shown mercy or exceptionally bad aim. One camera rested on a tripod before her. Another would be over her right shoulder and the third, the main camera that viewed the expanse of the chamber, stood across the room, also on her right. The fourth camera had been positioned in the hall they'd just left.

Mack stood facing the far wall. Something in his posture made her slow. She knew this was the part of the wall where Mack had positioned the thermometer, but he wasn't looking around with excitement. He wasn't tapping the device. In fact, he didn't even seem to be reading it. He stood straight staring at blank plaster.

"What did you find?" she asked. She crossed the room and passed in front of the primary camera's lens. "Is the thermometer working?"

"No," Mack said, quietly. "It's broken."

Melanie reached the wall and gazed at the digital temperature gauge. A shiny fluid covered the plastic case and the LCD screen. A single drop slid down the cable that attached to a transmitter on the floor.

"What is that stuff?" Melanie asked.

"I don't know."

Melanie reached out her finger and pressed it into the slick covering the top of the thermometer. The fluid was sticky, but thin, like the residue of a cola, and it felt cold. Behind her Yvonne entered the ward, and Reg followed, his eyes fixed on the small screen of his digital camera.

"Is she here?" Yvonne asked. "Has she come forth to greet us?"

"No," Melanie said, studying the tacky substance on her finger. She raised it to her nose and took a whiff, careful not to touch her face with it.

"But we have something," Mack said. "She left something behind. I think it's ectoplasm. It's all over the thermometer."

"Really?" Reg asked in surprise.

"Yeah, I think she—"

"It's not ectoplasm," Melanie interrupted, turning to Mack. She presented her fingers to him, but he stepped away. "Not unless ectoplasm is orange flavored and comes frozen on a stick."

A Popsicle.

Melanie shook her head for the twentieth time. Some idiot had put a Popsicle on the top of the thermometer. As it melted the cold liquid seeped into the device, cooled the sensor, but ultimately shorted the thing out. The others had spent fifteen minutes arguing over who might have pulled such a stunt—random vandals; a competing paranormal group; the owners of the dilapidated hospital, hoping for a bit of publicity—but Melanie already knew the name of the mastermind: Kee Ulrich. The lame ass producer of *The Haunt Club* had snuck into the dilapidated hospital and used the back hallway so he wouldn't be detected. Her co-host, Mack, swore he had no personal knowledge of the stunt, but Melanie wasn't convinced. He'd been standing on the damned popsicle stick so she wouldn't see it. Infuriating. This was the same kind of stunt Kee had pulled in Atlanta when he'd done some exceptionally crappy stop motion animation to show a toy car moving across a tabletop. Or the time in Mobile when he threw a black sheet over his head and wandered up and down a hallway, just distant enough from the camera to make it look like the darkness had taken on a life of its own, but not quite far enough away to obscure the fact that the darkness was wearing calf-skin deck shoes. In both cases, Mack had been privy to the shams; he'd defended Kee and spouted off about ratings and keeping the show "fresh."

Melanie wrapped a cord. She was doing her best to keep her temper in check, but a thick vine of humiliation moved through her belly and chest.

"Hey," Reg said. His arm slid around her shoulder. "You okay?"

"You know I'm not."

"Yeah, but I had to ask. It's in the job description."

Melanie smiled and leaned into Reg's firm chest, laying her head on his shoulder. Across the room she saw Yvonne on one of the beds. The woman sat with her head down, picking at the ragged edges of one of the mattress's many holes. She looked disappointed like a child who hadn't gotten the gift she'd expected for Christmas. Melanie knew how she felt.

Fortunately, Mack had decided to disassemble the control room so Melanie didn't have to endure the pretty boy, calculating new ways to undermine the show's credibility. The ridiculous little creep had already proclaimed Kee's trick, "Brilliant."

"It's just getting so frustrating," she said.

"I know," Reg said, "but we also knew this shit was going down when we signed on for season two."

She dropped the coiled cord on the ground and turned to press her chest against his, hoping to find some comfort in a familiar touch. "It doesn't make it right," she said.

"Nope." Reg kissed her quickly and rested his head on her shoulder. "It doesn't make it right, but it does make it our decision."

"Quit being logical."

"We have a six hour drive ahead of us," he told her. "I don't think I could sustain a rant that long, so logic is all I've got."

Melanie thought back, trying to remember if Kee Ulrich had ever taken them seriously, and further wondered if it mattered. She'd signed on to co-host *The Haunt Club* because the Shiver Channel had stepped up to finance her passion, and though she was never going to get rich off of what she made on the show, she was saving a fortune in travel, lodging, and meal costs, not to mention the high-priced tech toys Reg collected like action figures were now being provided by the show's producer. Did it matter if that producer actually thought they'd discover occupants of the afterlife? Did it make any difference at all if he laughed his way to the bank at their expense week after week? Kee wasn't exactly scaring the spirits off. They'd had no more or less luck in finding actual presences since Ulrich began following them around than they'd had before. Melanie still picked the locations, the local myths that inhabited them, and the methods of investigation. These things hadn't changed in the year and a half since Kee Ulrich had entered her life. The only real difference was a viewing public, witnessing her excitement, her fear, and her failure. Well that and the occasional bullshit prank Kee played on them in the name of ratings.

Mack entered the ward noisily. "Control room is wrapped. You guys ready to bail or what?"

"You ready?" Reg asked.

"Nothing to hang around here for," Melanie said.

"Good, we've got a long drive ahead, and I want pancakes."

4

Stuart sat at his desk, a cup of coffee growing cold next to his clasped hands. He watched the interview with Colleen Taylor on his computer monitor, his eyes locked on her face, looking for any sign of guilt to emerge from her expressions or her words.

"Walk me through your day again," Stuart said on the recording. The dowdy Colleen looked annoyed and tired. She wiped at her eyes and asked, "Again?"

"Yes please."

"I woke up and dressed for Pilates. Then I went to pick up Rachel Cobb at her house on Rolling Oak."

"Did you see your husband before you left?"

"Of course I saw him. He was lying right next to me when I woke up."

"But he wasn't awake when you left?"

"No, he doesn't usually get up that early."

"So you didn't say goodbye to him?"

"I thought I'd see him later."

"But you didn't talk to him at all before leaving the house?"

"No," Colleen said. She leaned on the table, appearing exhausted. "I didn't want to wake him. Pudge likes his sleep."

"Okay. So you dressed and you left the house. Did you see any cars or trucks in the area? Any unfamiliar vehicles at all?"

"No."

"Please try to remember."

"I *do* remember and there was nothing. No one parks on the street out there, so I would have noticed."

"And then where did you go?"

"To Rachel Cobb's house on Rolling Oak."

"Did you make any stops along the way?"

"No."

"And how long were you there?"

"A few minutes. I don't know. Rachel wasn't quite ready to go. She asked me to get her a bottled water, and after she was ready we left."

Stuart smiled while watching the DVD. He'd interviewed Rachel Cobb after leaving the Taylor residence, wanting to seal Colleen's alibi airtight before following any other leads. Mrs. Cobb struck Stuart as flighty and hyper and beyond even the slightest deception. She just wasn't smart enough to pull it off.

And she had asked Stuart to grab her a bottled water from the fridge while she "prepared for the interview." It seemed perfectly natural to the woman to ask a complete stranger to bring her a beverage, though she didn't offer Stuart one in the process.

"Where did you go?" Stuart asked on the video.

"The Aloe Ranch Day Spa. And no, I didn't make any stops along the way. We arrived five minutes early, grabbed our mats and joined the class. When it was over, we left."

"And how long is the class?"

"Forty minutes. It ran a few minutes over this time."

"Did you shower at the spa? Stay around for any reason?"

"No, I did not," Colleen said testily. "I have a perfectly good shower at home. I see no reason to use a public facility."

Stuart stopped the recording with a click of his mouse button. He rubbed his eyes. He'd been through the interview a dozen times and nothing leaped out at him. Her story never changed, and so far it checked out. Rachel Cobb, a guy named Timmy who worked behind the reception counter at the Aloe Ranch, and the Pilates instructor all confirmed Colleen's story. So if not the wife, who?

The forensics team still sifted through prints and fibers, cataloging the vast number of samples taken from the Taylor house. All of these would have to be checked against Colleen, the staff, and known visitors. The blood spatter expert had given Stuart an unofficial report.

The killer had come up behind Pudge while he was standing in front of the refrigerator. The victim had turned and attempted to flee, possibly struggling with his attacker in the process. Pudge tried to escape by crossing the kitchen to the archway leading to the dining room, but for some reason—either disoriented from trauma or possibly, the sight of another intruder—he turned in the direction he'd come. Though Stuart had come to these same conclusions, one facet of the expert's report was useful.

"The initial stab wounds were all low and to the right, very tightly grouped. It reminds me of a prison hit. One con comes up behind another and wraps his arm around the guy's neck, then gets in a half dozen jabs to do a lot of damage fast. You get minimal spray because the weapon isn't swinging through the air, but your killer is going to be covered in blood unless they really jackhammer that blade and put some distance between themselves and the holes they've made. Looks like your perp might have spent some time inside, certainly spent some time on the streets. You don't just pick up this kind of technique."

All of which pointed away from Pudge's wife as the killer, not that Stuart was surprised. The medical examiner had put the time of death within a narrow window. Yes, Colleen could have murdered her husband before leaving to pick up Mrs. Cobb. But there was no evidence to support this theory. The search of the property and her car came up empty. If she had killed Pudge, Colleen would have had to stash stained clothing and a large knife in a short period of time, not to mention cleaning herself up before meeting her friend. Based on the time of the 9-1-1 call there would have been no significant amount of time after dropping off Mrs. Cobb for her to do these things—the coroner felt certain that Pudge Taylor had been dead for a minimum of one hour.

If Colleen had murdered her husband, she'd done it before her morning workout.

And then she took the knife with her to Pilates? The stained clothes? Not likely.

Besides, Pudge had himself a fine little arsenal in that house, Colleen knew how to shoot, and crimes of passion generally happened fast. If Colleen wanted Pudge dead, it would have been a hell of a lot easier to just shoot him, hide the murder weapon on her way to Pilates, and suggest Pudge had interrupted a burglary—happened all the time.

David Ballard walked into the office and dropped a pile of photographs on Stuart's desk. Pudge Taylor's doughy face, eyes open in a dead stare, looked up at him from the topmost photo.

"I'll go over these with you later," Ballard said. "I'm following up with Taylor's business associates. Back in a couple of hours."

Stuart looked at the photos on his desk. Most of them had come from the crime scene, Pudge lying face down in his own blood, crazy dance steps circling his head, his great gut smushed to the side like a balloon pressed under a palm. Another set showed Pudge lying on his back on a metal table. The blood had been washed away, leaving shiny pale skin and a brush of white-blond hair covering his chest and belly. No wounds there. The killer had kept the attack to Pudge Taylor's back.

After flipping to the next photograph, Stuart recoiled. He shook off the startling sensation of déjà vu and brought the image closer to his face for a better look. The picture had been taken from the end of the coroner's table, and in the foreground Stuart saw the bottoms of Pudge Taylor's feet. A red sharpie had been used to circle the left foot. The coroner had made a note next to the bubble, reading:

Pre-existing: Scab indicates 3-4 days.

The dark lines on Pudge's foot were roughly in the shape of the letter A. It wasn't a good A—the right post of it veered well away from the center bar. In fact, more likely than not, Pudge had scraped his foot on a carpet tack or stepped on broken glass. Guys cut their feet all the time.

But Baxter and Thomason had used the letter A to mark most of their victims.

Pre-existing.

His phone rang, startling Stuart into dropping the eight-by-ten sheet.

The cuts had to be accidental. Just a coincidence. Stuart lifted the picture again, looked at it and decided the wounds didn't really look like an A at all. He put the photograph down and answered his phone.

"Stuart," Hannah Bolger said.

"How are you?"

"I'm fine, Stuart."

But she wasn't fine. Stuart had been married long enough to know when a woman used the word "fine" in place of the term "you fucking asshole." The edge of dissatisfaction came through loud and clear.

"What can I do for you?" he asked.

"Well, we didn't see you at the funeral this afternoon."

Funeral? Stuart flipped through his mental calendar and a series of faces, wondering who had died. Then it came to him: Alan Means. "Hannah, I barely knew Alan. It wouldn't have been appropriate for me to attend."

"I attended," she countered.

But you knew the guy, Stuart thought. *Besides, you would have gone anyway.* Hannah believed she was part of a great and living creature called the human race. As such, she felt a connection to everyone walking the earth. She took on problems that weren't hers and slotted herself in lives with which she had only the most tangential connection. Of course that wasn't the case this time. She and Alan had been close, but Stuart and Alan had not been. She would never see it that way, though.

"I'm sorry, Hannah, but there's a new case and I really can't pull myself away from it."

"Pudge Taylor," Hannah said. "I saw a news clip on the Internet."

"Yes, Pudge was murdered this morning."

"And don't you think that's odd?"

"Well, yes. Murder is odd. That's why we have laws against it."

"You know what I mean, Stuart."

Stuart rubbed the back of his neck furiously. Sometimes talking to Hannah Bolger was like being scolded by his mother, and he felt the same embarrassment and weakness he'd always felt when his mother laid the stink eye on him.

"No," he said, leaving his neck in peace so he could straighten the low pile of photographs on his desk. "I don't know what you mean, Hannah."

"First Alan and now Pudge. You can't tell me you don't think that's strange."

Both men had suffered loss at the hands of Baxter and Thomason, but Stuart couldn't see any conspiracy in it. "Alan burned himself up, along with the house on Ash Street. He wasn't murdered."

"You don't know that."

"Yes as a matter of fact, I do. We know where he bought the cans and the gas to go in them. His car was parked in front of the house. Now I'm not saying it was his fault exactly. He was sick. He didn't really know what he was doing, and I'm sorry as hell he got himself caught in that blaze, but he entered the house of his own volition with the intent of arson. Jeez, Hannah, if anyone should know how bad off Alan's head was, it should be you."

That argument seemed to work. Hannah remained silent for several seconds as she processed what Stuart had said. He was relieved but he couldn't help but think about the mark on Pudge Taylor's foot. Lifting the photo again, he stared at the cuts and told himself they didn't resemble the letter A one bit.

"Pudge Taylor wasn't burned alive," Hannah announced as if she'd just slapped a trump card on the table. "That was no accident."

"Exactly," Stuart replied. "You just proved my point—two different crimes with two different motives. Alan accidentally killed himself, and we'll know who killed Pudge soon enough. There's no connection here, just a coincidence."

Again Hannah fell silent. Stuart took this opportunity to try and get the woman off of the phone. Honestly, he liked her and under different circumstances might have made the time to chat, but he'd been put on the defensive from the get go, and he wasn't fond of feeling like an inept adolescent. Besides, he had work and the day was slipping away.

"I really have to get back to this. Let's talk next week."

"I never see you anymore," Hannah said.

"We'll fix that soon."

"Why don't you come to dinner tomorrow night?"

"Can't. I have plans."

"Well, Sunday doesn't work at all. Dinner at my place Tuesday?"

"Done." Stuart began scribbling the information on a post-it pad. "You have a good weekend, Hannah. I'm really sorry about Alan. I know you two were close."

"Thank you. And don't try to get out of Tuesday."

"Wouldn't think of it."

Stuart hung up the phone. He tore the post-it free and slapped it on the bottom of his computer monitor, then he lifted the stack of photographs and began to go through them with a more focused eye.

5

Hannah Bolger turned on the kitchen light. She put a mug of water for tea in the microwave. She couldn't sleep. It was very late, but Alan's funeral had woken too many emotions and cleared trails for a number of thoughts, and Hannah found the idea of sleep preposterous. She thought about her dear friend warmly, saddened because so few had attended his funeral. He'd been a lovely man and deserved a grander farewell than a handful of family and a few old friends, but the details surrounding his death couldn't be overlooked. To many people, Alan was nothing more than a sad old man who'd finally lost reason—someone to be pitied then quickly forgotten. Maybe that's what had kept Stuart away. Despite what he'd said, Hannah thought Stuart should have attended. He said he hadn't felt close to Alan, but they *were* close; they had both survived terrible tragedies and had shared their stories in Hannah's group. Granted, Alan had been far more willing to share than Stuart—the detective wasn't the expressive sort—but still he should have understood their bond. When the microwave beeped she retrieved the steaming mug, plunked a bag of mint tea into it, and sat at the kitchen table. Absently, she poked at the tea bag with the nail of her index finger.

Alan's last act, burning the house on Ash Steet, had stirred her mental pot, bringing up bits and pieces of weathered emotion. She couldn't help but think about her husband, Ben. She missed him. Ben had been a scoundrel and a bit elastic when it came to the truth, but she'd adored his bohemian ways.

Early in their relationship, they'd gotten quite an earful from her parents about the nature of their relationship. Silly really. They'd lived together without the burden of a formal marriage. No paperwork. No unwanted government sanction of the union. They'd had two beautiful children together, and though Eric was struggling to find a career that engaged him, Brianna was married and happily running a successful jewelry company she'd created with a friend from school. Despite forsaking a traditional ceremony and all of the hoopla of a wedding, Hannah had called Ben her husband for thirty-four years. They'd had a wonderful life together, even if Ben had become infuriating in those last few years.

Hannah didn't know what had gotten into the man, but his extramarital interests had positively exploded. Once the children were gone, Hannah had felt at peace. She'd given new life to the world, made a career of helping others. It had been like a long pleasant walk, and though she hadn't reached its end, she felt entitled to a rest, like stopping on a mountain trail to peer out over the path of her trek, giving her a chance to reflect on the journey and replenish her energies. With the children out of the house, Ben had grown restless. He'd joined a gym and become obsessed with his body. He drank protein shakes and had his back waxed. He even dyed his hair once, but the results were so dreadful, he never tried it again. Hannah smiled at the memory of her husband looking like Groucho Marx and jabbed the tea bag with her finger.

The police said Selma Baxter had lured Ben to her house with promises of sex. Hannah wasn't surprised. When Stuart Lancaster had informed her of this he'd paused, as if he expected Hannah to break down or throw a fit or do something equally ridiculous. Neither she nor Ben had believed in monogamy. They'd entered into their union as free spirits and he'd left it a liberated, if perhaps overly promiscuous, man. Her mournful, otherwise unfazed, demeanor seemed to bother the detective, but that was his problem; he wasn't the one hearing about the murder of his love. He had gone on to tell her that Derek Thomason was waiting in the house, lurking in the shadows until Selma maneuvered Ben into the basement.

His body was discovered in a culvert running along the south edge of Carter Park.

The months following Ben's murder had been dreadful. Not only had Hannah had to relive the sorrow with every news report, but those Hollywood vultures had appeared the day after Derek Thomason and Selma Baxter were sentenced in the murders.

Those damned producers, all tight suits and shiny hair—she despised them. Of the three proposed movies she'd heard about, only one was ever made. Fortunately it was shown on an obscure cable channel that couldn't have had a very large audience.

Hannah had watched that pile of steaming lies: *Lethal Lovers*. It was a cheap and amateurish film, obviously rushed through production to take advantage of the ongoing news coverage. Hannah would never forgive Ben's sisters for allowing the producers to use his name in their movie. Ben hadn't accounted for them in his will, so the vindictive slobs went about picking over his carcass in their own way. Those embarrassing harpies allowed the filmmakers to paint Ben as some kind of hypersexual sleaze. The actor they hired to play him, some soap opera veteran, had chewed up the scenery, glaring and licking his lips and acting like a low life lounge hound. He even slicked his hair down with pomade to make him look greasy and vile (not unlike the film's producers). That wasn't Ben. Not one bit of it. Ben had never leered in his life. He loved women, and while Hannah was willing to concede that perhaps he'd loved too many of them, he had always been a gentleman. How dare those hateful sisters allow Ben to be memorialized as a letch in that garbage drama?

Hannah had refused to sign the producers' release, so they'd presented

Ben as a loner, preying on any woman that crossed his path. Bastards. As infuriating as it was, sometimes when she thought of Ben, she pictured him as the slimy character that mediocre soap opera actor had created for *Lethal Lovers*. Such instances startled and sickened her, made her angrier at the hateful media.

Hannah rose from the chair and crossed to the refrigerator. She retrieved a bottle of Smirnoff vodka from the freezer and poured a generous shot into her tea.

And then there was Stuart. There was something about that man. He had secrets and they filled his eyes.

She'd met Stuart Lancaster the day Ben's body had been found in Carter Park. The detective had been waiting in the morgue when an officer led Hannah in to identify Ben's remains. At the time, she'd barely noticed Stuart. He spoke in a dry voice that struck Hannah as manufactured though in no way cold; he'd been trained to speak that way, but genuine concern buoyed his words. Stuart and an intimidating detective named Ballard showed her into a tiled room. At the center of the room was a metal table draped in a white cloth. The identification took only a handful of seconds. Despite the mutilation to the right side of the face, Hannah recognized the man she'd loved. Hannah had clearly identified the corpse as Benjamin Walker Locke. Then she'd surprised the detectives by leaning over and kissing his forehead. "Be warm and safe," she'd told her husband, a phrase Ben had used to end his many letters to her when they were dating.

She'd sat with Stuart and his partner, Ballard, for three hours. She'd answered their questions to the best of her ability. Little about that conversation remained with her, even later that night as she lay in bed sobbing over Ben's death. She recalled almost nothing the detectives had asked, less about her responses. It was all a smear of memory. Stuart had been all but forgotten until he became grief's casualty himself.

One day during group, a striking man in a pair of jeans, a white dress shirt, and a narrow-cut navy blue sports jacket walked into the room. Hannah recognized the detective immediately, and it was then that she saw the secrets in his eyes.

Alan Means was also there. He hadn't seemed old then, certainly not feeble. Others were there as well—parents, children, brothers, sisters, life partners. The "lethal lovers" had been indiscriminate in their killing spree.

She drank the rest of her tea in a single gulp. At the sink she rinsed out the mug and set it in the drainer. Leaning on the counter, she looked out the window and was surprised to see movement in her backyard. A pale figure raced from the privacy fence across the yard to the hedge. It startled her so badly she pulled away from the counter with a gasp and patted her chest. The clock on the oven told her it was three-twenty in the morning. Who the blazes was running around her yard at this time of night? Hannah walked to the kitchen door. She thumbed the switch beside the jamb and a series of floodlights burst on.

In the corner of the yard stood a naked man. He had positioned himself next to the cherry tree Ben had planted to celebrate their first anniversary of living together. The man's skin showed a pale blue-gray in the harsh light. He looked so terribly sad. He also looked exactly like her dead husband—his body destroyed with haphazard gashes—the way he'd been found in a culvert south of Carter Park. Hannah's heart rapped quickly in her chest as she stepped closer to the window to get a clearer view of the apparition.

"Ben," she whispered.

Unable to take her eyes from the figure, Hannah blindly grasped for the doorknob. The lock was engaged but Ben's image so distracted her, she didn't look at the knob to figure out why it wouldn't turn.

"Ben," she said more frantically.

Finally she thought enough to consider the doorknob and released the lock. Hannah threw open the door and stepped into the hot night air, hurrying toward the figure, but he slipped backwards into the fence. With each step forward Ben vanished just a little more.

"Hey," a man shouted from a neighboring yard. The voice was deep and threatening.

Hannah stumbled and turned to find her neighbor, Terry, running from his back door, wearing nothing but a pair of boxer shorts. His thick fist was wrapped around the handle of a baseball bat and his eyes were wide as he raced toward the hedge, separating them.

"Where'd he go?" Terry asked breathlessly.

Terry Haskins was a man in his mid-forties, who had lived next to Hannah for a dozen years. He kept his head (and apparently his body) smooth either through razor or wax. He was muscular and handsome and single. Hannah knew little else about him. But there he stood hefting a baseball bat, ready to take on whomever had trespassed on Hannah's property.

Just then the importance of his presence occurred to her. Terry had seen Ben. Well, Terry had seen *someone.*

"You saw him?" Hannah asked, just wanting to be sure.

"I saw him," Terry said. He tuned his head to search the yards. "Where'd he go?"

"Gone," Hannah replied, noting the sadness in her own voice. "Thank you for the help."

"Did you get a good look at him?" Terry asked.

"Yes, I think so."

"Do you want me to call the police?"

"No, but thank you."

"Are you sure?"

"I'm sure."

It was because she had seen the figure so clearly that Hannah didn't want to involve the authorities. Ben had come home. The thought was so exciting. She wondered if she should be frightened. She imagined most people would be if they'd just seen a ghost, but the strongest emotion she felt was anticipation. She wanted to see him again.

Distracted by her thoughts Hannah didn't immediately register the fact that her neighbor was talking to her. "Excuse me?" she said.

"I was just saying that I work strange hours." Terry lifted his hand and pointed at a window on the second floor of his house. "My office is right up there. I usually stare out the window when I need to get my thoughts together. That's how I saw the guy. I mean, I don't want you to think I stay up all night watching your house or anything weird like that."

"What in the world would you *want* to see over here?" Hannah asked, amused by her neighbor's exposition. "I certainly appreciate your concern, though. Thank you."

"You're welcome. If you need anything just holler."

"Are people saying 'holler' again?" Hannah asked distractedly. She smiled, but it was fostered by the wonder of what had happened before her neighbor had appeared and not his interesting vocabulary.

"I suppose so." Terry returned the smile. "Well, I guess I better get back to work."

"And I should get to bed."

They said goodnight and Hannah returned to her kitchen. She turned off the yard lights and locked the door behind her. Then, as an afterthought, she unlocked it.

Just in case Ben wants to come in, she thought.

That night as she entertained curious dreams of her husband, Hannah's sleep was disturbed by the impression that somebody was tickling the bottom of her foot. At first it startled her into a half waking, but she quickly attributed the sensation to her dreams.

Ben had always liked her feet. She often thought it was one of the odder fetishes people pursued but many nights had been spent with Ben's tongue tickling her arches and working between her toes. He used to enjoy rubbing his penis between her feet once the soles were slicked with spit. Hannah was incredibly ticklish so it wasn't always the sexiest thing for her, but she allowed it, if only to see the pure joy on her husband's face.

She looked around the room, nothing but blur and shadow. No one knelt on the floor at the foot of her bed, and she found herself disappointed.

Hannah lay back down and closed her eyes.

6

Stuart's day began with a headache and a struggle to get out of bed. Pudge Taylor's murder had kept him at the office late, and he'd carried the details home with him, where they'd rattled around his mind until exhaustion finally silenced the thoughts just after two a.m. Though pre-existing, the cuts on Pudge's feet—the ones that may have been a letter A or may have been absolutely random—kept appearing behind his eyes. Clarissa, his late wife, had been marked in this way. The lines of the letter so deeply cut as to have severed tendons in her foot. Considering Pudge's connection to Baxter and Thomason, and Alan Mean's recent death, Stuart couldn't keep the killers out of his head, nor could he keep Clarissa's memory silent. So all night he'd followed winding trails of thought from Pudge to Alan to Selma Baxter and Derek Thomason and then to his wife. Every time sleep would approach, Clarissa would appear cold and pale on the autopsy table, replacing Pudge and dredging up sour memories and bitter regrets.

After breakfast and a shower, Stuart dressed and left the house. He drove to the supermarket on the corner of York and Peters and bought a dozen white roses, and then he drove east, across Barnard to the freeway and took the onramp to the northbound lanes. Shopping centers and generic chain restaurants covered the land on either side of the freeway. These gave way to car dealerships and fast food joints, then lower-end shopping centers took over. He exited at Crowell Drive and continued on the service road until he reached the drive of the Harris Ranch Memorial Park, onto which he turned and followed the narrow lane into the cemetery.

He hadn't visited Clarissa's grave in nearly seven months; whenever he thought about it, a list of chores, suddenly very necessary, cropped up, and the visit would be postponed, but after a long night with her intermittently on his mind, dismal recollections of her corpse sandwiched between those of Alan Means and Pudge Taylor, the need to visit had overwhelmed him. If nothing else, it might quell the insistent memories of her, might relieve a touch of his guilt.

The thing he never spoke about after Clarissa's murder, the thing he found so difficult to deal with himself was the fact that their marriage hadn't been a happy one. He knew that in the aftermath of tragedy, people often idealized what was lost. So many people had come up to him to tell him how wonderful Clarissa was, and he'd thanked them and agreed. He believed she was wonderful, but their last four years together had been a nightmare, and the relationship hadn't been particularly contented before that. Fifteen years of marriage had chipped away at their personalities so that the grooves and teeth of them no longer worked together like synchronized gears, but rather ground and rattled revealing their broken machine. By the time Clarissa stormed out of the house that last night, they'd entered what Harlan had called the "Tourette's Stage" of the relationship. Clarissa would shout at him, insult and demean him until he'd felt compelled to respond in kind. She wouldn't let up until his temper rose to the same level of anger as hers, and profanity was as much a staple of their dialogues as the accusatory "You always…"

That was one of the reasons he hadn't gone to more than a few of Hannah's group meetings. If he'd continued with them, he felt sure something would slip out, and though he wasn't worried about incriminating himself—he hadn't killed his wife—he didn't want to tarnish Clarissa's memory by pointing out exactly how miserable she'd made him in the end. Some of his buddies at the station knew about it, and Harlan certainly knew it, but except for those few, Stuart had kept the information to himself.

He parked and climbed out of the car, walked away and then remembered the roses dripping water all over his back seat. Once he'd retrieved them, he set off across the freshly mowed grass, its scent clean and soothing in his head. The cemetery was relatively modern, which meant few tombs rose from the lawn. Instead, neat bronze plaques lay nestled in the emerald blades covering the field closest to the drive, and beyond these over a low hillock, more traditional stones of marble and granite, the majority of them small and tasteful, hardly larger than a carry-on suitcase, stood. Throughout the cemetery, well-placed oak trees cast shade and broke up the starkness of the lawns. In the distance Stuart saw Clarissa's marker and was surprised to note that someone already stood before it.

Of course, he recognized the man immediately as Clarissa's brother, Philip Tate. Phil stood six-foot-five-inches tall and had to weigh somewhere north of three hundred and twenty pounds. He wore a close-cropped graying beard, though his hair was in a state of tangled curls. Phil preferred to be called "Thumper," a name he'd earned as a lineman, playing high school and college football, and had only tolerated his given name when it was spoken by his sister. Thumper had visited the house a lot in the first several years of Stuart's marriage. They had sat around Sunday afternoons drinking beer, watching the games. Sometimes they'd head up north to the river and do some fishing. Thumper was a good guy, if a little less than ambitious. But after things went south with Clarissa, she preferred to meet her brother at his shabby apartment. Stuart had seen very little of the man in the two years since Clarissa's death, but Thumper always greeted him warmly, and Stuart imagined the death of his sister still hurt the man quite a bit.

He followed the walking path around an oak and then stepped onto the lawn to cross to Clarissa's plot. Thumper lifted his head, noticing Stuart's approach. His brow furrowed for a moment as if questioning Stuart's presence, but it smoothed and Thumper reached out to shake his hand.

"Thumper," Stuart said.

"Stuart. Nice to see you."

"It's been a while."

"I didn't know you still came out here," Thumper said.

The statement hadn't been meant as an accusation, but once it had filtered through Stuart's guilt it felt like one. "I get out here when I can," he said, looking away from the bearded man to Clarissa's marker. "Not as often as I should, I guess."

"Well, it's not like she's waiting for you to bring her a sandwich," Thumper said. "I only get out here about once a month myself these days, but I got Ma and Daddy to visit as well. And it's only a few blocks from the store."

Thumper worked at Barnard Stone where he fashioned countertops and tabletops from granite, marble, and other slabs of rock. He'd insisted on making his sister's headstone, and he'd done a fine job of it, using a piece of marble that revealed a pinkish hue in full daylight. A sconce attached at the side was meant to hold flowers, and a nice bouquet of brightly colored blossoms jutted from it. Stuart looked at the white roses he carried, then to the finely etched face of the marker.

"She loved roses," Thumper said.

"I know," Stuart said. "White ones because red ones were too predictable."

Early in their relationship, Stuart had been the romantic sort. He'd brought Clarissa flowers and candy, the way he'd always seen on television, but after the wedding he'd grown less diligent and over the years, on those few occasions when he did surprise Clarissa with a bouquet or a box of pralines—her favorite sweet—she'd accepted the offerings with suspicion. The last time he'd brought his wife a bunch of white roses, she accused him of having an affair and smashed the flowers on a table, beating the surface with them until the bouquet had been reduced to stems. He'd never tried again.

"She also liked the peach-colored ones," Thumper said, "but those are harder to find, and white was her favorite."

"Yeah."

They stood there for some time, neither knowing what to say. Stuart felt uncomfortable. He hadn't expected to find Thumper in the graveyard, eager to talk about his sister, and an overpowering urge to leave rapped inside Stuart's chest. He hadn't come here to reminisce and exacerbate his regrets; he'd come to placate them.

"It's a shame you two never had kids," Thumper finally said. "Someone to carry on after you."

Stuart clenched his teeth and nodded.

"I know you two decided not to have them," Thumper said quickly. "I'm not trying to start anything. It just would have been nice is all."

It would have been, Stuart agreed silently. Apparently Clarissa hadn't told her younger brother everything, the way he'd once suspected.

While it was true they'd agreed to hold off on having children for a while, what with them both just starting out on their careers, and Stuart's time as a patrolman being particularly stressful, their abstinence from parenthood had always been, in Stuart's mind, provisional. He wanted children, and after he'd been promoted to detective, he'd tried to convince Clarissa that their household and careers were stable enough to try, but she'd balked at the idea, saying the time wasn't right. This had gone on for years until Stuart had confronted his wife on the matter. Instead of a rational discussion, it had turned into a shouting match. He'd tried to stay calm and explain why a child meant so much to him, but that had only made things worse, and finally she'd confessed that she wasn't physically able to bear children, and how dare he make her feel inadequate and selfish for her medical condition. His response to this confession, delivered to him at striking distance with all of the subtleness of a rattler bite, was fury. She'd lied to him. For over a decade, she'd pretended that it was a practical matter, something they would resolve in time, knowing full well she could never have a child, and his temper got loose.

In the wake of this argument, their relationship had gone from strained to pure shit. He'd thought about leaving her—thought about it a lot—but there was too much love and familiarity to just walk away. He resented her and at times downright hated her for the deceit, but he hadn't abandoned her.

"We should go fishing," Thumper said, changing the subject completely. "Maybe catch a game some weekend."

"We should," Stuart agreed, though he knew it wouldn't happen. Every conversation they had would be as tense and miserable as this one, and not just for Stuart. He could see the discomfort in Thumper's eyes as well. They stood on either side of a wound and any attempt to communicate just tore it open.

"I've got to get back to the shop," Thumper said, backing away from Clarissa's marker.

"Yeah," Stuart replied. "I should get to work soon myself."

"It was good seeing you again, Stuart."

"You too, Thumper."

"Be sure to stay in touch."

"I will."

Thumper plodded away, and Stuart began to feel foolish standing there, holding a bouquet of flowers. No, he felt more than foolish; he felt like a hypocrite, because while he'd told only a handful of people about the problems he and Clarissa had shared in the last years of their relationship, before she was abducted from Carter Park and taken to the basement of that house on Ash Street, there was something he hadn't been able to confide in anyone: amid his sadness at losing a companion so near him and his anger at the butchers who'd made her last moments so terrible, in the wake of Clarissa's death, Stuart had also felt relief.

7

Mike Addison sat in his room, eyes fixed on a television screen on which monstrous aliens jumped from the dilapidated remains of an office building to charge his gaming character. He used the game controller to move a gun sight over the creatures and flicked the trigger rapidly, creating blossoms of sickly green wounds on their bodies. It was an old game, one he knew by heart, but the noise and the brilliantly gruesome colors provided familiar distraction. He'd moved his chair into the corner, further away from the television than he would have liked, but the joining of the two walls protected his back. Dory couldn't sneak up on him unless she passed through plaster and paint.

He thought about this, his mind going so far as to picture Dory hovering over his shoulders as he played. Mike turned quickly to find the corner empty, then returned to the game. His momentary distraction proved lethal for his character, however. A sickly yellow creature with a face full of teeth eclipsed the scene and the screen turned red amid the sounds of moist crunching.

Mike looked at the television with only the vaguest interest, thinking that it would be nice if the real world worked liked one of his games. Lessons could be learned with no true mortality at stake. Death only meant returning to the beginning of the level or being revived in some imaginative, and impossible, medical device to face the monsters with greater skill and the prescience of repetition. Dory could play the level over again and stay in the house or scream her head off when she saw Selma Baxter crossing the yard for her. But the only similarity his games shared with the real world were victims and the monsters that hunted them.

Instead of resetting the level and shooting his way through the office building again, Mike dropped the controller between his thigh and the arm of his chair. He yawned widely and rubbed his eyes.

He hadn't slept the night before. Whenever he'd neared sleep he thought about Dory's visit, and a flare of panic had sent enough adrenaline into his system to push it away.

Mike stood from the chair and walked to the bedroom door. He pulled it open and leaped back in surprise when he saw the girl standing at the threshold.

"Shit," he said.

"Sorry," Gwen Clermont said, looking embarrassed. "I was just about to knock."

"Nah," Evan Lord said, skirting Gwen and walking into the room, "she was listening at the door hoping to hear you beating it."

Mike followed Evan with his eyes. His friend crossed the room and dropped into Mike's desk chair, leaned back like it was the most natural thing in the world.

"What are you guys doing here?"

"It's an intervention, man," Evan announced. "Work from a place of love."

"Ignore him," Gwen said. She walked into the room and faced Mike. "We missed you, and we know you're still pissed at us, but we wanted to talk."

"There's nothing to talk about," Mike told her.

Ever since the night they'd broken into the house on Ash Street, defiance had formed a ragged scab over his emotions. He'd told Gwen and Evan to leave him alone, but here they were. Complicating the matter was the fact that he wanted them to stay, because he sure as hell didn't want to be alone.

"Obviously, there is something to talk about," Gwen replied.

"Whatever," Mike said.

"Oh, boo-fucking-hoo," Evan cried, "Mikey's all distant and tormented… again. Look, you're freaking us out, okay? The way you've been acting is totally borderline, and Gwen thinks you're going to be found hanging in your closet or in a pool of blood or something. Now, if some stranger wants to off himself that's between him and his razor blade, but you don't sit back and let your friends sink. So are we friends or not? Simple question. Simple answer."

"Evan," Gwen warned.

But Evan wasn't backing down. "Answer the question, Mikey."

Mike stood in the middle of the room, feeling trapped. He should have told them to go to hell and get out of his room, but why? They hadn't done anything to him. Evan had suggested they go to a house, and Mike had agreed.

"Maybe we should come back later," Gwen said.

"No," Mike said. "Evan's right. We're friends. Let's hang."

"Cool," Evan said, happily. "Let's hit Porter's for some caffeine. Mike is buying."

They'd been at Porter's Coffee Pot that other night, too. Three weeks ago. Before his arm was cut and his grandfather died in the blazing remains of the house on Ash…

Hannah pushed the sliced cabbage into the frying pan, covering the sizzling onions and strips of beef. The cabbage hissed and popped. After using the spatula to evenly disperse the shredded leaves about the pan, she frosted the cooking vegetables with a thin layer of mashed potatoes and covered the skillet. Ben had called the dish "Bubble and Squeak." His mother had handed down the recipe to Hannah thirty years ago, the night the two women had met for the first time. Hannah couldn't stand the smell or the taste of it, but it was Ben's favorite meal. Janis Joplin wailed through the sound system, offering another little piece of her heart. A gin and tonic sweated through its glass on the edge of the kitchen counter. The back door stood open and a warm, grass-scented breeze pushed through the screen, blending with the nasty stench rising from the pan. Late evening light, pink and amber, bathed the backyard. Insects, motes of pollen, and flecks of dust floated through the air like miniature fish traversing a pastel sea.

Hannah hoped she hadn't prepared the meal too early. It had been very late the first time her love had appeared to her, and she wondered if, like Hamlet's father, Ben could only appear in the early morning hours before dawn. The idea that levels of illumination might limit a spirit's movement struck her as more than a bit silly—After all, what harm could sunlight do a soul?—but still she did not count paranormal studies among her fields of expertise, and as such, she accepted the fact that her kitchen might reek with Ben's precious "Bubble and Squeak" for many hours to come. It didn't matter. She wanted her Ben to know he was welcome and if that meant preparing the awful dish every night for the next six months, then so be it. Naturally, Hannah hoped it wouldn't take that long for Ben to return. She so wanted to see him, to talk to him. Even if the message he brought her was terrible and heart breaking, she would hear it and do what she could to ease his spirit.

Porter's Coffee Pot was designed to resemble a New York coffee house with exposed brick walls and bookshelves carefully painted to look cracked and worn, carrying cheap copies of the works of Plath, Mailer, Kerouac, Woolfe, Vidal, and dozens of other authors the bulk of the clientele had no interest in reading. Faux velvet couches in tragic shades of violet and crimson occupied the center of the main room beneath a ceiling fan that resembled an airplane propeller. Fake columns ran floor to ceiling. Their paint too was cracked. The whole place looked remarkably calculated, and though the owner wanted to get the feel of an authentic New York coffee house, she had missed by a mile, though few in Barnard would have noticed.

The regular patrons were a mix of high school students and artistically adjacent sorts, who sat gazing for hours at their laptops, occasionally grinning knowingly and tapping a few keys or hoisting their mugs for sips of coffee before again returning to their serene paralysis. Others also used their laptops, taking advantage of Porter's wifi connection, cruising the web for information and sharing conversation with people hundreds, sometimes thousands, of miles away.

Mike sat at a table by the tinted front window, waiting for Gwen and Evan to return with their coffees. Conversations, some loud and others hushed, carried on against a backdrop of boring guitar music. Mike watched a blond guy whose clumped hair jutted oddly from his head punch his laptop's keys, looking furious. Mike wondered why these idiots sought out a public setting to pursue wholly introverted behavior. It was like they wanted to be *among* people but not *with* them.

Evan and Gwen worked their way around the purple sofa, and Evan accidentally bumped the blond guy's shoulder. The guy shot a bitter look Evan's way, but it quickly broke into a wan smile and a light wave—*No problem.* His friends dropped into chairs on either side of him, and Mike took the large cup of coffee Gwen offered. Evan immediately shrank into his customary sit-slouch, draping an arm over the back of his chair as if he would collapse without its support.

"So, dudelet," Evan said. "How's the arm gash?"

"Fine," Mike replied, lifting his coffee to his lips. It was too hot to drink, but instead of setting it down, he kept it at his mouth as he said, "It itches."

"That was a totally fucked up night," Evan mused, like he was remembering a kick ass party featuring beer and girls rather than a nasty bit of breaking and entering complete with dust and ghosts. "The last of its kind."

Mike bristled at the comment. The night had been the last of its kind because his grandfather had gone flame-happy on the place—and died in the process. Of course, Evan didn't make this connection in his mind. The jerk was incapable of following the path of the verbal spears he randomly lobbed and wholly unaware of who they struck or the damage they caused.

Fortunately Gwen jumped on the comment, because Mike's thoughts were in knots. "You're not allowed to talk," she told Evan. "Your contributions to the conversation are now limited to nods and grunts."

"*What?*" Evan asked, sounding genuinely confused.

"It's cool," Mike said.

And he wanted it to be cool, but it wasn't. His feelings had less to do with Evan's recent idiocy, though. As he sat there, looking at his friends, Mike still felt disconnected from them. The feeling had begun the night he'd cut his arm and seen the ghosts in that terrible basement on Ash Street, but he'd fully expected the sense of dislocation with his friends to pass given a few days. It hadn't. If anything, he felt farther away from Gwen and Evan. The more they reached out, the greater his withdrawal, like a toy bobbing on a lake and their attempts to bring him closer only created ripples pushing him further away. Mike hated the feeling, because it wasn't really a feeling at all. It was a cold and numb hole centered behind his ribcage, and everything he'd once thought important fell into it.

Evan was his best friend. Evan was exactly two months younger than Mike. They had met in the third grade, thinking it a sign from the universe that they had both brought identical Spider-Man action figures to school. Evan wanted to design video games. Evan thought Tia Ingram was hot, and he acted like an even bigger ass around her than he did around anybody else. Evan liked his pizza with everything, even anchovies. These were facts. Statistics. Mike observed his friend as he might a specimen in science class with all of the pertinent details listed in bullet point fashion.

Gwen brought a different, more detailed, list to mind but if any emotion accompanied that list, it fell into the hole behind his ribs before touching him. He'd loved her once; the memory of it remained, as easy to access as his cell phone number. He'd tried to kiss her, and her sharp rebuke had forced his overt longing into dormancy for the sake of their friendship. The mental mementoes of those days had not vanished, but the feelings associated with them had. This persistent numbing scared him. It was inside of him, part of him, which made it inescapable.

"Jillie's getting an eye full o' Mikey," Evan said, smirking.

Mike craned his neck and saw the girl Evan meant, sitting with two other girls at a small table in the corner. She was a pretty brunette with dark skin and brown eyes named Jill Ironside, and she'd carried on her unreciprocated crush since last year. Her head notched noticeably downward when Mike looked in her direction.

"I think we know how Mike feels about that," Gwen said.

Nothing, he thought. None of the embarrassment or pride he had once felt came with the knowledge that this attractive girl had feelings for him—just another bit of data, another statistic.

"He should be hitting that," Evan said. "I'd totally be hitting that."

"Jill wouldn't let you near her, even if she was up to her neck in quicksand," Gwen said.

"Cold," Evan replied. "You're a cold, cruel woman, Gwendolyn."

"Call me that again and you won't be hitting anything, because I'll rip your dick off."

"Mmm," Evan hummed, rubbing his stomach. "Dirty talk's as good as candy."

"Savor it," Mike said, surprising his friends with the comment. "It's as close to sex as you're ever going to get."

"Mikey comes back swinging," Evan said approvingly. "I can only assume that the gloves are off and we can proceed with the smack down?"

"Bring it," Mike told him. He smiled and reached for his coffee.

As Evan tore into him with a series of good-natured insults, Mike played the game. None of it amused him the way it would have before his grandfather's death. In fact, every word Evan or Gwen spoke hit his ears like jagged glass, and every reply Mike fashioned tore along his throat, painfully, but he needed to be among his friends, and though the façade was exhausting, Mike kept it up.

Maybe if he pretended to be okay long enough, eventually he would be.

8

Melanie woke late in the morning. A bar of light from a break in the curtains cut across her face, blinding her when she opened her eyes. She rolled over and pressed into Reg's back, kissed his shoulder, and slid out of bed. Pulling the white t-shirt she slept in down she crossed the room and walked into the hall, to the kitchen and on into the living room. She looked around for a moment, uncertain as to why she'd walked into this room instead of the kitchen where the coffeepot waited to be filled. Confounded by this break in her morning routine, Melanie turned back for the kitchen.

As the coffee brewed, Melanie opened the utility room door. Two minutes later, she wore ankle socks, a pair of green sweatpants, and a royal blue t-shirt that fit her snugly. She filled a chrome travel mug with coffee, splashed in some milk and emptied a packet of sweetener into the container, swirled the whole thing around, and then left the house. The sun was bright outside and Melanie considered going back in for her sunglasses, but didn't want to take the chance of waking Reg.

When she'd been employed by Mercury Parcel, she'd walked to and from the office. She'd considered it her contribution to saving the planet, not to mention saving a bunch of money on actually owning a car of her own. The walks, particularly those to the office, had served to clear her mind for the day ahead. Once she'd signed on for a second season of *The Haunt Club* and was able to give up the office job, Melanie had continued the practice of walking every day. She never gauged the distance. It might have been two miles or five miles. It didn't matter. She walked until the sleep was out of her eyes and her mind felt clear, then she headed home. It wasn't exercise at all, really. More like therapy.

This morning, as with most recent mornings, she thought about Mack Durham and Kee Ulrich. Their stunts had grown more blatant and annoying with each passing episode. She still fumed over last night's Popsicle incident.

She turned the corner on to Lloyd Street and faced the city park. Late morning on a weekday, the expanse of lawn was unoccupied and save for a single jogger just disappearing down a dirt trail on the north side of the park, the place could have been deserted.

"Hey," a voice shouted behind her. "Hey, ghost girl."

Oh great, Melanie thought. She paused on the sidewalk and turned to the voice.

A man of approximately her age, wearing a sharp-edged brown suit with a perfectly knotted yellow tie trotted toward her. His leather briefcase swung from its shoulder strap to hit his hip like a handbag. He wore a bright smile. The grin and his clothing made her think of Mack, and Melanie disliked the guy instantly. "Ghost girl" comment aside, he wore the arrogant veneer of someone who skipped blithely over his fellow man in pursuit of his own victories, and Melanie had met enough of this sort to know them on sight.

"Hey," he called again as if he didn't already have her attention. "Didn't you hear me back there?"

"I guess not," Melanie said.

"Well, I've been chasing you for a block."

"Sorry. My head was a million miles away."

"Yeah," the guy said as if extremely put out. "Whatever. Look my kid loves your program. I haven't seen it, but he talks about this ghost shit all day long. Bradley saw you walking by and wanted to get your autograph or something. He kept saying you guys lived in town. Whatever. You are her right?"

"I think so," Melanie said.

"Anyway, if you've got a signed picture or something my kid would like one."

Melanie looked down at her outfit. "I don't carry that sort of thing around with me."

The guy rolled his eyes as if this was simply the latest in a hundred disappointments she had delivered upon him. Appearing frustrated and impatient, he yanked on the zipper of his briefcase and reached inside.

"I guess I thought you were like a television star or something," he muttered digging around in the bag. "My kid makes it sound like you're the next Jennifer Aniston or something."

"Different kind of show," Melanie replied.

"Yeah well it wouldn't kill you to make it a little easier on the fans you *do* have."

The fans I have aren't assholes, she thought.

Most of the show's fans were considerate and interested in the investigations. Some suggested locations for future programs, going so far as to offer interesting—if likely embellished—tales of their own paranormal experiences. They weren't well-dressed dicks, trying to prove to their kids that nothing was beyond Daddy's power.

The man yanked out a yellow legal pad and shoved it at Melanie. Once she took the tablet from him, he reached into the breast pocket of his dress shirt and produced a Mont Blanc pen. This too he shoved at her.

"Bradley?" she asked, grudgingly removing the pen from the guy's grip. "Traditional spelling?"

"How many spellings are there? B-r-a-d-l-e-y."

Melanie wrote: To Bradley, who will be haunted for the rest of his days.

She signed her name and handed the pen and pad back to the man.

The man looked at the pad like a bill he wasn't expecting. "You think that's an appropriate thing to tell a kid?"

"He watches the show," Melanie said. "He'll understand."

"Whatever," the man said. Without a thank you, he turned away and trotted back the way he'd come.

"Poor poor, Bradley," Melanie whispered.

Above her, a pale blue sky spread out like a comfortable blanket. The sun appeared as a melting white ball high above the line of trees, rising beyond the park's lawn. The thick emerald green field stretched from the running path at the base of the oaks to the sidewalk across the street from her. The blades were lush and welcoming and immaculately trimmed. On her left, the playground rose like a tentacled beast with plastic globe eyes. Slides and ladders erupted from the central mass of the structure, which stood on stilts growing from a pit of sand. The playground was deserted. Children were in school. This place wouldn't see life until late afternoon.

Melanie crossed the street and climbed the sidewalk. She stepped onto the grass and began walking toward the running path and the stand of trees.

Though she'd initially felt some spark of satisfaction at the inscription she'd written for Bradley—who would be haunted for the rest of his days—Melanie now felt guilty. The petty slam against the kid's father now struck her as cheap. Maybe it had been an inappropriate thing to write for a kid. She should have kept it light and fun, but the father's aggressiveness and her own feelings of shame at the way the show was evolving had put her on edge.

The thing was, the audience didn't seem to care. They tuned in every week, even though Melanie and the other Para-Troopers had yet to discover a single presence they couldn't explain away as dust motes, light reflection, bad wiring, ancient plumbing, a settling building, or calculated tampering by the show's producer. Every week she expected to lose the audience, who would see her as a fraud and would see her life's work as silly and pointless, but the audience remained. It grew.

The ratings swell shouldn't have surprised her, but it did. It seemed like the audience knew it was all a sham, and they expected it to be. Over the years they'd become desensitized to deceit. A spate of "reality" shows that were no more real than scripted dramas poured through their flat panel televisions, blurring the lines between truth and melodrama. Celebrity secrets, all of them precisely calculated by public relations gurus and image managers, were exposed week after week on a dozen entertainment news programs, and the audiences ate them up as candid truths. Even elected officials played the game. Once the public had demanded integrity from their leaders, but now they seemed satisfied with a good performance and the occasional wink. Politicians had no more credibility than polyester-suited used car salesman, and the public knew it, yet they still cast their votes, never looking too closely lest they see the fingers crossed behind their candidates' backs.

The Haunt Club was part of the culture. For Melanie the show was a *victim* of this culture, but Mack and Kee treated it like a champion of the form.

She wandered through the park for another twenty minutes, her thoughts focused on the accepted superficiality of life. Then she left the park, carrying her concerns with her. An hour later she was home, walking through the front door to hear Reg stirring in the kitchen. Melanie crossed the living room and met her boyfriend at the dinette table. She leaned in to kiss him. He'd just shoved a spoonful of Coco Puffs into his mouth and she tasted milk and chocolate on his lips during the awkward kiss.

"Mail came," he said from the side of his mouth, as he struggled to keep the breakfast cereal from spilling out. Even before he swallowed the last mouthful, he was spooning another onto his tongue.

"Bills," Melanie dismissed, headed for the coffeepot to refill her mug.

"The studio," Reg said, his voice garbled. "They sent over the show's mail. It's on the counter."

"Don't talk with your mouth full."

Melanie turned to the counter and saw a green plastic tub overflowing with envelopes. As always the sheer volume of correspondence from the show's fans, and those with less kind things to say, amazed her. Even more amazing was the fact that the bulk of *The Haunt Club's* communications came via email. The contents of the glutted green tub represented only a fraction of the comments and condemnations of the show's viewers.

"Crap," Melanie said, turning back to Reg. "It'll take two days to get through all of that."

"You got other plans?" he asked.

"Shut up and eat your breakfast."

Reg dropped his spoon in the bowl, sending up a low splash of milk. He stood from the table and placed the bowl in the sink. "Breakfast done," Reg said, the words growling deep in his throat. "Now want woman." He hunched over and held his arms out, stalking across the kitchen toward Melanie. "Want woman now."

"Are you doing a caveman or Frankenstein?" Melanie asked with a smile.

Reg backed her into the counter and wrapped one of his burly arms around her waist. "I do you," he said, pulling her close and pushing his lips into the soft skin of her neck.

"I haven't showered yet," Melanie said.

"Mmm," Reg hummed into her throat. "Me like woman stinky."

Melanie laughed and nuzzled him back.

"You know, I don't think the problem is the show or the audience," Reg said, shifting his body against hers.

They lay on the kitchen floor. The air conditioning chilled the sweat on Melanie's stomach, making her shiver and push in closer to Reg.

"Yeah, then what's the problem?"

"I think it's you," Reg said. "And don't freak out. I don't mean there's anything *wrong* with you. I just think we've been doing this for a while, and we haven't really found anything. I think you're starting to lose faith."

"I'm not losing faith," Melanie said. "I just think I'm the only one who takes the investigations seriously these days."

"Yvonne takes them seriously."

"I love Yvonne like a sister, but the girl isn't exactly grounded in the real."

"And you don't think I take them seriously?"

"Not the way you used to."

"Well, maybe I'm just more reasonable about it. I mean, we go to a place for a couple of days and expect the spirits to appear on command. It's not like these things have calendars or work to a particular schedule. They aren't floating around waiting for their close-ups.

"Like that house on Baker Street we did last year. Over the last sixty years, they've reported—What?—twenty sightings? That's like three a year. We go in and spend a couple of days and when the entity doesn't show, we consider it a myth we've just debunked. I don't buy it. If we had equipment set up for a few months, and really monitored these cases, really invested the time and effort in them, then we could make educated assessments, but we don't have that luxury."

"I know."

"So, you may think I'm not as serious as I used to be, but you'd be wrong. I'm just seeing the flaws in our methodology. And no, I don't think we're going to find anything, not if we keep doing things the way we have been."

"What choice have we got?" Melanie asked. "Kee isn't going to let us spend an entire season on one location."

"Yeah, but I'm not worried about Kee or Mack or the audience. I'm worried about you. When we started the Troopers, you couldn't wait to get to a location. Every time someone sent us an email about a possible case, you'd light up like a kid at Christmas, and you'd start researching the property and the people involved. You don't do that anymore."

"I'm still thorough," Melanie countered.

"But you're not enjoying it. It doesn't drive you the way it used to."

Reg was probably right, but Melanie figured you could only hit a brick wall so many times before starting to realize the wall wasn't going to give and the only thing your drive offered were more bruises. She didn't say anything. She pushed in close to Reg, feeling the hairs on his chest tickling the soft skin of her breasts.

He kissed her nose and then looked into her eyes. "The universe is a big place. We aren't the total of it all. We're just parts," he said. "Don't let the job fuck with your beliefs."

Melanie sat at the dinette table going through the tub of mail. She'd showered with Reg, who'd left her under the spray so he could get downtown to buy another thermometer for the show. She glanced over the letters quickly and placed them into one of three piles: general fan mail, which could include everything from, "Great shows. Keep 'em coming," to more suggestive passages which often included less than subtle double entendres about possession, "If I could get inside of you…" and some outright, "Let's fuck," notes; general hate mail, which usually started with a pleasant greeting before rapidly descending into outrage at one perceived slight or another; and the final stack which was for suggested "cases" to be featured on future shows. Not surprisingly, Melanie found this last pile the most interesting.

The letter from Alan Means lay amid the correspondences near the middle of the tub. Melanie noticed nothing interesting about the envelope or the return address. It had been postmarked nearly two weeks ago, which seemed like a very long time for the letter to have been hovering in postal limbo, but it wasn't exactly unheard of. She opened the envelope and pulled two sheets of notepaper out with the intent of giving them a quick glance before deciding which pile they belonged to, but the handwritten note—the tight scrawl of the man's penmanship, the direct nature of the message—intrigued her, and Melanie read the letter all the way through. Then she read it again.

Dear Miss Bell,

My name is Alan Means, and I don't sleep well. As such, I find myself up late at night, watching the television. That's how I first saw your show. You seem sincere, and I'm asking you to help me.

I live in Barnard, Texas. There is a house here. It's on Ash Street, and something terrible is happening inside. Terrible things have always happened there.

Ash Street

The house used to belong to a pair of monsters named Selma Baxter and Derek Thomason. If you haven't heard of them, you can find out anything you want to know on the Internet, so I won't use up paper describing them or what they did. I will say that my granddaughter fell victim to these two just over three years ago. Dory was a good girl. She was only ten years old when they took her. Both Baxter and Thomason are in prison now, but the house is still there, and their victims are still inside.

I know how that sounds. I'm a practical man and I didn't believe in all of this supernatural hooey before, but I do now. I've seen the ghosts. I've seen Dory.

My grandson, Michael, visited the house the other night. He went with some friends. Only God knows why. He was inside that house and something attacked him. When he told me about the incident, I assumed the attack came from some addict, hiding inside to get high, but Michael told me he saw Dory. He saw her and the others.

The following night, I went to the house on Ash Street. I was afraid to go inside. I knew all of the terrible things that had happened in that place, and though I told myself I wouldn't enter because it was against the law, the truth is, the place scares me. Looking at it was like looking at the grill of a car racing toward me, knowing it would run me down. Just staring at the front door made me about sick to my stomach. Then a face appeared in the window. It was the face of a black girl. She looked hurt and scared. I didn't recognize her immediately, but I knew she needed help. She looked so desperate. The yellow dress she wore was torn and barely hung on to her body. I ran forward, across the overgrown lawn and cracked walkway. As I drew closer, I began to realize that I knew this young woman.

Her name was Regina Wolcroff. You can find a lot of information about her on the Internet, too.

Once I recognized the girl, I stopped running for the front door. I turned around and fled. All night I was haunted by that young woman's face. She had been a victim of Baxter and Thomason, just like my Dory had been. I thought about my granddaughter trapped in that horrible place, and it sickened me. I couldn't let her stay there.

The next night I returned, and Dory was there. Michael had told me that he and his friends had entered the house through the kitchen window, so that's what I did. At first, the place felt empty.

I said Dory's name. I could barely whisper it, because I felt so silly about the whole thing, but then I really shouted. I needed to find her, needed to get her out of that house.

I heard a sound on the stairs to the basement and turned to the open door. Dory stood on the threshold, looking at me with frightened eyes. She spoke to me. She wanted out.

She took my hand and I led her to the kitchen door, but she recoiled from it, terrified. She screamed and ran back to the basement. A second later, she was gone.

I've been back to that house three times, and each time I see a different victim of Baxter and Thomason before Dory appears. They are all lost, some of them raving. I don't know how to set them free, so I wrote you this letter.

I want you to come to Barnard and see the people trapped in the house on Ash Street. I want you to free them, if you can. You have to get Dory out of there.

I don't know what else to do.
Sincerely,
Alan Means

Melanie put the letter down and stood from the desk. She paced the room quickly as if caged between its walls. The note had her excited, not that she believed the old man's story, not entirely, it was insane, but the possibility of it, even if a fraction of the letter was true, she knew it would make a phenomenal investigation. These weren't some antiquated spirits who had shuffled around a gothic inn for the last hundred and fifty years. They were contemporary, and though she doubted the apparitions Alan Means described in his letter—those were likely a hoax or the fabrications of a weathered mind—the back-story was fascinating.

She'd heard of Selma Baxter and Derek Thomason. She'd followed the case for a while; it was impossible to be wholly oblivious to it. A couple of years ago it was the biggest story on the news. She'd even seen a terrible Made-for-TV movie about the killers.

Melanie hurried to her computer and plugged their names into her search engine. Tens of thousands of pages came back. Most of these were true-crime sites and serial killer fan pages. They would help to fill in the history of the crimes, but they weren't the kind of legitimate documentation she needed. She clicked through the "News" link and was surprised to find recent articles about Baxter and Thomason.

Then, she read the second headline down and her heart sank: *Arson Destroys Serial Killers' Den.* Tentatively, she clicked through to the article, and sure enough, the house on Ash Street was gone, reduced to cinder and rubble by a mentally unstable senior. His name was Alan Means, of course, and he had been killed in the blaze.

Melanie closed the web page and leaned back in her chair, disappointed. She'd thought about going to Barnard even before finishing Alan Means's letter. Not to scout for the show, but to follow an investigation of her own. If Mack and Kee knew about the story, they'd peck and caw over the glittering sensationalism of Baxter and Thomason, grabbing the shiny bits to line their nests. They wouldn't be concerned with the victims, except so much as their brutal deaths would spike the ratings. No, she'd wanted this investigation for herself.

But Alan Means was gone. The house was gone. How could she investigate a house that wasn't even standing anymore?

"Shit," she whispered, rocking her office chair lightly. "Shit and damn."

9

Roy Dermott stared out the plate glass window at the front of the furniture store. Except for his Spyder and his boss's gas-swilling Suburban, the lot was empty. The store had closed ten minutes ago, nearly an hour after the door had shut behind the last customer of the day. Now, Roy waited for the clock to rundown. In the back office, his boss was tallying the daily receipts.

Little in life sucked quite so much as working late on a Saturday, not that Roy had made plans for the evening, though he would likely hit a bar or two before heading home for the night. His current boyfriend—if a closeted guy still clinging to a girlfriend and the myth of bisexuality could be called a boyfriend—had plans and wasn't coming over, so Roy had the night to prowl. At least he enjoyed his job. Selling furniture may not have been glamorous or particularly lucrative, but Roy excelled at it. Besides, it was an easy job and the people he worked with didn't annoy the shit out of him. His boss, Wally Pepper, sole-owner and manager of Pepper Fine Furnishings, was easy to get along with.

He took a seat on the edge of a chaise in the window display, and then a flash of memory—erotic, yet sad—sent him back to his feet. The chaise had been in the store for years, probably longer than any other piece of furniture outside of the chairs and desks in the offices, and though Roy had suggested they send the piece back to the manufacturer on more than one occasion, Wally had refused to Roy's distress. It reminded Roy of a few good moments, but a whole lot of bad as well. The piece was bland and overpriced, but it had also been a prop in a particularly heated fuck session he'd shared with Chance Whiting. Chance had been Wally Pepper's son-in-law and the manager of the furniture store. One day, Chance didn't report in for work, and two days later they found his body in an abandoned building downtown.

Roy had been distraught at the news, but it had crushed Wally Pepper. The reaction was natural enough. The two men had been exceptionally close. Roy had envied their relationship, mostly because he didn't think he'd ever been that close to another living person in his life. The two men had worked together; the two branches of the family had vacationed together; and every Sunday Wally and his wife, Veronica, had eaten dinner at Chance's place.

Roy hadn't thought about Chance Whiting in a good long time, and it made him uncomfortable for a number of reasons. He'd liked the man, no question about that, but memories of Chance confused him. They stirred up conflicting emotions, and often enough guilt dominated the others.

A noise at the back of the store drew Roy's attention away from the window. Checking over his shoulder, he watched Wally Pepper crossing the far end of the showroom, holding something—floor lamp?—in his hand. The store owner's posture seemed off.

Wally Pepper always stood and walked with his shoulders back and his head up. He didn't exactly strut, nothing so arrogant, but Wally was a contented and proud man, and his stride reflected this confidence. He was also, Roy often pointed out, a remarkably unattractive man. Wally Pepper was tall with narrow shoulders and a marked paunch, like a creature Dr. Seuss might have drawn to populate Whoville. Further Wally had been cursed with acne and the divots and scars of this teenage affliction remained. His unpleasant appearance played in direct counterpoint to his son-in-law's, whose square-jawed masculinity had been a constant source of temptation for Roy. Not to mention Chance was a brick shithouse, well-muscled from years of hauling furniture for his father-in-law before Wally promoted him to store manager and hired a couple of Hispanic kids to do the heavy lifting.

Roy walked deeper into the store, navigating through a mock living room with black leather sofa and chairs. He paused at the end of the sofa and flipped the price tag down, so that it hung face out from the arm.

Generally, he found the store peaceful, doubly so when it was empty. He could pass from one faux domestic scene into another, imagining the life of the people who might live amid such accoutrements. Certainly a dusty old lawyer would want the burgundy leather suite with the cherry-stained armoire. He'd drink whiskey straight, served by his thin and severe wife in a cut crystal rocks glass. This boxy set in taupe leather would sell to an upwardly mobile couple, who didn't want the hair of their rescue shelter greyhounds to show. He could place people in these spaces, among the distinct furniture designs their social niche required. Sometimes he wondered why he always pictured couples and families in these settings, but often enough he didn't linger on the question. He was just daydreaming, and daydreams were about seeing the things you didn't have.

When his cell phone rang, he stood at the edge of a truly awful suite featuring Scandinavian design furniture upholstered with a brilliant, somewhat grotesque, red.

"Hello?"

"Hey, Roy, it's me," his friend, Tom, said. "What's up? I went by your place and you weren't home."

"Wally asked me to stay late."

"Cool. Look, do you have plans with Mr. Closet tonight or are you going out?"

"Going out."

"No late night romp on the lawn mower?" Tom asked.

"Ha. Ha."

A month ago, Roy had hooked up with his current flame in the guy's backyard. His girlfriend had been asleep inside, and he couldn't get away for long, so he'd talked Roy into coming over and slamming in the gardener's shed on the far side of the yard. It had been hot, with the possibility of the girlfriend walking in on them, but Roy wished he'd never mentioned that incident to Tom. His friend had given him shit about it ever since.

"So where are you going?" Tom asked. "I'm bored and need some eye candy."

"Same as usual," Roy said, spotting Wally Pepper working his way through a series of dining rooms toward him. "The Piston at ten and then Harry's after midnight."

"Ugh," Tom grunted. "Why do we always have to go to the old man bars?"

"I'll explain my aversion to twinks to you later. Boss man is coming. I gotta fly."

Roy ended the call, cutting off Tom in mid whine. As he was sliding the device into his front pants pocket, Wally sidestepped a sleek, bleached-oak cocktail table and held out his hand.

"Can I borrow that?" Wally asked, his voice low and hoarse. The corner of his mouth twitched, and a deep line had formed across the pitted terrain of his right cheek. "Mine's on the blink."

"Sure," Roy said, handing over the phone to his boss.

Surprisingly, Wally took the phone, but instead of poking the screen to dial a number, he turned his pear shape around and retreated to the back of the store. Roy thought to ask what was going on, but it occurred to him that the call might be private.

So why not use the landline in his office? Roy wondered.

Waiting for his boss to return, Roy crossed the center aisle of the store and entered another living room. This one featured a sofa as big as his car covered in a shockingly white fabric. Matching club chairs faced it across a nickel-plated and glass table. He sank into the sofa and let his head droop back against the soft material.

Eyes closed, he was surprised when Wally Pepper's calm voice poured through the speakers above the showroom.

"I want to talk to you, Roy," Wally said. "I know what you did to Chance. I know how you perverted him, and you should know a few things. He was like a son to me, Roy. Like my own flesh and blood. You don't fuck with a man's flesh and blood."

The comments so startled him, that Roy felt certain he hadn't heard them correctly. Mouth-dry nervous he opened his eyes and surveyed the showroom. The posed furniture no longer comforted him but rather brought to mind abandonment and despair.

"Chance was a good man," Wally went on. "He was a *real* man, not like you, Roy. Now is it right that he's dead, and you're alive?"

Roy pushed himself out of the sofa, struggling to rise from the deep cushions. Once he had his feet under him, he turned for the entrance. The insinuation in Wally's voice, echoing through the all-but-empty store like an announcer at a ball game, was more than a little threatening. Wally had asked him to stay late—had asked him to wait while he locked up. The son of a bitch had taken Roy's cell phone.

The bank of lights on Roy's far left clicked off, and then the next. Eight panels in all went dark in rapid succession, running over his head and to his right. Muted daylight struggled through the tinted glass at the front of the store, and Roy made his way toward it. Yes, the doors were locked but the whole front of the store was made of glass, and Roy was just fine with smashing out a pane or two. Some folks might have tried to reason with Wally, but Roy heard the arid hate riding his boss's words. This was no joke, no simple man-to-man confrontation. Too much planning had gone into this particular scene for Roy to think anything positive was coming out of it, so he ran down the aisle, skirting a round table with the circumference of a redwood trunk, and then poured on the steam until a man stepped from behind an oak china cabinet near the front of the store. Glare on the front windows cast the man in silhouette, allowing Roy only an impression of the figure. His heart tripped, and he skidded to a stop on the slick tiled floor. He backpedaled frantically, thinking the man ahead of him must be Wally Pepper.

But a moment later, Wally's voice returned to fill the room through the public address system. "He had a wife and children, Roy. He had a normal life. Then you corrupted him. You ruined him. You left my daughter a widow."

No, Roy thought, *no. That wasn't right.* Chance had come on to *him*—more than once. They'd seen each other cruising the park off of Holly, and Roy had promised himself that he would do nothing about it. Roy knew better than to slam his cock in the cash register. But Chance wouldn't let up. He'd pursued Roy with a vehemence that would have been infuriating if Roy hadn't found the man so attractive.

Eventually, Roy had given in to the persistent flirtations. At first, it had been amazing. They'd fucked in the warehouse and in one of the moving trucks and on a third of the sofas that Pepper's Fine Furniture displayed in the showroom. When it came to sex, Chance was without boundaries and seemingly without satiation. After several months, once the initial heat of the affair had burned itself out for Roy, Chance had started talking about leaving his wife, began to imagine a long-term life with Roy, who had taken the news as he often did in such situations: he broke the relationship off.

"How did you do it, Roy?" Wally asked. "How did you pervert him?"

Feeling exposed in the center aisle, Roy shot to his left and back, away from the silhouette of the man standing between him and the front of the store. He passed from one bedroom to another. Sleigh beds gave way to what looked like broad iron ladders with mattresses, which gave way to ornate brass frames and then simple wooden headboards like smooth white tombstones.

"When I was a boy, my daddy would send me out with a twenty-two to bag coyotes if they got too close to the house. Well, think of yourself as a coyote, Roy. And you got way too close to my house."

He made another bid for the front of the store, but again the dark shape of a man appeared between two chests of drawers, like a void cut from the lighted glass ahead. Now, Roy saw the difference in this man's shape. He wasn't tall and round-hipped like Wally; this man was strongly built with broad shoulders and thick arms.

"Who are you?" Roy called, but the guy didn't move. He didn't reply. "Help me," he cried. The man shook his head, saying nothing.

Shit, Roy thought. The guy was part of this. A friend of Wally's or just some redneck recruited with the promise of beer and violence? How many more of these guys prowled the store?

Roy slid out of the aisle and ran through the last of the bedrooms. On the south end of the showroom, where they kept the entertainment centers, standing bars and other large pieces of cabinetry, he stopped and crouched down behind a mirrored credenza.

He had to do something. He had to fight his way out of this.

But you don't know how many are out there, he thought. *Wally could have a single partner in this crime, or he could have a dozen.*

It didn't really matter, Roy had to get out of the store. Considering the layout of the place, he realized it wouldn't be easy. Wally hadn't wanted it to be easy. The showroom ran fifty yards from entrance to sales counters. Behind the counters on the north side of the store were the offices, and that was where Wally had to be. The public address system and the light switches were housed back there. The front of the store was his only real chance. As far as Roy knew, only one man stood between him and the wall of glass.

"Roy," Wally Pepper called. This time his voice wasn't electronically amplified dispersed through a dozen speakers embedded in the ceiling. Instead, it emanated from a single point on the north side of the showroom. He'd left the offices and come hunting coyote.

Why was all of this happening now? Roy wondered. Chance had been dead for years, and he'd stopped seeing the man months before his death. The affair had ended simply as far as Roy could tell. One of the reasons he dated married guys was that they were generally low maintenance. Their need for discretion made them perpetually pliable; they didn't rock the boat for fear of exposure. Chance had been comfortingly predictable in this regard. If the asshole had confided all of this to his apparently psycho father-in-law, why had Wally waited so long to take action? It didn't make sense, and furthermore it wasn't fair. Roy hadn't done anything wrong.

"He had a perfect life, Roy," Wally called. "He was going to inherit the store. He had a good family, but you don't respect that kind of life. You want to destroy it, smear shit on it and make it stink."

Roy pushed closer to the credenza. A towering black entertainment center blocked his view of the showroom.

He couldn't see Wally's position, but Roy wasn't about to move—sound carried in the high-ceilinged chamber. He heard Wally stalking through the center of the place, near the living room suites, the soles of his cheap dress shoes clicking on tile.

"Generally I got no fight with your kind," Wally said, his voice seeming much closer than it had only a minute before. (*Is he already in the bedroom section?* Roy wondered). "You keep to yourselves and do what you do, and everyone gets on just fine. But that's not enough for you. You got a sickness about you, Roy. You got a need to corrupt. Well, you damn well corrupted the wrong man when you went after Chance."

Roy's body thrummed with panic, and he wanted to shout his defense, but he wasn't ready to confront Wally, and any sound would give his position away. But shit, he couldn't stay crouched by the credenza all night either. Wally would find him; he was likely only a few feet on the other side of the black entertainment center.

"I loved you," a man whispered in his ear.

Roy recoiled from the sound, slamming the side of his face into the credenza, then turning frantically toward the voice. What he saw there wasn't possible.

Chance Whiting crouched next to him. Fluids and organs spilled from the cuts in his flesh. A sharp bone poked through the scabbed pulp of his shin.

Roy shrieked and sprang to standing. He backed into the credenza away from the impossible man. Then he rocketed forward, no longer thinking about Wally Pepper or the weapon he carried on his hunt. All that mattered was putting distance between himself and the slaughtered man. Roy rounded the massive entertainment center blindly and collided with his boss.

Stunned by the impact, Roy stumbled back. The gloomy showroom seemed to tilt to the side and then right itself, just as Wally Pepper recovered from the collision and rose to his full height in front of Roy. No longer capable of rational thought, Roy struck out. He punched Wally in the throat and then the chin. The storeowner's eyes lit up with surprise. He fumbled with the shotgun in his right hand, trying to bring it around to aim, but Roy kept pummeling the older man. As Wally backed away, apparently surprised that his prey had turned on him and unaware of his surroundings, the low television stand caught the back of his knee.

Seeing an opportunity, Roy lunged forward and planted his palms against Wally Pepper's chest, sending him toppling backwards over the television stand. Wally crashed through it. Glass shattered and metal joints squealed in protest. His ass hit hard on the floor and the shotgun flew out of his hands, clattering on a bit of tile before bouncing onto a green area rug and skidding to a stop.

"You fuck," Roy wailed. "You crazy old fuck! I didn't corrupt Chance. He was sucking cock long before he met me. He did it because he liked it. You understand that?"

His shoes crushed shards of glass as he worked his way toward Wally Pepper. He shouted at the top of his lungs, hoping to take what little opportunity he had to explain things, but as he drew closer, Roy noticed something about his boss's position, something about his eyes.

In tripping over one television stand, Wally's head had come down with tremendous force on another. He'd shattered the glass surface of the unit, and one of the metal supports had punched through the back of his head. Wally lay propped up, mouth open and eyes wide, staring vacantly at Roy, who was just then realizing the man who used to sign his paychecks was dead.

"Oh shit," Roy whispered, running his palms through his hair. Sweat dripped down his brow and into his eyes, and he wiped it away furiously.

Movement at the corner of his eye reminded Roy that he wasn't alone. There was the other man—the *impossible* man: Chance. He whipped around, certain that he'd find the lacerated face bearing down on him, but the nook beside the credenza was empty. He continued his search looking in every direction, squinting against the gloom like trying to find his way under water, but he saw nothing. The impossible man was gone, leaving Roy alone with the corpse of Wally Pepper.

10

Stuart sat in a vinyl lounge chair holding a bottle of Shiner Bock, gazing at the sparkling water in Harlan Teague's pool. Harlan busied himself at the grill with a couple of ribeyes, jabbing the steaks with a long fork and scooting them across the hot iron grate. Though it provided a relaxing and comfortable atmosphere, Harlan's backyard lacked landscaping of any note—a few crape myrtles, a pear tree, and half a dozen hackberry trees. There was the redwood deck on which sat the grill, a large glass table and six wrought iron chairs with thick sand-colored cushions. The table and chairs were stationed beneath a broad umbrella, also sand-colored. Stairs ran down to a concrete lip surrounding the pool, and a field of perfectly manicured grass—not an easy feat with the heat and Barnard's endless water restrictions—ran from the concrete frame to the distant fence. Far to the back of the property stood the requisite garden shed and a small garage for Harlan's motorcycles, including a custom job that had set him back about thirty grand, a couple of dirt bikes, and a restored Harley-Davidson. It was eight pm and the sun still blazed, yellow and hot, melting like a pat of butter in the western sky. After a day of frustrations—beginning with his encounter of Thumper Tate at Clarissa's graveside and continuing on through the dead ends he'd faced in the Taylor case—Stuart could think of nothing better than a good steak and a few beers with his best friend.

"Where'd you say Gretta was tonight?" Stuart asked.

"Her Intro-to-Ballet class has a recital. Gives the parents a chance to see where all of that money is going."

"You still taking lessons, Esther?"

"Don't start with me, Lancaster," Harlan said lifting the fork and pointing the tines at him. "Those lessons gave me grace, and they gave me Gretta. You got neither, so shut your hayseed face about it."

Stuart apologized, but he couldn't help but laugh as well. It was true that Stuart had given Harlan a hard time when he'd first started taking dance classes. Six years ago, a few punks from a rival contractor had introduced Harlan's left knee to a length of pipe. Dissatisfied with the slow progress his physical therapy offered, Harlan had joined a therapeutic dance class taught out at the community pool in the Beresford District. Most of the students were geriatrics whose fragile bones and joints couldn't take the impact of traditional exercise, and Stuart had always smiled when thinking about his stout friend whirling and kicking in a pool full of blue hairs. After his knee had recovered, Harlan continued with the therapy for another four months, though he said it was only because he wanted to, "Bang the ballerina," (meaning his current girlfriend, Gretta). Stuart imagined dance was just another one of Harlan's "things," like fixing motorcycles and pottery. Truth was Stuart was jealous of his friend's hobbies—not only the willingness to try new things, but Harlan's invariable proficiency at them.

"So everything's good around here?" Stuart asked.

"What? You mean Gretta and me?"

"Anyone else live here?"

He noted his friend's hesitation in answering and the way Harlan's brow furrowed as he drove the fork into one of the steaks. "You want any blood in this thing?" he asked, voice casual as if they'd been talking about steaks all along.

"No," Stuart told him.

"Dry as a bone?"

"You already know the answer, why do you always ask?"

"It's polite." Harlan skewered one of the steaks and set it on a warming rack above the grill while the other continued to cook. "And no, things aren't great. Not lately."

"Is Gretta giving you a hard time?"

"Gretta's not the problem," Harlan said. "Gretta's a dream."

"So what's the problem?"

"I'm waking up."

"I don't follow."

"Nothing," Harlan said. "I think it's one of those mid-life crises you hear about, only not."

"That's pretty vague, Harlan."

"It's the best I can do right now."

"Are you fucking around on Gretta?"

Harlan looked up startled and burst out laughing. His whole face lit up. "God, if only it were that simple. Look, until I get a handle on this, I'm not talking. Trust me, when the shit hits the fan, you'll be the first one I call."

"I'm honored."

"As it should be," Harlan said. "Anyway, it's not like I'll be taking relationship advice from you. Your current relationships seem to end about the time you flush the rubber."

"I'm not ready to get involved right now."

"Bullshit."

"Okay, I don't *want* to get involved right now," Stuart said.

"So all of these women are just keeping your dick warm until you decide you're ready?"

"Drop it."

"It's dropped. Now, what the hell are we going to talk about?"

Stuart didn't know, but he didn't want to get into his personal life.

After Clarissa was murdered and her killers were apprehended, Stuart had tried a number of things to dilute his viscous, often caustic, emotions. Distractions as diverse as crossword puzzles, fishing trips, and building a shed in his backyard had all come and gone. He'd even tried to write a book but gave up after seven pages. He followed the Baxter-Thomason case closely, but his captain and colleagues at the station continually tried to shield him from the details, as if he hadn't already known them. The Feds came in, and in six weeks, Baxter and Thomason were brought down by their own vanity. They'd shot a video for YouTube, and though it showed none of their victims, one viewer had recognized Derek Thomason, identified him as the driver of the car Ella Taylor had climbed into the last time she was seen alive. Then six months had passed. Baxter and Thomason plead guilty to everything to avoid the death penalty. The case was closed, but it wasn't over.

Reporters and authors and television producers wanted Stuart's story. Except for work, Stuart learned to hate leaving his house. Once-simple tasks like going to the grocery store or the barbershop took on the stressful equivalency of running a gauntlet, as men and women with impossibly styled hair bombarded him with one question after another. So Stuart stayed in and his natural fascination with observation led him to the Internet, and his loneliness refined the search to single's sites. The women that visited his house for casual dates were pretty and fun, with smooth personalities that provided no traction for a serious relationship. They didn't seem to want one, and neither did Stuart, though he'd made no proclamation to that effect. It simply was. Only looking back could he see how attracted he'd been to the superficial. There was nothing wrong with the women, quite the opposite, but they were young and hadn't decided what part they'd play in the theater of life. They were stops along the way, none of them a destination.

"Hey," Harlan called. "You never told me about the dead guy."

"Which one?"

"How many'd you have yesterday?" Harlan crossed the patio and set an oval platter holding the steak and an enormous baked potato in front of Stuart.

"Pudge Taylor."

"Are you shitting me?"

"Don't you watch the news or are you too busy ironing your tutus?"

"I've been up to my ass in that new development south of Austin," Harlan explained. "Oh, and fuck you."

Harlan turned away from the table, wandered inside, and returned with a beer in each hand. He set one beside Stuart's nearly empty bottle and carried the other to his side of the table.

"You got any ideas about what happened?" Harlan asked.

"Only that Pudge took about a dozen knife wounds to the back."

"Damn," Harlan said, shaking his head and sawing into his steak. "Knives are the worst. Give me a bullet any day."

"I've thought about it." Stuart cut into his own steak, trying not to think about Pudge Taylor.

"Maybe you should get the rest of the shit out of your mouth before you start eating."

Stuart chuckled. "I think it's gone now."

"Good to hear. So any idea about who'd want Pudge cold?"

"Can we discuss this after dinner?" Stuart asked.

The fact was, he didn't want to discuss it at all. He'd spent the last two days interviewing neighbors and business associates of Pudge Taylor. Forensics was still sifting through the evidence, analyzing fibers and blood, but so far they'd found nothing that could be considered a lead. All of Colleen Taylor's clothes were negative for blood spatter and the widow hadn't changed a single word of her story. That morning Stuart and David Ballard ran down Eddie "Fish" Throckmorton, because one of Pudge's business contacts brought the number runner's name up in connection to some gambling the victim had done, and while it was true Pudge wagered hefty sums on his alma mater's football team, and just about anything else that crossed his mind, his debts were paid in a timely manner. ("I'm going to miss that fat old loser," Fish had said. "Bought me a new Lexus off what he threw away on UT alone last year.") Pudge Taylor seemed to be an above-board guy who just happened to be in the wrong place at the wrong time, the randomness of which only making Stuart's job tougher.

Besides all of that, Harlan's curiosity was uncharacteristic. He never asked about the cases Stuart was working on, because Harlan knew a fair number of shady people, and he had a homicide detective as a best friend, and Harlan liked to keep conflicts of interest to a minimum.

"What's going on, Harlan?"

"I'm having a pleasant meal. What's going on with you?"

"Are you holding out on me?"

"Yes. Now, eat your dinner."

Stuart set down his utensils and stared at his friend, knowing the only way he would get Harlan to talk was if he said nothing at all. Harlan had an aversion to silence that made questioning him almost too easy. It didn't take long before Harlan, too, set his fork on the table and tossed his head from side to side like a dog with a tick in his ear. Finally, he fixed an exasperated expression on Stuart and began talking.

"Look, I might know something that can help you, but I'm not spilling a word if I don't have to. It's all just hearsay anyhow, and Pudge had himself a good reputation."

"I'm not a reporter, Harlan. I'm not going to broadcast anything you tell me, but if it can help, you might best spill it."

Harlan chewed on this for a minute. He looked off to the sunset and took a drink of his beer. "Okay," he said. "It's about a girl. Actually, it's about a lot of girls."

"He cheated on his wife?

"If what I've heard is true, yes. But right now it's little more than gossip. I'd want to check this out before you start stirring the shit."

"Infidelity isn't exactly uncommon, Harlan. These days it seems to be a given."

"Maybe, but Pudge may have been fucking around on the green side of the pasture."

"Meaning?" Stuart wanted to know.

"The girls met Pudge before they met high school."

"Pudge had a thing for underage girls?" Stuart asked, though the question had already been answered. "So this could have been done by a parent."

"Yeah," Harlan said. "Maybe. But before you run off and make a thing out of this, I have a few calls to make. It might take a couple of days. In the meantime, keep it quiet. I'm not about to torpedo some guy's memory for a bit of locker room small talk."

"Who would I tell outside of the station?" Stuart asked.

"No one," Harlan said, "but those are the people I'm worried about."

At home, Stuart walked through the kitchen and dropped his keys in the piece of Native American pottery Clarissa had used for a fruit bowl. His day had gotten considerably better, particularly if Harlan could back up his supposition regarding Pudge. A parent who'd found out their daughter was being violated by a middle-aged businessman made a solid suspect. He just wished Harlan could have told him more, but his friend had had nothing else to offer.

Stuart continued through the living room, into the hallway and came to a dead halt on the threshold of his office. Even with the light out he saw the disarray. The realization that his home had been burgled landed in his throat like a rock. His nerves erupted, sending waves of uncomfortable tingle over his skin. Suddenly, he felt someone in the house. Whether this sensation was based on anything more than a justified sense of violation, he couldn't say, and he didn't care. Pulling his sidearm, he released the safety and eased down the hall, ears alert for any warning. His heart beat thickly, like the whirring of a copter's blades. The sound filled his ears. He moved down the hall to his bedroom and pushed the door open with his foot, and for a moment, everything seemed to stop, even the whump-whump of his heart as he peered into the darkness of the room. When no one charged out of the gloom for him, Stuart thumbed on the light switch and entered, checking possible danger zones—behind the door, beside the bed, the closet.

A nagging voice told him to get on his cell phone and call the station, but Stuart ignored it. There were things in his study he didn't want his colleagues to see; things he would have a difficult time explaining away.

He made his way through the house one room at a time, carefully checking every possible hiding place. At the front door he tested the knob and was surprised to find it twisted freely in his palm. The lock was disengaged; the deadbolt the same, even though he knew without question that he'd checked both before leaving the house to meet Harlan. He never entered or exited through this door. He didn't even use it to get the morning paper; that was retrieved from the drive on his way into the office. The door was always locked unless someone came to visit. After Clarissa, he'd become a lot more cautious.

He opened the door and ran his fingers over the jamb, searching for evidence of tampering, splintered wood, cracked paint, anything to indicate someone had gone at the door with a bar or flat out kicked it in. The paint was smooth and unmarred. Not so much as a smudge of dirt.

They picked my locks, Stuart thought. A professional job. But what the fuck were the thieves looking for?

He closed and locked the door; threw on the security chain. Stuart returned to his office, the only room in the house showing signs of disturbance. He turned on the light and surveyed the disarray over the barrel of his gun. Video cassettes and DVD cases littered the carpet. The shelves they'd once occupied were now empty, leaving only ghosts of dust. Cautiously, he stepped around the worst of the mess and headed for the closet. He pulled open the door, certain he would find the intruders within, but it too was empty.

His second trip through the house was slower, more methodical as he checked for any valuables the intruders might have taken, but Clarissa's jewelry still rested in a box in the bottom drawer of the dresser, Stuart's televisions and audio equipment were untouched, even his laptop computer, which sat on the edge of his desk, remained.

So, some idiot came in to throw my movies on the floor? he wondered.

Placing his sidearm on the desk, Stuart turned to the task of picking up the strewn media. Instincts, long exercised and honed, insisted he not touch anything. He was contaminating a crime scene, but this *wasn't* a crime scene because he would never report the break in.

He couldn't exactly call it a hobby, nor could he truthfully justify his possession of the video archive as a function of his job, though much of the material had come from the station.

And that was the problem.

In his collection of moving images, Stuart had security camera tapes, crime scene recordings, interrogation clips. He also had the only remaining footage, outside of the District Attorney's office, of the Baxter-Thomason crimes. Sure some had leaked to the media, but they only managed to get their hands on a thirty second clip of Thomason and Baxter laughing over the bound figure of Regina Wolcroff, before they cut into the woman. Stuart's collection contained over ten hours of the psychotic couple's crimes—everything they'd confiscated on the day of Thomason and Baxter's arrest, which amounted to only a fraction of the videos the killer's had taken.

The two had been found in the basement of the house, the place they'd taken their victims. When officers entered, the two were furiously scratching a pile of DVDs with sanding blocks. They'd already erased all of the files from their computers, going so far as to destroy the memory cards of the machines just in case wiping the hard drives didn't do the trick. They'd managed to destroy dozens of hours of footage, but they hadn't finished the job. Barnard Police Officers confiscated six DVDs, containing more than enough visual documentation to prove the couple's guilt.

Before the evidence was handed over to the DA, Stuart got his hands on the discs. He downloaded the files, burned them onto discs as he'd done with a hundred other bits of recorded malfeasance.

Four different victims appeared on the recovered discs. Clarissa was one of them.

He gathered up the cases, starting with the DVDs. Not being an idiot, he hadn't labeled the discs, nor had he kept them in jewel cases for curious visitors to inspect. Rather, he hid his collection in the inconspicuous packaging of movies one might expect to find in his home. The Baxter-Thomason recordings hid in a boxed set of Clint Eastwood films.

And they were gone, the entire set. He finished straightening up with his heart ticking desperately in his chest as he searched for the cases holding *Dirty Harry* and *Magnum Force* and others, but they were not among the scattered boxes.

Another disc was also missing, this one far more personal and far more damaging to him.

How could you do this to me?

"Shit," Stuart hissed looking around the room to make sure he hadn't missed any stray cases. He bent low and checked below the desk, going so far as to tear the closet apart in the hopes the thief had kicked the disc under the door in his haste.

"No, no, no," he muttered.

Then he started the futile search all over again.

11

Pamela Carney, "Pam" to her friends, of which she had few, belched and scratched the underside of her breast where the bra cup had grown itchy. She thought about doing some laundry. Clothes were stacking up. Hell, the whole place needed a good cleaning, but she was exhausted. All day, she'd argued with the assholes at the insurance company about the house that senile geezer had torched. They were trying to screw her, but wasn't that always the way? They heard a woman's voice on the phone and they figured they had themselves a sucker, an easy mark, just some lame-brained broad who didn't know her ass from a calculator.

First the city tried to steal the property—offering her a fraction of its worth—because they were all squeamish about what had happened in the house, as if it was the house's fault, like the stairs and siding and carpets were evil and dragged innocent idiots over the threshold. Of course, they *said* it was because all of those lookie-loos were creating a public disturbance, but Pam knew better.

The two freaks who'd done the killing were gone, arrested and locked away forever. There was nothing left of them in that house. Hell, the cops had stripped the place clean. Every scrap of clothing was yanked from the closets and chests of drawers. All the personal possessions of Selma and Derek had been confiscated in the name of evidence. The police took everything that wasn't nailed down, even some of the furniture because they thought blood might have gotten on it. Didn't leave a damn thing for Pam. She'd lost two year's rent on the place because of all the hoopla, and she hadn't got so much as a matchbook out of the place to sell on eBay.

That wasn't right.

Not that Pam wanted to go into the house. No sir. No thank you. That house and her had enough history—even before Thomason and Baxter turned it into a torture chamber—to last her a lifetime. After the cops snagged all the important shit, the stuff that would have really made her some money at auction, she'd hired a cleaning crew and a couple of border jumpers to do maintenance on the place. They'd probably stolen a lot of shit, kept it for themselves. Fucking men.

She stood from the sofa and yawned, scratched her chest again, then her head. The properties were about all she had. The city didn't understand that. The cops didn't understand it either. They thought she was just being difficult, but she had to protect her investments. It wasn't like some man was going to come along to take care of her. That was romance novel bullshit. The only things men gave you were headaches, bruises, and a few loads of spunk. Beyond that, they took, they drained, they wore through your skin with their constant demands, creating more holes because the ones you got weren't enough for them.

Pam knew plenty about men. She didn't care to know any more. At this point in her life—thirty-eight-years and counting—she had been through enough of them to know she'd *had* enough of them. Fucking cock caddies were all they were, hairy and ignorant fools with a single redeeming feature located just south of their navel. When she picked a man up at Brock's or The Tin Whistle she didn't ask his name; why the hell would she care what to call him? It would be like naming a vacuum cleaner or a dust mop. She wasn't even nice to them. She didn't have to be. They were usually too drunk to care about courtesy, their heads swimming in beer and hormones. All they wanted was a warm place to park their dicks.

In the kitchen, which was strewn with pizza boxes, wine bottles, and empty cookie packages, Pam walked to the sink and looked at the dishes piled there, frowned with disgust as if someone else had left them dirtied for her to wash and turned away.

Standing in the next room was a man, though she could not see him clearly. If anything what she saw would more accurately be described as a man-shaped shadow, and her heart leapt into her throat as she squinted to make sense of the intruder. No matter how she tried, the details of his face eluded her. He was big and wearing dark clothes, and beyond that, he might have been any man on god's green ball. Still, she didn't need to see the asshole's face to know he didn't belong in her house. Pam opened her mouth with the intent of threatening the prick if he didn't get his shit maker out her door, but then she saw that he wasn't alone and her heart again skipped north.

A young guy emerged from behind the first. He was a sickly looking prick with blond hair, bad teeth, and not an ounce of fat on him. Pam thought he was a methhead, coming to rob her, but the scrawny man walked up to the dinette set, barely noticing Pam at all, and set a stack of DVDs on the table. He flashed her a nasty grin; his watery, green eyes twinkled; and he turned and walked out of the dining area, through the living room and out her door, leaving Pam alone with the shadowy figure.

"What the hell?" she asked, spinning toward the sink. The handle of a long filet knife jutted from a pile of cereal-crusted bowls. She yanked it free and turned back to the shadow. "You got three seconds, asshole."

"Pammy," a high voice said.

It wasn't a woman's voice. It sounded more like some homo talking in falsetto, mimicking Judy Garland or Marilyn Monroe, only more shrill. The tone hit her ears like blades of ice, cutting cold straight through to the center of her head. Her entire body began to tremble as if suddenly freezing. She stuck the knife out, waving the blade slowly before her.

"Don't be that way, Pammy."

Pammy? Even the name chilled her. The only person who had ever called her that was Selma Baxter. When the girl had wanted something like an extension on the rent or needed something fixed, she got all cutesy and adopted a baby-doll voice:

Oh pweese, Pammy?

We wuvs you, Pammy.

The freaky little bitch managed to make it work for her, but who the hell knew Baxter had called her that? And what difference did it make?

"I don't have any money here," Pam said. "Not a damn dime."

"I didn't come to take," the shrill, vibrato voice said. A glass-sharp titter of laughter cut the gloom. The man moved away from the dining table, sliding like a cloud of smoke sent billowing by a gust of wind. "I've brought you things. Lovely valuable things."

"Where'd your friend go?" she asked.

"He served his purpose. He has more important meetings to attend." The shadow moved, but Pam didn't hear footfalls. "Look at the lovely things I've brought you."

He's doing that fucked up thing with his voice so I won't recognize it. Do I know him or is he just afraid I'll be able to identify him later?

"And why would you do that?" Pam asked, leaning to the side to see around the archway, making sure the man wasn't trying to sneak up on her. He stood in the center of the living room, barely visible in the gloom.

"Because you suffered so much for them."

"Who's them?"

"You know."

"No, I do not know," Pam insisted.

"Look at what I've brought. Imagine what these are worth. Imagine if there were more."

Pam squinted into the murk and saw the DVDs on her table, and a sharp curiosity led her forward, but the man moved, and Pam leaped back into the kitchen, kicking a stray wine bottle with her heel. The bottle skittered across the kitchen and came to rest against the baseboard beneath the sink.

"What are they?"

"Lovely and valuable."

"So you say."

"There are more. There are dozens. When I leave, you come see how lovely. There are more in the house."

"What house?" Pam asked.

"Ash Street, where we first met."

"Who are you? You can't be Derek; he's still locked up."

"Very true," he said.

"You're a friend of his?"

"I am."

"Did he send you?"

The man backed toward the door. "There are more at the house," he said.

"The house is nothing but char and crap," Pam told him. "There's nothing left."

"In the basement, behind the stone. The police never found them. Never did."

"Found what?"

The man fell silent again. Pam's front door opened and closed quietly, but she wasn't going to believe some asshole had just popped in for a chat and to give her presents. *He didn't leave, he's trying to fool me.* Pam felt the certainty in her chest, beating with her heart.

Pam glanced at the stack on the dining table—*What the hell?*—then continued into the living room. She launched herself through the archway, led by the slender blade of her filet knife, ready to cut off a big chunk of the asshole if he charged back into her apartment. She ran to the door and threw the locks, and then she crossed to the window and looked down to see if the freak loitered on the stoop of the building, but she didn't see anyone below. Checking the window latch to make sure it too was secure, she breathed deeply to slow the rapid pulse of her heart.

Once convinced the intruder was gone, Pam returned to the dining room. On the table sat a stack of DVD boxes. She put her knife down and lifted the topmost case, turned it over in her hands.

"Some lovely and valuable gift," she said and dropped the case on the table. "I don't even like Clint Eastwood."

12

"Oh! You know what we should do?"
"No, baby, what should we do?"
"We should send this vid to her mama."
"Oh, baby, that's awesome. But we better make it a good show."
"It'll be good. Hand me that box cutter."

Melanie stared at the computer screen. On it, a twenty-three-year-old man and a nineteen-year-old girl grinned at one another as Selma Baxter handed Derek Thomason a utility knife. With his perfect skin, a winning smile that made his cheekbones swell, and fashionably tousled hair, the man resembled an Abercrombie & Fitch model. The girl was also beautiful with straight brown hair and voluptuous lips painted the color of bubblegum, adding intensity to her illusion of adolescent sensuality. Grim adoration blazed in their eyes. Behind them, in the corner of an unfinished basement with symbols painted on the walls, an African American girl in a yellow dress squirmed. The harsh beam of a lantern flashlight bathed her face. Wires had been tightly wrapped around her arms and legs, securing her to the chair. Wide eyes, filled with tears, stared in terror from above a dirty white bandana, which was being used to gag her. The couple in the foreground kissed as the man took the weapon from his lover's hand.

Ever since she'd received Alan Means' letter, Melanie had felt compelled to find out what she could about the house on Ash Street and the crimes that had been committed there.

On the screen, the two parted and walked across the room to where their victim waited. The girl's name was Regina Wolcroff. She had been twenty-two years old when Thomason and Baxter abducted her from the side of a road, less than a mile from the rehab center she'd escaped only an hour before.

The streaming video, the only clip of the two killers at work to reach the public, stopped as Derek Thomason was bringing the razor-edged cutter to Regina's eye.

Melanie closed the video window and leaned back in her chair. She sipped from her cup of coffee and rubbed the back of her neck.

Opening the thick folder, she gazed down at the face of Selma Baxter, grinning pleasantly from her senior yearbook photo. Selma had been a striking girl. Lovely. Bright blue eyes shone from the photograph above a narrow nose and a brilliant white smile. She was the epitome of the wholesome high school student, if such a thing ever existed. No one would have suspected her of shoplifting let alone murder, and that was part of the perplexing nature of the case.

According to media reports and the editorials of an army of Internet "experts" neither Thomason nor Baxter had exhibited early indicators for violence, and certainly nothing to suggest the extremes of brutality they would go on to show their victims. Both had been raised by solid middle-class families in the Beresford District in Barnard, Texas, reputedly a swanky zip code. No history of abuse was evident in either of their lives. Both of the killers were strong students, deeply involved with school activities. Thomason had played on the baseball team, and Baxter had been a cheerleader. Both were popular kids, well socialized, and courteous. Following their arrest, a slew of character witnesses presented themselves to the media, clearly stating there had been a mistake; there was no way the two young people could have committed such ghastly crimes. Though good intentioned, their pleas were meaningless. The guilt of the two parties could not be questioned. Ten hours of video had been recovered in the aftermath of the crimes; the content of those tapes showed two young people with a taste for torture and death. Once the video clip of their abuse of Regina Wolcroff went public, the couple's supporters quieted and slipped away.

Civic groups claimed that the two had been warped by violent movies and suggestive music, but there was no indication that either Thomason or Baxter had any great interest in popular, if dark, forms of entertainment. Religious groups blamed satanic worship and black magic, and that might have been closer to the truth.

Rituals were involved, though experts who'd viewed the tapes found no clear system of belief. The symbols Baxter and Thomason had carved in their victims were meaningless, except for the heart that held their initials, found on the bodies of two of the eleven victims. The wounds they gave each other fit into no known cult or religious text. Most experts agreed that the two were simply insane and had created their own form of cruel worship.

The case was baffling, confounding detectives and federal profilers alike. The victims of the Thomason-Baxter killings were absolutely random. Men and women and children. They came from diverse socio-economic backgrounds. Some were abducted and others seduced. They all died, though. That was one thing they shared.

Melanie returned her attention to the list of victims. She read as if expecting some clue to emerge from the roll, but they were only names.

13

Hannah Bolger hummed a bouncy tune as she poured the remains of a bottle of reconstituted lemon juice into a pitcher. It soaked the mound of sugar waiting at the bottom of the carafe, turning the crystals into yellow mud.

"I saw a ghost."

The claim had come from Richard Wolcroff, an African-American gentleman who'd begun attending Hannah's grief counseling sessions two months after his daughter's murder. The news, which might have otherwise caused her alarm had she not recently seen the specter of her own lost husband, thrilled her. Richard's assertion confirmed Hannah's belief that Ben had returned to her, perhaps to say goodbye, perhaps to assure Hannah of his spirit's wellbeing, perhaps with a philosophical message from the other side of life.

Since the night she'd spotted Ben in her backyard, Hannah's emotions had run chaotically. In addition to fixing Ben's favorite meals and leaving the kitchen door open for the scents to waft out so he would know he was welcome, before going to bed each night, Hannah set out a gin and tonic—Ben's usual drink—on the kitchen counter, like a child offering bribes to Santa Claus. Every sound in the house was Ben. Every flicker at the corner of her eye was her lost husband finally finding his way home. She hated leaving the house and avoided it whenever possible, fearing the thirty minutes it would take her to run to the supermarket and shop would be the very same time frame Ben chose to make another appearance.

He hadn't made another appearance, not since that first night, but Hannah knew he would; the certainty of it filled her chest like warm stones.

When Richard arrived, Hannah was in the kitchen dropping cubes of ice into the freshly made pitcher of lemonade. She'd been giddy all morning, ever since Richard's call, eager to hear his story and share her own, but she knew better than to show too much enthusiasm. Richard was a reserved man. Like Stuart Lancaster, he kept his emotions off his sleeves. It must have taken every ounce of his strength just to call her and tell her what he had seen.

Hannah answered the door and greeted Richard with a hug. Richard was a large man in height and girth. He had a round face, framed with a well-trimmed white beard and short white hair. His stature and composure always made her think of prestigious professions, a judge or lawyer or college professor. Generally he wore suits, a habit many men of his generation—which was also Hannah's generation—clung to, despite the fashions having trended to the far more casual over the years. Today, Richard wore a crisp red dress shirt, cuffs neatly buttoned, and a pair of gray pleated slacks. Seeing him again, knowing what they shared, Hannah had felt compelled to wrap her arms around him. The embrace was sincere, but she kept it brief, feeling Richard bristle against her. She ushered her guest back to the kitchen where the morning light cut a wedge across the dinette table and offered him a seat.

"I have coffee or lemonade," she told him. "Oh, or tea if you'd prefer?"

"What I want is a scotch," Richard said wearily.

"I have that, too."

He fixed her with a wry look. "It's not even noon, yet. I think coffee would be more appropriate to the time of day."

She presented him with a mug and fixed herself a glass of lemonade before joining him at the table. Richard poured a splash of milk into the coffee and followed this with a spoonful of sugar from the bowl.

"How have you been?" Hannah asked.

"I've been well," Richard replied. He sipped the coffee. His lips turned up slightly, all but sneering at the contents of the mug. Hannah noted the reaction but it didn't bother her. She'd never been able to make coffee worth a damn, because she didn't drink it herself. Still, Richard took a second sip before he continued. "With the notable exception of having lost my mind."

"Now Richard that isn't a healthy thing to say."

"Seeing ghosts isn't exactly a healthy thing to experience, is it?"

"Why don't you tell me what happened? We'll see if we can't figure out what it means."

"You know that Delia left?" he asked.

"Yes." Hannah had spoken with Richard just after his wife had announced she was leaving him, returning to Houston to live with her sister's family. "I'm very sorry about that. Have you two spoken?"

"Not in months. I tried calling several times, but Lil, her sister, always says she's out. Delia isn't out. She just doesn't want to talk to me. She still blames me for what happened to Regina, but you know all about that. It seemed to be the only thing she wanted to talk about in group."

"Yes."

Hannah remembered Delia Wolcroff as an angry woman, always targeting blame for even the tiniest misfortunes in her life. On one occasion, she arrived at group with the heel of her shoe in her hand. She had broken it off, slipping on the sidewalk outside of her office building. She went on to blame Hannah for scheduling the meeting on a rainy day, though the weekly meetings always took place at the same time. It was simply her way. The woman rationally knew Richard was no more responsible for their daughter's death than anyone else in that room, she'd needed a focus for her emotions, and not the obscure concept of "a killer." She needed a face and a name to purge her hurt on, and those had belonged to her husband.

"So you know what she can be like?" Richard said, simply to confirm that Hannah agreed with him. She showed him that she did by nodding her head. "But I still miss her. The house feels wrong without her there. It's like the air is too thick because there's only me breathing it. With the girls gone, now Delia, the place can be depressing, so maybe I've been drinking a little more than I should, and I wanted to believe I was drunk last night when I saw *her*. But I wasn't. I know I wasn't."

"Who did you see, Richard?"

He didn't answer immediately. The grizzly bear of a man just gazed into his coffee cup, tears pooling in his eyes. Sniffing lightly he clutched the cup tightly between his palms. "I only had the one drink. It was early in the evening, not even seven o'clock."

"Who did you see?"

"Regina." The name tumbled from his mouth as if he'd been choking on it and only a tremendous act of will had dislodged it from his windpipe. "I was sitting on the patio behind the house and saw her through the kitchen window. She stood by the refrigerator. We still had full light outside. I saw her clear as I'm seeing you now."

"What happened?"

"Nothing. Nothing happened. I just sat there and tried to convince myself I wasn't seeing my murdered daughter."

"How did you feel when you saw her?"

"How did I feel? I felt shit scared. Her mother was the one that had to identify her, because I was down with the flu. Delia blamed me for that, too. I never saw what happened to Regina, what Thomason and Baxter did to her. I never wanted to see that, but last night I saw."

"She looked *injured*?" Hannah asked, trying to soften the word as much as she could.

"She looked torn apart, Hannah. Now, what the hell is going on? Is this just some kind of post-traumatic hallucination or a manifestation of guilt or what?"

"It very possibly could have been a ghost, Richard."

"I don't believe in ghosts."

Hannah smiled tightly and put her hands on the table. Richard's expression was a mixture of sadness and bewilderment. "I'm going to tell you something," she said. "It might change your mind."

She described her own visitation and did so with the utmost earnestness in her voice, knowing Richard might take anything else as insincerity or even mocking. She also mentioned the arrival of her neighbor who had witnessed the apparition of Ben in her yard. Richard's expression didn't change, and he didn't move. He seemed to be paralyzed by all that he'd said and all that Hannah was telling him. Only when she mentioned that Ben too had worn the wounds of his death did Richard move, and that was nothing more than a twitch of his lip.

"I can't say I know what is happening," Hannah told him. "But I think the ones we love have a message for us."

Richard sipped his coffee, lowered his head and stared at the table. As for Hannah, excitement welled, making her heart trip and her head light. Amazing things were happening, and yes she understood how they might seem frightening, but she couldn't help but believe she and Richard and maybe Stuart and who knew how many others, were on the brink of something startling and fantastic. After all, how wonderful was it that they might have one last chance to speak with their loves, to tell them goodbye? What a rare and special thing.

"I know this must all seem very strange, but I don't think we need to be frightened. I think we should embrace their return."

"Embrace them?" Richard asked incredulously. He shot her a hard look and then slid his chair back.

Hannah thought she'd offended him and struggled to find words so he wouldn't leave. But Richard wasn't leaving. He was untying his left shoe.

"Richard?" she asked.

Carefully, he removed the black oxford and slid his thumbs into the cuff of his sock. He gathered the material in his fingers and pulled it off. Then Richard grasped his ankle, crossed his leg, and presented Hannah with the sole of his foot, which was covered by a fat bandage. He pulled the dressing away, revealing three deep cuts. They formed the letter A.

"What happened?" Hannah asked. Her excitement was sapped, drained away by the sight before her.

"After I saw Regina, once the initial shock wore off, I had a few drinks," he said quietly as if ashamed. "Then I had a few more. It took half a bottle of Johnny Walker before the shaking in my hands stopped. I stumbled up to bed and passed out a little after ten. At some point, I woke. My ankle was locked up. I thought it was tangled in the sheets, but I couldn't kick my foot free. It was like someone was holding me. I didn't even feel the cuts, not until I came to this morning. There was blood all over the sheets at the foot of the bed, but there weren't any tracks. What I mean is I didn't sleep walk and gouge myself somewhere else in the house. It happened in my bed."

"Did you see who did it?"

"It was Regina. I dreamt about her, heard her giggling this shrill, awful sound as she clutched at my leg. But it wasn't a dream. You think our loved ones want to give us a message? Well, here it is carved into my foot."

14

At one a.m. Mike woke to find his sister crouching like a cat on the bed next to him. He bucked the covers loose and rolled away from her, a shot of adrenaline rapidly clearing his sleep-burdened mind. Because his flight was propelled by reflex, he didn't navigate the course well and hit his head on the edge of the nightstand before tumbling to the floor. When he recovered, rising to his knees and peering over the edge of the bed, he found that Dory hadn't moved. On the opposite side of the mattress, she faced him with an expression the gloom made unreadable.

"What do you want?" Mike whispered.

Dory didn't reply.

His fingers clamped the edge of the bed, fabric gathering between them like dry flesh. Anxiety sent his body to trembling, and Mike thought to call out for his parents, but could not bring the words to his tongue. In addition to his fear, an inexplicable rage welled up in him, silencing him by constricting his throat like a garrote, but he was not angry with his sister; the fury was directed at himself. An argument was beginning in his head as if he were two people, two *enemies*, existing in a single body.

"You should have been watching," Dory finally said. "Why weren't you watching me, Mik-Mik?"

Because you were real, Mike thought, then wondered on the oddity of the notion. *No*, he corrected. *Grandpa Alan said he was going to watch you.*

It doesn't matter, Mike argued to himself, *she was your little sister and you should have been watching.*

She was just playing in the front yard.

She was tied to a chair, you selfish fuck. They kept her alive for hours, Mik-Mik. Do you know what they did to her?

The argument raged in his head, and he stood up. Dory didn't move, just glared at him, her lips moving as if in silent prayer.

He couldn't remember the brief moments between leaving the bedroom and standing on the cold tile of the bathroom across the hall, staring at his reflection in the long mirror above the sink and counter. His face appeared skeletal and sickly beneath the bath of jaundiced light cast by the bathroom fixture. The arm reflecting back to him was outstretched, palm up. In it rested a small pile of pills as if the boy in the mirror were a drug dealer, offering Mike his wares. Mike looked down and saw a mound of Xanax tablets in his hand. His doctor had prescribed them after Dory's murder, something to help Mike cope. They'd sat in his medicine cabinet, untouched for the most part, for nearly three years.

But they were touched now. They were present and necessary. He lifted his palm to his mouth and pressed the pills to his lips. On his tongue, the pills felt dry and tasted bitter—the small desiccated carcasses of his sanity. One mouthful of water and one brief swallow and he could forget about guilt, forget about all of the fucking pity and playing the part of a normal boy in a normal world. Maintaining the act was just too hard. Easier to sip water. Easier to just swallow.

The fire in his mind buffeted, leaving Mike with a moment of crystal sharp clarity.

This is death, he'd thought. *This is the last moment, all the rest is memory.* He'd then thought, *it's not enough* and lowered his palm. He crossed to the toilet and spat the small dry pills into the still water. Working up a mouthful of spit, he swished it over his tongue and spat this out too.

He returned to the mirror and stared at his reflection. The hate for the face he saw remained, but he saw how irrational the emotion was. Guilt was creating this loathing—guilt for something he could never had foreseen and couldn't help. Mike held to this logic, even as the urge to smash the face in the mirror swelled. He continued to stare into his own eyes until the logic overpowered the anger, and once the rage was beaten back and the fire receded, he dropped forward, clutching the lip of the bathroom vanity with clawed hands.

Each day he edged a bit closer to a final act, and he was scared as hell that the next time, or the time after that the moment of clarity would come too late.

Hanging out with Gwen and Evan helped, but they weren't always around. Time with his friends was like standing in light, but the moment he separated from them, darkness encroached, surrounding him like a wet black fog.

Maybe he should talk to someone. Not his parents. He couldn't talk to them. His mother would break down into tears if he even mentioned Dory's name and his father would throw a fit, telling Mike to "Snap out of it." Hannah Bolger had run the grief-counseling group his parents had attended. They spoke highly of the woman and her approach. He might be able to talk to her.

If it happens again, I will.

Don't let it happen again.

Michael looked at the cut on his shoulder, now just a purple line running across the meat high on his arm. He touched the wound and remembered when he'd received it.

It began with Dory and the other victims, but his visiting that house with Gwen and Evan had woken something. What had they done there? What door had they opened? He had to remember, wanted to remember while the bitter flavor of the pills remained on his tongue.

The house was a simple two-story frame design, with a basement. It looked right at home on the block, just another bland suburban house in a bland suburban neighborhood. It even looked pleasant, harmless. The same could have been said for its former tenants; they'd looked harmless, too. Selma Baxter had been the epitome of high school popularity, while Derek Thomason had looked clean and sleek, like a successful young stockbroker or a lawyer. And the house looked like the perfect place for such a young professional. The shingles were a deep green and the siding wore a clean coat of white paint with brown trim. Mike remembered his father railing about the owner, a woman named Pamela Carney, who'd fought the city council's attempts to buy the property, but they'd finally succeeded. The house on Ash Street was coming down.

"Lucas told me there's a broken window in back," Evan said.

"That doesn't mean it's legal," Gwen said.

"Have another drink."

Mike told himself he was cold because the AC was cranked up. Evan ignored him, pressed down on the gas pedal, and drove to the corner. He parked on the side street, half a block off Ash.

"What about the neighbors?" he asked.

"We go through the back yards," Evan said. "The house on the corner up there is for sale. The owners moved to Dallas. So it'll be easy enough to slip along the side and go through their fence. We go around back of that and then just stay low until we're in the right yard."

A harsh voice in Mike's head started nagging him for what he was doing. Your sister died in that house, *it said.* She was murdered, probably tortured like the others. Now you're here killing time like the place is some kind of mall or amusement park? Are you hoping to see her blood? Bits of her left on the floor?

Mike parked the car, ignoring the voice as best he could. Evan took a big swig from the bottle of vodka and slid it under the front seat before leaping out. A gust of hot air rolled in through the open door.

"We don't have to do this," Gwen said. She leaned forward in the backseat and grasped Mike's shoulder. "Let's go back to Porter's."

"It's cool," Mike told her.

He opened the door and felt the hot night greet him. Gwen looked out at him, her eyes all but pleading for Mike to reconsider. Seeing that this wasn't going to happen, she shook her head and followed him out.

Evan's plan worked well enough. The house on the corner was empty and the gate at the side, leading to the backyard, didn't have a lock. Lights burned in the house next door, but the three scurried along the fence line from shadow to shadow. The next house was dark, except for the blue-white glow of a television on the second floor. Then they were in Baxter and Thomason's backyard, and Mike felt the cold return to his skin. His flesh pimpled with it.

Unlike the front of the house, which had been carefully maintained to present a good face to the neighborhood and prospective renters—though no one was foolish enough to actually sign a lease on the place since Baxter and Thomason's arrest—the backyard was overgrown, with brown grass climbing up to Mike's knees. He thought about snakes. Mice liked this kind of field and rattlers liked mice. He stepped carefully but quickly until he was out of the grass and standing on the concrete patio rolling like a tongue from the kitchen door. Evan was already sliding up a window.

"Why are you doing this?" Gwen whispered at Mike's back.

"Because it's here."

Despite his casually defiant tone, sweat soaked through the collar of his t-shirt and wetted his palms, chilling him further. Ahead, Evan slipped through the open window like a professional burglar. He turned, his form a smear of movement against a pitch-black backdrop. Evan waved and stepped to the side, disappearing as if the dark had swam forward to engulf him.

Ignoring the voice in his head, which was beginning to sound like Gwen's, Mike approached the window. He hesitated, his hands trembling on the sill. Peering inside he noticed Evan had already moved deeper into the kitchen, a wisp of smoke amid cloying darkness.

Do it or don't, *he told himself.*

A moment later, he stood on the kitchen's linoleum floor. It was furnace hot in the house. The doors and windows had been shut for days, maybe weeks, and the air, baked by days of triple-digit temperatures, seemed to have lost its oxygen. Mike could barely breathe. He'd expected the place to smell foul, like old blood and rotting meat, but a flowery, nauseating aroma filled the place. Plug-in room deodorizers, he thought. His mom used them and their odors, never quite like the scents they were trying to imitate, always made him gag. It seemed like a dozen of the things were being used in the kitchen alone, their reek amplified by heat and captivity.

Gwen slid the window closed behind him. Mike's heart stuttered, and he suddenly wanted another drink of vodka. His buzz hadn't followed him into the house; it had remained on the patio as if afraid to enter.

"Okay," Gwen said, "we're here. Now what?"

Evan leaned against the counter ahead of them. "I don't know. I never thought we'd actually come inside."

"Let's look around," Mike said.

"Mike," Gwen protested.

He crossed to Evan and slapped his arm lightly, "Give me the flashlight."

Evan grinned through the gloom like a kid staring at a cookie. He yanked the small maglite out of his pocket and handed it to Mike.

"What are you doing?" Gwen asked.

"Checking the place out."

"Why?"

Because it scares me, *Mike thought.* It has scared me for over two years and I'm sick of it. I can face this place. I can deal with it. Once I do, once I see that it's just wood and plaster and metal and wires and paint and pipes—once I see that it's just a house that happened to shelter two psychopaths, it won't scare me anymore.

"Come on," he said, thumbing on the light and slicing the darkness with its beam. He stepped into a hallway.

Leading his friends toward the living room, Mike kept telling himself the house was nothing. It wasn't exceptional in any way. It was okay. The hardwood floors were clean. The owner had had the interior painted once the police were done with their investigation, but the color was white or off-white. Bland. Stupid. Boring.

He played his light across the floor, careful not to shine it on the living room window in case a neighbor caught sight of it. Of course, a neighbor would see the light inside regardless if they were looking, but to Mike's mind, if he didn't shine the light on the glass, if he kept it inside, there wouldn't be a problem.

"I can't believe we're in here," Evan whispered.

"Yeah, well we shouldn't be in here," Gwen replied.

Mike ran the disc of light up the front door and traced along the floor to where he stood. Had they brought Dory in that way? he wondered. No. They would have parked in the drive at the side of the house and brought her through the backdoor.

"What was that?" Gwen asked.

"What?" Evan said, his voice equal parts amusement and fear.

"On the front door," she said.

Mike shined the light on the door again but he didn't see anything; it looked like a thousand other doors. But Gwen walked toward it, pointing.

"Look, something's bleeding through the paint," she said.

Mike walked closer and joined his friends. Gwen was right. There in the center of the front door a stain marred the perfectly white surface. The stain itself was white, but whereas the rest of the surface was flat this other shape was shiny.

"How did you even see that?" Evan asked.

"I don't know, the way the light hit it. It kind of twinkled."

"What is it?" Mike asked.

The symbol was about the size of his fist, shaped like a figure eight laid on its side with a bar through it. Each end of the bar had a little flag pointing away, and Mike thought about a swastika, or at least half of a swastika bisecting the two bubbles of the reclining number.

"It's a different finish," Gwen said.

"What?" Evan replied with a chuckle.

"I accidentally did the same thing painting my bedroom. I used glossy paint samples, but covered the walls in flat. The gloss bled through. It even looked shiny like this. My dad was so pissed. He had to hire a professional to come in and sand and resurface and paint the room."

"Yeah but… what is it?"

"Who knows? This could have been here for years and no one thought it was a big enough deal to fix. I mean, you'd hardly notice it."

In any other setting, Mike might have accepted the explanation, but in this place, he saw the symbol as ominous. And there it was again, carved into the threshold. Maybe Baxter and Thomason had used this kind of image in sick rituals. Maybe they'd carved it into their victims—into Dory.

"Can we go now?" Gwen asked.

"Getting scared?" Evan wanted to know.

"Getting bored," she corrected.

"I'm going upstairs," Mike said.

"I'm not," Gwen said quickly. "No way. You guys wanted to come here and we did. That's it. I'm done with this Buffy shit. I want another drink and I want it someplace BTK wouldn't hang."

"Then wait here," Mike told her. "Come on, Evan."

"Nah," Evan replied. He looked away when Mike shined the light in his face. "Gwen's right. There's nothing here. Let's bail."

Gwen was already returning to the kitchen, and Mike knew she was doing the right thing, but he felt a strange anxiety, a need to stay in the house, to see every inch of it. It was inexplicable and powerful. Evan set off after Gwen, leaving Mike standing in the middle of the living room, feeling edgy.

"Are you coming?" Gwen asked from the hall.

Mike peered into the gloom but he didn't have an answer for her. The urge to stay was just so strong.

Finally, when he heard Gwen—or Evan, Mike couldn't tell which—opening the kitchen window, he set off across the living room to follow them. Invading this place was dumb enough. Exploring the dark house alone would have been idiotic.

In the hallway a noise startled him. He thought it had come from beneath his feet. Mike thought about the basement. That's where they took their victims. That's where they took…

The sound came again and pushed Mike forward. He crossed into the kitchen in time to see a figure pass through an open door on the far side of the room.

"Hey," he whispered, swinging his light to the now empty doorway.

The figure had been shorter than either Evan or Gwen. A child?

Mike walked to the open door. Wooden stairs descended to the basement. He played the light over the walls and the stairs. A voice came up behind him.

"Let me out," it said.

He turned away from the basement to see the sad and damaged face of his little sister, who stood in the middle of the kitchen. Mike nearly dropped the flashlight.

"It's so hot in here," Dory said. "And it's always dark. I'm afraid. Let me out."

"Please," another voice begged.

Mike stepped back, his heart beating heavily in his throat.

"So dark," a third voice said.

The kitchen began to crackle as if with electric charge. Mike continued back until he realized he stood on the threshold of the basement. His little sister spun on her heels and ran into the hall, where a terrible scratching sound, like thick claws on wood rose. The impossibility of the situation washed over him with the sudden silence. His shoulders relaxed, and he shook his head in disbelief. That hadn't just happened. There was no way in hell that had just happened.

Then a muscular, old man bore down on him from the hall. The man's face had been torn apart and his body carried a dozen vicious wounds. He charged Mike like a bull seeing red. Mike stumbled back and lost his footing. He fell and fell until he slammed against the staircase, hitting the steps hard as he crashed into the basement.

He rolled off of the last three steps onto the concrete floor. Dazed and shocked it took a moment for the pain to wake. When it did, every inch of Mike's body cried out. A bright pain radiated from his left elbow and wrist. His back ached in four distinct places, each beating like a separate heart. His head throbbed behind his right ear.

Voices surrounded him, all of them demanding release. The flashlight had skidded halfway across the floor and cast a cone of light toward the center of the dark room. Things moved in the darkness. Wisps of form appeared and vanished in the gloom. Each spoke for a moment, but before Mike's eyes could settle on a figure another appeared at a different point in the basement.

Then the old man with the mangled face appeared before Mike's watering eyes. He held something in his hand, something sharp.

"Let me out, you stupid little fuck," he said with a high falsetto voice.

The man knelt down. A severe wound on his lower abdomen opened like a mouth then squeezed shut with the motion.

"Fuck," Mike cried. Fuck, this isn't real.

"Let me out," the man roared, his arm swinging at Mike as if he intended to slap his shoulder. Mike scurried back against the wall. Something tugged at his shirt and arm. He turned to find a protruding nail; blood dripped from its rusted point. Then the room went darker and darker. He didn't want to think about this place, didn't want to remember any of it. It couldn't be real. It wasn't real. It was just a dark hot place. Full of nothing but black air and pain. Mike retreated into unconsciousness, the only place he felt safe.

When he came to, Gwen was shouting his name and crying. He opened his eyes and was instantly blinded by the flashlight beam.

"Oh god, don't move. Don't move," she cried. Her hands went to either side of his face and she looked deeply into his eyes, though why Mike didn't know.

He hurt all over. Where the hell was he?

Then he remembered Evan had suggested they go to the house on Ash Street. He'd gone to the house and he'd fallen down the stairs because the ghost of a…

No, he thought, stopping the idea before he could consider it.

He fell down the stairs. That was all.

"Dude, are you okay?" Evan asked. Suddenly Evan's hand was in his face making a peace sign. "How many fingers am I holding up?"

"Two."

"Oh god, your arm," Gwen yelled in his ear.

Mike winced. He looked at his shoulder and saw that his shirt had been ripped. The light fell on the ragged edge of the torn cloth, and he saw the wound beneath. Blood belched out of it, sliding like lava down his arm.

"Shit," he whispered.

Then he closed his eyes and returned to the safety of sleep.

15

Pamela brushed the cigarette ashes off of her laptop's keyboard and looked up at the television screen, and what she saw there, despite its lurid and monstrous content, made her smile. The shadow man who had visited her house to deliver a stack of DVDs hadn't lied. He'd promised lovely and valuable things and that's exactly what he'd left for her, secured in their folding plastic boxes and burned onto high-def Sony discs. The movies her guest had left had nothing to do with Clint Eastwood.

These were the killing tapes.

Pammy now possessed the largest digital record of Selma and Derek's basement torture sessions outside of the Barnard Police Department, and they were fucking incredible. Having no stomach for the violence, but eager to confirm the value of the discs she'd muted the television and only looked up occasionally to make sure the entire "show" featured Selma and Derek and didn't include old episodes of *American Idol* or *Lost* after a few minutes of lead in. She'd already fast-forwarded through three of the six recordings, and was stunned, sickened, and pleased to find each had over an hour's worth of video. She returned her attention to the computer resting on her thighs and continued to scroll through the auction listings, all of which featured her former tenants' names in the item description. Some of the things were stupid as hell, like a Barnard High yearbook with Selma's signature: "Have a great summer, Yo!" An idiot from California had already bid $350 for the damned thing. What would that same goofball pay to see Selma slapping her titties against an old guy's face before she carved off a significant portion of his cheek? A hell of a lot, Pamela figured. Hell, even beyond the serial killer groupies, idolaters, and wannabees there was a whole perv underground filled with rich sleazes eager for snuff films. She didn't know a thing about contacting such fuck wads but the Internet answered all questions, opened all doors, and was about to pay all of her bills for life.

The key was exclusivity. Rarity meant value. Once the recordings got out, it was sure as shit falls down that some idiot would copy the hell out of them and sell them cheap. Then they'd show up all over the internet, and they wouldn't be worth squat. That was the thing about the web, a thing had no value unless everyone knew about it and wanted it, but once everyone had it, it wasn't worth a jiz stained Kleenex. Besides, the discs had to be illegal, and she didn't want to invest in some drawn-out retail situation that would put cops on her doorstep. She wanted to get good money for the recordings, and then get out.

Ash Street

Pamela checked the TV again, winced and jerked her chin down. The events on the screen were just too gross, but the world was full of deviant pricks, and a lot of them were willing to spend a few bucks to get their twisted, blood-hard rocks off. "Sick fucks," she whispered.

Pamela turned off her laptop, closed the lid, and set the machine on the sofa. She reached for the remote and turned off the television before standing up and hurrying to the kitchen.

The freak had said there were more recordings, more discs. They were in Pamela's house. Yeah the old shit had burned the place down, but that didn't mean a damn thing. That house had been in Pamela's family for a good lot of years and she hadn't gotten a thing from it after Selma and Derek were busted, but that wouldn't matter if she found those discs. It wouldn't matter at all.

She took the flashlight from the junk drawer, turned it on to make sure the batteries and bulb were still working, and then she started to leave, when as an afterthought, she returned to the far corner of the kitchen and pulled her slender filet knife from the dish drainer. She gripped the handle tightly. Then, giggling, she slashed the blade through the air as if engaged in a swordfight with an invisible pirate.

Pamela locked the house and walked to her car. She drove the two miles to the burned-out property and then sat in the car, looking at the black-lipped hole where her house had stood. The police or fire marshal had set up chain link fences on three sides of the charred pit but the front was unobstructed except for a couple strips of that worthless yellow emergency tape. Last week when she'd driven by, the day after that Means asshole torched her house, the place had been swarming with people, but most of those were cops and firemen sifting through the wreckage for clues or to extinguish smoldering remains. They'd erected their ridiculous fence and put up their tape and left the place, which meant any jackass and his brother could have slipped onto her property and looted her house. She should have come back the night that freak had left the discs for her, but Pamela hadn't believed his story. Why would she? A guy breaks into her house and hides in the shadows, talking about giving her things in that high and squeaky, homo-on-helium voice; how was she supposed to know he was telling the truth? She hadn't even bothered with the discs until this afternoon, and at first she hadn't understood exactly what she was watching, but it didn't take long for Pamela to realize that what played on her television was money in her pocket.

And now she sat in her car, staring at the lot, telling herself that she was being cautious, checking things out before she approached the ruins. Naturally, her inaction was actually and directly attributed to fear. The house, even reduced to a pile of burned up shit the way it was now, unnerved her. Everyone talked about the bad things that Selma and Derek had done in there, but they weren't the first to pollute the house with sickness and violence; they were just the ones who got caught.

"Either climb on or go the fuck to bed," her father shouted.

Pamela started behind the wheel. The remembered voice came like a blow to the back of her head, sending ripples of anxiety over her shoulders. She shivered and closed her eyes, but that was worse. With her eyes closed she could see her father's red face, his scowl filling the room like a moon.

She'd been eight years old. Her mother was gone that night, off visiting a sister in San Antonio, giving her bruises a chance to heal before Myron Carney could add to their numbers. Myron had left Pamela alone with the television so he could go out drinking, and she'd fallen asleep on the sofa, watching M.A.S.H. Late that night, terrible sounds had woken her. Screams and grunts and curses raced down the stairs. These awful sounds—bright and sharp one moment and deep and blunt the next—surrounded her, and Pamela sat up on the sofa, dreading the cause of the horrible din. She wanted to go to bed and climb deep below the covers, way down where monsters couldn't reach her, but going to bed meant approaching those noises and coming into the orbit of the beasts that made them, so she lay back down on the sofa, curling herself into a tight ball, waiting for the cries to end.

When they did, she waited some more. She drifted off to sleep again but woke only moments later. The house was quiet, and she wondered if the terrible sounds had been nothing more than a nightmare playing at an exceptionally high volume. She climbed off the sofa and headed for the stairs, wiping the sleep from her eyes.

"Bullshit," Pamela announced to the empty car. She shook away the bad memory, refusing to follow her child-self up those stairs.

Instead, she started the car and drove up the block. At the corner, she turned right and parked. If the police came along and found her rooting through the remains of her house, she could tell them that she was just looking the place over for posterity's sake. After all it had been *her* house, but Pamela would prefer to not have to explain anything, so it was better to park out of sight and walk to the lot.

After she locked the car, Pamela walked toward her property, keeping her head down but her ears alert. She wanted to appear casual, in case some nosey neighbor was up late, getting his jollies by spying on the neighborhood. It was the end of the weekend so the scent of freshly cut grass hung in the air, and the hour was so late—or so early, depending on your perspective—the street was silent, except for the hushed slap of her tennis shoes on the sidewalk. She reached the band of yellow tape and shook her head at its impotence before bending low and sliding beneath it. One corner of the house still stood, jutting from the ground like a black-edged trowel. The front lawn was trampled down and covered in debris. Large slabs of burned wall and ceiling were stacked like a giant's overcooked waffles; timbers formed a mound that would still make an impressive bonfire; and bits of rubbish littered the grass in a hundred places.

Pamela picked her way through the wreckage until she reached the far side of the house. The foundation had been cleared here, revealing the well where a wooden staircase had once run down to the basement. Now the steps were gone, but the beam attached to the foundation—the one that had supported the stairs—was intact and didn't look badly damaged. She'd have to be careful so she didn't break her stupid neck falling off the thing, but at least she didn't have to jump to the concrete below.

As the adult Pamela worked her way down the beam, her mind filled with her child-self climbing the stairs that had once risen from the living room to the second floor.

Barefooted, she mounted the staircase, having only the vaguest recollection of horrible noises. At the top of the staircase she noticed the light on in her parent's bedroom; something moved in there. Intending to say goodnight to her father, Pamela continued past the door to her room and followed the corridor. New sounds came to her then, muffled eager sounds that were just as alien to her, but not nearly as disturbing as the ones she'd attributed to a nightmare, so she kept padding along the upstairs hall carpet until she reached the threshold of her parent's room.

She found three people within. Naked. Sweating. Ugly. All of them so ugly. Her father knelt at the end of the bed, his face buried in a fat woman's crotch. The bloated woman moaned and panted as Myron Carney shook his head back and forth like a dog trying to rip the throat out of a squirrel. A man lay on the floor between her father's legs, his head pistoning forward and back, taking Myron's cock deep into his mouth. This man was the first to see Pamela in the doorway. He stopped the eager filatio, and her father looked up from his task. At first he appeared surprised, but then the anger came.

"Either climb on or go the fuck to bed," he shouted.

Confused by the sight before her and terrified by her father's tone, Pamela had been frozen in place. The fat woman laughed and snatched for a pillow to cover her face. The man on the floor, no longer interested in her presence, returned his attention to Myron's cock.

"Fine," Pamela said to the wreckage, "Daddy was a perv."

She reached the bottom of the support beam and stepped on the concrete slab, then realized there was nowhere else to go. Most of the floor and a good part of the landing above that had crashed through to fill the basement. Blackened timbers with burned scraps of drywall lay haphazardly against the sides of the room and entire walls had collapsed, leaving tiny gaps, barely large enough for a small dog, let alone a person to pass through. Pamela dug the flashlight out of the pocket of her shorts and thumbed it on. Sweeping the beam about the miserable and impenetrable debris, her anger swelled.

"Well shit," she hissed. This had been a total waste of time. She thought about the other DVDs hidden somewhere behind this mound of crap and grew absolutely furious.

Then the beam of her flashlight fell on an opening in the rubble. It wasn't very wide but it seemed to stretch high enough for her to slip through, though getting there was going to be a chore. Determined to make this trip worth her efforts, Pamela climbed over a mound that had once been part of the kitchen floor and banged her hip on the remains of a crumpled oven range. She muttered a curse and attempted to get her footing on the uneven litter. Again she shined her light on the opening ahead and from this new angle, it appeared to be an even more likely passage. Careful to avoid jutting nails and spear-sharp splinters, Pamela navigated through the forest of dead wood and melted linoleum until she reached the mouth of the opening. She pointed the flashlight into the corridor and stopped cold.

"Son of a bitch," she whispered.

A man stood in the cramped space ahead. The idiot was naked as the day he'd been born, and his flesh was so pale the flashlight beam seemed to reflect off it. He stood straight-backed, facing the wall, like a corpse propped against the timbers. He was very short. In fact, if he'd had another inch of height on him he'd have had to crouch in the vault. As it was, the pronounced bald spot on the back of his head all but touched the slanting timbers above.

"Who the hell are you?" Pamela asked.

The man didn't reply. He made no movement at all.

"You're trespassing," she said. "You can't be here."

Pamela thought to press the point further, but the peril of her situation finally sank in. Though startled by the man's presence, her initial reaction had been rage at his nerve, but now the anger was ebbing enough for her to realize exactly how bizarre and dangerous this situation was. She took a step back. The flashlight beam swept over the broad, motionless back and a deep chill coursed through her, bringing needles to her neck and brow. She turned to flee, but struck the side of her head on a collapsed beam. Soot broke loose of the board and filled her nostrils. She pulled away and scraped her elbow on a protruding nail.

"Fuck," she cried, suddenly feeling trapped by the charred debris. Panic flared in her torso like lightning conducted through ice, and Pamela whipped the flashlight through the air. She needed to keep the strange man in her sights. He might give up his possum game at any moment and come after her. The beam found his muscular back again, casting a drape of shadow on the wall he faced. Though unmoving, the man seemed closer to the gap in the boards than he had.

It's just an illusion, Pamela thought. *My view of the chamber is different and the light is hitting him from a different angle. He didn't move.*

Whether the creepy man had moved or not hardly mattered. She wasn't sticking around to confirm or refute the possibility.

Pamela turned to leave and her t-shirt snagged on a jagged fragment of wood. She snatched it away, tearing a long hole in the fabric, and then stumbled along the path that had brought her so deeply into the wreckage of the house. She could come back for the DVDs, if she could even find them in this mess.

Her flashlight beam fell on another figure ahead, framed by a jumble of trash including the oven range. This time, the body was that of a woman with long, straight strawberry blond hair. She too was naked and faced away from Pamela. Her buttocks had been slashed and tiny black holes, cigarette burns, ran in a grotesque constellation across her back.

"I knew you'd come," the falsetto voice whispered. Pamela turned to confront the high-voiced freak, but found no one near her save the woman blocking her way out of the maze of charred waste. "Oh Pammy, we're going to have such fun."

16

The phone call ended another night of brief and restless sleep. Stuart rolled over in the bed, reached out blindly for the headset and pressed it to his face. "Yeah?" he said.

"Wake up. It's time to go to work."

"Harlan?"

"Who else?"

"It's been days," Stuart muttered. "Is this about Pudge?"

"Yeah."

"What have you got?"

"First the rules," Harlan said.

"I don't need games first thing in the morning."

"Then go back to sleep and forget I called," Harlan told him. "I'm serious, Stuart. This is some nasty shit and a few very well-connected citizens are involved, and some of those well-connected citizens can make my life a living hell if this falls through. So rule one: my name doesn't come into this…ever."

"Deal," Stuart said. He yawned and rolled onto his back, then checked the alarm clock to see that he'd overslept. He sat up and wiped the sleep from his eyes. "You are officially an anonymous tip."

"Rule two: No questions. I'm telling you what I know, and that's it. And you don't ask where I got my information. You wouldn't like the answer anyway."

"Fair enough," Stuart agreed. Climbing out of the bed, he nearly dropped the phone, but recovered it in time to hear Harlan's rule number three:

"Don't say anything to anyone on the force, until after you get the information you need."

"Harlan…"

"Hey," he interrupted, "respect rule two."

In the hallway, on his way to the kitchen to make coffee, Stuart shook his head in exasperation. "Okay," he said.

Then he came alongside his study. The door was wide open, the way he'd left it after spending another evening shuffling through DVD cases, certain he had simply overlooked the recordings. It was a denial tactic, one that he had employed each of the three nights since having discovered his home office in ruin.

In the end, truth was truth: the discs were gone. The Baxter-Thomason recordings, and another recording that was far more personal.

Maybe Hannah Bolger hadn't been as far off the mark as Stuart wanted to believe. Pudge Taylor; Alan Means; and now the theft of the Baxter-Thomason recordings: they all tied into the crimes on Ash Street. But how had the thief known which DVDs to take? What were the odds that a random miscreant would steal those precise discs? For that matter, what were the chances that anyone, even someone so thoroughly committed to aligning themselves with the Lethal Lovers, would know Stuart had pirated those recordings and kept them hidden in and among a set of Hollywood blockbusters? The odds were astronomical and fell far outside the realm of coincidence. In fact, it was impossible.

Stuart mentally gnawed on this idea until he realized Harlan wasn't speaking. He said his friend's name, and then continued down the hall.

"Fine." Harlan paused. He sniffed loudly like a boxer trying to keep blood in his nose. "Early this afternoon, a man named Winston is going to be setting up shop in a house on Bluebonnet Street. He's like a gypsy, moving around all the time, so he'll only be there for a couple of days before moving on. I don't know much about the set up, but you need to use the word 'Puppies.' Don't say anything else. That will get you in the door. Bring about a grand in cash for cover."

"Wait a minute," Stuart said. "What kind of shop is he setting up?"

"Which brings us back to rule number two."

"Harlan, you can't send me in there blind."

"I can't tell you what I don't know, and I'm not going to speculate because that could get you killed. That's all I got, buddy."

"Do you have an address on Bluebonnet."

Harlan read it off, then said, "Remember, don't head over until after noon. You get there too soon, and he's likely to hightail it out of there."

"Thanks, Harlan."

This must be the place.

Stuart eased his car to the curb and looked across the street at the house. The number 620 was visible above the door. Ghosts of the numbers outlined in filth remained where once there had been wooden, perhaps even brass numbers tacked to the siding. The yard was an overgrown mess with bits of litter visible through brittle and brown weeds. Boards covered the windows on the ground floor. The framed glass on the second story had been broken out long ago, revealing sheets of slate gray paper buffeting in the wind.

He crossed the street. He tested his weight on the stair leading to the porch, and it creaked threateningly, so Stuart grasped a wooden support and hoisted himself up. Instead of knocking, he simply pushed the cracked and stained front door inward, revealing a gloomy hall of crumbling plaster and cracked paint. The air trapped between these walls seemed alive with dust and pollen, like pale plankton caught in an ocean's current.

With great effort, he pictured Pudge Taylor entering such a place, a hovel long since abandoned by anyone remotely civilized. He imagined the big man with his oil-money swagger lighting a cigarette in the hall—maybe he smiled around the butt, maybe he frowned with shame—as he waited for… for what?

"Hello," a reed-thin voice whispered.

Stuart tensed and turned to an opening that led to what had once been a small living room. A slender Caucasian man, holding a cigarette between two fingers, regarded Stuart, examined him with a cool intensity. Stuart assumed this was the man named Winston. A familiar ratchet—the sound of a shotgun being pumped snapped over his right shoulder. Stuart turned to find a Hispanic boy, who couldn't have been more than fifteen years old, standing on the staircase sighting down the barrel of an ancient Mossberg shotgun. The gun was too big for the kid, and he'd probably blow his shoulder out of joint if he pulled the trigger, but that wouldn't help Stuart any if he got off a shot. The kid was too close to miss.

"Hello," Winston repeated.

"Puppies," Stuart said, using the word Harlan had given him.

"I don't know you," the slender man said. His head moved slowly on his neck like a snake assessing the best angle to strike. Putting the cigarette between his lips, he squinted through the gloom. The end of his smoke burned orange.

"Puppies," Stuart repeated. He didn't know what else to say, and the presence of the shotgun so near his back wasn't helping him think straight.

"Are you sure?" Winston asked. "You don't strike me as a dog person."

Fuck, Stuart thought. *This is wrong. This whole scene is wrong.*

Pudge would never come to a place like this. If he needed to play out his hebephilia fantasies there were a dozen more practical ways to do it. He could fly to Mexico, or Morocco, or Bangkok, and buy the company of a dozen youths. Entertain them in a nice hotel room that didn't smell of hate and cat piss.

Stuart felt his confidence tremble, but he wouldn't let it collapse. He had to face this *wrong* place, had to make himself part of it. The slender man with the insect eyes, the corded neck, and the crisply pressed white cabana shirt and slacks; the broken and crumbling walls of the dismal room behind him; the little boy who should have been in school but was instead ready to blow a hole in Stuart's back: he'd made a mistake coming in here alone. He didn't know his way around a place like this, but there was no way to leave. He couldn't just walk out. Not now.

"Puppies," he said for the third time.

The slender man shrugged and nodded his head. He broke his pose in the grimy living room and stepped forward. "Julio," he called with a wave of his hand. Stuart turned to the armed youth, who nodded rapidly and lowered the shotgun. Then the boy, having been relieved of duty, raced up the stairs as if eager to return to his toys or a cartoon series he was missing on television.

Stuart followed Winston down the dingy hallway, alert for any more gun-wielding juveniles. The entire house smelled of must and damp and animal waste. The place had rats. Stuart could hear them moving behind the shoddy walls. No doubt termites had colonized the frame. Harlan had told him that this son of a bitch was like a gypsy, keeping his caravan of children moving from one run-down property to the next. What Stuart didn't know was if the slender man and his "family" actually struck deals with the owners—whether paying rent or bartering services—or if the pervert just scouted out fresh places to squat. Stuart didn't think so. Even though the neighbors were likely to keep their mouths shut, not wanting the police to interfere with their business any more than they did Winston there would always be the chance of a property owner spotting the action in a house, seeing men dressed too well for their neighborhood traveling from late model sedans over unkempt lawns and into their houses. They'd get curious, and if Julio didn't blow their heads off with a round of buckshot, they'd likely cause some trouble, at least financial hardship, for Winston. Stuart imagined the places were rented by the week, the landlords welcoming what little cash their shacks brought them.

"You never mentioned who referred you," Winston said as they passed into the kitchen.

"True enough," Stuart said, "but I don't imagine he'd appreciate having his name bandied about any more than I would."

"You're a man of discretion," Winston noted. "First timers are often more talkative. It's the nerves. They get themselves all wound up and can't seem to keep their traps shut. Then after they finish their business, they're as quiet as church mice running out ahead of the parishioners. Guess all the nervous gets used up. But when they come in, they talk a mile a minute on account of them nerves."

"You nervous about something?" Stuart asked.

Winston paused and threw an amused glace over his shoulder at Stuart. "You're a sharp one. Best you don't cut yourself."

They entered a small kitchen, barely larger than the master bath in Stuart's house. All of the cabinet doors were gone, exposing empty shelves. The appliances had been scavenged long ago, leaving voids between the chipped formica countertops. The place reeked of rotten vegetables, and flies swarmed over the sink. Beneath their buzzing was another, lower hum.

A generator, Stuart thought. He looked around the gray room until he noticed a small red light in the base of a coffee pot. Behind the pot a white cord ran along the corner of the counter and met up with a black socket that had been punched through the siding and the interior wall.

"Some place," he muttered.

"Don't you worry none. I got the basement and the rooms in front done up clean and proper. You ain't going to be lying in any shit stains, I guarantee that. The wife keeps all the linen good as new."

The wife, he thought. *Jesus, this is a family business.*

"Also got some of those little plastic air fresheners in there, so you don't have to sniff rat piss while you're visiting," Winston said. "And we'll run the fans so it don't get too hot. You'll be comfortable enough. The only thing we can't offer you is a shower, but most of our clientele just stops by their health club on the way home if they feel the need. Otherwise, we got baby wipes and paper towels to sop up the worst of it."

Stuart's stomach lurched. It was bad enough to imagine someone like Pudge Taylor taking this disgusting tour, and following it through to its thoroughly fucked up conclusion, but how in the hell had Harlan known about this operation? Stuart reminded himself that Harlan had grown up on the low side of the tracks and that a lot of his oldest acquaintances were something less than law abiding, but this shit went over the line. He swore that the next time he saw his friend, he was going to get answers.

Winston opened the door to the basement and walked over the threshold immediately disappearing into a wall of gloom. From below, Stuart heard the soft, high voices of children. His already uneasy gut flipped. He took a moment to quell the rising sickness. Then he started down the stairs.

Halfway along the descent he paused. He saw them. The children. He counted six in all: four girls, all wearing cheap summer dresses; and two boys wearing blue jeans and plain white t-shirts. Stuart estimated their ages at between eleven and fifteen years old. They were all Hispanic and all appeared to have been freshly scrubbed, with their black hair neatly combed and shining beneath the harsh glow of a single tall lamp, obviously running off the generator, that stood in the corner. The children sat on plastic chairs or on the floor. One little girl, clutching a rag doll, turned away as Stuart descended into the obscene showroom. The boy closest to him continued to roll a plastic truck over the filthy concrete. He looked up only briefly, sad distant eyes registering Stuart, before returning his attention to the toy.

"Do you want to see them play?" Winston asked. "Some of our clients like to see them play a game of tag or catch."

They want to see the innocence before they take it, Stuart thought. *They want to pretend they're at the edge of a playground instead of a moldy basement, observing happy carefree children, rather than slaves imported into the country for this sick endeavor.*

Stuart checked the perimeter of the chamber. Deep bruises of shadow fell on the floor behind the water heater and a stack of collapsing cardboard boxes. Another shotgun-toting boy could easily hide among them, might hide beneath the stairs. Stuart shifted his eyes and again checked the six children. They looked frightened, tired, and despondent, but they didn't look threatening.

"No play?" Winston said. "Good enough. You pick one of the puppies, we only have two right now, but more come through all the time. It'll be eight hundred for the afternoon."

Stuart nodded slowly. It dawned on him then that "puppies" was code for the boys. The girls were given a different designation, probably kittens or some equally demeaning moniker. "Eight hundred," Stuart repeated quietly, his eyes fixed on a dull-faced little girl with large brown eyes, wearing a sheer, powder blue dress. Her hair was pulled back into a neat ponytail. Her hands crossed in her lap.

"Eight hundred for the afternoon."

Stuart reached into the flap of his jacket as if going for a wallet. Instead, he grabbed his service revolver and yanked it out, leveling the barrel at Winston's face.

Below and behind him, the children screeched and scrambled. He heard their shrill voices and their tiny feet retreating deeper into the basement. Stuart threw a quick look at the panicked boys and girls. None of them had taken up weapons against him. Their only plan seemed to be to get as far away from the crazy man with the gun as they could manage.

"I'm Detective Stuart Lancaster with the Barnard Police Department, and you're under arrest for pandering, child endangerment, and a shitload of other offenses yet to be named. I'm sure INS will have a list of their own."

Winston looked as if he'd been slapped. His hands were up on either side of his shocked expression, and what little color his cheeks had possessed drained away. "We can work something out," he said quickly. "How much do you want? Five grand? Ten?"

"You sick fuck," Stuart said. "This isn't a negotiation. You smuggle these kids over the border to be violated, and you think there's enough money in the world to keep me from shutting this down?"

"Everyone has to earn their way," Winston said, now attempting to be cool. "This is America, detective. Capitalism and supply and demand. They want out, then they have to pay for that privilege and the farmers got more than enough hands pulling cabbage."

"You're lecturing me? You're trying to justify this shit?"

"Everyone has to earn their way," Winston repeated.

"Tell me about Pudge Taylor," Stuart said. "You have one of your puppies go at him with a knife?"

"Never heard of him. We're not big on names around here."

Stuart wanted to hurt the man, wanted to send a bullet into each of the pervert's kneecaps. No. That wasn't enough. Not nearly enough. He wanted to put a bullet in the guy's face. He never wanted this prick to walk free again.

He fished in his lapel pocket for a photo of Pudge Taylor. He removed it and shoved it in Winston's face. "Look close. Talk fast."

"He's the dead guy," the thin man said.

"That's right and you're at the top of the suspect list."

Winston rolled his eyes dramatically and then sneered. "For a cunt, you're not a very good liar. If he was a customer, and I'm not saying he was, why would I cut off a regular cash supply?"

"Maybe he was feeling guilty," Stuart said. "Maybe he thought shutting you down would help his conscience."

Winston laughed. "The men who come here don't listen to their consciences. They listen to the calling. It's like a fever and the only cure is a tight little body with big eyes and a whole future ahead of them, a future those men have the power to irrevocably fuck up. Boys. Girls. Doesn't make a fucking difference. That's the key. Get it? They aren't here for sex, at least, not just sex. They're seeking converts. Your fat, dead friend was one of countless sick and broken men who don't want to feel alone so they build a cult by creating more like themselves. They share their calling and pass it on, increasing the ranks of their parish, building a church of damaged souls."

"And you're their priest."

"I don't even share their faith," Winston said.

"But Pudge Taylor did?"

"He was devout. He broke in quite a bit of my stock. Some couldn't even work anymore, but there's always new product coming over the border to line the shelves."

Stuart shoved Winston against the wall. The man's foot slipped on the stair, sending him to the side, and Stuart reached out reflexively to steady him. Winston took the opportunity. He uncoiled, landing a fist in Stuart's belly, and then the thin man shoved, and Stuart dropped back against the railing. Before he could regain his balance, Winston was racing up the stairs.

Stuart tried to aim at the fleeing man, but again lost his balance. He shuffled down two stairs before getting his feet firmly under his weight.

By then, Winston had reached the basement door. He threw it open and it hit the wall with a deafening explosion—a sound far too loud to have been created by wood hitting old plaster. It was an explosion, a hammer dropping on a shell packed with powder. The thin man spun back toward Stuart, who saw the crimson blossom on the chest of Winston's cabana shirt. The man looked startled. Then he crashed down the stairs, sliding along the planks until his body's momentum was stopped. Winston lay wedged in a semi-fetal position between a spindle and the wall three steps up from where Stuart stood. A device with a plastic case, no larger than a garage door opener, clacked on the wooden slats and skittered across the floor.

The children screamed again. They pushed into a tight knot in the far corner of the basement.

Stuart hurried down the stairs toward the device that had fallen from Winston's hand. He lifted it from the floor. A red light blinked on its facing. Stuart wasn't certain exactly what the controller did, but he assumed it was a makeshift alarm, something that had alerted Julio or another boy to impending trouble. Then they'd accidentally gunned down their meal ticket when he burst through the door, which meant that at least one youth waited above with a shotgun trained on the doorframe. There could be more.

Stuart worked his way toward the children in the corner, never taking his eyes off of the light at the top of the stairs. He pulled out his cell phone and dialed for back up.

Stuart sat in his office, his thoughts weaving and knotting, colliding like drunken gnats in a dense fog. He hadn't slept well in days, and after the adrenaline tweak at Winston earlier in the day and the ensuing statements and paperwork, he could barely keep his eyes open. Images of crying children, some holding him tightly and whispering phrases in Spanish, a language he didn't know well, blended into a grotesque collage featuring Pudge Taylor's morgue shots and similar images Stuart remembered from the Baxter-Thomason case. One moment he thought about the little plain-faced girl who held tightly to his leg, whispering "gracias" into the fabric of his slacks, and the next he was assaulted by the open wounds on the bodies of Regina Wolcroff and Sam Locke and Dory Addison. Amid this provocative mental picture show, his friend Harlan would appear, skewering a grilled steak and asking Stuart if he wanted any blood in it. Stuart imagined some of these images were connected, but he no longer believed Pudge Taylor's murderer had originated among the vagabond Winston or his child slaves. Granted, Winston had been free with information about Pudge, because he assumed Stuart would be taking a chest full of buckshot before the conversation was done. Still, the pimp had made a good point; there was no reason for Winston to eliminate a steady source of cash.

When Stuart still believed that Pudge might have exercised his disgusting behavior on local girls, incurring the wrath of their parents or the girls themselves, then it seemed likely his behavior would more than suffice for motive, but Winston's girls had no immediate family. They were precious to no one but Winston and his clients, and the pimp needed Pudge more than he needed any one of his little girls. …*there's always new product coming over the border to line the shelves.*

Not that this lead was being written off. It would be pursued thoroughly, but Stuart wasn't holding out much hope of it producing a solid suspect. What it did was provide confirmation of Pudge's twisted needs. Maybe there was a local girl (or boy) who had endured Pudge's advances. Maybe the child had told her father, mother, or an older sibling. Maybe she'd picked up a knife herself.

A lot of maybes. The case was getting uglier, but no clearer.

He'd completely forgotten about his dinner plans with Hannah Bolger until the woman's call broke his miserable reverie. Looking at the caller ID he found himself unable to make sense of the display. Foreign glyphs had replaced letters. He wiped his eyes harshly and again checked the readout. Now, he could read Hannah's name and he debated answering the call, but he knew he should.

She reminded him about dinner, and he told her that he would be late. She shouldn't hold the meal for him, but she insisted. Hannah had already seen the news report about the house at 620 Bluebonnet.

"You just come over when you can get away," she told him.

17

Hannah Bolger opened the front door and smiled out at him like a mother seeing her son for the first time in months. Always uncomfortable under this maternal gaze, Stuart stepped over the threshold quickly. He leaned in to hug Hannah, and then offered her the bottle of wine he'd picked up at Truck's Liquor on his way to her house.

"You look tired," Hannah said, leading him through the cluttered living room to the kitchen at the back. "Haven't you been sleeping?"

"Maybe not as much as I should," Stuart replied. In truth, he was hardly sleeping at all. Between his frustration over the Pudge Taylor case and the burglary of his home, the last few nights had found Stuart lying awake well into the early morning hours, often sliding his hand beneath the pillow next to his, checking for the loaded firearm he kept there. Sleep would approach and then scurry away like a frightened animal with every creak of the house and every car that rolled down the street. His mind hit overdrive every time he closed his eyes, and once he'd bolted out of a shallow doze, convinced he'd solved the Taylor case, only to realize the solution was no more substantial than the dream that had produced it.

In the kitchen, Hannah spun on him, wearing a broad smile. "Have you been visited, too?" she asked.

"Visited?" Stuart asked. His first thought was that Hannah's house had been broken into the same way that his had. Maybe the serial killer collectible crowd had taken things to the next level. Maybe they were breaking into the homes of victims to scavenge personal items to add to their sick treasures. Maybe one of these collectors had surprised Pudge Taylor at his fridge and decided his life wasn't worth as much as something intimate to his daughter.

Stuart sat down at the small table in Hannah's kitchen and mentally chastised himself for creating the weakest motivation for murder he'd ever conceived of before. He really did need some rest. Otherwise he wasn't going to be good for anyone.

"Yes," Hannah said, "visited."

"Have you been burglarized?"

"Leave it to you to think I'm talking about a crime."

"Then what are you talking about, Hannah? Sorry, but subtlety is going to be lost on me tonight."

"Richard Wolcroff was here the other day," Hannah said. "Now, I don't want you to get upset. Listen to everything I tell you so you have all of the information. Then we can discuss it like enlightened adults."

"Discuss what?"

"As I said, Richard was over the other day and he told me about a visitation he'd had."

Stuart didn't like the sound of the word visitation. This was probably more of Hannah's groovy new age weirdness, and he didn't feel up to dealing with any of that tonight.

"He told me he saw Regina."

The name didn't immediately register with Stuart. He was checking it against a mental list of people he might know—living people. It didn't occur to him that Hannah might be talking about the daughter Richard had lost to Baxter and Thomason.

"And I've been visited by Ben," Hannah told him. "I fully expect you won't believe me. Of course, I didn't believe it myself. I assumed it was a delayed grief reaction or perhaps a strong jolt of wishful thinking, but my neighbor, Terry, saw him too. It wasn't just me. Now, I have several theories about why this might–"

"Wait," Stuart said, once the significance of what Hannah was saying crept through the fatigue born mist clouding his thoughts. "You saw Ben? Ben Locke?"

"Yes, and Richard saw Regina."

"His dead daughter?"

"Stuart, before you write us off, I want you to listen to what I have to say."

"I'm here thirty seconds and you spring this shit on me?"

"I don't think it's just us," Hannah added quickly. "I think Alan may have been the first. I think that's why he went to the house on Ash Street."

"Alan didn't just go to the house on Ash Street; he torched it. Are you suggesting a ghost told him to do it?"

Hannah prickled under the question. Her broad rectangular face tightened into a disapproving glare—the stink eye Stuart remembered from his own mother—and she cleared her throat quietly as if waiting for an apology. When none was forthcoming, she said, "Yes. That's exactly what I think happened."

Stuart couldn't even work up the energy to laugh at the ridiculous idea. He'd already hurt Hannah's feelings, but there was nothing he could do about that. She sounded only a couple steps closer to sane than Alan had been, and they weren't giant steps.

"You don't have to believe me," Hannah continued.

"That's a relief."

"And you don't have to be rude about it."

"I'm sorry," Stuart said, shaking his head. "But don't we have enough real world problems without dragging in the supernatural? I mean, Christ, Alan killed himself. Pudge Taylor was murdered." *And someone broke into my house to steal digital recordings I don't want anyone to ever see.* "I'll concede that someone—a real person—might be obsessed enough with Baxter-Thomason to start a crime spree of their own. But ghosts? Isn't it possible that these deaths dredged up a lot of memories? Feelings? Let's face it none of us has done a great job of moving on since the murders. Maybe no one ever does, but you can't start letting this stuff creep into your head. It can take hold and severely fuck you up."

"So you think it's all in my head?"

"Hannah, what other answer is there? Come on. Really."

A click sounded beneath the table and Stuart pulled back. A moment later, Hannah was presenting the bottom of her left foot. She just dropped it on the table like she was serving it for dinner. He saw the three cuts on the sole of her foot, cuts that looked like the letter A. Stuart closed his eyes and breathed deeply. The autopsy photos of Pudge Taylor swam into his thoughts. The tee-pee shaped wound on his foot. The coroner's Sharpie notation in red: *Pre-existing.* It wasn't possible, Stuart told himself. He was just exhausted, and he hadn't really seen anything except an old woman's wrinkled foot. Slowly he opened his eyes. The mark remained.

"Richard had a mark just like this on the bottom of his foot," Hannah said. "Now I don't know about him, but I'm not in the habit of going around and cutting myself. They want us to know they're real. They're trying to communicate and we have to listen."

Stuart considered what that might mean to him. *Clarissa*? The name cut into his mind like an icy scalpel. The sick feeling in his belly grew and hardened into a painful stone behind his navel. He dreaded the message she might have for him.

How could you do this to me?

"You know what this mark means, don't you?" Hannah said.

"Yes. It was something we managed to keep out of the media, something about the murders. Baxter and Thomason marked some of their victims. They scratched, sometimes carved, the letter A into the foot, sort of like branding them."

"Why an A?" Hannah asked. She removed her foot from the table and leaned forward.

"You remember the trial," Stuart said. "The defense made a weak attempt at an insanity plea early on. They had three different expert witnesses testifying that neither Baxter nor Thomason were individually capable of committing the crimes. It was only when they came together that it caused this sort of psychological catalyst, essentially creating a totally different mentality that was not only capable of murder, but also insistent on it. The experts called it a Third

Personality Disorder, and taking their cue from the psychologists, Baxter and Thomason named this third personality, 'Andy.'"

"But they were marking the victims long before the therapists became involved."

"I know, but..." Stuart paused. He wasn't remembering the series of events properly. He scratched his fingers deep into his scalp, hoping to wake up his tired memory. "No wait. That's wrong. When they were taken into custody, they mentioned the name Andy. And they used it while they were torturing some of their victims. You remember they recorded a lot of their crimes? On one of the recovered discs they were talking to this Andy like he was in the room with them, asking him what he wanted them to do. Christ, I can't believe I forgot that.

"Anyway, we originally thought Andy was a real guy. We figured these two psychos had found a third to play with. We didn't know if he escaped or turned out to be another victim of Baxter and Thomason. But soon enough, we discovered Andy was a fabrication, a game they played, probably just another mind fuck for their victims. Once the psychologists started talking about this Third Personality Disorder, they changed their story and named the personality Andy."

"You said they marked *some* of their victims?" Hannah said.

"Yeah," Stuart told her, "the last seven victims were marked. They didn't do it to the first four."

"Why do you think that is?"

"They never explained it," Stuart said. "We assumed that their methodologies evolved along with their confidence. Once they got past the initial hesitance of killing it got easier for them. Early on it wasn't clear that we were dealing with serial killers. Once the connection was made and released to the media, they might have wanted to make sure they got credit for the people they'd murdered. I don't know. We thoroughly checked their pasts and considered a possible religious or occult connection to the letter A, but outside of the novel by Hawthorne, the letter seems to have no significance."

"Do you think *The Scarlet Letter* influenced them?"

"I doubt they ever read it," Stuart said. "I read it three times, looking for something that might be considered a link, but came up dry. They certainly weren't driven by religious or moral frenzy. They never thought their victims deserved to be punished, at least not because of misdeeds. From all that we could gather, they killed because they could and because they liked it. The victims were totally random. Convenient."

"But maybe there was more to it," Hannah suggested. "Maybe that's why they're back."

"More to what?" Stuart asked. "They were murdered and their murderers have been caught. Both of them are going to be in prison for the rest of their lives. What else could they want to tell us?"

"They might be warning us," Hannah said.

"Warning us? About what?"

"That Andy is real."

18

Stuart woke to the sound of snoring. He felt angry and on edge. The alarm clock in front of him read six in the morning, so he'd barely slept three hours, and his groggy mind took a minute to process what he was hearing. Once he recognized the sound, he rolled over and found no one in the bed next to him.

"What the hell?" he muttered. He fell back on his pillow and rubbed his eyes. When he pulled his hands away he saw movement across the room and bolted upright, but the movement played on the television. In fact the high-definition television was also the source of the snoring.

Stuart focused his bleary vision and was surprised to find that the picture on the screen was a video of him asleep. The camera angle was wide, covering half the room and taking in the bed and nightstands. In the center of the scene, he tossed restlessly beneath the sheets.

Stuart climbed out of bed and walked toward the screen.

In the video, he rolled over and clutched a pillow. Then a woman walked on screen. She was naked and badly wounded with burns dotting her back like thick moles. Dried blood stained her hips and buttocks. She crossed around the bed and stood next to the nightstand staring down at Stuart's sleeping form. From this angle he could clearly see her face. It was slashed at the brow and chin. Her left eye was missing. Two deep puncture wounds just below the rib cage were caked with thick clots of blood. These had been the killing wounds, Stuart noted. The forensic report on Clarissa had gone into great detail about them.

In the video, Stuart snorted loudly and one leg kicked at the covers. His dead wife just watched.

The dread of what he was witnessing hit Stuart like a fist. He stumbled away from the television and tripped over the end of the bed. He fell backward on the mattress but before his body settled Stuart rolled and leapt away, fleeing the room and bolting down the hall toward the front of the house.

"Shit," he muttered. "Shit. Shit." His skin crawled into chilled gooseflesh as the image on the video sank in.

Rationally he knew Clarissa had not been on that tape, could not have been in his room, regardless of the spook stories Hannah had told him. It wasn't possible. He was imagining things. Maybe he was still asleep. Stuart scratched his head with both hands sending cascades of chills down his neck, but he hadn't needed this tactile sensation to prove his wakefulness. His mind began to reel through possibilities, any piece of logic he could hang what he'd witnessed on. Someone doctored the tape, he reasoned. It was possible. Someone could have snuck into his house one night and filmed him sleeping only to add computer animation later, but who in the hell would go to such extremes for a sick joke? It was too elaborate, too brutal. He wasn't important enough to warrant such attention.

Stuart anxiously paced the living room as he tried to sort through his thoughts. He was a cop for god's sake. He'd faced knives and guns and the fists of drunken idiots with eighty pounds on him. Taking deep breaths, he quelled his nerves and settled his thoughts. Slowly his confidence returned and Stuart walked back to the bedroom. The picture on the television screen hadn't changed. Clarissa still stood by the bed staring down. Stuart lay asleep, absolutely oblivious to her presence, absolutely helpless. *How long was she here*? The chill returned to his neck, but Stuart kept calm. He attempted to bring a rational analysis to the situation.

From the angle of the scene, whoever had taped this encounter had to have been operating the camera from the hall. (*Unless they used a tripod or ghosts don't need fucking cameras to record shit.*) This last point went a long way in further unnerving him. Stuart knelt down and found his own digital video camera perched on the shelf of the media center. A cord ran from the unit to the back of the DVD player. He snatched the camera up and saw a smaller version of the picture that played on his television. Then he replaced the unit on the shelf and stood. No magic there. The image had been recorded like a million others, but who had operated the camera while Clarissa watched him? Had she set it herself? Was it even her?

Stuart stared at the figure next to the bed. It was impossible for him to deny the identity of the woman. He knew her face and body far too well to entertain denial. Further, he knew what Thomason and Baxter had done to her. It was Clarissa. He reached out a trembling hand toward the screen and just as his fingers grazed the picture, she lifted her head and glared at him.

"How could you?" she asked, her voice cold and flat. "How could you do that to me?"

Stuart jerked his hand away from the screen. He quickly knelt and turned the camera off, and then backed away from the media center. So much for rational, he thought as his calm vanished into a mire of dread and uncertainty. Hurriedly, he dressed and left the house. He would shower at the station. He just needed to be among people right now, needed to be among the living.

19

Mike made it through fourth period before he thought his head would explode. The night had been as restless and bleak as a stormy ocean, and he'd again found himself standing in front of the bathroom mirror, only instead of pills he surfaced to a moment of clarity and found the point of a utility knife dimpling the skin at his wrist. He'd placed the instrument on the bathroom counter and fought to hold back tears.

He'd always assumed that suicide was a destination, the place that lonely, depressed, and hopeless people ended up when no other place else would have them. He'd never seen the act as a force that had to be analyzed and fought and run from. Deep down, maybe he wanted to die, certainly there was a part of him that wanted to be removed from his life, taken up and away from the pitying stares, the hushed conversations that ended when he entered a room, his dysfunctional and separated parents, but in those few moments when he was clear-headed and able to rationalize both his situation and his future, he understood death wouldn't cure his problems; it was simply an amputation removing the sick him from the population's body.

After Dory's murder, and all of the media bullshit, Mike had kept it together, though he'd often felt like screaming. It was different now. Since his grandfather went pyro, since his butchered baby sister returned with taunts and accusations, Mike could only touch self-control with the tips of his fingers; it was barely within reach.

Now, sitting in class and exhausted from lack of sleep, Mike felt as if wires had been pushed through his skin, each one sending a tiny charge of electricity to his extremities, making his leg bounce beneath his desk and his fingers tap a-rhythmically on its wooden top. During fourth period, the feeling became too much to bear, so when the bell rang, he made his way to the parking lot. He spent ten minutes wandering through the vehicles until he remembered that his mother had taken the car today. She'd dropped him off and driven it away. The realization confounded Mike, like facing a room that had neither windows nor doors, yet knowing he had to escape it. He could have found Gwen and Evan; they would shuttle him away from the school, but Gwen would treat him like a patient—all soft-eyed concern and pity—and Evan's abrasive humor would further aggravate his raw nerves. They'd miss him at lunch. No doubt they'd text and call until they tracked him down. By then he might be ready to see them, but he couldn't stand in the parking lot for the next hour waiting.

Ash Street

A cool breeze blew, and Mike walked into it, away from the school, with no destination in mind, but feeling a renewed sense of control in his decision to move. He walked through the suburban neighborhood bordering the school grounds with unfocused eyes, stumbling more than once on uneven patches of sidewalk, but he kept moving forward. He felt drunk and sick, as if enduring a hangover while still inebriated. Though the worst of summer's heat had passed, he sweat profusely at the neck, and perspiration slid down his back in prickly rivulets.

Mike considered the possibility that he was really sick, might have contracted the flu or some other fever-inducing ailment, but more than likely his symptoms were nothing more than the product of fractured sleep and a near-constant dread. He needed a safe place to hide, a place where ghosts could not find him, so that he could sleep through the disorienting illness. But where?

He thought about the question for thirty minutes as he blindly walked from one neighborhood to the next. The answer came to him when he stepped onto Brown Street, the upscale shopping district in the center of Barnard. Despite the awkwardness of the request, Mike would ask Gwen for sanctuary. If he had to sleep on her floor or in the bathtub, he would consider himself lucky.

The Brown Street shoppers milled. Mike thought they all looked like ghosts, fuzzy and frayed at the edges, moving slowly as if performing a play under water. He tried to get his bearings, checking the street signs, which seemed to sway before him. He knew where he was, but at the same time he felt completely lost.

What am I doing here?

Mike had not intended to come to Brown Street. It had not been a conscious destination, though he felt certain he had wanted something here. When the answer wouldn't come to him Mike decided to walk down to Porter's Coffee House, someplace to sit and think with a cup of coffee. If he sat the world might not feel quite so elastic beneath his feet.

A scream rose across the street, and Mike jumped back to the wall of a women's shoe store. The cry had come out of nowhere, piercing the city sounds of traffic and pedestrians. He searched the road until he found the source of the disturbance. Across the street, on the patio of a fancy restaurant, a woman backpedaled, knocking over chairs and bumping into the table behind her own. Her eyes were wide and she pointed at the road frantically. Mike followed the direction of her finger, and when he saw what had frightened the woman, he pressed closer to the wall, hoping it would engulf him and shield him.

An African-American woman, wearing a shredded yellow dress, walked down the street. She moved as if on two broken feet, each step an exercise in balance and agony. The black woman didn't face Mike but rather looked at the source of the scream. Other patrons on the patio similarly cried out and scurried away from the filigreed iron fence that separated the terrace from the sidewalk. Mike didn't know what they were seeing in the woman's face, but he knew why they were scared.

Like his sister, Dory, this woman wasn't alive. At first, Mike had nothing but instinct telling him this. He looked at her shambling form and thought, she's dead; she's another ghost of another murdered girl. His confirmation came a moment later when the woman skipped. No other word could accurately define the movement he witnessed. The ghost walked forward, then she was suddenly three feet back, repeating the tortured march down Brown Street. She didn't vanish completely in that split-second. Instead she seemed to unravel into a thousand threads of purple-black light veined with sickly yellow strands, which slid and writhed and regrouped, but it happened so quickly that if he had blinked in that moment, he would have seen nothing but the apparent transportation of the woman.

A young man with hair like the fronds of a palm tree raced to the rail of the patio, shoving his cell phone at the apparition. Excited rather than afraid, the guy was taking the apparition's picture.

A dull throb of fear beat at Mike's temples as he witnessed the chaotic scene before him—shoppers dropping their purchases, children crying, cars slamming on brakes to avoid the dead woman in the yellow dress—because he suddenly understood that whatever this woman was—ghost, demon, unknowable thing—was made of the same material as his late sister. Until now, the possibility that his sister's visitations were no more substantial than a particularly horrific daydream had been his only comfort. On some level he'd believed the new Dory (the terrible Dory) was nothing but a mind fuck fabricated from loss and guilt, but now that hope was gone. Dory was as real as the woman bringing panic to Brown Street.

The ghost skipped again, forward this time. Its unnatural motion proved disorienting, and like the surrounding crowd, Mike found himself looking about in alarm as if keeping the thing in sight somehow nullified its threat. He caught a flash of yellow from the corner of his eye and Mike saw the apparition had taken the turn at the corner and was no longer on Brown Street at all. He stepped off the sidewalk and ran across the road.

He followed the being down a side street, compelled to observe it, to understand it. Fear had affixed to his chest like a plate of ice, but Mike wouldn't indulge the fright. He wanted to know about this thing—what it was, where it came from—because it might help him understand the reappearance of Dory. He *needed* to know, and he'd follow until he dropped from exhaustion if there was even a chance of getting answers.

The woman led him away from the boutiques and cafes and into a neighborhood of pricey town homes, duplexes, and apartments. Her jolting progress, the skipping Mike had noted, increased in frequency, giving her speed, but Mike managed to keep up, hiding behind buildings and landscaping. In the presence of pedestrians, she vanished, or rather, skipped from her place on the road to take a position in the shadows of yards so as not be noticed, as if the prospect of being seen now frightened her.

Mike wondered why the spirit didn't vanish. If this ghost had had enough of people, why didn't she simply dissolve and go unseen? It occurred to him then that she might know he followed, that he felt compelled to tail her through the streets. She could be leading him into a trap. Mike pushed on, anyway, curiosity stronger than fear.

The African-American woman moved down and to the east, away from the city center, toward Hacktown where lower rents and violent crimes coexisted in a hidden corner of town. She approached the side of an old apartment building, and in its shadow, she changed.

The transformation was so abrupt and so disturbing, Mike questioned it and entertained the terrible prospect that he'd been hallucinating this whole time. His sleep-addled mind and weary eyes had sent him on a wild goose chase, except the goose now changed into something else. He pressed in close to the trunk of an oak for camouflage and stared in disbelief.

Where the battered African-American woman in the tattered yellow dress had stood, now appeared a middle-aged man—the man from the basement on Ash Street who'd come at him with a knife. A grotesque wound covered the right side of his face, more muscle and bone than skin. Long gashes ran over his chest and belly, and his cock had been sliced to a grotesque nub. The man peered about, taking in his surroundings, and then he too vanished.

In his place, stood Dory. She surveyed the landscape, then walked from under the shadows of the building to continue the journey to Hacktown.

Mike breathed deeply. He closed his eyes for a moment, feeling a vague and bizarre sense of relief.

It's not Dory, he thought. *She doesn't hate you.* The city wasn't being haunted by a legion of spirits. *There's only one.*

Mike stepped from behind the tree and continued to follow the being, wondering what else he might learn.

20

Melanie thought Kee Ulrich's office looked like the bedroom of a wealthy twelve-year-old boy. Posters of teen television starlets and NASCAR racers hung from the walls; a variety of bottom-level television awards covered a shelf; on the credenza below Kee had carefully placed sports memorabilia, including a baseball card in a plastic case. Melanie knew nothing about the game, but the card looked old and was probably worth a bundle. The furniture was high-tech Italian, and a seventy-inch high-definition television hung like a window on the wall behind Kee's desk. She sat in an hourglass shaped chair with a leather seat. Mack sat in a matching chair beside her, punching the screen of his iPhone as he chatted with Kee. Her co-host made himself right at home in the office, but Melanie felt like a babysitter who'd been invited into her charge's bedroom so the little brat could hit on her.

To add to her unease Kee had called the meeting but hadn't scheduled Reg or Yvonne, which meant this wasn't a standard production meeting. Of course Mack was there, his lips never too distant from the ass they worshipped.

"So are you going to tell her?" Mack asked. He didn't bother looking up from the screen of his phone, but a smirk curled the corner of his mouth. The bastard was trying to keep from laughing.

A stone dropped in Melanie's stomach. Any conversation that began with that question, particularly a subject that Mack found so amusing, couldn't be good.

"Two words for you," Kee said. He leaned forward, resting his elbows on the desk, his face alight with glee. "Edinburgh Castle."

Melanie took a moment to process this. At first, a litany of information about the castle surfaced. It was considered one of the most haunted places in Europe; it was still in use as a military facility; known apparitions included French prisoners, a spectral piper who seemed to only appear when gusting winds whistled through ancient battlements as if called by the musician's pipe, and a headless drummer. Edinburgh Castle was something of a Mecca for paranormal investigators, which was to say it had been thoroughly investigated a hundred times. Picked over. Old news. They might as well consider doing a show on the Loch Ness Monster or Bigfoot. This wasn't to say that Melanie wasn't excited about the prospect of travel. The fact that Kee had convinced the network to bankroll this trip was an encouraging sign. Melanie just wished the subject were a little more interesting.

"We're going international," Mack said.

"It's all set," Kee added. "You and Mack leave on the Fourteenth and you're there for a week. We're setting it up as a two-hour season finale. If we get the ratings I'm expecting, we'll be considering additional locations in Europe, Asia, and Latin America for Season Three."

"So how much does that rock?" Mack asked.

"It rocks," Melanie said, "but why Edinburgh? Scotland has a dozen more interesting locations that haven't been raped by every 'Haunted Europe' television special ever produced. There's Dunvegan and Fyvie. Hell, Glamis Castle alone has…"

"It's a done deal," Kee said. The excitement had drained from his face and he leaned back in his chair, obviously disappointed that his news hadn't been met with the level of enthusiasm he felt it warranted. "Mack's already done all of the research on Edinburgh and we've gotten the appropriate clearances."

It figures, Melanie thought. Mack probably punched the words Haunted Europe into Google and followed the first link that came up. *Damn it.* She lamented the loss of such an opportunity, wishing there was some way to convince the producer that a less familiar setting, one with some actual mystery to it, would make a better show. There was nothing new to be found at Edinburgh Castle; all of the legitimate paranormal teams had already been there—and could confirm nothing.

"You know, you should be thanking me," Mack said. Finally, he'd tired of his iPhone, and he set it on Kee's desk. "I busted my ass pitching this show. You have any idea what kind of dance I had to do to get the network on board? This show is going to be huge."

"I know," Melanie said, "it's just that for the money, we could do an actual investigation instead of a retread."

"You're just pissed you didn't think of it," Mack said. His tone was dismissive and thoroughly infuriating.

"Excuse me?" Melanie said. "You think this is some kind of competition? Do you honestly think I want to be Mommy's favorite?" She threw a searing look at Kee. "I don't give a shit about Q Scores or market share or being The Star. That's your ego-crack not mine. I want to *find* something. I want proof that every apparition that's ever been reported isn't a trick of the light or swamp gas or some lonely old idiot's hallucination."

"And I want to stay on the air," Mack said bemused. "We already know what we're going to find, Mel: nothing. We've done enough of these investigations to pretty well put a nail in that coffin, but if we keep the show fresh, keep doling out the eye candy and keep the investigations popping, then maybe the audience will stick around for another season or two."

Melanie was about to respond. Her indignation had built up to a fine, lid-crashing boil, but Kee jumped in before she could say a word.

"I cannot believe you are even questioning this. It's like a paid vacation to walk through the Holy Grail of haunted houses, and you're complaining because you won't be the first paranormal investigator on the scene?"

"The first? We won't be the thirtieth team to explore that place. It's a dead horse."

"Whatever," Mack said. He retrieved his iPhone from the desk and stood. "Are we done here? I've got a thing with a girl, and I don't need my happy fucked up by this negativity."

"We're done," Kee said, looking at Melanie like she'd just pissed on his rug.

"Cool. Keep it tight, brah," Mack said. He waved as he crossed the room, making a clear show of ignoring her. At the door, Mack stopped and said, "Be sure to tell her about the other thing." Then he opened the door and called, "I'm out," before closing it behind him.

"What other thing?" Melanie asked.

"It's about Yvonne and Reg."

Budgetary limitations my ass.

Melanie pulled into the driveway and killed the engine. What she wanted to do was punch the gas and drive the SUV through the wall of the place if only to hear it crunch and smash. Better yet, she wanted to get Kee and Mack in front of the grill, but that wasn't an option.

The network had signed off on the Scotland trip based on a "limited talent" clause, which excluded Yvonne and Reg. Both were welcome to appear on the episode but none of their expenses, including travel, would be covered. Reg would take it in stride, probably just laugh it off and buy a plane ticket, knowing he could share Melanie's room, but Yvonne would be heartbroken, not only because it was unlikely she could afford such a trip, but also because this exclusion would be the latest in an extensive list of slights she'd endured at the hands of Kee Ulrich. Yvonne had always made Kee nervous, sometimes scared the hell out of him; it was just one of the reasons Melanie loved the woman so much.

She was livid when she entered her house. The urge to pick up the phone and call Kee to tell him where he could shove his Limited Talent clause, along with the rest of *The Haunt Club* thrummed in her chest like a palsy. She went to the refrigerator and grabbed a bottled water before stomping into the home office. She killed the screen saver on her computer and saw a number of News Alert messages in her mailbox. She'd set the search agent up years ago, so stories about hauntings would come to her, rather than making her surf the web for hours a day.

She clicked through to one of the news pages and saw a blurred picture of what looked like a black woman wearing a yellow dress. The image itself was nothing special. Though several witnesses claimed it was a ghost, it looked like a terrible picture of a battered woman. Even if it was meant to be a ghost Photoshop or a thousand other photo manipulation programs could have been used to mock it up. No, what caught Melanie's eye was the city designation at the front of the article: Barnard, TX.

Alan Means had sent her a letter from Barnard. Barnard was the home of Selma Baxter and Derek Thomason and where a house had been built on Ash Street, a house that the two psychopaths had turned into Hell.

A warm current ran through Melanie's veins. She read the story and then clicked through to the next. After gleaning as much information as she could from the internet news, she opened her desk drawer and retrieved Alan Means' letter.

Scotland and all of the hassles that trip promised were forgotten. She had other travel plans in mind.

21

Stuart wouldn't return to his house. He spent the bulk of his day answering the questions of the vice officers and INS agents—who had come in to clean up and close the Winston child prostitution case—instead of focusing on the reason he'd gone to Winston's traveling hebephile show in the first place. The leads they had in the Pudge Taylor case were getting chilly and if something didn't break soon, they'd be starting over. Back to zero. Stuart was less and less likely to believe that anyone involved with Winston Tucker had been responsible for Pudge's murder. The man's wife, Angelina, had been taken into custody at their home, where police found her screaming at an eleven-year-old girl who spoke no English and who had apparently only been in the country for a matter of days. The timing of Winston Tucker's death was fortunate for the girl as she would not have to earn her keep as a player in his perverse enterprise, but the girl was already traumatized and would be sent back across the border, where she would likely be sold to some new lowlife by her parents—the people who had negotiated with Angelina Tucker in the first place. As for the shooter, Julio, he had fled the scene. Officers found his shotgun in the yard, but there was no sign of the boy, and except for a basement full of frightened children, the decrepit house had been empty.

All of the questions he couldn't answer, the frustrated expressions on his colleagues' faces and their insistence he give them something helped keep Stuart's mind off of the nightmare he'd woken to that morning. It was during the quiet moments, alone in his office, that he thought about Clarissa and looked around the room to see if she had decided to appear again.

At lunch, reporters had tried to swarm him for comment about the Winston case, but Captain Gann had made the official statement to the press, and Stuart directed the screaming mic-wielding journalists to him. He just ducked his head and repeated, "No comment," before dashing down the street to Lulu's for a quick lunch.

When his workday was complete, Stuart lingered at the office, but eventually had to leave, unless he felt like answering more questions about why he was afraid to go home. But he *wouldn't* go home. Clarissa might be there, and for all of the difficult questions he'd answered in the course of the day, hers would be the most terrible. Instead, he drove eight blocks to the Majestic Hotel and checked in. He showered and wondered what he'd do about fresh clothes before dropping onto the mattress with the intent of sleep.

That was when Harlan rang his cell phone.

"Where are you?" Harlan sounded mildly perturbed.

"What are you talking about?" Stuart asked. He tried to remember if he'd had plans to meet his friend, but nothing came to mind.

"I've been at your place for the last twenty minutes. I figured you'd be home by now."

Oh shit, Stuart thought. How was he going to explain his presence in the hotel without coming off as a total nutjob? Maybe it didn't matter. Maybe he could talk around it.

"Haven't made it home yet," he said. "I'm waiting for one of the techs to get back to me with some information. What's up?"

"I need a place to crash tonight. Gretta and I aren't managing our issues well. Actually, it's more like Gretta isn't managing my issues so well."

"What?"

"I'll tell you later," Harlan said with a chuckle. "Am I going to see you or should I check into the Majestic?"

"Probably both." He told Harlan where he was staying. He avoided Harlan's questioning, changing the subject and outright lying until he got the man off the phone.

Twenty minutes later, Aaron Talbot from the forensic lab called with news about the Taylor case. Stuart perked up when the tech introduced himself, but the man's news sufficiently tamed his excitement.

"Not sure if it's good news or no news," Talbot said. "A kid was playing in the greenbelt behind his house in the Beresford District and found a knife."

"I'm assuming it's a match for the wounds on Taylor's body?" Stuart said.

"Almost identical," Talbot said. "Same blade dimensions at any rate."

"Then how can you say this is no news?" Stuart asked.

"This isn't our knife," the tech said. "It is nearly identical—probably the same make—but the murder weapon's blade wouldn't be this clean. We found frags in some of Taylor's wounds where bits of edge chipped off. Plus, this knife is raw. It's never been used."

"Never?" Stuart asked.

"Not even to skin an apple. No material on the blade or the handle, except environmental detritus: dirt, grass, you know. No detergent residue in the handle recesses. No bleach. Nothing. If I had to guess, I'd say it came right out of the package and landed in the woods."

"What about fingerprints?"

"Nada. Well, except for the kid who found it and his mother who took it from him."

"So it's intentional," Stuart said. It was hard enough to buy the idea that someone would just throw a brand new, and apparently expensive, kitchen knife into the woods, but to do so without leaving a single print? "We were supposed to find that knife."

"That's for you big smart detectives to figure out. I just tell you what I know."

"Where was it found? You said in the Beresford District?"

"Green belt bordering Marley Drive."

"Thanks, Aaron. Look I'm not at the station right now. Have you told Detective Ballard about this?"

"He just left to visit the scene. I told him I'd pass the news along."

"Get a message to Aguilar and have him start tracking down dealers for that brand and model of knife."

"It's late. Aguilar isn't going to be at his desk."

"Email him and flag it. Top priority. I'll talk to him first thing."

"Whatever."

"You're very helpful," Stuart said and hung up the phone.

He walked to the window and looked out over the city. Pink and violet light ran in ribbons across the horizon. The sun dipped low, burning angry orange as night encroached.

An urge to race out to the scene struck Stuart. Not only did he want to see the location the knife had been found in, but also it was his job to do so. If he weren't expecting Harlan at any minute, he'd already be out the door.

Though not the murder weapon, the knife was valuable to the investigation. Only the killer would go to the trouble of buying a double of the blade used to kill Pudge Taylor, probably hoping somewhat naively that the weapon would be entered into evidence as the murder weapon, knowing their defense counsel could tear it apart in court.

Harlan arrived wearing a black short-sleeved shirt that made him look like a bowling ball with appendages and a Houston Astros baseball cap. He stormed into the room carrying a paper bag filled with cheeses, cold cuts, kettle chips, and a bottle of Macallan scotch, a twenty-one-year-old single-malt that ran over two hundred bucks a bottle.

"I thought we could use the good stuff tonight," Harlan said making his way to the small table beneath the window. "Get glasses."

"Harlan, I just got word from the station…"

"It'll wait," Harlan insisted.

The sharpness in his friend's voice cut through Stuart's need to meet Ballard. For all of his personality issues, Ballard was a good detective. He'd ask the right questions, come to the right conclusions. Harlan wanted to talk about Gretta, so Stuart could give him an hour before heading out to the Beresford District or the station if the team had already finished up at the scene.

"You need ice?" Stuart asked.

"Fuck ice," Harlan said. "This isn't pleasure drinking, my friend. This is full on drink-til-the-world-goes-black drinking. And I'm smoking, so get used to the idea now."

"Non-smoking room," Stuart informed him.

"Then I'll buy the fucking hotel." Harlan looked around distractedly, his eyes fell on the king size bed, and he sneered. As promised he pulled a pack of Marlboro reds from his shirt pocket and lit one up. Then he looked at the bed again. "Shit. I'd better call down for a room of my own. I was hoping you'd have doubles up here."

"What's the big deal?" Stuart asked. "We've shared beds before."

"Yeah," Harlan said, drawing deeply on his cigarette and releasing a blue-gray cloud into the air. "But that was before you knew I was gay, and I'm thinking you're opinion on the matter might be somewhat altered."

"Before I knew what?"

"I can't help but think you use the word *what* far too often," Harlan said. He took another ample drag from the cigarette. As he exhaled he said, "If you listened closely when people were speaking, you'd find it unnecessary. I am gay. I came out to Gretta, and as predicted, she didn't take the news well. Now, if I'm going to get shit from you about it, I'm taking this bottle and leaving."

"Just slow the fuck down," Stuart said, trying to make sense of Harlan's rant. "You're gay?"

"Yes."

"And when did this happen?"

"Last week I was in the crystal section at Macy's and thought, well isn't this fabulous?" He was being facetious, but he was also more wound up than Stuart had seen his friend in a long time. "How the hell do I know how long? It's always been there, but a few days ago my buddy Roy nearly got himself killed, and after he told me what happened, I finally understood what people meant when they say life is too short. So this morning, after I talked to you, I poured Gretta a cup of coffee and sat her down and told her." He eased the baseball cap off, revealing a bandage the size of a postcard running over the crown of his head. "Her reaction was less than civil."

"Jesus," Stuart said, walking toward his friend, "what did she do?"

"She smashed a bottle of Bombay Sapphire over my head. I was checking my email and the next thing I knew, *Bam*! She had me face down on the floor bleeding like a pig. After two hours in the emergency room and thirty-some-odd stitches I concluded that home was not such a homey place."

"Fuck," Stuart mumbled.

"Fuck, indeed."

"Did you press charges?" Stuart asked.

"Don't be a dumb ass," Harlan said. "I had it coming. I know that. I hit her with this ton of pink bricks and she lashed out. I get that. I've had my whole life to think about this. She had thirty minutes, and she decided to come out swinging." Harlan chuckled and shook his head. "I do love that woman."

"She could have killed you," Stuart pointed out.

"If she'd wanted to kill me she wouldn't have gone for the rock on my shoulders. No. She did what she had to do, and I figure she's allowed a couple of sucker punches for the way I handled it. I imagine you are too."

"Nah," Stuart said. He didn't know how he felt about the revelation. If anything he just felt numb. What Harlan did with his dick seemed rather insignificant compared to Clarissa's reappearance and the murder of Pudge Taylor. Still, Stuart couldn't help but think this was a shock reaction, nerves dulled to accept unnatural abuse, and his opinion on the matter might change at any minute. Somewhere in the back of his head, he understood something grave was happening to his longest standing relationship. "Let me get those glasses."

Once they were situated at the table, drinks in hands, Harlan said, "So now you know what I'm doing here. Why are you here?"

"No wonder Gretta clobbered you," Stuart said. "You drop this kind of news and then you try to change the subject."

"I'm taking the bandage approach," Harlan replied. "Get it over with. Rip it—fast and clean."

"Yeah well, try that with the bandage on your head and see how you fare."

"Point taken," Harlan said. "Do you actually want to talk about this?"

The truth was, Stuart didn't. He wasn't sure what Harlan might reveal; he figured it was probably more than he wanted to hear right now. "No," he admitted. "But maybe talking about it will help."

"It won't," Harlan said. "It is what it is. I could do the emotional rant, but I've looked at this from every angle: business partners, friendships," he lifted and eyebrow and toasted Stuart, "family and Gretta. I know I'm going to take some shit, and there's going to be a lot of guilt."

"Have you actually…?"

"Actually?"

"Never mind."

"You want to know if I've sucked dick? Taken it up the ass?"

"God, you really don't make this easy, do you?"

"No," Harlan agreed. "I don't know how to make this easy. Sorry. I'm kind of wired to the defensive right now. Can't seem to shake it. That's one reason I'd really rather talk about something else. When I talk about this, I feel like I want to punch someone. I'm hoping it's a temporary reaction, or I'm going to have trouble keeping a boyfriend around." Harlan fell silent and looked at the carpet.

He tapped his glass on the table and nodded his head to the rhythm of it.

They could sit there in silence. Maybe that was the best thing. Stuart didn't know what to say. Too many strange thoughts and questions rose in his mind, and he knew that, like Harlan, he was in no position to speak rationally on the matter, yet. Harlan had removed a mask, and the face beneath looked just like the one he'd pulled away, or nearly so. Stuart couldn't help but acknowledge the deceit to himself if not to Harlan, but he didn't want to deal with it.

"I saw Clarissa this morning," Stuart blurted.

Harlan stopped his glass in mid-rap and looked at him. Stuart took a long draw on his scotch and let it warm his throat. Then he told Harlan how he'd woken up that morning—the snoring, the video, the appearance of his dead wife.

"You win," Harlan said.

"Win?"

"The surprising revelation game. You win. Gay has nothing on that shit."

"I'm serious."

Harlan bobbed his head. "I can see that, Stuart. That doesn't change the fact I don't know how to respond to it. You said you saw her on a video?"

"Yeah."

"So you can show it to me?"

"If it's still there."

"Where else would it be?" Harlan asked.

"I don't know. I'm almost hoping I imagined it."

"That would certainly be more comforting." Harlan tapped his glass some more and nodded his head. Then he said, "Why don't we take a drive out to your place and see if that video is real? If nothing else, we'll get the whole you're-crazier-than-a-rat-on-acid out of the way."

"It isn't pleasant," Stuart warned.

"That seems to be a theme today."

They were in the lobby of the hotel when Stuart heard the word, "Ghost." The voice sounded amplified and amused. He turned toward it and found a television screen suspended above the lobby bar. A blurred image appeared next to the smiling face of a blond anchorman.

"That's right, Barnard," the anchorman said, "witnesses are claiming that the image behind me belongs to a ghost. The incident occurred earlier this afternoon in the Brown Street shopping district. Witnesses claimed to have seen the form walking down Brown Street only to vanish moments later."

"I don't know what to think," a pudgy woman with short brown hair said. "I thought I was losing my mind, but everyone else saw it too."

"Yeah, yeah, right," a skinny pale man with red cheeks gushed, "it just flashed past me, and I felt this like—this like cold, you know? It totally freaked me out. I was all, what the hell?"

"It wasn't a person," a Hispanic woman said. "People can't move like that."

"What do you think it was?" the reporter asked.

"I don't know," the woman said, beginning to cry. "I don't know."

The blurry image filled the screen. Stuart clearly saw an eye and a mouth. He noticed the shredded yellow fabric that draped from the shape's shoulders and cinched around its hips. The skin was dark.

Regina Wolcroff, he thought.

"I guess we don't need to see that video," Harlan muttered.

"Yeah," Stuart replied, "but now, I want to."

"You're awfully damn quiet," Harlan said.

Harlan drove, so Stuart had let his mind wander. He considered the knife a little boy had found in a greenbelt, a weapon identical to the one used in the Pudge Taylor crime, but his partner and a team of well-trained investigators had that particular issue in hand. Once he shared the video of Clarissa with Harlan, he'd drop his friend at the hotel and get back to work. His primary concern was the appearance of ghosts in Barnard, the fact that his wife's spirit was among the recently resurrected made the situation all the worse. People didn't come back. There was no heaven, no matter what they'd tried to force down his throat in Sunday school, and equally there was no hell. You didn't look at the world with any clarity and seriously believe that some almighty power of good oversaw the whole mess. So if not these fabrications of faith what was left? Stuart had always thought death was a true end, providing darkness and peace if only because the neuroses and pains of life were left behind in the rotting brain tissue. It wasn't a comforting philosophy but it was pragmatic and the only one he'd ever been able to invest any real belief in. Of course, Harlan's disclosure carried its own weight, and Stuart felt it gnawing in there with his thoughts on death, but it was something else he didn't want to think about. Realizing he hadn't responded to Harlan's comment, Stuart shifted in the passenger seat and rested his head on the palm of his hand.

"Hello," Harlan said, breaking Stuart from his reverie.

"What? Sorry, I haven't slept much in the last week. I'm riding on adrenaline, and it's running out."

"Yeah, and I seem to have plenty to spare."

"Do you believe we have souls?" Stuart asked.

"Of course," Harlan said.

"Really?" Stuart replied.

"Yes."

"So you believe in heaven and hell?"

"Those are different questions."

"Well, do you?"

"I don't know," Harlan replied. "I've been to church just about every Sunday of my life, and I don't know. Needless to say, recent events have forced me to reevaluate the content of a few of those sermons, but that's not really what's in your head. My guess is you're trying to figure out where these things are coming from, and you figure if you get a handle on that you'll figure out what they want."

"Maybe."

"I would imagine we'll all know soon enough, what with them making public appearances in the middle of town."

"It's probably some kind of hoax."

Harlan made a fart noise though his lips. "You don't believe that. I mean I don't blame you for *wanting* to believe it, but you don't believe it. Shit changes whether you want to see it, believe it, or turn your back on it. If we go back to your place and find that video, and it's the way you described it to me, you're giving up any hope of denial."

"That's why I want to see it."

"And then what?" Harlan asked.

"I guess that depends on her," Stuart said. "You know how bad things were between us before she was killed. After her message this morning, I'm not thinking she's back with glad tidings from the great beyond."

He fell into silence, dropping his head against the cool glass of the passenger window and peering out at the simple houses all lit up for nighttime. He wondered if the people inside those unassuming homes were scouring the news channels and the Internet for information about ghosts, or if they'd already gotten back to their normal lives, eating and drinking and watching television, maybe humping away the blues.

When Harlan turned onto his block, Stuart's stomach clenched, and he thought he might actually vomit. He took deep breaths to calm the rising sickness and closed his eyes. His eyelids remained firmly clenched until Harlan turned into his driveway and stopped the car, and then Stuart lifted them to see the familiar panel of his garage door, which did not comfort him the way such a familiar sight should have.

"You okay?" Harlan asked.

"Honest to god's truth? I'm scared shitless."

"Yeah well you're about to step on the tail of Schrödinger's cat and that son of a bitch is likely to let out a less than friendly screech."

"Harlan, what the hell are you talking about?"

"Never mind. It'll take too long to explain, and I'm thinking the best bet is to haul our asses in and out of there as fast as our feet will carry us."

"The bandage approach," Stuart asked, pointing to the white dressing on Harlan's head.

"Damn straight," Harlan said, already climbing out of the car. "We go in, see what we see, and then we get the hell out of there. We can discuss what we did or did not see elsewhere and elsewhen."

"Sounds like this is getting to you, too."

"Yeah, it is," Harlan said looking across the walk at Stuart's front door. "I got that goose on my grave feeling, and the fucker's tap dancing."

"Then let's get this over with."

"Holy shit," Harlan said, when he saw Clarissa walk across the screen to stand at the side of the bed.

Stuart was beyond speech. He knew when to expect his dead wife to show up, but there had been no way to prepare himself for seeing her again—her cut skin, the blood, the face and body he knew too well to deny. Again he closed his eyes against a tide of cresting nausea. Harlan's confirmation pushed the truth of it deep into Stuart's gut and worked it around like a narrow blade.

"I'm going to grab a few things," Stuart said abruptly and crossed to the closet. He didn't think about what clothes he might need, but rather grabbed half a dozen hangers holding dress shirts and a sport coat because they were clustered together. He took these to the bed and laid them down, the sound of his snoring filling the room. At the dresser he clutched a handful of boxers and picked a bunch of socks from the drawer. They dangled from his palm like freshly unearthed carrots. He tossed these on the pile of shirts and returned to the closet to retrieve a selection of pants. He'd buy new clothes if he needed them. What he wouldn't do was look at that screen again.

"How could you do this to me?" Clarissa asked.

The question fell over his shoulders like a freezing ocean tide.

"Turn it off," Stuart muttered, rushing back to the closet for a pair of shoes.

"Are we taking this with us?" Harlan asked.

"Yes," Stuart said, though he didn't want the recording anywhere near him. He wanted Harlan to erase the thing and break the damn camera, but Stuart had spent too many years examining digital images for evidence, and there was no telling what he would discover if he could actually force himself to study the tape. There might be some clue. Something.

"I'll take this on out to the car," Harlan said, holding up the camera.

"Wait for me," Stuart said, his voice weak with fear. The sound of it in his own ears was embarrassing as hell, but Stuart didn't care.

"Sure," Harlan said.

With trembling hands, Stuart shoved the pile of clothes into a leather satchel and hoisted the shirts and slacks by their hangers. The shoes fell off onto the floor and he looked at them for a second before deciding he didn't need them. He rushed from the room, and then through the house and out the front door. He handed the satchel to Harlan so he could lock the door, and then the two ran for Harlan's car like a couple of kids racing away from the site of a fulfilled dare.

22

Richard Wolcroff pressed the remote with a trembling finger and the television screen went black. His phone rang, and he knew it was Hannah Bolger wanting to talk about the news report, and he thought that maybe he should speak to her, but he ignored the phone anyway.

They're coming back, he thought. Ben and Regina. What about the other victims of Baxter and Thomason? Were they coming back, too? Why now? What did they want?

None of this played into Richard Wolcroff's philosophy, not a bit of it. He was raised to believe that you lived and you died and if you lived a righteous life you bathed in God's glory and if you squandered that life on sin you became a victim of the Devil's eternal torments. Ghosts weren't in his bible. Zombies were equally absent, and while he had an aunt who lived in the bayous of Louisiana who held that spirits and zombies were as real as bankers and advertising men, Richard had never believed in the dark creatures his aunt wove into colorful stories. But he had seen Regina in his house and again on the television not two minutes ago.

The cuts on his foot hurt. He flexed his toes, hoping to ease the uncomfortable sensation. He felt the emptiness of the house on him like a hot blanket, too much air, choking him with its density. He wished Delia hadn't left him alone in the place, wished she'd take his calls so he could find some modicum of comfort in her voice, but she blamed him for what had happened to their daughter. She blamed him for everything.

In his statement to the police after his arrest, Derek Thomason had said that he and Baxter had lured Regina to their house with the promise of drugs. Richard had been forced to divulge his daughter's ongoing chemical dependence, had told Stuart Lancaster that he'd admitted Regina into a rehabilitation clinic three separate times, the first when she was just fifteen years old. It wasn't as if he could hide the information, wasn't like his daughter's reputation could be further tarnished by her father's disclosure. Regina had struggled with the demon of drugs for nearly a decade, the same as him.

Unlike her father—who had given up control to a single narcotic: cocaine—Regina would take whatever was at hand to flee reality. Puffing smoke and huffing paint, snorting meth and shooting smack all provided satisfactory transportation for his daughter's escape. He'd done what he could for her. Richard had tried tough love and tender love and poured thousands of dollars into counseling and doctors, but something about this world, something he could never get Regina to reveal, was just too awful for her to face with any level of clarity. He could relate to the dependency but not the motivation. When he was downhill racing on snow, Richard wanted to enhance his sensations, wanted to stay awake and see everything. He excelled at his job, working late into the night, fueled by the powder. It was the eighties and you couldn't afford to fall behind in the rat race. Everything needed to be faster and faster.

Thinking about those days, back before Regina was born, Richard's stomach clenched. The pang was for the white fuel. It hit him hard whenever he thought about the drug, but he'd walked away from cocaine. He hadn't needed counseling or institutionalization; all he'd needed was Delia's disapproving glare. She'd told him to stop or she would leave, and he'd stopped. The cravings remained to this day, but he could turn them off simply by picturing his wife's stern face.

When Regina's problems started, Delia was rational and focused on their daughter, tried to help the girl through her problems, but as time went on and Regina's dependencies worsened, Delia gave up. Instead of trying to help Regina, searching for a key that might unlock her chemical chains, Delia had decided to blame Richard for their daughter's addiction. Their little girl had inherited the weakness from him. She'd been born soulless because Richard had danced beneath the snowfall. God wouldn't have Regina because Richard had forsaken Him to snort his fucking cocaine.

Though his wife's accusations sounded preposterous in retrospect, Richard had accepted responsibility for Regina. He'd bailed her out of jail, driven her to the methadone clinic, made sure she took her dose before chauffeuring her into town for an ice cream sundae. When Regina moved out, he checked on her every night after work, and for a while there, it looked like his daughter might be emerging from the narcotic tunnel she'd drifted through for so much of her youth, but she met that boy. Tim Ohnegian—that lousy son of a bitch—came into Regina's life, and she was right back in the hole, wandering down a dim road carved through rock.

Richard crossed the living room and lifted the bottle of Johnny Walker, tipped a good shot into a glass, and then walked away without touching the drink. He needed to get out of the house. He couldn't spend another night in the stifling air alone with his thoughts. Isolation was just another addiction, a way to avoid the world, a way to pretend everything was going to be okay.

Thoughts of his daughter and that punk Tim Ohnegian chased him to the front door and out into the warm night. He looked at the garage and considered driving; it didn't matter where he went just so long as he was moving, but he decided against it. Walking would be better. It was a pleasant night and too many months of Chinese take-out, microwaveable entrees, frozen pizzas, and Johnny Walker had added pounds to his already substantial build. No, he would walk and breathe fresh air thinned by the inhalations of thousands of other people, not the thick hot air trapped in his house, air he couldn't breathe fast enough to thin out. And out here, walking, his footsteps and the sounds of distant traffic comforted him, even though his thoughts scraped jaggedly against the soft tissue of his brain.

Why couldn't Thomason and Baxter have taken Tim Ohnegian?

It was an unkind, certainly an unchristian, thought, but he'd entertained it so often over the last two years, it had lost the power to disturb him. Ohnegian was a rich boy who played on the low side of life because he was bored and wanted to infuriate his parents, because they'd made his life so difficult, what with being rich and all. Ohnegian was an unrepentant addict who had more than enough money in the bank to support his habit and, for a time, Regina's. He'd flown her off to Las Vegas for a long weekend, bought her jewelry, not because he cared about her, but because such things meant nothing to him. They were disposable trinkets meant to instill gratitude and assure subservience. Regina hadn't thought twice about the relationship, and Richard's warnings were met with lines like "You just don't want me to be happy," and "I've finally got myself together and I don't need you anymore and it pisses you off."

Got herself together, Richard thought. She had simply used better drugs in fancier locations.

After six months, Ohnegian got bored, the way Richard had always suspected he would, and he left Regina, heartbroken and so lost in her addiction she wouldn't even try to find her way out again. She overdosed just before her last Christmas, and Richard had sat in the hospital for two days, making himself sick. She went into rehab one last time. He brought her Christmas presents to the clinic and sobbed as she tore into the packages, discarding one after the other with comments like "Crap," and "How am I supposed to get any real money for this?" Then he went home and fell into bed with a mind smearing flu. He'd been dazed and blurry eyed when he answered the phone the next day—an administrator telling him that Regina had escaped the facility. He'd thought it was all part of a terrible dream.

He'd thought the same thing when Stuart Lancaster appeared at the side of his bed two days later to tell him that Regina was dead. Delia wouldn't even come in the room.

Strolling on the familiar streets, Richard felt a brief flash of anger at his wife, but he refused to entertain it. He understood her weakness, knew full well the only way she could manage her grief was to make him the cause of it, and he wanted to believe she would see this herself, but with each passing day, he found it less likely she would. His two remaining daughters were doing well, living comfortably. He loved them.

But he was alone.

Richard walked for an hour, from one block to the next all but oblivious to his surroundings. He knew the city so well that every now and then he'd look up and see the neighborhood he was in, remember a friend who had lived in this house or that one, and then Richard would move on.

Wandering in the direction of his home, Richard thought about leaving this city. If the financial demands of his family hadn't been so great over the last handful of years, he could have retired without a second thought and moved to Florida or San Diego or some other warm place that didn't hold so many memories, but Regina had needed help and the rehab clinic hadn't been cheap. Bail and lawyers hadn't been cheap. Now, Delia needed money, and Richard sent the check dutifully every month to cover her expenses. He didn't question her demands. Yes, she was living with her sister, and Richard couldn't imagine what she needed so much money for, but he sent it along anyway. She was still his wife, still his responsibility, and he loved her. He'd do whatever he could for her, just as he'd done all that he could for their daughter.

Back at his house and standing on the front porch, Richard fitted the key into the lock and pushed open the front door. The glow from the television in the next room greeted him, and he paused, feeling certain he'd turned the thing off before he'd left the house. Obviously, he hadn't or it wouldn't be on now, but the flickering light made him uneasy. He dropped his keys on the small mahogany table by the front door and walked down the hall to the kitchen. There he lifted the phone from its cradle on the wall with the intent of calling Delia, but a gray wave of despondence washed over him and he replaced the phone. He just couldn't handle his wife's rejection right now.

Instead, he walked through the dining room and into the living room, where the television played. On the screen, a petite and attractive woman and a man far too pretty to be male, wandered down a gloomy hallway, their flashlights playing through the darkness and bathing chipped peeling walls as they discussed the history of the house in which they roamed.

Richard wasn't familiar with the program. Usually he watched political shows on one of the news networks. When he wanted lighter viewing, he watched old sitcoms on TV Land or soft-core B movies on one of the premium cable channels. This show seemed to be about ghosts, and that was the last thing Richard wanted to think about. He retrieved the remote control from the arm of his chair and turned the television off.

"I was watching that," a man said from the corner of the room.

Richard spun to face the intruder. He stood about five-foot-eleven and wore black clothes. His build, which was stick-thin and spoon chested, wasn't in the least bit intimidating, but the face, a lumped mess of bulging and wrinkled skin with sunken eyes and fat, cracked lips sent a bolt of dread to Richard's chest. It took him a moment to realize he was looking at a Halloween mask; a scary visage cast in rubber and nothing more, but with this realization came another:

the man in the mask was holding a gun.

Out of reflex, Richard lifted his hands to shoulder height, palms out. His heart tripped loudly in his chest and the sound rolled up his arteries to pound in his ears.

"What do you want?"

The man stepped away from the corner of the room. The rubber masked bobbed loosely on his head. "Is that any way to treat a guest?"

"Take what you want and go," Richard said. "I won't give you a hard time."

"Oh, I know that," the man said. "You're too much of a pussy to try anything. Hell, you couldn't even keep Regina off the junk, because you were afraid she'd hate you for trying."

"Who are you?" Richard asked.

"A friend," the masked man said, "not yours, of course. You've always been a prick. Since day one and from the beginning of time… prick! But I'm not really interested in the past. What's done is done. Dust in the wind and that shit. No, I'm interested in the future. My future. So why don't you just take me to the safe, and I'll get out of your hair."

"Safe?" Richard asked. His surprise was genuine. There was no safe in the house. He kept valuables in a deposit box at the bank. In fact, now that Delia had left and taken her jewelry, there was very little of value in the house except for the appliances.

"Now don't play dumb," the man said with a laugh. "Just take me to your study and open the fucking thing. Otherwise, Mr. Pistol goes bang."

"I don't know what you're talking about," Richard said. Slowly, he lowered his right hand and reached behind his back. "I'm just getting my wallet. You can have it. There's about a hundred and fifty dollars and credit cards. I won't report them missing for a few days. Just take it and go."

"A hundred and fifty dollars? Credit cards? Fuck that, Pappy. I want the real cash."

"There is no real cash," Richard insisted. The name, "Pappy," jabbed at his brain like a tack, sticking and piercing his thoughts. It meant something but he was too confused, too frightened to put it together. His fingers grasped his wallet, and he pulled it free. He cautiously presented the leather case to the intruder and waved it unthreateningly in the air. "This is all I've got."

"Now that's not what I heard at all. I heard you got about fifty grand in that safe. For a big shot like you, that ain't very much but it's enough for tonight. You get me that and I'm a dream you can wake up from."

"I don't know where you got your information, but you're mistaken. I keep my money in a bank like everyone else."

The man in the mask lunged forward and knocked the wallet out of

Richard's hands while swinging the gun at Richard. It clipped the side of his head painfully and sent him off balance. Once he regained himself, the barrel of the gun pressed into his forehead. Cold steel dimpled his brow. Richard felt the hole in the muzzle on his skin and the gentle trembling of his body became a full-blown rattle.

"I don't have a safe," he said, voice shaking. Richard peered through the holes of the mask to see icy green eyes looking crazily out at him. Amid the lumps of formed rubber and the nests of cheap man-made hair, the eyes took on an inhuman quality.

And then Richard knew who this man was; he knew why the name Pappy had punctured and clung to his thoughts.

"I know you," he said through a tight jaw.

His face grew hot and the fear in his chest hardened into absolute rage. Richard tried to control the fury, but it was beyond him. The skinny thief was Tim Ohnegian. This prick had manipulated Richard's daughter; he'd blinded Regina with drugs and fancy vacations; he'd abandoned her like a car he'd wrecked one too many times, leaving it to rust out and rot on the side of a road.

"Good for you, Pappy," Ohnegian said. He sounded amused and cruel at the same time. "That don't change the way of things. You take me to that safe and you open it or your walls are going to get good and messy."

"There is no safe, you dumbshit."

"Take me to it. Regina said you got a safe."

"My daughter was deluded."

"Maybe she was, but she isn't anymore. She knows where you hide the goodies. She told me."

Ohnegian was insane, Richard understood. The little shit had doped up once too often and was totally out of his mind. He didn't even talk about Regina in the past tense, making it sound like they'd just had this conversation earlier in the day. Only offhandedly did he remember his own visitation from Regina, but he didn't connect this personal haunting to the skinny thief's insane ramblings. Furthermore, he began to believe his own life would be in irreparable danger once Ohnegian realized there was no safe, there was no money, there was no point in his intrusion at all.

Panicked, Richard balled up his fist. He canted to the side, so the barrel of the gun slid along his temple and then slammed his hand into the soft rubbery mask, covering Ohnegian's face. His knuckles hit home with a satisfying crunch, and Ohnegian stumbled back, shouting nonsensical syllables, which soon became intelligible curses.

"You fucking old asshole. Son of a bitch."

Richard used this moment of victory to build his courage. Ohnegian hadn't even pulled the trigger when taking the blow. Richard waded forward, both hands balled tightly.

Ohnegian spun away. He aimed quickly and fired the gun.

The report deafened Richard. After the flash of light at the tip of the muzzle, he stumbled back as if a leash was attached around his waist and it had played out. Richard's breath rushed from his body in the same moment the pain erupted near his naval. He looked down and saw glistening scarlet blossoming over his shirt. Dropping to his knees, Richard continued to look at the creeping stain in disbelief.

"You stupid fuck. All you had to do was give me the money. That's it. You can't spend it if you're dead." Ohnegian ranted as he stomped back and forth in front of Richard's kneeling form. "Don't you know how this works? I come in and show you the gun and you get scared and give me what I want. Then I leave. No harm. No foul. No fuck up. What kind of numbnut dickhead *shitforbrains* are you?"

"Fuck you," Richard said. "You destroyed my daughter's life."

"But she still loves me," Ohnegian replied. "She hates your fucking guts, but she still loves me. Now, why is that, Pappy? Hm? You got an answer for that?"

Then Regina entered the room behind Ohnegian. A fresh pain gripped Richard's heart when he saw his little girl, beaten and cut. Regina appeared serene as she glided up to her ex-lover's back. She gazed at Richard with the one eye Baxter and Thomason had left her, but it was the empty socket, behind badly abused lids that drew him in, as if this void were the truth of his daughter and the rest—her face, her body, her dress—were nothing but insignificant tissue.

"Why didn't you love me?" Regina asked, her voice sounding so pained and soft. "I just wanted someone to love me."

"Regina," Richard muttered. A flash of pain from the wound in his stomach bent him forward, but he struggled against it and righted himself. He needed to tell her that he did love her, had always loved her. All he'd ever wanted was for her to be happy and to have a good life, a real life, not the milk and honey illusion her drugs had built.

"See what I mean?" Ohnegian said through a smug grin.

"Go to hell," Richard told him.

Ohnegian laughed. He pulled the rubber mask off his head so Richard could see the damage drugs had done to the kid. They had ruined his once boyish appearance. His cheeks were gaunt and shadowed. The skin beneath his watery green eyes was black. He'd lost half a dozen teeth and those that remained looked small and gray like tiny tombstones planted in his gums.

Regina wrapped her arms around Ohnegian's neck and leaned on him. She laughed, too.

"Don't let him do this," Richard pleaded.

The pain in Richard's belly receded then burst forth with greater severity. He groaned, clutching at the hole in his stomach. Blood poured over his palm and through his fingers.

"Bye, daddy," Regina said.

Ohnegian fired five times. Each bullet tore into Richard's head, shattering bone and ripping flesh, rocking him backward on his knees. When the hammer fell on empty chambers, Tim Ohnegian continued to fire. He laughed and shook his head and kept pulling the trigger.

PART TWO
In Cold Blood

23

Melanie reached Barnard, Texas just after four a.m. She stopped at a gas station on the edge of town and filled the SUV's tank. Alone at the pump, with nothing for company but the beeps of the electronic credit card reader, she began to feel uneasy and decided to wait in the vehicle while the fuel glugged its way through the hose. As she sat behind the steering wheel, she remembered the newscast and the smeared image of a young African American woman in a yellow dress. It still had the power to chill her. Staring through the windshield, she projected the woman's image on the dark field ahead and trembled. Melanie closed her eyes until the pump announced the gas tank was full.

She had programmed the GPS with the address for the house on Ash Street. (Ground zero, as she was beginning to think of it). But it was still dark and would remain so for another two hours, and though she was eager, even compelled to see the center of this new mystery, she didn't want to go to the remains of that house alone, not at night, though she saw little alternative.

Eventually, it could be today or tomorrow, Mack would be following her to Barnard. He'd likely have *The Haunt Club* crew in tow. Kee would want the show to be taped as fast as possible, before all of the other paranormal investigation teams and a swarm of journalists descended on the city. Locals would have to be interviewed before they'd completely burned out on the intrusion of inquisitive strangers, and fresh footage would have to be shot to augment the shot of the young woman's apparition, which by the time the show actually aired, would be considered tired.

Melanie knew Mack and Kee were only interested in what would make a flashy show. Their focus would not be her focus, so she had to make the best use of her time before they swooped down to erase the substance with the sensational.

The electronic voice of the GPS unit guided her from the gas station through a run-down retail district. The buildings were single story boxes with peeling paint, fading signs, and dirty windows. Corner groceries butted up to pawnshops and bail bonds offices. The streets were deserted, which didn't surprise her, but the sight of the dismal structures added weight to her unease.

After a mile, the seedier buildings gave way to a middle-class residential neighborhood with small, but neat, homes. When the GPS instructed her to turn right, she found herself on a block of larger houses. They were pleasant in their commonplace way. This street might have been lifted from any suburb in the country. Two-story homes with clean siding stood evenly spaced on the sides of the road. Lawns were kept manicured and free of debris, except for the occasional child's toy. Late model sedans and SUVs stood in driveways, and Melanie felt her agitation subside a notch.

She chastised herself for being a snob. The presence of a few liquor stores and pawnshops wasn't evidence of a ghetto, any more than the sight of bland suburban houses should have been considered comforting and safe. The house she drove toward had been as quaint as any other suburban domicile, but what those two did in the basement…

The GPS instructed her to turn left and Melanie spotted the sign at the intersection: Ash Street. A thrill tingled in her chest, and her hands suddenly tightened on the wheel.

The place was easy enough to find. Like the street she'd just left, the lots held nice frame houses with fresh paint and lovely lawns. That is, all lots except for one.

Melanie pulled to the curb next to a series of stakes that had been planted on the grass. Yellow police tape formed a rippling fence between the wooden shafts. Already a flimsy chain link fence had been constructed on the sides and back of the condemned property, caging the burnt remains on three sides. Jagged and charred walls, none standing more than six feet high, jutted from the foundation. The entire front of the house was gone. Shrubberies and a single pecan tree had been burned down to black sticks. Seared beams and serrated floorboards stuck up behind the toasted foliage.

Grabbing Reg's DVR unit, Melanie climbed out of the vehicle. She turned the camera on, framed the destroyed property on the small screen, and then walked forward as quietly as she could manage. She paused at the yellow tape. Trepidation tickled her stomach. This was not only a condemned property, but it was also a crime scene. Alan Means had performed arson on this place, and Melanie knew that the moment she crossed the waving yellow line, she would be breaking the law. It caused her pause.

With her determination on hold, Melanie stood on the edge of the lawn. A strip of the yellow tape brushed her stomach. She looked at the camera's view screen to see if the decimated house even registered with so little light. Satisfied that the streetlamps cast enough illumination, Melanie played with the zoom feature. The broken and burned remains of the house on Ash Street raced toward her, just as a voice spoke at her back.

"Can I help you?" a man asked.

Startled, Melanie spun around to find a stern-looking man, wearing a white button-down shirt and faded blue jeans. Her heart thundered against her ribs as the man's presence sank in. He stood at least six feet tall and was built thick through the shoulders with a face that revealed little about his age. His weathered, yet attractive features could have belonged to a man who was anywhere between forty-five and fifty-five years old, though she assumed he was on the younger edge of that spectrum. She thought about cowboys and policemen, or rather the clichéd representations of these archetypes.

He repeated his question.

"No," Melanie said quickly. "I was just…"

"You were just recording the place for posterity," he interrupted. "A morbid video clip to add to your collection of Dahmer cookware."

"What? No. It's part of my job to…"

"To document misery and shove it down the throats of your viewers? I know. I know, it's your job and the people have the right to know."

Melanie realized this man thought she was a journalist. Her initial fear began to melt into annoyance. She prepared herself to respond but he wasn't finished yet.

"Eleven people died in that house," the man said, "No wait, twelve now. They all died violently, terrified of what was happening to them. Can you imagine what they went through? Do you ever take even a single moment to wonder how absolutely powerless they were at the end? Or doesn't that translate into ratings?"

"Are you going to let me say anything?" Melanie asked, furious now. She could tell the man was exhausted. He looked as if he hadn't slept in days, but there was no way in hell she was going to let the guy paint her with the same brush that colored assholes like Mack Durham and Kee Ulrich.

"I imagine I've heard it all before," the man said.

"Must be some imagination," Melanie replied. "But on the off chance you skipped over a couple of scenarios, why don't you shut up and let me finish?"

Though not cowed, the man shrugged and crossed his arms, waiting for her to go on. An officious little smirk cut his mouth as if he were amused that a woman should be so assertive.

"A man sent me a letter and asked me to come here. He thought something was happening in this house, something bad. In fact, he believed that whatever was inside was so bad he burned the place to the ground."

The information sank in and the smile faded from the man's face. "Alan wrote to you?"

"Yes. He thought I might be able to help, but I didn't get his letter until it was too late."

"So are you with the state police? The government?"

"No," Melanie said. She was about to explain her profession but paused. This guy thought she was a law enforcement officer, maybe an investigator. She couldn't imagine his reaction when she revealed the true nature of her business. He'd probably laugh her off or his disdain would become even more insufferable. Still she wasn't going to lie, so she said, "I'm a paranormal investigator."

The shadows on the man's face shifted. He didn't burst into laughter as Melanie had expected but rather seemed to be digesting the information slowly, letting it sink into his mind as a bit of candy might melt on his tongue. Finally, he nodded and held out his hand.

"I'm Detective Stuart Lancaster," he said. "Maybe we can help one another."

They sat in an IHOP next to the interstate. Melanie drank coffee and ate wheat toast while Stuart picked at a plate of eggs and sausage. In the restaurant's harsh light, the man's exhaustion was even more apparent. He seemed to be keeping his eyes open by a sheer force of will. Melanie was used to pulling all-nighters with the show, so she felt fine, even after the long drive. Her body clock was in a constant state of adjustment, and she'd gotten to the point where she could sleep when she wanted to. Most people, including the detective, didn't have that luxury. Stuart speared a link of sausage, appraised it unhappily, and returned the meat to his plate.

"Not hungry?" Melanie asked.

"Not much," Stuart said. He lifted his mug and drained the coffee from it before leaning back in the booth.

"Are you always up this early?" Melanie asked.

"These days, yeah," Stuart replied. "I was at the station most of the night." He looked like he might expand on the statement, but his face wrinkled. He shook his head and said, "Tell me something."

"That's why we're here."

"Have you ever found anything real? I mean, you go on these ghost hunts and walk around empty houses, but have you ever come across a real ghost?"

"We've experienced things we couldn't explain," Melanie told him.

"But that's not the same thing. Have you ever actually seen a ghost? Have you caught one on tape or heard its voice?"

"Yes and no. When I was a little girl, I believe I saw a ghost, but if you're asking for hard cold evidence… no. Generally our investigations are geared toward debunking supposed hauntings, which is to say, we are looking for anything that could rationally explain the things people have seen or heard. For example, a person hears footsteps on the second floor of her house. We come in and find the pipes are old and they creak. It sounds like footsteps. End of investigation. Someone else sees an apparition. We go in and find light playing off of a mirror and a window in such a way that it looks like something is moving at the end of a corridor. End of story. We have occasionally come across situations where nothing in the location explains the noises we hear or the things we see. We use an EMF detector to document disturbances in the atmosphere and often enough the electrical field is being influenced by exposed wiring or a bad fuse box, but sometimes nothing explains the variations we've experienced. In those cases, we don't call the house haunted, but we do keep the possibility open."

"So you don't believe in ghosts?" he asked.

"I didn't say that," Melanie said. "I do believe, but you were asking for evidence, and I don't have any. At least none that I'd consider unequivocal."

"What do you think they want?"

"Excuse me?"

"These people, why would they come back? Why would they stay in the first place? Why don't they move on?"

"You're assuming they have a choice. For that matter, you're assuming they're motivated by the same things that motivate us. I don't think that's the way it works." Melanie finished her own coffee and used the carafe on the table's edge to fill both their mugs. "There used to be a popular theory about apparitions remaining earthbound because they had unfinished business with the living—a loved one they wanted to say goodbye to, a document they left hidden in the walls of a house, the identity of the person who killed them. It's all Hollywood nonsense. There's nothing in the paranormal studies arena that supports the theory. That way of thinking was likely derived from the egos of the living, who believed nothing could happen unless it directly affected them. Spirits had to mean something to *them* or want something from *them*, but again I've found nothing in my research to support the idea. Current thinking suggests that what we're seeing when we see ghosts is actually residual energy, moments captured and frozen in time that play over and over again. These are emotional images of a person with no consciousness and no purpose like a movie clip that loops randomly. Locations of intense electrical activity are particularly susceptible to these phenomena. In fact, some researchers believe that when human beings are exposed to tones of approximately 18.9 Hertz they get the experience of seeing ghosts."

"Really?" Stuart asked, looking somewhat amused.

"Yes," Melanie said. "That is also the resonant frequency of the human eye, meaning that our eyes vibrate when exposed to a sound of this particular frequency, which might cause abnormal light refraction, blurring… And you think this is all bullshit."

Stuart chuckled and shook his head. "I don't mean to be an ass, but I've had some recent experience of my own. Believe me, I find your explanations far more comforting, but they don't exactly hold up."

"Are you talking about the apparition on the news?"

Stuart sipped his refreshed coffee and nodded. "Her name was Regina Wolcroff. I worked her murder case."

"She was a victim of Baxter and Thomason?"

"You know the case?"

"I followed it when it was happening, then refreshed my memory after Alan's letter."

"And what did Alan say?"

"That he saw a number of the victims, including his granddaughter, Dory, in that house."

"Did he mention why he went there in the first place?"

"He said something about his grandson getting hurt. Someone cut the boy when he broke into the house with friends. He told Alan about it and Alan went to see for himself."

"Stupid kids," Stuart whispered. The detective gazed into his coffee cup for a moment and then looked back at Melanie. "I have a question for you."

"Why stop now?"

"Nothing Alan wrote could have been supported by your theories and experiences. I mean, spirits that cut and talk and roam the streets don't exactly fit into the classifications of residual energy or eyeball shakes, so why are you here? Why didn't you just write the whole note off as the ramblings of a deluded old man?"

"Because I'm not jaded enough to believe I know it all, Detective Lancaster. If I were, I'd find a new way to make a living. Now there's the apparition of Regina Wolcroff to consider as well."

They sat silently for a minute. Both drank their coffee and did their best not to make eye contact. Melanie figured they'd reached the point in the conversation when they would decide to work together or to go their separate ways. She didn't know if she needed Stuart's help, but she suddenly realized she wanted it.

When Stuart spoke, his question surprised her. The answer was so obvious.

"Don't you want to know what my interest in all of this is?"

"I already know," she said. "Your wife was the tenth victim of Baxter and Thomason, and since the other apparition was a victim of those crimes, I have to figure you've seen her recently."

"You're pretty sharp," he said. "And call me Stuart."

"Do you want to talk about what you saw?"

"No," Stuart replied. "Not just yet. But there is someone I'd like you to meet. In a way, she's the cog that holds all of us together. Her name is Hannah Bolger. We'll swing by her place tonight. My guess is, she's already in touch with the other family members. She probably has a lot of information we could use."

"Then why are we waiting until tonight?"

"Because I have a job," he said. "I'm in the middle of an investigation, and even though I'm beginning to think it's not as far away from this Ash Street business as I used to, I can't exactly file a report that includes ghosts."

"You think one of these apparitions was involved in a murder?"

"I don't know," Stuart replied. "But if I keep telling myself it's just a coincidence, someone else could get killed."

24

Stuart walked from the parking lot to the station. Dawn smeared pastel colors over the front of the building, and he turned to the sunrise, staring at the orange ball working its way into the sky. The light hurt his eyes, but his tired mind didn't make the connection between the action of watching the sun and the pain it brought to his head, so he kept looking until his head grew so heavy his chin dipped down to his chest, startling him enough to break the sun's spell.

Inside, the ceiling bulbs were equally as harsh, casting glare and discomfort. He felt nauseated, and his head hurt. His eyelids fluttered. Melanie Bell swam into his thoughts. She was an attractive woman, a strong woman, who pursued her profession in earnest. Stuart liked her, but thought she was wholly out of her league. She was hoping to find residual human energy—spirits who had long since given up interest in interacting with the living, but what haunted Barnard was something else, something focused, something motivated, something malicious. Stuart knew it.

Clarissa's face pushed through the haze, shoving Melanie away. Stuart rubbed his eyes and continued down the hall.

He made it to his office, to his desk, to his chair. Stuart sat down and a moment later, he was sleeping with his face on a low pile of manila folders. If the phone rang, he didn't hear it, and if he dreamt, the subconscious images came and went without disturbing him. The slumber was deep and peaceful, which made giving it up all the more difficult.

"Hey," a man's voice whispered.

Stuart surfaced from sleep as if rising from a nighttime lake. When he opened his eyes, the room around him—not immediately recognizable as his office—was blurred and seemed to melt at the edges as if he were viewing the room from somewhere beneath that dark water.

"Stuart?"

He blinked and rubbed the sleep from his eyes. Before him stood Detective Brian Hall, a slender, neatly dressed man in his early thirties with prematurely gray hair that made his face seem all the more boyish. Stuart had often wished he'd been partnered with Hall instead of David Ballard. The guy was sharp and personable, thorough and dedicated.

"Brian," Stuart said. He forced a laugh and leaned back in his chair. "You caught me napping."

"Sorry," Detective Hall said, "but I figured you'd want to see this."

"What can I do you for?"

"We got a call last night. A robbery gone bad. The victim took five to the head, one to the gut. We caught the perpetrator fleeing the scene. He's screaming innocent, but he was carrying the murder weapon. His gloves are covered in powder marks and he's got blood all over him. Plus, he had a history with the victim. It shouldn't take us but a minute to get this in front of the D.A."

"You said there was something I needed to see?"

"Yeah, Stuart. It's the victim. His name was Richard Xavier Wolcroff."

He pushed a breath over his lips and leaned forward on his desk. "Shit," he muttered.

"Now I know you've seen the news," Hall continued. "We both know who that girl in the yellow dress is supposed to be, the one they're calling a ghost, and I think we can file coincidence away in the bullshit cabinet. We got attacks on Pudge Taylor, Roy Dermott, and now Richard Wolcroff, all family or associates of people killed by Baxter and Thomason, and all of them dead in less than two weeks."

Don't forget Alan, Stuart thought. Alan Means had been another survivor; now another corpse. But one of the names didn't click with him: Roy Dermott.

"He was involved with Chance Whiting, the fifth victim. They were 'special friends' if you get my meaning, but they weren't together at the time of Whiting's murder, which is probably why the name never came up. We got it when we were questioning Selma Baxter, so we talked to the guy, but according to Dermott his relationship with Whiting only lasted a couple of months."

"What happened to him?"

"Chance Whiting's stepfather is Wally Pepper, the furniture guy. He attacked Dermott in the store. Dermott fought back and the old man fell through a glass table, impaled himself on an iron post."

The details sharpened in Stuart's head. He remembered the talk around the station and the news reports. The case had been open and shut, self-defense, occurring only a day after Pudge Taylor's murder. Stuart's mind had been focused on his own problems, and since the Dermott attack wasn't ongoing, closed and tucked into bed, he hadn't given it much thought. Still, he was shocked that there was a name associated with the Baxter-Thomason case that he didn't immediately recognize. There was something else familiar about the name, but when Stuart tried to recall it, he flashed back to a conversation with Harlan and couldn't give the name any context.

"You said the perpetrator in the Wolcroff case also had a history with the victim?"

"Yeah, his name is Tim Ohnegian. He used to date Wolcroff's daughter."

"I remember him," Stuart said.

Tim Ohnegian's name had been bandied around a hundred times during the investigation of Regina's murder. It had come up again, frequently, in Hannah's counseling group, as Richard Wolcroff spoke the name with venom. Stuart had run into the kid before all of the Baxter-Thomason crimes as well. He'd watched in furious dismay as the kid had avoided any real punishment for his ongoing drug-related crimes. Ohnegian's father, Chester, was a big shot in the computer business, running a major facility in the foothills to the east of Barnard. Tim represented a lot of bad PR for his father, yet the old man had always been quick with the cash for payoffs and bail outs.

"Right," Detective Hall said. "Ohnegian's a big fan of pharmaceuticals. He's got some priors for possession, but his daddy always bailed him out. Charges never stuck. Apparently, neither daddy nor daddy's lawyer are taking Tim's calls these days.

"Last night, Ohnegian broke into Wolcroff's home. He had himself a Beretta nine-millimeter and enough meth in his system to light up an entire high school football team. Ohnegian copped to being wired out of his mind, but he's screaming innocent to the homicide charge. Smug little fuck. Considering he had about thirty-eight cents on him when we pulled him off the street, we're thinking he hit up Wolcroff for some cash and things turned ugly."

"Can I talk to him?"

"He lawyered up—public defender. They're in counsel right now. It'll be a few hours, at least. My guess is the PD will demand we let his client rest and de-ice before we continue the questioning."

"Let me know when he's available."

"Will do." Detective Hall turned from Stuart's desk. Then he paused and turned back. "Oh and Stuart," he said. "Get some sleep. You're looking like Elvis on the crapper."

"Thanks, Brian," Stuart said. "Duly noted."

Alone in his office, Stuart slid a notepad across the blotter and snatched up a pen. He considered what Detective Hall had told him and then quickly jotted down his thoughts:

Pudge Taylor ----> Ella Taylor <---- ?
Alan Means ----> Dory Addison <---- Alan Means
Roy Dermott ----> Chance Whiting <---- Wally Pepper
Richard Wolcroff ----> Regina Wolcroff <---- Tim Ohnegian

In the cases of the last two, the victims had been attacked by people with whom they'd been familiar. They weren't random crimes, perpetrated by strangers. Further, in each case both the victim and the attacker had been close to a victim of the Baxter-Thomason killings. Chance Whiting's stepfather had attempted to murder Whiting's ex-lover. Tim Ohnegian, Regina Wolcroff's ill-chosen boyfriend, had succeeded in murdering Regina's father. This was the pattern. So, if all of these crimes were connected—and like Brian Hall, Stuart was unable to believe any of this was a coincidence—then Pudge Taylor knew his killer and both of them had been close to Ella Taylor.

Stuart looked at his simple, quickly sketched diagram. He wrote a name next to Ella Taylor's. It looked right and felt right, but he didn't have a shred of evidence against the suspect, not so much as a hint in her statement or a moment unaccounted for in her alibi, but still he knew Colleen Taylor had murdered her husband.

Now, he just had to prove it.

25

Colleen Taylor stood at the living room window, smoking a cigarette and looking into the rain. Not far away, the sun shone. She could see it clearly through the pelting gray drops. A mile distant, maybe two, a hill wore a cap of golden light, but storm surrounded the Taylor's house. She left the window and stubbed her cigarette out in a crystal dish on the coffee table and then continued across the room, its ornamentation soft-edged and indistinct. She would miss the house's comforts. Walking up the stairs to her bedroom, Colleen thought about her family—Pudge, her sons, and her daughter, Ella.

The ghost of her daughter, her beautiful little girl, hadn't appeared since the morning of Pudge's death. Maybe Ella was free now, and that should have pleased her mother, but instead Colleen felt panicked, like sitting in a car that had lost control and spun crazily across the lane into oncoming traffic. If Ella had only told her she'd done right. If her daughter had returned just once to ease her mother's mind, she would feel differently.

In the bedroom, Colleen circled to the far side of the bed—Pudge's side of the bed—and opened the nightstand. Inside she found one of her husband's guns. It was large, and light winked at her from its chrome barrel. Twenty years ago, he'd taught her how to shoot. Colleen remembered the weight of the weapon and her initial difficulty in managing its thick handle, and she remembered the terrible thrill she'd felt squeezing the trigger to unleash thunder. She lifted the gun and pressed it to her chest, cradling the weapon like a kitten. Leaving the nightstand behind, Colleen strolled to the door. She cast a final look at the bed, but could conjure no comforting memories. Despite his growing belly and softening features, Colleen had continued to want her husband. Seeing him naked had aroused her right up to the morning she'd put the knife in his back the way Ella had taught her. The sight of his cock brought memories of the pleasure she'd taken from it, and the bulk of his chest reminded her of the comforting compression of his weight on her. But Pudge had lost what little passion he'd felt for her years before. His lust for her had been a rather shallow puddle to begin with, and it'd quickly evaporated. From the beginning Colleen had suspected she'd married into convenience, but she'd stored this hurtful possibility in a dark nook at the back of her mind. If the issue was convenience, it had been Pudge's convenience. She'd adored the man.

Colleen followed the stairs back down and crossed through a stone arch to the foyer. In the guest bath, she deposited the gun in a drawer and pressed her face to the glass door of the shower. It was cold on her cheek. She trembled and detected the scent of ozone bouncing from one marble-tiled wall to another.

Ella? she wondered. But more likely, it was just the storm. Her daughter had moved on; her soul at peace. Colleen wanted to feel proud she'd managed this last duty as a mother, but she only felt empty and scared.

Back in the living room where she could see the distant sunlight through the rainfall, she lit another cigarette and blew the smoke against the glass. Life's lies, the small conciliatory fictions she'd long told herself, settled with the nicotine in her system.

She'd been an idiot—a cruel idiot. She'd turned her eyes away from what was happening to her daughter to pretend Pudge was a good husband. She'd brushed away all of the clues to the contrary, choosing to ignore the painful reality of the man and her life with him. At times, she'd even bolstered her fragile convictions with thoughts like—Does it matter? Monogamy doesn't equal love. A marriage isn't sex. But these had been arguments against digressions she couldn't accept, tilting at dragons like Don Quixote, though in opposition to Cervantes's madman, Colleen had painted windmills over the dragons and accepted them as harmless pieces of landscape.

Pudge had been unfaithful. Colleen accepted that now, and she could have lived with it. She knew she could have spent the rest of her life letting the information burn her heart and mind, but what Pudge had done to their daughter…

What he'd done to Ella when she was still a child…

How could any mother accept that? How could any mother forgive it? How could any mother not right that wrong?

Behind her a soft noise drew her attention. Colleen clasped the cigarette between her lips inhaling deeply as she quit the gloomy scene at the window.

The sight that greeted her when she turned to face the living room made no sense. A woman and a man fucked on the low marble table in the center of the room. Colleen was not initially disturbed by the image as she felt certain it had been disgorged from her subconscious. Both figures were steel gray, details of their form made clear by shadows and light. The woman lay back on the table; her hair draped over the edge nearest Colleen. Her legs were spread to accommodate the muscular body of a man, who had no facial features save for a ghastly smile. His face was a smooth plain cut with a toothy crescent that ran from cheekbone to cheekbone. As her mind truly registered this scene, Colleen began to hear the voices.

"Did daddy do it like this?" asked the grinning man.

The woman on the table whimpered and screamed, but the sounds were muffled as if a cloth had been shoved in her mouth.

"You hated him for it," he said. "You hated it when daddy put his rod in you, but you love me. Tell me you love me."

The crying woman acquiesced with mumbled words. Her response was greeted with a particularly violent thrust of the man's hips. The woman slid on the table, her head dropping back over the edge.

Colleen gasped when she saw her daughter's face, staring desperately at her. Ella's hair pooled on the floor as her body quaked, jostled by the violent intrusions. And though the grinning fiend looked nothing like him, Colleen knew the thing violating her daughter was Derek Thomason. She'd heard what that man had done to her little girl—she'd heard every sick detail.

"Stop it," Colleen whispered. She had no breath and the smoke tickled her throat. She coughed violently. Tears stung her eyes.

The man turned his grin to Colleen. A strangled cough like a yelp caught in her throat. Then his shape began to change, melting and broadening. The muscular form grew softer, inflating as if he were nothing more than latex filling with air. His tight abdomen expanded, his washboard stomach bloating, turning smooth and round. Firm pectorals became fluid and engorged. Wisps of blond white hair sprouted across the blossoming torso. The face was the last to change, but even before the cheeks filled in and a blunt nose and large eyes appeared above the monstrous smile, Colleen knew what form the specter was taking.

"Pudge," she groaned miserably.

During this grotesque transformation, the rape continued. Pudge's girth further displaced Ella's legs, pushing them wider. His fat hands grasped at her breasts, grinding them and squeezing them. Ella screamed, her voice still muffled. Through the violence to their daughter, Pudge kept his smiling face turned to Colleen.

Her head grew light and the room canted beneath her feet. Only the sharp pain in her chest and the burn of tears kept her from giving in to the dizziness. Colleen reached out to find a wall or a table to support her weight, but her hand slapped uselessly through the air. She stumbled and made it across to the sofa, but this vantage revealed more of the terrible abuse. She squeezed her eyes closed against the perversion, but she could still hear her husband's watery grunts and snorts and her daughter's pleas.

"Don't you close your eyes," a strange voice yelled. It sounded nothing like her husband's voice. It was too high, too sharp. "Don't you close your eyes when I'm giving it right. Look at me. Look at me, you fucking bitch."

Colleen's eyes shot open, terrified by the shrill sound of the voice, thinking the apparition would soon finish with her daughter and move its cruel attention to her. The grinning man glared back at her, still wearing her husband's face.

"That's better," he said. "Getting close now. Always happens fast with the young ones."

"Stop this," Colleen said.

"We should have had more daughters," was Pudge's response.

Colleen thought she might be sick. Nausea twisted in her stomach, bringing another layer of dislocation from the event transpiring before her.

Then Pudge was gone and the man with his well-built body and his smooth face returned. One of his arms elongated and narrowed. The hand and fingers melted away leaving a smooth tube tapering up to his collarbone: a shotgun. The butt of the gun pressed into the man's shoulder and the barrel disappeared into Ella's mouth. Colleen's daughter choked on the weapon.

"Stop it!" Colleen cried.

"Just about there," the man said. "Just about…I'm gonna blow. Fixing to pop… right…about…"

A sickly groan filled the living room and the grinning man leaned forward, resting heavily on the stock of the shotgun, pressing the barrel deep into Ella's mouth. Colleen watched in disgust.

"You're a good one," the grinning man told Ella. "No wonder daddy liked that ass. I couldn'ta kept off it even if you were my own little girl."

"Go away," Colleen yelled. "Get out of my house."

"You done good getting me to pop," the man continued. "Now it's your turn."

He leaned back, seeming to use the shotgun in Ella's mouth to support his weight.

"No." Colleen squeezed her eyes closed again. She waited for the explosion that would kill her daughter again, but the report never came.

She finally made herself look, the anticipation far worse than anything she might see. The surface of her cocktail table, all gleaming polished marble, held a fan of magazines and the crystal dish holding half a dozen cigarette butts. Ella and her abuser were gone.

"They're coming for you," her daughter whispered in Colleen's ear. "You're going to prison. They won't care why you did it. They won't care that you did it for me."

Colleen sniffed loudly and nodded her head. She wiped the tears from her cheeks with trembling hands.

"I know," Colleen said. "I know."

"Is that why you got daddy's gun?"

"Yes."

"Are you going to use it, mommy?"

Colleen straightened her shoulders and swallowed a thick paste of fear and disgust. She swept away the last tear from her eye and said, "They aren't taking me anywhere."

26

It wasn't a ghost, Mike knew. The thing that haunted him, despite looking like his sister, was not Dory. The sweet little girl's spirit had nothing to do with the monstrous apparition except for the fact it wore her face, but the thing Mike had seen scurrying along neighborhood streets, leading him toward Galveston Drive wore many faces; it changed them as easily as Mike would change a shirt or a cap. He thought back to what he'd seen in the house on Ash Street, all of the ghosts that had begged him for release—fakes.

Once he'd reached Galveston Road, he'd lost sight of the creature, and despite a thorough search of the sidewalks and yards, found nothing, so he'd walked home and turned on his computer and tried to identify the monster that pretended to be his sister.

Hours passed as he read page after page about shape shifting entities, but in each of those tellings, the monster began as human or animal, or at least existed in a solid form, and the transformations that were described all bore striking similarities to the sensational skin warping, bone snapping changes he'd seen in films.

His cell phone rang. Mike answered it absently, distracted by a word he found on the webpage he was searching. The word was *doppelganger*, and it sounded familiar, but he couldn't immediately recall what it meant.

"Don't you go to school anymore?" Gwen asked.

"Doctor's appointment," Mike lied.

"What's wrong?"

"Nothing," he told her. "Just haven't been sleeping. Mom's worried. I'll be in class tomorrow."

"Do you need anything?" Gwen said.

"I'm good, thanks."

"Be sure to download the assignments off the web."

"Yeah," Mike said. "I will. Look, can I call you later? I have to head out."

"Sure."

"See ya," Mike said, then ended the call before Gwen could reply.

He returned his attention to the strange word—*doppelganger*—but the doorbell interrupted his investigation a second time. He wanted to ignore the noise and whomever it announced, but he didn't.

Mike recognized the woman on his front porch immediately. Her name was Melanie Bell and she was famous, or pretty damn near it. She hosted a program on the Shiver Channel called *The Haunt Club*, a television series about paranormal investigations, and suddenly he felt self-conscious about the way he looked. He hadn't showered and was still wearing the clothes he'd had on yesterday. He checked over Melanie's shoulder to make sure that Reg guy, the one who always videotaped the shows, wasn't behind her, capturing his fatigue and poor hygiene for a future episode.

"Mike?" Melanie asked.

How does she know my name? he wondered. "Yes," he said.

"I'm Melanie Bell."

"I know." Mike didn't know what to make of her standing there on his doorstep. His thoughts clanged and skipped like gears in a broken machine, and he couldn't think of anything to say.

"You're home from school," she said awkwardly.

"Yeah. I-I was going to a doctor's appointment."

"Well, I don't want to keep you."

"No. I mean you're not," Mike said.

"This might seem strange, but I was hoping we could talk."

"With me?" he managed.

"I won't take up too much of your time, but I received this letter from your grandfather," Melanie handed him two sheets of folded paper, "and I was hoping you could tell me a little about your experience."

Experience? Mike wondered on the word as he took the letter. "Come on in," he said, stepping back for Melanie to enter. He started reading before she made it over the threshold: *My name is Alan Means, and I don't sleep well…* Absently, Mike closed the door, his mind engrossed in his grandfather's letter.

My grandson, Michael, visited the house the other night. He went with some friends. Only God knows why…

Mike winced with embarrassment when he read this part and threw a quick glance at Melanie, whose face showed interest, without a hint of pity or aggression in her eyes. He liked her for that.

After finishing the letter, Mike said, "No one cut me."

"Excuse me?"

"Granddad said one of those things cut me, but it didn't happen that way. I was trying to get away and tripped. My arm was cut on a nail when I fell. I might have confused things when I told him because I was on some painkillers. If I hadn't been, I wouldn't have said anything to him at all."

"But you did see these apparitions?"

"I guess so," Mike said cautiously. "I saw something."

"Can you tell me what happened?"

"Do you want to sit down?" Mike asked. The rapid change of subject took Melanie off guard and it showed in a humorous, rapid blinking. "I've got some coffee if you want some."

"Coffee'd out, thanks."

Mike didn't want to talk about that house, and he knew he didn't have to talk about it, not with Melanie. After all, it wasn't like she was a cop and he was obstructing justice or anything, but he felt a strange sense of obligation like talking to a teacher. So he didn't ask her to leave, but he wasn't comfortable with her staying either. Mike felt familiar walls erecting in his head. He liked Melanie. She seemed cool, but a lot of reporters had acted cool to him, when they were trying to pry more shit out of him about Dory.

"I'll believe whatever you tell me," Melanie said.

"I'm not going to be on television am I?"

"I hope not. I hope none of this gets put on my show."

"Really?"

"Long story," Melanie said. "This is a personal investigation. If my producer gets his hands on it, it's going to turn into a mess."

"Like that show with the stop-animation car?" Mike said wryly.

"Worse," Melanie replied. "This isn't a goof at some random homeowner's expense. Those are bad enough, but this would be playing with people's tragedy, broadcasting pain for the sake of ratings, and I'm not going to let them do that, at least not with me on the show."

"Except for the thing about one of them cutting me, it's all in the letter," Mike said. "I went into the house and thought I saw those—what did you call them?"

"Apparitions."

"Yeah, apparitions. I got confused and fell into the basement, and when I tried to get out I gouged my shoulder on a nail."

"How many did you see?"

"I don't know. Three. Maybe four."

"And you saw your sister?"

Mike went silent.

"I'm sorry," Melanie said. "Just tell me what you want to tell me."

I already have, Mike thought.

"Have you seen any apparitions since that night in the house?"

There's only one. It's one spirit pretending to be all of them. "I saw the woman on Brown Street," he said. "The one on the news."

"You were there?" Melanie asked, her eyes sparking with interest.

Mike backpedaled with a lie. "I mean, I saw it on the news. Look, I really have to get ready to go. Sorry I couldn't be more helpful."

"You were very helpful," Melanie said. She reached into her jeans pocket and produced a low stack of bent and dog-eared business cards. Handing one to Mike she said, "I'm staying at the Majestic Hotel, so if you want to talk some more please call me, but if you run into Mack, the other guy on the show, or a man named Kee Ulrich, you might want to be careful what you say. They might just put you on television." She smiled and shook his hand and left.

Mike watched Melanie Bell walk to the end of his drive and climb into a black SUV. An anxious vibration in his chest made him want to call out, to have her return so he could spill everything he knew, everything he believed. Maybe she knew what to call the thing he'd seen; she was an expert wasn't she?

But he didn't call her back. Mike watched her pull away from the curb and drive away.

27

He knew he was in no shape to be interrogating witnesses. Stuart could barely keep his eyes open, and he felt certain exhaustion would take its toll on the investigation: he'd say something foolish, or overlook an important piece of information. He could barely focus, and the world seemed to have turned soft, all of the surfaces under his feet unstable as if made of mud or rubber. It was entirely likely that his sleep-deprived mind had made connections his rested mind would not have made, but he'd read through Colleen Taylor's testimony, and when he factored in the pristine knife found in a greenbelt only three miles from the Taylor home, he strongly suspected the knife he wanted—the murder weapon—had been hidden in plain sight. Last night he'd gone over Aaron Talbot's report and the notes David Ballard had left for him. All of the Taylor cutlery had been examined, so that left a single, now obvious, location.

Looking at Rachel Cobb reminded Stuart of perusing magazines at the supermarket checkout stand—specifically tabloids with headlines like "Make-over Tragedy" and "Plastic Explosive." Cobb resembled a past-her-prime actress who, over the years, had made one too many trips to her plastic surgeon's office. The woman's face was swollen and tight as if she were having a dangerous reaction to a bee sting, and her lips, smeared in a soft pink lipstick, were almost comically pouty. Her eyebrows were little more than razor-thin arches over her wide—what the hell is happening?—eyes. Even her hair suffered. Stuart couldn't imagine what a woman had to do to hair to make it look so fragile. Maybe it was too much bleach, or too much time with a curling iron. Whatever the case, Rachel's attentions had resulted in strands with the texture of fiberglass, carefully molded to look like human hair.

"Detective," Rachel said with a flirtatious blink of her eyes. She clutched her robe close to her neck and smiled with such false demure, a shock of pity ran through Stuart. "It's so early," she said, attempting a sex-kitten purr. "I'm not even dressed."

"I'm here about Colleen Taylor," he said, barely registering the note of flirtation in Cobb's voice. "More specifically, I'd like to go over her alibi with you again."

Rachel Cobb looked momentarily confused. Given even the slightest flexibility Stuart imagined his disinterest in her seduction would have caused her face to fall, but instead, her expression didn't change. Her posture however stiffened, and she kept the robe clutched to her neck as she stepped back and pulled the door open.

"Come in," she said, curtly. "I need to put something on. Would you be a doll and get me a bottled water from the kitchen?"

"Of course," Stuart said, grateful Rachel hadn't suddenly found hospitality in the week since they'd last chatted.

Ms. Cobb attempted a dramatic departure, spinning on her heels and causing her robe to spread out like a cape, revealing green lace panties and a fine pair of legs as the fabric of her gown billowed, but her feet weren't up to the motion and she stumbled, ever so slightly, before hurrying across the foyer to the stairs. Stuart caught her clumsy misstep but thought little of it. Instead, he turned and walked to the kitchen, where he knew he'd be alone for at least five minutes.

Colleen Taylor had known the exact same thing.

He pushed open the heavy wooden door and entered the gloomy room. After a moment, he found a bank of switches on the wall to his right. He slid his palm over the plate, knocking every toggle upward, and the lights burst on all around the kitchen. Heavy stainless steel appliances occupied recesses in the black granite countertops. An island with a matching black stone top and a deep metal sink stood in the center of the room. A broad oak cutting board had been sunk into the granite and next to it stood a block of knives.

Stuart's theory was simple: Colleen Taylor murdered her husband, using a butcher's knife that matched the set her best friend owned; after the killing, she put the knife in a plastic bag or wrapped it in some other protective material and placed it in her gym bag; knowing she would have ample time while Cobb prepared for their Pilates class, Colleen disposed of the protective material, washed the knife off in the sink, and exchanged the murder weapon with her friend's cutlery, which she then discarded during her drive home. Every minute of the morning of her husband's death would be accounted for, and the murder weapon would remain well hidden in the house of a woman no one had any cause to suspect.

Of course, there was the issue of blood spatter on Colleen's person. She could have cleaned away the worst of it with disposable wipes, perhaps depositing them in the same bag as the knife. Stuart considered the light lycra fabric of a leotard, common enough clothing for an exercise class. The stretchy material could easily be balled up and hidden away—even burned with little left for examination. How easy it would have been to hide a spare in her purse to change into after a shower at the spa.

He knew he was missing something about the clothes and Colleen's removal of blood evidence—he just couldn't get all of the gears in his head to sink up—but that wasn't important just yet. He had the murder weapon. Its black handle jutted from the pale oak block only inches from his hand. Colleen knew Ms. Cobb would make her wait while she gathered her things for the exercise class—she had more than enough time. Likely, whatever Colleen had done to clean herself had happened in this very room.

He pulled a handkerchief from his pocket and carefully lifted the butcher's knife from its slot. He played the ceiling lights off of the blade. Cold flashes pierced his eyes. He saw subtle damage along the curved blade of the cutlery. Small nicks etched the slender edge of the knife; multiple scratches marred its surface. Carefully he replaced the cutlery in the block.

Stuart was eager to call a forensic team. Even after a week, they could turn something up, but he didn't want to hassle with a search warrant. It would be so much easier if Ms. Cobb simply allowed the investigators into her house. So, Stuart waited for the woman to return. When she did, she wore a pair of jeans that tightly clung to her shapely legs and a sheer pink blouse that parted at her midsection, revealing a gleaming gold loop affixed to her navel.

"Couldn't you find any water?" Ms. Cobb asked, sounding perturbed.

"I'm sorry," Stuart said. "I was just admiring your kitchen."

"Oh, that's sweet," she replied. "I'm almost never in here. John and I always eat out or order something in. I just never got the hang of the whole food thing. My hips and ass are eternally grateful for that." She laughed at her joke and flipped her hair back over a shoulder. It moved like a molded plastic wing, lifted away, then fell back to its previous position. "Now, what can I do for you?"

"As I said, it's about Colleen Taylor."

"Lord," Ms. Cobb responded dramatically. "Can't you leave the dear woman alone? She's been through so much."

"I know," Stuart said, "but I just have a few more questions."

"Oh, all right," Ms. Cobb said, attempting to sound like a petulant child. She leaned forward on the island, chin in hands.

"Now, you say you never cook in here?"

"No, never. Why?"

"Can you tell me about these knives?" Stuart asked. He kept his voice modulated, calm and conversational.

Ms. Cobb chirped a laugh. "You want to talk about Colleen? I'll tell you something about her. I love her like an older sister, but she has crap taste when it comes to gifts."

"What do you mean?"

"She knows I don't cook. She knows I'll never cook, and what does she get me for Christmas?" Ms. Cobb pointed at the block of knives. "Might as well have bought me a gift certificate for a vasectomy."

"These were a gift from Colleen Taylor?" Stuart asked.

Rachel Cobb opened her mouth to reply but no words came out. Her gaze shot from Stuart to the block of knives, then back to him. The ping-pong glances happened twice more as Rachel began to understand why Stuart had asked the question, and under other circumstances, Stuart would have found the gesture amusing. Though not amused, he felt considerable relief. Colleen Taylor would be in custody within the hour.

28

Ballard was already at the Taylor house when Stuart arrived. He parked behind his partner's Ford truck and climbed out of the car. A cruiser had been dispatched and would be arriving soon. Aaron Talbot had already taken possession of the knife, and his report would be waiting for Stuart when he brought Colleen in for questioning.

The woman didn't strike him as a psychotic mastermind, but she'd covered her tracks expertly, left no real evidence at the scene. The ploy with the knife absolutely amazed him, and he knew only blind luck had given her away. If Rachel hadn't made a habit of having her guests fetch bottles of water, he never would have found the damned butcher's block or the recognizable design of the handles jutting from it.

Though solving the case did nothing to alleviate the nausea and ache of sleeplessness, it still proved comforting. A murder of passion was no less awful than any other murder, but at least it made sense.

Inside the Taylor house, he found Ballard in the living room on the left of the foyer. Colleen Taylor sat with her hands folded in her lap on the sofa. She gazed at the carpet expressionlessly.

When Stuart stepped into the room, the woman's head whipped up and her eyes locked on him. She leaped to her feet and said, "Him. I'll talk to him."

Stuart recoiled from the display, finding himself suddenly off guard.

"You'll talk to both of us," Ballard said.

"No," Colleen said. "I'll tell Stuart Lancaster whatever he wants to know, but not with you in the house. You get out."

Ballard shook his head. "You don't seem to understand how this game works."

"Of course I do, detective," Colleen said. "It's *my* game."

"We have…"

"You don't have shit," Colleen spat. "You can't connect me to one fucking thing, but I'll make it easy for you. So easy. I just need a few minutes alone with him, and then you both can celebrate a job well done. Now, do we play my game or do I call my lawyer and sit my ass back down?"

"Nice language," Ballard said.

"Hey," Stuart said. "Give it a rest, Ballard. Nothing that happens here is going to change our case. Just wait outside until the wagon gets here."

Ballard shot a perplexed look at Stuart. Grudgingly, the towering detective stomped out of the room, shaking his head. The front door slammed.

"What a big baby," Colleen said.

"Colleen, you have about two minutes to tell me what's on your mind. Once the cruiser arrives, we'll have to follow protocol, and this kind of interview is not standard procedure. Before we begin, I'm going to read you your rights. I don't want you to think you have to say anything to me."

"This isn't the kind of thing that will make it into a police report, Stuart."

"Everything makes it into a police report." He proceeded to read Colleen her rights and asked if she understood them. Colleen grunted in response. "Do you understand these rights?" he insisted.

"Yes," Colleen hissed. "For fuck's sake, yes. Consider this my confession."

"You're confessing to the murder of your husband Pudge Taylor?"

"Yes. But I want you to know why it happened." Colleen paused. She began to pace in the narrow alley between the sofa and the cocktail table. She threw a look at the table and Stuart saw her visibly tremble before turning away. "He molested our daughter. Our Ella. It went on for three years; from the time she was thirteen until she turned sixteen."

Stuart considered what he'd already uncovered about Pudge Taylor's sexual practices, and the accusation, while certainly repellent, wasn't surprising. A lot of twisted fucks brought their sickness home. It didn't excuse Colleen Taylor's actions, and for all Stuart knew, she'd discovered the same information about Pudge's indiscretions and was using them to build a sympathetic defense, but to the best of Stuart's knowledge, none of Winston's client's names had leaked to the media.

"And how long did you know about this?" Stuart asked.

"I found out a few days before I killed him."

"And how did you come by this information?"

"Ella told me."

"Ella?" he asked, cautiously. His mouth went dry and tremors ran uncomfortably through his muscles.

"Yes, Stuart. My daughter."

"Colleen, she's been dead for over three years."

"I'm aware of that."

"If you intend to build an insanity plea, I'd suggest…"

"Times wasting, Stuart," Colleen shouted, flapping her arms once like a bird. "Ella told me you'd understand. She told me you'd believe me because you'd seen things yourself. Because you'd seen your wife. *Have* you seen your wife, Stuart?"

He looked at the floor as if the answer whirled in the pattern of the travertine marble. "My personal life has nothing…"

"Time is wasting," Colleen cried again. "My daughter was butchered. Your wife was butchered. And now they're back, but instead of taking out their fury on the two fuckers that murdered them, they're coming after us. Does that make sense? Is it even logical?"

"Colleen, you have to calm down."

"Don't you understand? It *is* logical if what we did to them was worse than what those butchers did."

"Nothing could have been worse than what Baxter and Thomason did to those people."

"You're a fool, Stuart Lancaster" Colleen said. "We betrayed them. Their trust. Their love. Pudge raped our daughter and I didn't want to see it happening. I refused to see Ella's pain. And she is right, I am every bit as much to blame as that cocksucking husband of mine. Andy did them a favor. Andy took their pain away."

"Andy?"

"What did you do to your wife, Stuart?"

"Did Ella talk about Andy?"

"What did you do to your wife?"

"I'm done here," Stuart said quietly. "I'm… done. You can give your statement at the station."

"She won't rest. She won't stop. She'll take her pound of flesh."

"That's enough, now," Stuart said, straining with every cell of his body to remain calm. He turned away from the woman. He would get Ballard back inside, and his partner could deal with the ravings of the widow. Behind him, Colleen Taylor started to laugh hysterically, a shrill insane sound that hit Stuart's eardrums like needles. "Enough," he whispered. He repeated the word endlessly as he walked to the front door, hoping it would be loud enough to drown out Colleen's cackling, but of course it was merely a distraction and didn't mask her hysterics in the least.

He opened the front door and waved for Ballard to join him. A noise at his back sent him spinning, and Stuart watched Colleen dash across the foyer to a door. Her shrill giggles grew dense in the confines of the room before the door slammed shut to cut off the sound completely.

"She went rabbit," Ballard said, hurrying across the foyer to the door.

"It's a bathroom," Stuart told him. "No exit to the exterior of the house."

"Should we break it in?"

"No," Stuart said. "Let her cool down until backup arrives. She isn't going anywhere."

A single gunshot followed the statement, punctuating and confirming Stuart's claim. The report hit him like a bolt of electricity, short-circuiting what remained of his rational thought.

David Ballard ran to the bathroom door and began pulling on the knob. He pounded on the door, but did he expect the dead woman to answer?

Stuart turned away from the scene and peered into the Taylor's living room. In the room beyond it, Clarissa stood in profile, like a defiled statue adorning the distant chamber. Everything about the posture radiated contempt. Even her wounds were accusatory. His skin tightened uncomfortably. Otherwise, he remained unfazed. His exhausted system simply couldn't take any more.

Hello, honey, he thought bemused. *Having a nice day*?

His mind had had enough. Without a word to Ballard, Stuart walked out of the house. He climbed into his car. He felt dizzy, and a buzzing sound rattled in his head, and the landscape around him smeared into an abstract of browns, grays, and greens. He drove away, ignoring his partner, who called and waved from the threshold of the Taylor's house.

29

When Melanie met Hannah Bolger, her first impression was one of discomfort. The striking woman, with her tight helmet of gray hair and her flowing white tunic over tan slacks made of a rough cotton fabric stared down on Melanie with a barely concealed smirk and hard, disapproving eyes. Hannah's big hand wrapped around Melanie's, engulfed it for a tense moment, then was quickly withdrawn.

Eclectic mixes of furniture and art adorned the house. A new sofa, covered in an earthy green fabric sat beside an ancient brown leather recliner with most of the corners worn through. Brightly colored paper fans, cheap landscape prints in wooden frames, and Native American dream catchers hung beside African-inspired ceremonial masks and a series of framed postcards. Pungent incense hung thickly in the air, assaulting Melanie's nose with the dueling scents of jasmine, pine, and patchouli.

Stuart had arrived before her and sat with a drink in his hand. He introduced the two women, and Melanie noted the detective's advanced exhaustion. Slumped down in one of Hannah Bolger's armchairs, he looked beaten and worse; he looked scared.

"What happened?" she asked.

"Stuart thinks he's solved our mystery," Hannah said, "but he wouldn't explain a thing until you arrived." She turned from Melanie to the detective. "And now, she's here, so why don't you tell us what you've found?"

"We're not safe," Stuart said into his glass before emptying the contents. "Nowhere near safe."

"Oh for Pete's sake," Hannah said. She sighed loudly like a mother frustrated with her child. "What are you talking about, Stuart?"

"You said it yourself. Remember? After you heard about Pudge Taylor, you thought his murder was somehow connected to Alan's death. Well I think you're right. I also think both are connected to Richard's death and an attack on Roy Dermott."

"Who is Roy Dermott?" Hannah asked.

"He's a young guy, used to date Charles Whiting. Whiting's stepfather tried to kill him the day after Colleen Taylor took a knife to her husband's back."

The cold description of the crime needled Melanie, who still stood at the edge of the living room. She crossed her arms over her chest, noticing that Hannah had made the exact same gesture next to her.

"Colleen killed Pudge?" Hannah's voice trembled.

"Yeah," Stuart said. "Solved two mysteries today. Time to celebrate." He pushed himself from the chair and crossed the living room to a low table. He lifted a bottle of whiskey and filled the rocks glass in his hand. "Colleen murdered Pudge because Ella returned from the grave to say Pudge had molested her. Now, here's the kicker… he probably did. While investigating his murder, I discovered that Pudge frequented a particular service here in town, a sort of traveling kiddie brothel."

"You're saying the apparition had an actual conversation with Colleen Taylor?" Melanie couldn't believe it. This sort of manifestation was unlike any she'd encountered before.

"You need to put your excitement away," Stuart said sharply. "Whatever you thought you knew about ghosts and spirits and shit? It's wrong. These things aren't residual energy. They're not lost souls. They have a purpose, and they are pissed off."

"Maybe each soul has a different purpose," Hannah said. "There's no reason to believe that they're all malevolent. I mean it's perfectly understandable that Ella would seek justice for what Pudge did to her, and though he certainly did nothing wrong, Richard's relationship with his daughter was hardly a happy one."

"Maybe," Stuart conceded, "but so far, the numbers don't support your theory. Alan is dead. Richard and Pudge are dead. Colleen Taylor is dead; she killed herself this afternoon after confessing to me. So we have five bodies—if we count Wally Pepper —presumably all the result of these visitations. Who did Alan hurt? What the hell could Roy Dermott have done to deserve to be attacked?"

"But you're forgetting something," Hannah told him.

"What's that?"

"Ben," Hannah said.

"Who's Ben?" Melanie asked.

"My husband," Hannah said. "He's been here and it wasn't to threaten me. It certainly wasn't to kill me."

"They don't kill anyone," Stuart said. "They have other people do it. Ella had her mother kill her father. Regina Wolcroff sent her ex-boyfriend to kill Richard. Apparently being dead for a few years has taught them what buttons to push."

"It doesn't always work that way," Melanie said. Both Stuart and Hannah cast hard-edged looks her way. She understood. She was an outsider, never having shared their pain.

"You mean Alan?" Stuart said.

"Yes."

"Bullshit," Hannah chirped, her tone in counterpoint to the word. The sound was so joyous, it startled Melanie, who turned to the surprising woman. "Bullshit, bullshit. You can't talk someone into killing himself. You simply can't. Alan was a very sick man," Hannah said.

"Well, you've certainly changed your tune," Stuart said. "When you heard about Pudge you…"

"I know very well how I was," Hannah said. "That was before Ben. That was before we knew our loves were coming back. I refuse to believe they mean us any harm, not all of them at any rate. You make it sound like they were simply waiting for the chance to get revenge on us, and I am not cynical enough to believe that."

"Cynical or not…" Melanie began, but was cut short by Hannah.

The woman spun on her like a lynx. "I am not interested in your opinion, young lady. This hardly concerns you. You didn't lose anyone to those savages. You run a little ghost program, making fools of innocent people who just want the chance to believe their loved ones aren't gone forever. You take their hope and crush it. And what gives you the right? What right do you have to make a joke out of their loss? Their loneliness?"

"I don't…"

"I am not finished!"

Melanie stepped back. Hannah was in a rage, and she didn't know the woman well enough to anticipate exactly how far her anger would take her.

"Hannah," Stuart said, weakly.

But she didn't even look at him. Her attention and fury were for Melanie. "You proclaim to being some kind of expert in the paranormal, but you don't know any more than we do. You probably know less. Do you have any idea what these souls feel? Do you know what they've seen?"

"No, b-but…" Melanie stammered.

"No, you *don't*, because you spend all of your time trying to convince yourself they don't exist, or if they do exist, you're intent on driving them away."

"That's enough," Melanie said.

"It most certainly is not enough."

"Yes, it is. You don't know me or what I believe. I haven't been in your god damn house for five minutes and you've decided you know me? Well, you don't and the more you bellow at me the more foolish you look. I'm not trying to debunk these visitations, and I'm not trying to exorcise them. I simply want to experience them and understand them, if that's even possible. Now, you think the souls of your loved ones have come back with good intentions. Stuart has very solid reason to believe they haven't, and based on the body count, I'm more likely to agree with him right now, but like you said, this isn't about me. I didn't know any of the victims of Baxter or Thomason, so I'm removed from it. I can be objective, but if Stuart is right, you'd better start working out some plans to protect yourselves."

"Protect myself? From my Ben?"

"No," Stuart said. "From whomever Ben sends to kill you."

Melanie noted that Stuart was beginning to slur his words. She had no idea how much he'd had to drink before she'd arrived, but his eyelids were at half-mast, and he looked like he might keel over with exhaustion or inebriation at any moment.

"Ben loves me," Hannah whispered, sounding shocked by Stuart's words.

A deep silence blossomed in the room. Melanie felt it spread in the wake of Hannah's claim. It seemed to ripple through the air, buffeting Melanie's face and chest like a dry wind. The three looked at each other and then away. Hannah touched her cheek and slid her hand upward to push a thatch of hair away from her temple. All but engulfed by the thickly cushioned armchair, Stuart appeared diminished and weak. He sipped from his drink.

The silence passed when Stuart pushed himself out of the chair and set his drink on the small wooden table next to it. "Well, this was a great idea. Glad I thought of it."

"Where are you going?" Melanie asked.

"Back to the hotel."

"You're not going anywhere," Hannah said. She crossed the room and grasped Stuart at the shoulder and elbow as if leading an invalid. "You can barely walk."

"I can manage a ten minute drive," Stuart said, twisting himself out of Hannah's grasp. "I can't think straight, and I'm getting pissed off. I'm not going to be any good to anyone tonight. We'll regroup in the morning. I have some paperwork to finish up at the station tomorrow and then I'm taking a few days off so we can focus on all of this." He stopped next to Melanie. The mingling odors of sweat and whiskey rolled off of him, overpowering the dense scent of potpourri. "Hannah, regardless of your opinions on this matter, I want you to put together a list of the people who attended your counseling group, and I'd like you to consider calling them to find out if they're experiencing what we are. I'd do it myself, but you know these people better than I do. They're more likely to talk to you."

Hannah nodded. "I spoke with several of them at Alan's funeral. I'll find out what I can, but I don't want you harassing them or scaring them."

Stuart didn't reply to this. Instead he turned to Melanie. "Did you get a room at the Majestic?"

"Yes," she said, "I'll drive you back."

"I'll be fine."

"I'm sure that's true," Melanie told him. "But since I have to go back there myself and even cops can do time for vehicular manslaughter, I think you'd better let me drive."

"Manslaughter," Stuart muttered with amusement. "They'd be lucky to make a reckless driving charge stick."

"Which changes nothing for the guys bleeding out on the pavement. I'll drive."

Melanie turned on the ignition. Through the side window, beyond Stuart's head, she saw Hannah Bolger standing at her front room window. The intimidating woman held back the curtain with a hand and stared across her lawn at them.

"Is she always so intense?" Melanie asked.

"No," Stuart replied. "No, she's not, which is why I wanted to get the fuck out of there."

Melanie pulled the SUV away from the curb. "I didn't mean to upset her," she said at the corner.

"Hmmm?" Stuart asked drowsily. "Mmm. It wasn't you. The second I stepped into that place, my skin started tightening up. I figured it was another side effect of being awake for a few days straight."

"But you think there's something else going on there?"

"I don't know. Yes. I don't know."

Melanie had more questions but she kept them to herself, allowing Stuart to drift off in the passenger seat. At the hotel, the valet took her car, and she helped Stuart up the steps, through the lobby, and into the elevator. In his room, Stuart's disorientation seemed to worsen. He stumbled over the threshold, and Melanie grasped tightly to him, keeping him from taking a nasty fall, but Stuart fought her grip and tried to spin away from it. This resulted in his shoulder knocking into the open closet door. He recoiled from the collision and backpedaled several steps, taking him into the middle of the room, where he teetered for several seconds before regaining his balance. He looked around with wide eyes, confused and concerned as if he'd just woken surrounded by armed thugs. Melanie's heart kicked at her ribcage when the detective drew his gun.

"How did I get here?" he asked. "What the fuck is going on?"

Terrified by the weapon in Stuart's hand, Melanie stayed in the alcove. She'd never faced a gun before, and if she could get this one out of her face, she'd feel considerably better. The door to the hotel's hallway was at her back. To her left the open closet door ceased its rattle, and beside her right shoulder the bathroom door stood open. Stuart was hallucinating, and she didn't know if this could evolve into violence, or if he would soon clear himself of it. Whatever the case, the man held a gun, and Melanie mentally ran through scenarios, all of which were designed to get a door between herself and the provisional lunatic in the middle of the room.

"Stuart," she said, calmly. "You're in your hotel room. I brought you back from Hannah's. Do you remember that?"

"I…" he said. He spun on his heels as if expecting an attack from behind. When he turned back to face Melanie, the wild look was gone from his eyes. His face fell into a mask of exhausted despondence. His shoulders relaxed and he holstered the pistol. "Shit. I was dreaming or hallucinating. We were in the car talking, and then… then, I was in the basement of the house on Ash Street." He began to unbutton his shirt as if he were alone in the room. "Baxter and Thomason had me tied to a chair. They were filming while they tortured me, and Clarissa was there. She stood behind the camera, grinning like a kid getting a bar of chocolate, like nothing could please her more than watching me hurt." He slid his shoulder holster off and hung it from the edge of a chair. A moment later, he peeled off his cotton shirt, revealing the thick hair that ran over his muscular chest. "I could hear the hiss of the camera, like it was old and still spooled film, but it was a new digital model like the one I have at home. And I could hear Clarissa giggling like a little girl." He unfastened his belt and the button on his slacks. After unzipping the fly he shed the trousers without the slightest hint of modesty.

A sudden flush warmed Melanie's face, and she averted her eyes, looking first at the neatly made bed, and then away at the armoire, which the hotel used as an entertainment center. Stuart still slurred his words, still looked dazed, but he had shelved the crazy for the time being.

He walked around the bed, pulled the covers back, and fell onto the crisp white linen. He didn't pull the sheet up to cover himself, but rather lay there exposed, wearing nothing but a pair of white briefs. "Clarissa knows I don't want her to come back," Stuart said. He closed his eyes. "Never want her to come back. I'm glad she's gone," he muttered. "Let her stay wherever she is. Glad… she's…"

A deep breath eased from his lips, and he fell asleep. Melanie crossed to the bed and looked down at the weary detective. She didn't even know the man, not really, yet she felt close to him, as if the unnatural events of the last day had joined them. She combed her fingers gently through his hair.

She turned away, and then left the room.

Melanie's room was two floors down. It looked exactly like Stuart's room, which wasn't surprising; neither was the red light blinking on her phone, greeting her as she entered the room. Mack and Kee would be in town by now. For all she knew they were drinking martinis in the hotel bar below, or sharing a joint in one of its rooms. She knew she couldn't avoid them forever, and knew that from a career standpoint, it wasn't a brilliant plan to try, but still she wasn't ready for their union of bullshit just yet. Instead, she needed some time to quietly digest the day—her visit with Mike Addison and the disastrous meeting at Hannah Bolger's house. Using the mini coffee maker, she set up a pot to brew and went to the window.

The view was pleasant enough, strings of lights spreading away from the hotel like a jeweled net placed over dark earth. A teacup moon hung above, and Melanie smiled humorlessly remembering what her aunt always said about them: You never know what kind of shit is going to spill out of a cup that size.

Shit is right, she thought. Michael Addison was clearly trouble, and Stuart seemed as close to a breakdown as any man she'd ever met. Some real sleep would restore his perspective, but she couldn't help but picture him wild-eyed and waving a gun at hallucinated monsters. He didn't even have the comfort of telling himself the monsters weren't real.

Melanie still didn't know what to make of Hannah Bolger. She couldn't say she hated the woman, who'd come off as rude and inexplicably aggressive, hardly the former-hippie her house's décor suggested, but she didn't trust the woman. Hannah's belief that her husband's spirit had returned with only the warmest intentions ran counter to what Stuart had found, and even if she hadn't experienced real threat from the specter, she shouldn't have written Stuart off so casually.

The visitations were changing them, Melanie knew, damaging them. What must it do to your head to spend years mourning and weaving acceptable explanations to yourself, only to have the focus of your grief return and undo all of your hard fought coping mechanisms? In his dazed state, Stuart had said he was glad his wife, Clarissa, was gone. Had he meant that? Had Clarissa been a bitter, manipulative shrew? Had she cheated on him? Or had he simply found her an aggravation after so many years of marriage? Clarissa had visited Stuart, but what had her spirit wanted?

Melanie listened to the messages on the hotel system and her cell phone. Yes, Mack and Kee were in Barnard, but they were staying at a hotel closer to the Regina Wolcroff sighting. Melanie was relieved to hear it. At least there was no chance of running into them in the hotel elevator. Yvonne called, saying she would be along tomorrow, and Reg called half a dozen times, wanting to know where she was. As it happened, he *was* in the hotel bar, seven flights below, waiting for her to return. She considered ignoring his calls, letting him wait for another hour, maybe two, so she could focus on the mystery before her, but she didn't.

She left the room, rode the elevator down, emerged into the lobby, and crossed to the bar. A large television over the racks of alcohol showed a baseball game, which none of the clientele seemed to be watching, but she didn't find Reg. She surveyed the lobby and off of the main room she saw a plaque that read: Restaurant and Lounge. She found Reg inside the lounge, sitting on a stool, a near empty pilsner of beer before him. A good-sized crowd drank in low club chairs, booths, and at the bar. Couples and groups of businesspeople chatted in the dimly lighted space, flickering candlelight playing over the screens of their faces. At the end of the bar, three seats down from Reg, a burly little man with a van dyke leaned over the bar and threw back a shot of whiskey. Melanie paused to notice the man, because she found him oddly attractive and because he looked thoroughly wound up, as if a single word, even one as innocuous as "hello" could set him off.

She took the barstool next to Reg and leaned forward for a kiss, and then he listened closely, smiling, frowning, and nodding in all of the right places as she recounted the events of her day, and more than once, she marveled at the idea that little more than twenty-four hours had passed since she'd left him in the living room of their house in Louisiana. Every so often, she gazed over Reg's shoulder at the wound up man, the way his foot tapped a manic rhythm while perched on the barstool footrest, the way one hand clutched his glass and the other tapped nervously on the bar. His agitation was contagious, needling her.

"Let's take a walk," Melanie suggested.

"I'm beat," Reg said. "The drive wore me out, and even though I've been sitting here for two hours, I'm not exactly craving exercise."

"Did you come out with Mack and Kee?"

"They flew."

"And they made you drive?"

"They didn't make me do anything. They didn't even want me to come, but I figured I should run interference for you." He sipped his drink. "I also know about the Scotland deal. Sounds like they're streamlining."

Melanie tried to find accusation in Reg's voice but there wasn't any. "I should have told you before I left."

"You were in a hurry. I don't blame you. You had a very short window before those douchebags swooped in and turned everything here into shit, and it sounds like you made the most of it. All we have to do now is keep Kee and Mack away from your cop friend and that Hannah woman. I'll do what I can to give you the space you need, but Mack is ready to sink his teeth deep, so I may not have much luck."

"They're planning to interview the families of the Baxter-Thomason killings?"

"Oh yeah." Reg took another drink. "I could hear Mack popping a hard on when he heard about that Wolcroff guy getting killed. He wants to see if the other survivors are afraid, or more accurately wants the audience to see it. Just more sex and violence as far as he's concerned."

"Mack is going to look like a ghoul."

"Oh, but that's not all," Reg said. He hoisted his glass and downed the remains of his beer. "In an effort to be completely dense and perverse, tomorrow Kee is going to try getting a permit for us to film in the house."

"It's just a burned out shell with a basement. There is no house."

"The basement is all Kee's interested in."

"They'll never give him the permits," Melanie said, realizing it was based more in wishful thinking than any knowledge of the matter. "It's a death trap."

"Ah, but think of the ratings." Reg slid his glass across the bar and draped his arms on Melanie's shoulders. "Don't sweat it. I'll break Kee's legs before I let him send you in there."

"Caveman protect woman."

"Always."

Unfortunately, this was exactly what Kee and Mack wanted. If Melanie refused to play their game, Mack would get all the screen time. Soon enough, they'd push her out, the way they were trying to freeze out Yvonne and Reg, and everything Melanie had worked for would be taken away. The worst part was those assholes knew it; either way, they won. She had no choice but to go into the basement on Ash Street, unless she was willing to let the show completely slip through her fingers.

30

Stuart woke to a disturbing silence. Some silences are pleasant, like the kind experienced when sitting in a boat, floating on a quiet lake and caressed by the lightest of breezes, so gentle it wouldn't even whisper in the trees, but this silence was not one of those. This silence was more like drifting to the bottom of that serene lake. Last breath gone. Lungs saturated with water. Heartbeat eternal seconds in the past. Though genuinely rested for the first time in days, Stuart felt agitated, and he rolled out of the bed, checked his watch, winced at the lateness of the morning and continued into the bathroom. After relieving his bladder, he called room service and ordered a pot of coffee, then he climbed into a hot shower and stood motionless under the needling spray until the worst of the restlessness steamed out of his muscles. He didn't remember how he'd gotten back to the hotel, though he remembered (or had dreamed about) Melanie standing in the room wearing a fearful expression.

He ran the soap over his body and remained in the shower longer than usual, feeling a sense of comfort under the pelting water, knowing the comfort was transient and hardly genuine to begin with. While scrubbing his feet, it occurred to him that he had yet to receive any cuts, no letter A, identifying him as a target of Andy's (or Clarissa's or whatever the fuck was calling the shots) on his foot. He knew Richard had carried the wounds, and Pudge had had them. What about Hannah? Stuart rinsed the sole of his foot and wondered if he'd managed to escape targeting, or if he'd just made it more difficult for the spirit to leave its mark.

After drying himself and dressing, his cell phone rang. The call was from Harlan, the fourth in the last twenty-four hours, and like those other calls, Stuart let it ring through to voice mail.

"Not this morning, buddy," Stuart said, tossing the phone on the bed.

Room service arrived five minutes later and Stuart guzzled two small cups of coffee, then decided to take the rest of the carafe with him to work. He was going to catch hell from his captain for Colleen Taylor's suicide and his subsequent disappearance from the scene yesterday afternoon. His superiors would never understand that he'd been crazy from lack of sleep (*Because my dead wife wants to have a come to Jesus with me*), nor could he be expected to create a functional script for the private conversation he'd carried on with Colleen two minutes before she cleaned out her skull with a high caliber handgun. It was all too fucking crazy. Then the strange scene at Hannah's, of which he remembered little save for a desperate need to be out of her house and away because the woman wasn't acting like herself—nowhere near herself, actually—and the apparent change in her personality, which might have been nothing more than Stuart's considerably altered perception of events, had scared the hell out of him.

You've spent way too much time scared lately, he told himself.

He knew he *had* been scared, and it had affected his job and his interactions in unacceptable ways, perhaps even irrevocably damaging ways. Further, he knew it was time to put scared away and start thinking smart, because he believed there really were monsters in Barnard, and while some of them were flimsy-essence mementoes of the living, the others were flesh-and-bone human, armed and angry.

Leaving the room, he reminded himself to call Hannah to get the list of names from her grief management group and see if she'd had any success in contacting them once he was done having his ass gnawed through by Captain Gann. With any luck the paperwork on the Taylor case would only take a few hours, then Stuart could request leave—if Gann hadn't already filed paperwork to have him suspended—and focus on the ghosts of Ash Street.

He didn't want to hear what Clarissa had to say. He'd indulge the spirit if necessary; endure that vile revenant tongue for however long it took the venom to milk from it. If it would bring his wife's spirit peace, he'd listen, but if she intended to exact revenge for his perceived injustices against her, then he would do everything in his power to drive her soul back to whatever afterlife it had seeped from.

Hannah called as Stuart stood in front of the hotel, wondering where he'd parked his car.

"Good morning, Hannah." He looked up and down the block, holding the room service carafe in his hand, trying to spot the misplaced vehicle.

"Stuart," she said. Her voice was clipped.

"How are you?"

"Just checking to make sure you made it back to the hotel in one piece."

"Fine," he said. Hannah's arctic tone reminded him of the scene in her living room the night before, and he again felt the need to distance himself from the woman. If he hadn't needed information, he would have found an excuse to end the call. "I was going to call you from the station," Stuart said. "We need to discuss the other members of the group, and I can call up more names from the case file, until we have a functional list. Then we can make some calls and see if anyone else is experiencing what we are."

"How's your little friend?" Hannah asked.

"Friend?" It took him a moment to realize she meant Melanie Bell. Of course, that's why he couldn't find his car. The young woman had driven him home. Stuart's car remained in front of Hannah Bolger's house.

"Coy is new for you."

"Sorry, I'm still a bit out of it," Stuart said. "I guess she's fine. I haven't seen her yet this morning."

"I'm sure she'll sniff you out."

He knew what Hannah was implying. She wasn't even attempting subtlety, but Stuart wasn't going to let his first conversation of the day turn into an argument. Hannah was wrong, and she probably knew it as well as he did.

"About that list," he said, "could you email me a copy? You have my work address, right?"

"I have it," Hannah said.

"Great. I'll be at the station until mid-afternoon, and then the rest of the week should be freed up."

"Lovely," she said.

Her tone was sarcastic and edged with annoyance. He didn't know what was happening to the woman, but seeing the ghost of her dead husband must have given her an emotional jolt, leaving her less than civil, and he decided that any future meetings would be held away from her house and its discomforting vibe. She wasn't seeing things clearly, and Stuart knew she needed to be protected. He simply didn't know how to manage that if she wasn't willing to see the threat.

"Okay," he said to break the cold silence. "I'll call you after I get done, and we'll figure out our next steps."

"Goodbye, Stuart."

"Yeah, Hannah. Bye."

Stuart returned the cell phone to his pocket and then turned back for the hotel. He climbed the stairs and entered the lobby, approaching the front desk to have them call a cab.

Hannah set the phone on her kitchen table and leaned back in her chair. Ben stroked her hair, his touch as soft as feathers; it felt wonderful and right. She preferred not looking at him. As much as she loved his face and body, she favored not seeing the damage he had endured; this way she could pretend he'd never been taken away, enjoying his presence without the terrible burden of seeing his wounds.

"They think you want to hurt me," Hannah said.

"They're afraid."

"I'm not afraid," Hannah said, rolling her head beneath Ben's delicate touch.

"Why should you be?"

"Where do you go when you leave?" Hannah asked.

The fingers left her hair. "I don't know," Ben told her. "Other houses. Other rooms. Blank spaces without décor."

"You should stay with me."

"I am with you."

"But really stay."

"There's too much to do."

Hannah laughed. Ben's voice had climbed into a higher register, thinned out so he sounded like he was impersonating a particularly shrill woman. "What are you doing with your voice?" she asked, still giggling.

The soft-as-feather touch returned to her hair. Hannah breathed deeply and lost herself in the sensation.

31

Mike woke in the middle of the night to the sound of Dory whispering in the darkness, and though he tried to find her shape in the room, he saw only shadows on shadows, none with a distinct form. She spoke his name and told him how much nicer it would be if he left his life behind and joined her in the afterlife, but for all of the dread of the experience, he didn't once entertain the notion of finding a new bottle of pills or a fresh razor blade. He felt no guilt when Dory said, "You should have been watching, Mik-Mik," because the accusation didn't come from his sister; it came from a third party, a fucked up spirit that manipulated its shape and its voice. The thing scared the hell out of Mike, but he didn't owe it remorse or self-flagellation. He didn't owe the thing with Dory's face one damn thing.

When morning came, Mike had already decided to talk about what he'd experienced, but he wasn't going to fish Melanie Bell's rumpled business card out of his wallet and spill his guts to her. No, he decided to tell Gwen, or more accurately to show her exactly why he'd been acting so strangely since his grandfather's death. If Gwen saw the creature with her own eyes, then he could tell her about the pills and the razor and explain why his world had become one fucked up and constricting knot.

After having spent the entire day trying to get the words out and failing either from uncertainty or because Evan was tagging along, he finally cornered Gwen in the halls before their last class, tried to convince Gwen to ditch their friend after school and go into town with him. It was important.

"I'd really feel better if you didn't ask me any questions," Mike said.

"Questions about what?" asked Gwen. "You haven't told me anything."

"You just kind of have to take my word for it, and I don't want Evan coming with us."

"Mike, you know I'll go with you, but you have to give me some idea what this is all about."

"I don't know, exactly," he said. He felt cornered and the urge to drop the whole matter hit him suddenly. But no, he had to get this shit out of his head, and if he was lucky, Gwen would see the entity, and it would all be easier to talk about. So he had to tell her something. "You know that woman who was on the news—the one everyone is calling a ghost?"

"It's all over the Internet and TV. Half the kids have it as wallpaper on their phones now."

"Right, well it got me to thinking a lot about my sister and granddad and I just need to talk about a few things. That's why I don't want Evan around because he's always joking, and if he cracks a joke about this, I'll dummy up."

Gwen's face lost its quizzical look and softened. She appeared proud as if he'd chosen her for a special award, and though Mike thought it was an odd response, at least she wasn't looking at him like somebody else had just died.

"Sure," she said softly. "And I won't say anything to Evan."

Mike began feeling sick about the plan only a few seconds after Gwen left him by a wall of lockers. He didn't know what he was going to say. It could be hours before that creature showed up, if it showed up at all. He'd have to find something to fill the time or else Gwen would think he was being a freak. Unable to concentrate during his last class, he focused on the clock, ticking like a timebomb on the wall, counting down the seconds to his humiliation. When the bell finally rang, Mike rose from his chair slowly, and again he felt a commanding urge to drop the matter, to sneak out of school and walk home, avoiding Gwen and the complicated story he had to tell her.

Again though, he chastised himself. He would talk to her. He had to talk to someone.

Gwen drove and Mike gazed out the passenger window, resting his head on the glass and watching the landscape roll by. He'd suggested they go to Brown Street for coffee, though that was a ruse, meant to get Gwen in the general area of the destination. There was nothing on the section of Galveston Drive except for old apartment buildings and run down houses, so he couldn't suggest it as a location without a complicated lie.

He wouldn't call it luck, but as soon as Gwen turned onto Brown Street, Mike discovered all of the excuse he needed for them to drive on. News vans took up half a dozen parking spaces along two blocks of the shopping district. Knots of people gathered on the sidewalks, many of them speaking into microphones held by well-groomed and well-dressed correspondents. As the scene of the woman in yellow's appearance, Brown Street had taken on the air of a street fair. Everywhere he looked, people were snapping pictures and pointing excitedly.

"Ugh," Gwen said. "I was worried about this."

"You knew this was going on?"

"Everyone knows this is going on. Don't you watch the news?"

"I was a little distracted yesterday," Mike said.

"Just yesterday?" Gwen teased. When Mike didn't respond she said, "Everyone at school was buzzing about the ghost. People were texting stupid crap like 'Boo!' and 'the dead are rising.' Really dumb. There was still a lot of it today, especially since the story went national. It was everywhere last night, and not just on the web, but on the news, too."

"Are you serious?" Mike asked. "Because of one picture?"

"Yes, I'm serious," Gwen said. "But it's not just the picture. It's all of the eyewitnesses. I mean it happened right here in broad daylight and nobody can figure out how it could be a hoax. Some experts on TV said it was mass hysteria, like a group hallucination, but that's just stupid."

"So you really think she was a ghost?" Mike asked, hoping he'd found a way to broach the subject of Dory and the thing that had stolen her face.

"No," Gwen said. She laughed and shook her head. "Come on. No way. I don't know, maybe."

"Go on up to Reichart and turn left," he said.

"You have another place in mind?"

"Yeah, just head on up. We'll never get into Porter's with all of this going on." He rolled his forehead against the cold glass and closed his eyes. "They aren't ghosts," he muttered. The words surprised him. He hadn't intended to say anything about this yet.

"What?"

The simple phrase had dropped from his lips and now it pulled a string of words out with it like an anchor leading a chain. Mike couldn't stop them. "Dory came back. My sister. I thought she was haunting me, trying to get me to hurt myself, but it isn't her. It's something else, the same thing that everyone saw on Brown Street, only it looked different then, but it's the same because I followed it to Galveston Drive and it changed into someone else."

The car swerved in the road, but Gwen managed to straighten the wheels before driving onto the curb. "What the hell?"

Mike breathed deeply and began telling her what had been happening to him since his grandfather's death. Occasionally he paused in the story to give Gwen directions, but he related his experiences with as much detail as he could remember in a clear chronological naming of events. They reached their destination as Mike finished telling Gwen about the night he'd snapped out of his daze to find a razor against his wrist.

"Park here," he said, pointing at an open space at the curb.

"You tried to kill yourself? Twice?"

"I can't explain it very well," Mike said. "I would be in this kind of trance, but I knew what was going on and I wanted it because I felt like shit, like nothing would ever work out and then I'd snap out of it and get scared."

"You've gone through a lot."

"No I haven't," he said. "I mean, no more than what a thousand other people go through. That's the thing. That's what snapped me out of this. None of this was happening to *me*. Dory was murdered. My parents split up. Granddad

Alan was sick. I had nothing to do with those things. There was no cosmic plot to fuck up my life. Bad things happened and would have happened whether I was there or not, but I blamed myself and felt sorry for myself because I kept thinking something—god, the world, whatever—was out to get me, but it wasn't. It was all random, until this thing showed up."

He saw the gentle look of concern on Gwen's face and knew she didn't believe a single thing he'd said. She thought he was as crazy as Granddad Alan had been, insanity just another trait that ran in the family. The sinking feeling in his chest told him he should have waited until they saw the spirit before he tried to explain any of this. Maybe he shouldn't have said anything at all.

Gwen reached out and put her hand on Mike's leg. A tingle of energy ran from her touch, setting his skin alight.

"You think I'm nuts," he said.

"Like I said, you've been through a lot. You're probably just confused right now."

"All of those people on Brown Street weren't confused. That woman they saw? Her name was Regina Wolcroff. She was another victim of the two who murdered Dory."

"You don't know that," Gwen said.

"Can we just sit here?" Mike asked. "Just for a while?"

"Why *are* we here?"

"I'm not sure. This is the last place I saw it. I was on Brown Street the other day when it appeared for its photo-op, and I think it kind of panicked and ran off, I followed. The last place I saw it was on this block. By then it had changed into a normal looking guy, but I couldn't see his face. He walked between two of the houses and disappeared."

"So you think a super-spook is renting a house on Galveston Drive?"

"Thanks for the sarcasm."

"I can see why you didn't want Evan along."

"What's the difference?" Mike said. "I'm still taking a ton of shit."

"Oh come on, Mike," Gwen said. "You're talking about a *thing* that pretends to be a ghost. Several ghosts. It's crazy."

"Look, you've been on my fucking back for weeks, wanting to know what was wrong. Well, *this* is what's wrong. *This* is why I wake up with pills on my tongue. If you want to act like it's all a big fucking joke, go ahead, but I can't."

Gwen turned on the ignition. Jaw set and eyes narrowed to slits, she refused to look at Mike. She didn't even check her mirrors before pulling away from the curb.

"Great," Mike said.

Angry silence rolled off of Gwen in waves as she navigated through town in the direction of his house. He didn't know what to say. Didn't even know if he wanted to say anything. Gwen was supposed to be his friend, and yeah, his story was out there, but it wasn't totally left field. People *had* seen Regina Wolcroff on Brown Street. Her damn picture was on a thousand websites, and she'd been dead for three years. Why was it so impossible for Gwen to believe his story?

She turned onto his street fifteen minutes later and parked in front of his house. She stared out the windshield, hands clasping the steering wheel so tightly it turned her knuckles white.

"So that's it?" Mike asked. "Game over?"

Gwen took a deep breath then sighed loudly. "You need help, Mike. I can't give it to you and I don't want to be around you until you get it. Things are hard enough."

"Yeah, you've got it so tough," Mike challenged.

Gwen whipped her head around to face him. Fury burned on her features and she looked like she'd lunge across the console and start tearing at his face with her fingernails. But the expression was gone a moment later. It melted away, seemingly under its own heat. Gwen's eyes grew wide and her tightened jaw fell open, slack, making a distinct O shape. She looked at Mike and then over his shoulder in the direction of his house, then back at Mike again.

"Shit," she hissed.

Mike turned and saw what Gwen had seen. The sight of it punched him in the chest, took away his breath.

The front door of his house stood open and a man leaned out, staring at the car with an expression of absolute glee. It took Mike a moment to make sense of the face because it was Granddad Alan's face. Mike's thoughts turned into icy streams, draining from his head in a torrent. On the verge of fainting, he pulled away from the car window.

Granddad Alan disappeared inside and slammed the door.

32

The Morgan Hotel, where Kee and Mack had taken rooms, was a serene and sterile boutique hotel at the end of Brown Street, only three blocks from where Regina Wolcroff had made her appearance. Earthy pastels—bleached mint greens, buttery yellows, and sand-beige browns—covered lightly textured walls. Subtle leaf patterns appeared here and there near the corners to suggest a woodsy spa atmosphere, and a hint of green tea deodorizer scented the air. Little placards on the front desk assured customers that The Morgan was a "Green" hotel and if they had any questions as to how they could "Help the Earth, during your stay," they should direct their inquiries to the front desk. The place pulsed with eco-snobbery, but was suitably tranquil, the way most dull things are.

Melanie sat in Kee Ulrich's room, breathing deep of the tea-scent and ground her teeth, while the producer of her show paced on the far side of the bed, excitedly waving his hands to Mack's amusement and Melanie's annoyance. Reg was at the house on Ash Street shooting B-roll for the show. Yvonne would meet him there to give an initial on-camera "Reading" of the property. Melanie was already exhausted. She'd spent most of the day interviewing random pedestrians down on Brown Street, one of whom called her a servant of Satan and fled from her microphone. Looking at Kee, Melanie thought the frantic woman might not have been too far off.

"Mack, that interview with the phone jockey was priceless. He was the only guy smart enough to snap a pic of this thing. Golden ticket shit," Kee said. "His bit about feeling its anger, like the thing was getting inside his head was phenomenal. Creeped me out. Skin-crawling-palm-sweating brilliant. It'll make a terrific tag."

"Every reporter in town has already talked to him," Melanie pointed out. "He's even got a website up and running with twenty-two pages about his experience."

"And we're going to paste that fucking URL all over the screen," Kee said, pointing one of his slender fingers at her. "That's collateral content. We drive visitors to his site and he drives them back to us. I already cleared it with him. He's putting up a major banner on the home page… 'As seen on *The Haunt Club*.'"

"It's a free ride on the Internet," Mack said, coolly, never looking up from his iPhone. "We catch the viral wave and ride it to major web presence. The audience grows. We feed them old episodes and outtakes. They get fat on it and multiply. It's a win-win."

"Fucking right, it is," Kee said. He rubbed his palm over his shiny bald pate and paused his pacing, trading this anxious motion for bouncing on the balls of his feet.

Melanie thought the producer looked like he was about to explode. Maybe that was wishful thinking, but despite her confidence that by the time they actually got the show on the air the story would be stale, Melanie tried to play nice. Save for the reflexive gaff of pointing out how uninteresting the story of the man who'd taken Regina's picture would be, she'd presented herself as a team player, ready to get out there and find a ghost, no matter what the cost. Rah-rah team. It was wholly insincere but necessary. She wanted to keep Kee and Mack focused on the superficial, feed their egos so they didn't get hungry for more substantive content. Their attempts to interview Stuart had failed miserably, because they couldn't reach him, and to the best of her knowledge they hadn't even thought of talking to Mike Addison. Many of the other survivors had moved or unlisted their contact information, which was no surprise considering the media frenzy that had followed the arrest of Selma Baxter and Derek Thomason. Those people wanted to be done with this story, and Melanie hoped they got their wish. So she smiled and nodded and said, "Great idea," when she actually meant, "Dumb ass," and she offered an expression of the sincerest disappointment when Kee returned with the news that the city would not allow them a permit to tape in the Ash Street ruins—though they were more than welcome to shoot from the sidewalk and adjoining yards, with owner permission of course.

"We need the house," Mack said, tapping a button on his phone and setting it down for the first time in an hour. "The shit we've got is cool, but it all revolves around that house. That's what holds the story together."

"No permit," Kee said shaking his head. "Country-fuck locals."

"That's why I'm thinking we go guerilla on this."

A sudden flare of unease erupted in Melanie's stomach.

"We can't take that chance," Kee said.

"It could jeopardize our insurance," Melanie pointed out. "Plus it's illegal."

"We've done it before," Mack said. He leaned forward and gave Melanie a wink before pushing himself from the chair. "Our audition tape? The Berloit Plantation? No authorization. No permits."

"Excuse me?" Melanie said. "We had permission from the owners and the county to be on that property."

"Not exactly."

"I saw them," Melanie said. "They're still on file at the house."

"Yeah, but they weren't exactly authentic," Mack said with a smile. "These new computers are fancy jig-a-ma-thingies. They can do all sorts a stuff."

"You forged documents? Jesus, do you have any idea what they could have done to us?"

"A fine or two. Maybe a night in jail if we couldn't get a lawyer on the line. That's about it, and it was a small chance to take that got us a television show. Besides, that footage never aired."

Though Melanie expected this level of contemptible behavior from Mack, it didn't change the seething in her chest. She dropped back in the chair, silent, biting on the anger to keep Kee and Mack on track and away from the real story.

"You son of a bitch," Kee yelped joyfully. He laughed and rubbed his head again.

"Best believe," Mack said. "Now, here's how this works. The production meeting ends now. Thanks for coming folks. It's been great. Officially, we are off the clock." He paused and checked Melanie and Kee to see if they were bursting with anticipation for what he was about to say. "Now, since there is some minor possibility that our hick hosts actually watch their televisions and one or more might get the idea to press charges, we need to separate ourselves from the show completely. That means we get a new camera that is not owned by our generous producer here, and we use no branded clothing, which is to say none of those fucking Haunt Club polo shirts. This is a private excursion by a couple of civilians out for a whimsical romp. We shoot the program and donate the footage to the show. No network or producer authorization, so no network or producer culpability."

"You're talking about breaking the law," Melanie said, keeping her voice low and even. "Then broadcasting it on national television."

"I'm talking about a minor infraction that may or may not even raise the eyebrows of the local authorities, then broadcasting it to the largest audience in the show's history."

"I can see a lot of problems with this," Kee said.

Melanie looked up at the producer, surprised. It wasn't like Kee to even question a move that could bump ratings. The most outlandish things—the stop-motion car, the popsicle on the thermometer, the shadowy apparition—were his ideas. It seemed nothing was beyond the man, short of having nude models parading around the sites, and he might have spearheaded that idea if he could have figured out a way to get it past the censors.

"As the producer of *The Haunt Club* my primary concern is the safety of my crew," he said. "I can't allow you people to put yourselves at risk for the sake of entertainment. I'm sorry; that's my official stance on this matter."

"Duly noted," Mack said. "But just for clarification… off the record, of course… we're cool?"

"Hell yeah," Kee said. "Get your asses in that house. This is golden ticket shit."

Ash Street

In the hall outside of Kee's room Mack followed Melanie. She was headed back to the Majestic Hotel to meet Reg and Yvonne for dinner and looking forward to spending time in more pleasant company. Mack was returning to his room, his gaze already locked on the screen of his phone.

"So what's the angle?" he asked.

Melanie turned. Mack still looked at the screen. "What are you talking about?"

"All that 'Go Team' shit in there. That's not like you, Mel. It was a good show until you nearly cried when Kee mentioned not getting the permits. A bit of overkill. A bit hammy. So, what's the deal? Why the sudden teamwork routine?"

"I don't know what you're talking about," she said.

"Fine," Mack said with a shrug. "But nobody is interested in your integrity. The camera won't read it, and the audience won't buy it. They don't want that shit. They may want the illusion of it, but they also want to know it's an illusion. The fucking idiots out there in ratings land create their own heroes and their own villains and they build them from the flimsiest shit they can find."

Her cell phone rang and she quickly retrieved it. The name on the ID wasn't familiar, but it was a necessary distraction. She accepted the call.

"Hey…uh…this is Mike," an uncertain voice said. "Mike Addison. You came by my house yesterday, and… I think… well… can we talk?"

Melanie felt Mack at her back, could all but imagine his ears pricking up to catch any useful word or telling phrase. He was such an ass.

"Yes," she told Mike, "but I'll have to call you right back. I'm about to get into an elevator and I don't want to lose the call. Will you be at this number?"

"What?... Yeah, oh yeah… I'll be here."

"Give me five minutes," Melanie said and disconnected.

"I smell an angle," Mack said. He'd stopped in front of the door to his room and was slotting his card key while maintaining his focus on the phone screen. "I'm not bitching, mind you. I've got an angle or two of my own. I'm just saying."

"Duly noted," Melanie said, pressing the elevator's call button.

33

Stuart had expected his workday to end with a bang, but it went out with hardly a whimper. He'd broken regulations in the Taylor case and had failed to return to duty, but he'd also solved the case and when added to his work on the child pandering case, he was, if not wholly untouchable, still bathing in enough glory to keep his ass out of a sling. Captain Gann accepted his request for leave with hardly a shrug, under the stipulation Stuart made himself available to Internal Affairs at their discretion, which he agreed to. The rest of his day had been filled with paperwork and keeping his head down.

Apparently, the picture of Regina Wolcroff's spirit had put blood in the media waters and the sharks were circling. Journalists and television correspondents were all over town. Though not as frenzied as the media attack after Baxter and Thomason had been captured, the reporters were eager. Stuart had walked into a pack of them on his way into the station. At first their presence had confused him, but then he'd attributed their facades of hungry concern to the Taylor case or maybe Richard Wolcroff's murder. But no, that would have been real news, so it wouldn't have whipped them into such a lather. They wanted to talk about Regina Wolcroff's ghost and what it meant to the survivors of Baxter and Thomason's victims. Only the local guy with the *Courant*, Hamilton "Hamster" Stoller, had made any connection between the two cases, and he'd surfed right over it, but word would get out. Someone would put it all together. Stuart was in no rush to help them, so he kept his mouth shut and stayed at the station through lunch.

Now that he was officially off duty, he hesitated to leave. He perused the list Hannah had emailed and hoped she was making progress contacting the people on it. Of course, she was convinced her Ben was an angel returned from heaven, so Stuart didn't expect her to actually warn the families, but maybe she could find out which of them had been contacted.

And that was another reason Stuart preferred to remain in the station, though his shift was well over and his obligation to the service had been put on hiatus—he felt safe here. Of all of the places he could imagine, this was the last where he thought Clarissa would appear.

But he was forced to give up that brittle security approximately two minutes after he took Melanie Bell's phone call. She wanted Stuart to meet her at the hotel. Mike Addison was with her and they needed to talk. Now.

She told Stuart they'd been wrong about everything.

He walked into Melanie's room and was surprised to find five people waiting there. Mike Addison sat on the edge of the bed next to a pretty red-haired girl who looked like she was awaiting punishment. Next to the redhead was an older woman with long blond hair and a dreamy look in her eyes. Her hands were folded in her lap, the tips of her index fingers and thumbs touching as if she were about to start chanting. A man sat in one of the chairs at the desk on the far side of the room. He was stout and balding and reminded Stuart a little of Harlan, though this man was a good twenty years younger than his friend. Seeing the unexpected people made him recall his fortieth birthday party. Clarissa had invited a houseful of guests to surprise him when he opened the door. It had been a surprise to be sure. The night had ended in screaming.

Introductions were made and Stuart took a position against the wall. Melanie returned to the far side of the room and sat down beside the man she'd introduced as Reg. He immediately wrapped an arm around her shoulders and slid his chair closer to hers, telegraphing the fact that their relationship extended beyond their working on the same television program.

After some gentle prodding, Mike began telling his story, and Stuart settled in to listen, wincing when the kid mentioned his little sister and her condemnation as well as her insisting on a fatal penance for his neglect. Each word seemed like it was made of glass and cut the kid's tongue as he released them from his throat. Stuart could relate to the boy's fear and confusion, and whenever Mike spoke about Dory, Stuart's chest tightened painfully, but when Mike described the events that had begun on Brown Street and ended on Galveston Drive, Stuart pulled back from the narrator. One ghost? A single vicious spirit pretending to be all of them? Impossible. He absently shook his head and crossed his arms, taking a pose he generally reserved for interrogating suspects.

Mike noticed and stopped talking. "You don't believe me," he said.

"It just can't be the way you describe it," Stuart said. "Look, each of us has been visited and the details are too specific. When my wife appeared, she knew exactly what words would do the most damage to me. Pudge Taylor's daughter implicated him in her molestation, something no one knew about. We had one victim that was a closet homosexual, and apparently he'd been pretty damn good about keeping his secret, but his ghost tried to have an ex-lover killed. And Mike, you yourself said that no one but Dory called you Mik-Mik, so how did this thing know to call you that? It couldn't have been following all of us for the last ten years gathering information for some monumental mind fuck. It doesn't make sense."

"Right," Mike snapped, "we're talking about ghosts and you want it to make *sense.* I can only tell you what I saw. Okay? I saw this thing looking like Regina one second and the next it looked like some old guy with half his face torn off."

"Maybe it's a concordance," the blonde named Yvonne said. Her voice was light and fuzzy like the buzz of a hummingbird's wings. "Perhaps they came together in death, their souls intertwined and struggling for dominance."

"How in the hell do souls get tangled?" Stuart asked. "That's like trying to make knots out of air."

"It's a theory," Yvonne offered. She shrugged and lowered her chin to gaze at her fingers.

"They're not ghosts," Mike said. "It's something else."

"Something else that knows all about the victims? All about us?" Stuart wasn't buying it.

Melanie interrupted then. Her voice was calm and direct. "We don't know what it is, or what *they* are. But Mike mentioned something interesting before you got here and I'd like to get back to it."

"The doppelganger thing?" Reg asked.

"Right," Melanie said.

"What?" Stuart asked.

"Doubles," Melanie explained. "Historically there have been a number of recorded instances of people seeing themselves across a crowded room or on a city street or right next to them. The double looks identical to them, like it's a copy. Or, have you ever been in a strange city and you were convinced you saw an acquaintance crossing the road ahead of you? But you knew there was no way it could be that person? Popular mythology suggests that the double is generated by the host, but some people think these doppelgangers are spirits or beings that imprint on a person, acquire their appearance and overt mannerisms, but may have malevolent intentions."

"And you think we have a pack of these things running around looking like murder victims?" Stuart asked. Exactly how ridiculous was this conversation going to get?

"No," Melanie said, "I think we could have one that is trying to copy all of them."

"For fuck's sake," Stuart said.

"Breathe deep, detective," Reg said, "that's the easiest part of this particular topic to swallow. Yvonne, bring him up to speed."

The blonde looked around like a child hovering over a present she had been awaiting permission to open. "The doppelganger mythology, in addition to many of the shape shifting legends can be traced back to a particular entity. It has a number of names, but it's considered rare even by occult standards. I've seen them referred to as Moljac and Venants and Hexekind."

"Witch children?" Gwen asked.

"You know German," Yvonne said, giving the girl a light hug. "You really have the prettiest hair. But no. Technically they're not the offspring of witches, but they are considered naïve spirits, easily molded and taught. This in addition to the fact they take their dominant behaviors from those they first encounter, like a spiritual genetic code, is one reason they are mistaken for the spawn or child of the witch. Initially, these spirits are empty. If they emerge into our realm, they become like sponges, soaking up the energy around them, taking on the traits and beliefs of those whose emotions form it, or manifesting in a way prescribed by the one who, for lack of a better word, "adopts" them. Destroying or banishing them can be a total bitch. They do not operate on the rules of the other realms. They are strictly guided by those it considers mentors, or using the Hexekind analogy, its parents."

"So if Baxter and Thomason raised this thing, only they know how to kill it?" Stuart said.

"If they ever took the time to design such a philosophy. Again, this is what makes Hexekind so dangerous. They only know what they are told or taught. Others construct their reality—from physical manifestation to manner of death. They are in every way the product of their influences—truly man-made monsters. If your killers didn't create the rules for its death, then there are no rules for it."

"But if they called this thing," Stuart said. "They have to know something."

"No," Melanie said. "You don't understand. These things can't be summoned or raised, not in the traditional sense. They're accidents. They can only be found. My guess would be one crossed into this realm very near the house on Ash Street. It may have crossed into the house itself, could have been there for years before it was acknowledged and as you said 'raised' by the killers. Once they recognized the spirit, they may have given it limitations, but they could just as easily have fed it their hate and left it at that."

"Andy," Stuart whispered.

"Who?" Reg asked.

"It's complicated," Stuart said. "During the interrogation of Baxter and Thomason, they tried to blame their crimes on a guy named Andy. The last seven victims had the letter A carved into the sole of their left foot, and both Baxter and Thomason claimed it was because of this Andy guy."

"Dory had one of those on her foot," Mike said.

"No," Stuart told him. "They didn't start the practice until their fourth victim."

"But I saw it," Mike said. "The first time she came into my room, she was sitting on the bed and I saw the bottoms of her feet. It was there."

"I can't explain that," Stuart said, but it seemed to corroborate what Melanie and the others believed. Andy may have assumed all of the victims were treated similarly, marked with an A, particularly if it wasn't there in the beginning. "But," Stuart continued. "There was no evidence to suggest a third killer, and they knew it, so after their psych-evaluation they changed their story, saying that Andy wasn't a person but rather a third personality they manifested in order to kill people."

"Is that true?" Mike asked.

"No. Two of the psychiatrists involved suggested something called a third-personality disorder. They misinterpreted what the doctors meant and decided that there really was a third personality with them, and they just kept the name Andy from their original claim."

"But it's possible they were right," Melanie said. "If this thing imprinted them during the murders then it would have adopted those mannerisms and emotions."

"It still doesn't explain how he... or it... knows so much about *us*," Stuart said. No one in the room responded. He looked from face to face and read varying degrees of fear, dejection, confusion and anticipation on them. "Look we can't just ignore what's happening. For now, let's say you're right, and we're dealing with a single spirit, this Andy. We need to track him down, whatever he is, and I suggest we treat it like any other investigation."

"Which means?" Melanie asked.

"We go over the witness testimony." He gazed at Mike and offered a supportive smile. The kid looked worried. "You said you followed Andy to Galveston Drive?"

"Yes," Mike said.

"Was it between Dassa Street and Brinker Street?"

"How did you know that?"

"Baxter and Thomason rented the house on Ash Street from a woman named Pamela Carney. She used the place as an income property. She lives on Galveston Drive in one of those old houses they cut up into apartments. With her connection to those two, it makes sense Andy might be out to get her too."

"Then let's go," Melanie said.

Stuart shook his head. "This isn't your kind of investigation, yet. It's mine. I'm not leading a caravan of six people to Carney's house and trying to explain what we're all doing there."

"So you're going alone?" Melanie asked. "Isn't that a little Bruce Willis considering the circumstances?"

"I'm not going at all," Stuart replied. He glanced at Yvonne, then Reg and finally Melanie. "You are."

"Come again?" Reg said. "I thought you just said this wasn't our kind of investigation."

"That's right. It's mine, and I call it undercover work. We don't know why Andy visited Carney. She could be a new victim, or she might be one of Andy's puppets being set up to kill someone. Whatever the case, if she sees me, she's going to be suspicious. From the outside, none of you have been involved, and since Andy appeared in public as Regina Wolcroff who died in Carney's house, it makes sense you'd want to interview her for your program. I'd be surprised if she hasn't spoken to a dozen journalists already today."

"He's right," Melanie said.

"I'm not good with confrontation," Yvonne muttered from the bed.

"We're just going to go and talk with her. Ask some questions and look around. We're not doing anything she might take as provocation." The plan seemed to excite Melanie, but next to her Reg continued to look uncertain.

"The fact is, you have no reason to go," Stuart said. "None of this concerns you outside of an academic interest. I'm not suggesting you have to go. It's up to you."

"Right," Reg said. "None of this concerns us now, but if we go over there and it turns out this woman is dancing with Andy, then suddenly we're on its radar. And *that* does concern me."

"This is the kind of thing we've been looking for," Melanie said. She stood from the chair and leaned over to kiss Reg on the cheek. "I'm going."

34

Melanie remembered Pamela Carney's neighborhood from the night she'd pulled into town. The gas station where she'd filled her tank stood less than a mile away. On first sight, she'd considered the neighborhood on the trashy side, nothing more than a suburban slum, and bright late afternoon sunlight did little to change her opinion of the district. The house Carney lived in stood three stories high. Based on the number of buzzers poorly affixed to the front door frame, it had been chopped into five apartments. Scraps of paper labeled with names had been poorly attached beneath each bell. Carney's was in the worst shape of them all, the ink so faded, Melanie and Reg identified her apartment by eliminating those with legible tags.

"This place feels cold," Yvonne said touching the jamb. "And it smells like dog food."

"Why in the hell would a woman who owned a property like the one on Ash Street live here?" Reg asked. "I mean, the house was long gone by the time I saw it, but the neighborhood was damn good."

"She could probably live off what she made in rent alone," Melanie said, pressing the buzzer. "At least until Baxter and Thomason turned the place into a real estate pariah."

Waiting for Carney to answer her bell, Melanie surveyed the neighborhood, but the streets were quiet. No children playing on the sidewalks. No people sitting on porches enjoying the end of the day and the cooling of the air. The block appeared deserted and Melanie drew an uncomfortable sensation from the emptiness. Stuart was right. The journalists who had come to town to cover the Barnard Ghost should have made the connection to Baxter and Thomason by now, and they should have been swarming around Pamela Carney, so where were they? Where was *everyone*?

She pressed the buzzer again. "She's not home," Melanie said. "I guess we'll come back later."

"Or," Reg said. He reached out and turned the doorknob. The latch clicked and he pushed the knob, sending the door open, revealing a shadowed entryway that smelled far worse than dogfood.

"We can't go in," Melanie said. "Besides, she's not home."

"She's home," Yvonne said, caressing the side of the building with her palm. "She's on the second floor on the left side of the landing."

"Are you having one of your feelings?" Melanie asked.

"Mmm, no," Yvonne replied, discreetly pointing a finger upward. "Don't look but she's at the window, watching us."

"How do you know that's Carney?" Reg whispered.

"Both times you hit the buzzer she closed the curtains."

"So what do we do?" Reg asked. "She obviously doesn't want to talk to us."

From the landing above a woman's scream tore down the stairs to fill the bleak entryway. It startled Melanie so badly, she leaped back, nearly knocking Reg over. Yvonne squealed and raced away from the house, and she kept running. Apparently the abnormal was far more terrifying for the woman than the paranormal. Reg made sure Melanie had her feet under her and then slid past, charging for the shadowy stairs. Melanie thought to call after him, but instead she ran, taking the steps two at a time. A second scream—like a terrified child—sliced the atmosphere, adding to the fuel of adrenaline forcing Melanie upward.

By the time she reached the landing, Reg was already putting his shoulder to the door. The scream came again, but it was abruptly muffled. Another female voice shouted obscenities. Something crashed, like a drawer holding silverware smashing to a floor.

"Fuck," Reg grunted. He stepped back and planted his foot next to the doorknob. The jamb creaked but held.

As he drew the foot back to deliver another blow, the door whipped open cracking hard on the interior wall. The body of a wiry woman with hair like a crushed tumbleweed filled the frame for a moment, then in a flash she was over the threshold diving for Reg while clutching a knife in her hand. She cocked her arm. Carney drove the blade down toward Reg, who stumbled back to the wall, but he caught himself just in time to raise his arm and knock Carney's attack wide. Then Melanie was in motion, lunging forward and slamming her palms into Pamela Carney's shoulder and side, sending the woman hard to the landing. The knife the crazy woman had been holding skidded along the wooden floor and *clicked* to a stop against the baseboard, but Carney's assault wasn't finished. She scurried like a spider from where she lay and latched on to Reg's shins, trying to sink her teeth into his leg, while making a high wheezing pant like a dog about to vomit. Melanie kicked the woman in the stomach, but she barely seemed to notice as she clamped her teeth into Reg's leg. He managed to end the scene with one hard stomp of his cowboy boot, punching the heel into the side of Carney's head and forcing her to release the hold she had on him. She groaned loudly, and Reg raised his foot to stomp her again.

"Don't," Melanie said. "It's okay." She turned to look inside Carney's apartment, and her stomach clenched.

A severe-looking woman with long straw-colored hair walked slowly toward the opening, her motion so smooth she appeared to be gliding. Her torso had been slashed terribly, though none of the wounds bled. Her empty eyes fixed on Melanie, and her cracked lips parted revealing a row of broken teeth.

“How could you do this to me?” the woman asked.

The question confused Melanie, whose first thought was to get the woman medical attention. Only when the woman began to hiss a high-pitched squeal did Melanie realize what it was she faced.

“Andy?” Melanie asked.

The façade of the woman lowered its chin and turned the head slightly in a gesture that was almost coy. “Do we know you?” Andy asked. The falsetto voice skittered into Melanie’s ears like insects.

“Oh Christ,” she said. She backpedaled to the wall and felt Reg’s arm snake around her waist.

“We know you *now*,” Andy said. The female shape fell as if suddenly emptied, leaving a void in the doorway. A moment later a middle-aged man with half of his face torn away appeared on the staircase. “Bye-bye, Pammy. We wuvs you.”

Then the man-shaped spirit leaped down the stairs and disappeared through the front door, leaving Melanie trembling. Her heart kicked against her ribs and her temples throbbed. On the floor at her feet, Pamela Carney whimpered.

“It’s gone,” Melanie said.

“Yeah,” Reg said. He nodded toward the open door of Carney’s apartment. “But look what it left behind. I think I’m going to be sick.”

Amid the filth which seemed to grow like mold along the windowsills, counters and shelves; and the discarded food containers now housing an assortment of insects and bacterium; and old beer cans baked in the hot apartment and reeking of boiled yeast; and furniture so badly stained it was difficult to determine any piece’s original finish, were the remains of a man and a woman. The man, who lay beneath the street-facing window, had been dead for some time—his body lacerated and bludgeoned into a misshapen fleshy lump. The woman died before Melanie’s eyes. She sat tied in a chair, wearing a shredded blouse and jeans stained with blood. Around the woman’s neck, Carney had affixed a cone—the kind veterinarians used on dogs to keep them from worrying their wounds. Bits of vomit formed a crust on the plastic shield under the woman’s chin, and below the lowest lip of the cone a wide gash oozed blood.

Carney had slit her victim’s throat to silence the screams before storming onto the landing. Melanie sobbed. A thick film of tears blurred the woman’s final expression, but the rattle of her death, like moist hiccups, was unmistakable.

Reg had managed to keep from getting sick. In the hallway, he shouted into his cell phone, providing the emergency operator with the address, the circumstances, and a slew of insistent obscenities. He loomed over Carney, raging like a storm, his eye fixed on the woman, body tensed to subdue her if necessary.

No longer able to look at the corpse, Melanie turned away. The first things to catch her eye were the sharp objects that had spilled from a box to litter the floor—kitchen knives, screwdrivers, saw blades. Melanie backed away from the dangerous implements. She saw Carney's sofa and her television set and a stack of DVDs on top of it. At the bottom of the pile, the DVDs were in proper boxes, the kind you'd find at any video store, but those on top were without cases.

"Don't you dare," Carney screamed from the hall. The woman looked at her, eyes blazing. "You leave my things alone. They're *my* things. Mine!"

Ignoring the raving woman, in fact, to spite her, Melanie crossed to the television and lifted a disc from the pile. Carney couldn't see her from the hall, but the woman must have known what she was doing.

"You fucking cunt," Carney yelled. "You bitch cunt. You leave my things alone. They're mine."

Melanie heard a cracking sound from the hallway, and Carney fell silent. She assumed Carney was making a move for the door, and Reg had subdued her appropriately. Melanie hoped so. She couldn't imagine hating anyone as much as she hated Pamela Carney in that moment. The feeling welled in her as if it were carried into her body on the fetid air. She wanted Reg to hurt the woman who had filled this room with pain. He could kill her for all Melanie cared.

A spark of reason caught her off guard. Her mind was so overwhelmed with anger, she wasn't thinking straight. She didn't want anyone dead, not even a monster like the ragged woman on the landing. Such thoughts were wholly unlike her, but then again, she'd never watched a knife arcing for her boyfriend's chest before, nor had she entered the scene of a double murder.

Melanie returned her attention to the disc. Someone had used a Sharpie marker to label the silver surface.

C. Lancaster, it read.

Melanie exchanged the disc for another:

R. Wolcroff

Then another:

D. Addison

Sirens wailed in the distance. Melanie gathered up the stack of discs and returned to the landing.

35

A soft rapping on the hotel room door interrupted Mike's conversation with his mother, who sounded typically distant. She didn't even ask why he was at the Majestic Hotel. Gwen sat looking out the window, apparently still shaken by the sight of Mike's late granddad, and she whipped her head around to the sound. Stuart spoke quietly to someone on his phone and glanced across the room at the door. The detective looked at Mike and shrugged, so Mike climbed from the bed.

"Hey, mom," Mike said. "I'll call you from Gwen's when we get back from the movie." He peered through the peep hole and saw Yvonne distorted by the small lens.

"Is everything okay, Mike?" his mom asked.

"Sure," he said. "See ya." He hung up the phone and pulled open the door.

Yvonne flew into the room, waving one hand above her head and clutching a large plastic sack in the other. At the bed, she dropped the sack and backed away as if it contained a rattler she'd managed to bag but no longer wanted near her. "There," she said. "I am so done."

"What's going on?" Stuart asked. He moved away from the window, past Gwen who cringed under his shadow, and approached Yvonne. "Where are Melanie and Reg?"

"Well," Yvonne said crisply, "they are either still at Pamela 'bitch-with-a-blade' Carney's or they're in police custody. I was waiting for them at the van, and Melanie shows up with an armload of junk she dumped on me." Yvonne pointed to the bag sitting on the bed. "She shoved it at me and told me to get it back here, because apparently Carney has been carving people up in her apartment, and she decided to add Reg and Melanie to the list, but Reg flattened her…Yay, Reg!... and Melanie found those discs and thought they might help you, but I don't see how, and it really doesn't matter because I am so done." Yvonne was already at the door. "And thank you *so very* much for the assignment, Captain."

Mike saw that the woman wanted to bolt from the room and the hotel and likely the city itself. The detective must have known it too, because Stuart dashed to Yvonne, grasped her arm, and then hauled her into the center of the room.

"Police brutality," Yvonne muttered.

"Assault," Stuart replied, "I'm not on duty. Now sit down and tell us what happened."

"Just did," Yvonne said.

"Are Reg and Melanie okay?" Stuart demanded. "Are they hurt?"

"I don't think so. I didn't see Reg, but Melanie said Carney went after him with a knife. I'm assuming that since he knocked her ass down, he's okay. Melanie was only at the van for like two seconds. She said she had to get back before the police came because she was a witness and Reg needed her because he was flipping out, but she thought the discs were important and she didn't want them getting held for evidence or anything, and she said she didn't want to call you because you'd do the Bruce Willis thing and show up, and then you'd be wasting time instead of watching those." Again, Yvonne pointed at the bed.

Mike watched the exchange, oddly amused by Yvonne's immature tone and the rapid delivery of information. She had seemed so mellow, so together. She put across this air of cool and bizarre spirituality, but that mask had cracked hard and fallen away, leaving behind a scared young woman who wanted nothing more than to return to a simple life of channeling non-existent spirits and chasing their vibes through old houses.

"What are they?" Stuart asked, nodding toward the bag.

"DVDs," Yvonne said. "Melanie didn't tell me what they were. I'm not even sure she knew, but she thought they might be important. Most of them are homemade. The others are like Clint Eastwood films or something."

Mike noticed the color draining out of Stuart's face. *What's that about?* The detective reached for the bag and yanked it open. Reaching inside he seemed to be pushing aside the contents until he found what he was looking for, and then his shoulders slumped, and he exhaled loudly.

"What are they?" Mike asked.

"I think they're the recordings Baxter and Thomason made of their crimes," Stuart told him.

"They recorded what they did?" Gwen asked from her place by the window.

"Almost all of it," Stuart said. "Before they were apprehended they managed to destroy a lot of the evidence, but some of the discs were recovered. There are more here, though. I'm not sure if they're copies or something else."

"We should watch them," Mike said. The idea was sickening but it was also compelling, like going to the house on Ash Street had been.

"I'll watch them," Stuart said. "I've looked through a lot of this material. You don't want to see it."

"True enough," Gwen said. She rose from the chair and met Mike at the far side of the bed, skirting Yvonne and Stuart in the process. She wrapped her arm through his and gently pulled him toward the door.

"Wait a minute," Mike said. "What are we supposed to do?"

"Well, I'm leaving," Yvonne said. "As options go, it's the best one I've got."

"You're just bailing?"

"We should all go," Stuart said. "There's no DVD player in the room, so I'm going to have to go home to watch these. I'll call Melanie and let her and Reg know how to find the house, but I think we're done for the day. It's almost dark, and I don't want any of you running around out there until we have some more information."

Disheartened, Mike huffed a sigh. "So that's it? You're going home to watch TV, and we're supposed to just hang out and pretend none of this is happening."

"Mike, the last thing I want is for you to pretend this isn't happening. What I'm saying is I don't have a plan beyond seeing what's on those discs, because we still don't know what we're dealing with. Maybe there's something on there that can help, but for now you should go home."

"He's right," Gwen said. "You shouldn't leave your mother alone. Come on. I'll drive."

Disappointed with his dismissal, but seeing no alternative and expecting no reprieve, he followed Gwen into the hall. The last place he wanted to go was home to his zombie mother and the possibility of encountering the visage of his baby sister—or his granddad—roaming the rooms of the place. But did it matter where he went? Lately it seemed that every building and every room he entered was haunted.

36

For three years Stuart had saved the video recording of his wife's torture and murder at the hands of Selma Baxter and Derek Thomason, but he'd never watched it. His compulsion to obtain the recorded images was just that, a compulsion; no rational explanation for the piracy ever emerged. Baxter and Thomason had already been apprehended by the time Stuart had made his copies, so he couldn't claim investigation as a motive, and though early on he'd told himself that the videos would make good research into the disturbed minds of Baxter and Thomason (and perhaps others like them), Stuart could no longer hold to this excuse.

Stuart sat in his home office with the stack of DVDs Melanie had stolen from a crime scene, and he methodically worked his way through them, maintaining a cool detachment from the ugly events captured on the discs. Now it was late and the DVD featuring his wife rested in his computer's drive, paused with the window reduced to a pulsing icon on his desktop.

He'd only viewed half of the recordings, those that included Chance Whiting, Regina Wolcroff, and a truck stop hooker named Blanche Parker, each one enduring two discs worth of humiliation and torture at the hands of Baxter and Thomason before being murdered, their killers laughing over their bleeding corpses or making out like high school students at a Homecoming dance as blood pooled at their feet. Many times, he'd heard a third voice, a high falsetto, speaking off camera, encouraging the brutality and suggesting creative ways to inflict pain.

The discs he was watching were not the recordings from the evidence locker or the copies Stuart had made for his private collection. Andy's shrill voice never appeared on those confiscated materials. Stuart couldn't even imagine what twists the investigation would have taken if it had. But these discs had taken a different path, whether squirreled away by Pamela Carney over the past few years or discovered recently by the woman in the charred remains of her home on Ash Street. Stuart had separated the familiar recordings—those that *had* come from his house—from the newly acquired discs, and they sat in two piles beside his monitor. The disc on the top of the familiar stack was labeled, *C. Lancaster.*

He didn't need to watch the recording of Clarissa's last hours of life. There was no point. He understood how Andy knew so much about his victims and their loved ones. It was all there, held for dreadful posterity. They hadn't just tortured and taunted their victims, Baxter and Thomason had pried into their personal lives, playing a sick and humiliating game of 20 Questions. But now, after midnight, Stuart felt compelled to watch the home movie. He closed his eyes and took a deep breath as if preparing to leap from a cliff into unknown waters below. Then he double clicked the pulsing icon and drew his chair close to the desk.

Clarissa sat tied to a chair. They had stripped her and already a shallow cut ran beneath her breast in a thumbnail moon arc. Her straw-blond hair fell over her face, and it looked as if she had passed out—head down, unmoving. Seeing her that way hurt so badly Stuart felt the urge to shut the program down, eject the disc, scratch its surface, and snap it into pieces so that it could never be read by another machine. He didn't want to see the fate of his wife. He had to, though.

The scene behind her was the basement of the house on Ash Street. Floodlights bathed the simple room in harsh illumination, bleaching out the shadows, making the basement look like a concrete interrogation chamber. The only ornamentations on the walls were a series of identical symbols, some no larger than a matchbox car and others as big as his computer screen. Some were etched sloppily into the concrete; others had been carefully stenciled on its surface. A clanging sound from off camera startled Stuart.

It was the audio component that bothered him most about these recordings, despite the disturbing images. The voices were raw, not processed like in movies and on television, and the crispness of tones sounded wrong, yet terribly true, especially when the subjects screamed.

Clarissa attempted to lift her head, and Stuart clamped the arms of his chair, his nails sinking deep into the leather. She moaned and sucked in a rasping breath.

"Yay," Selma Baxter cried from off camera. "Mrs. Detective is awake."

Derek Thomason, looking as if he'd just stepped off a billboard advertising high-end jeans, walked onscreen and positioned himself beside Clarissa's chair. Grasping her hair, Thomason yanked Clarissa's head back, and she stared directly at Stuart.

The fear in her eyes, the helplessness, pierced him. "Jesus," he hissed, before capturing his lower lip between his teeth.

"Smile for the camera," Thomason said. "This is your fifteen minutes of fame."

"Your last fifteen minutes," Selma Baxter added enthusiastically, racing into frame and leaning down to face her captive. "Better make 'em good."

"You want to say 'hi' to your husband?" Thomason asked. "You said he was a cop and he was going to get us. Do you think big badass policeman will get *us* before we finish with *you*?" He pulled a box cutter from his pocket and thumbed the blade free of the handle. Pressing the blade against Clarissa's cheek, he asked, "You *think*?"

Baxter leaned away and delivered a sharp slap to her cheek before ducking back in, her head eclipsing the camera's view of Clarissa's face. "Answer him," Baxter said. "You think you got a chance in hell?"

Clarissa sobbed and squeezed her eyes closed, producing a wash of tears that spilled down her cheeks. Her body shook uncontrollably, and the sight of it worked between Stuart's ribs like a dull blade.

"I hope this one doesn't shit herself like that black bitch did," Baxter said. "I ain't cleaning that up again."

Ten minutes into the recording Stuart had reached his limit. His jaw ached from grinding his teeth together and his knuckles throbbed from clutching so tightly to the arms of his chair. Baxter and Thomason spent those minutes humiliating Clarissa, verbally and physically, running their filthy hands over her body while accosting her with the most vulgar taunts Stuart had ever heard. *Enough*, he thought, reaching for the mouse with trembling fingers.

"So what were you doing all alone?" Thomason asked. "I mean, where was your husband? Does he let you cruise the streets for dick? Does he like watching strangers plowing your tired old cunt, or did he give up on that road kill, and you sneak out because you still need some rod?"

Stuart's hand paused over the mouse, then he drew it back to the arm of the chair.

"You better answer him, bitch," Selma Baxter said, leaning close to Clarissa's ear. She slid the flat side of her knife down Clarissa's breast. "This isn't some game show where you get to pass your turn."

"Twenty questions," Thomason announced, happily.

"Twenty questions," Selma repeated. "I love twenty questions."

Clarissa's eyes shot from one killer to the other, racing like a cat trapped in a box, desperate for escape.

In the course of watching the torment, Stuart had forgotten all of the animosity, the discontent, and the frustration of the final years of marriage to this woman. He wished he could have made those years better. He wished he could free her from that chair and…

Honey, Stuart thought. *I'm so fucking sorry. If I'd caught them sooner… If I hadn't…*

"The rules of the game are simple," Thomason said. "We ask a question and if you won't answer it or if we think you're lying, we cut something off. Why twenty questions?" he asked in a depraved mimicry of cheer. "Fingers and toes, bitch. Fingers and toes." Thomason stepped away from the chair. "Now, for your first question. Are you a dried up old cunt?"

Selma Baxter grinned, awaiting the response. She moved her knife over Clarissa's chest like a barber stropping a razor.

"Time's wasting," Baxter said. "You don't want to forfeit this round."

Clarissa nodded her head rapidly. Tears shook from her eyes, spraying her cheeks.

"We'll need a verbal clarification for the judges," Thomason said. "Are you a dried up old cunt?"

"Yes," Clarissa mumbled.

"I knew she was," Baxter said. "I knew it."

"Very good," Thomason said. "Now, why were you in the park?"

"I was taking a walk."

"Judges?" Thomason asked, looking to the ceiling as if a jury gazed down from above. "I'm sorry, but that is an incomplete answer."

"I was taking a walk," Clarissa insisted.

Selma Baxter grabbed Clarissa's hand. The ropes at her wrist hindered the victim's ability to struggle, and Baxter positioned the knife between the ring and pinkie finger and rocked it twice, the point digging into the arm of the chair. The blade creased Clarissa's pinkie below the third knuckle, then rocked sharply upward to prepare for the cutting blow.

Stuart closed his eyes. The scream came then. The too-real audio—too damn sharp, yet haunting—echoed as if his head had been emptied allowing the shriek to ricochet off smooth bone. Soft whimpers of pain caught in his throat, wholly drowned out by the scream of his late wife. He kept his eyes closed, only able to listen to the game.

"So, Mrs. Detective why were you in the park?"

"A fight… we had a fight. My husband and I had a fight."

"Much better," Thomason said, obviously amused. "And what was the fight about? Was your brave police husband fucking another woman?"

"No," Clarissa said. She sniffed loudly, then moaned.

"Did he want to fuck you in the ass?" Selma Baxter asked, giggling like they were sharing gossip.

"He made a movie," Clarissa said. "When we were young, he made a videotape."

"Oh really," Thomason said. "And what were you doing on that tape?"

Clarissa's sobbing took over the audio track. In the background, barely audible was the sound of a high-pitched titter like wind whistling through broken glass.

"Were you naughty on the tape?" Selma Baxter asked. "Were you a whore?"

"We…we…"

"Nineteen wrong answers to go."

"We were having sex. I didn't want him to make the tape, but we were drunk, and I asked him to erase it. I begged him to throw the fucking thing out, but he didn't do it, and I found it. After all these years I found it, and I hated him for keeping it."

"I'm sorry," Stuart whispered. His throat tightened around the words. Tears pooled behind his closed eye lids, salty and scalding. "I'm so sorry."

"But I shouldn't have been mad. We shouldn't have fought," Clarissa said. "We're always fighting. Always. I can't help it. I just want him to look at me instead of his goddamn computer. I want him to come home and talk to me and look at me, but he leaves one office and disappears into another. And I hate him for that, because I love him and want him to love me, but he's so distant that I know he can't. So I yell, and he yells back. Sometimes it's the only way I know he's there."

Stuart opened his eyes. Clarissa looked back at him. He shot his hand out and paused the image. Then he wiped at his eyes, clearing away the distortion of tears. Suddenly he felt trapped in the study. It was too small with walls that locked around the chair, pinning him to the desk, but he couldn't move or escape his wife's judgment. He stayed and he cried and he apologized until his throat was raw.

37

After three hours at the police station, giving statements in between extended bouts of waiting, a detective named Hall told Melanie and Reg they could go. The media was already all over the Carney murders and had gathered in front of the building like a swarm of wasps. Detective Hall kindly led Melanie and Reg to the back of the building and escorted them through the prisoner transfer dock, leading them into the parking garage where his car waited. Detective Hall drove them back to the Majestic Hotel. Melanie had gotten Stuart's message about checking out of the hotel and returning to his house, but her concern had been for Reg, who was shaken so badly by the events at Carney's apartment, he wept as Hall drove them away from the station. In their room Reg b-lined for his duffle bag, where he removed a fifth of Smirnoff vodka and began to drink. Melanie lay next to him on the bed, her arm draped over his stomach. He fell asleep around midnight, but Melanie remained awake through the night, too excited and frightened to sleep.

We know you, now.

The morning began with a call from Kee Ulrich. The producer sounded wired, absolutely thrilled that Melanie and Reg were "fortunate" enough to be on hand to witness the insane landlady's "killing spree." He called a meeting at the Morgan Hotel, so after having a cab drop them on Galveston Drive to retrieve the SUV, Melanie and Reg found themselves in the pretty sterility of the Morgan, listening to Kee as he turned a dreadful and traumatic incident into "golden ticket shit."

I signed my life away, Melanie thought.

Kee babbled about the copious free publicity, and Mack sat in his chair, nodding furiously; and next to her, Reg, who still looked green from the previous evening's events, remained silent with his head down, holding her hand under the table.

"Yvonne's out," Kee said. "I think we can all agree to that."

"We can?" Melanie asked. She was too tired to fight, but she didn't want either Kee or Mack getting it in their heads that she took their side in any of this.

"She went AWOL," Kee said. "Got an email from her this morning. She's already back in Baton Rouge, and according to her note, she's finished."

"Rat jumping ship," Mack said. "Whatever. It wasn't like she added much credibility to the show."

"The press on this is going to be huge," Kee said for the eighth time. "It's already going national."

"Yeah, but it fucks our production," Mack muttered. "These two are going to have reporters all over them wherever they go. No way we're sneaking into the place on Ash Street now. Plus, all of the assheads finally put the ghost together with the Baxter-Thomason murders, so any edge we had is blown to shit."

He's jealous, Melanie thought. The spotlight wasn't shining on him, even Kee's focus had shifted to Melanie and Reg, and it pissed Mack off. Maybe if he'd actually seen Carney's victims, that man and that poor woman, her head encased in a humiliating plastic dog cone, bleeding out onto the floor of Pamela Carney's filthy apartment he'd realize there was no warmth in this particular spotlight. *No*, she corrected. *He'd gladly suffer such a scene for a spoonful of publicity*.

The victims had been identified as Ronald and Olivia Aday, a married couple living in the apartment below Carney's. From what Melanie could glean from Detective Hall and the bits of conversation she'd heard at the police station, both had been lured up to Carney's apartment earlier in the week. Bound and gagged, they'd endured more than twenty-four hours in Carney's apartment. As for Carney, she'd been hauled from her building by the police, sobbing and insisting, "I couldn't help it. It's not my fault. It's him. It's *him*."

There had been a minor issue of accusations regarding a missing stack of DVDs—Carney had ranted and raved about "her collection" to the police, but Melanie had told the authorities she didn't know what the crazy woman was talking about. They didn't press the matter. Apparently, Melanie was a far more credible witness than the former landlady of Selma Baxter and Derek Thomason.

"So I guess your angle paid off," Mack said, thumbing an icon on his phone. "Except for totally killing the episode I was putting together."

"That's right, Mack, we set the whole thing up as a publicity stunt to fuck you over. We talked Pamela Carney into butchering the couple downstairs so we could catch her, because we're just that kind of brilliant."

"Shame Reg didn't have his camera," Mack said.

"Go to hell," Melanie told him.

"Can I say something?" Reg asked, his first words since stepping into the meeting. As such they carried weight and Melanie and Kee looked at the sullen man. Mack didn't take his eyes off the screen of his phone. "I think we need to scrap the Scotland finale and use Ash Street."

"What?" Melanie asked. This was the last thing she'd expected Reg to say.

He held up his hand in a calming gesture and continued, "Melanie and I sign an exclusive to the show for an appropriate bonus to be negotiated prior to on-camera testimonies. We don't say a word to the media until the show airs. That gives us plenty of time to fill in the background information on Carney, plus

Baxter-Thomason, and we may have additional sightings to cover by then. We've already got more than enough footage to pull it together."

"I like it," Kee said.

"We don't have an investigation," Mack argued. "Not unless we can get into the remains of that house. Jesus, we can't just use the interview footage."

"Why not?" Melanie asked. "Oh right, you're not featured in the interviews."

Mack shot her a furious look.

"What kind of bonus are we talking about?" Kee asked.

"To be determined," Reg replied. "Melanie's agent will work out the details, but there's one other stipulation."

"Go ahead," Kee told him.

"You have to keep the press off of us. We won't have a show if our faces are plastered all over the airwaves and the Internet. Even if we don't talk, they'll interpret shit and build stories around whatever footage they can shoot. We're going to check out of the hotel. If anyone asks we went back to Louisiana."

"But you're staying here?" Mack asked.

"I don't know," Reg said. He glanced warmly at Melanie. "We have to talk about it."

"Are you with Reg on this?" Kee asked, addressing Melanie.

"I-d... Yes. I'm with him."

"I'll make some calls," Kee said.

"Oh come on," Mack said. He tossed his phone on the table and leapt to his feet in a dramatic display. "We've got Scotland. A fucking castle! And you're going to trade that in for a story that's going to be as stale as year-old toast before we can bring it to air? This is not the kind of shit our fans expect from us."

"Maybe it's time for them to expect more than shit from us," Melanie replied.

Mack's cheeks burned red. He hurried around the table to face off on Kee. Reg let go of Melanie's hand and tapped her thigh. When she looked at him, he was nodding his head toward the door.

"We're gone," Melanie said. "We'll check in with you later."

"Right," Kee said, looking over Mack's shoulder. "Golden ticket, guys."

In the hall, Melanie pushed close to Reg and asked, "What the hell are you thinking?"

"Honestly, I'm thinking about retiring from television," Reg said. "Mack is right. This story is going to be stripped to the bone before it airs. We'll do what we can to keep it legit, but you know they'll spin it into cotton candy for the audience. So I don't think I'm going to be signing on for a third season. I have no problem with you going back, but I'm done. A decent bonus check will get me through for a while, and in the meantime it shuts down Mack's bullshit and keeps us out of the basement of that house. Plus, we can lay low and maybe do something real."

"Something real?"

"Andy," Reg said. He scanned the corridor for curious ears before continuing. "After seeing what it drove Carney to do we have to stop the thing. If it can be stopped."

With a couple of sentences, Reg had solved all of their immediate problems, and even accounted for some Melanie hadn't considered. "I love you," she said.

"You have impeccable taste," Reg said, nudging her with his hip.

Reg and Melanie checked out of the Majestic to avoid encounters with the press. If they decided to stay in Barnard another night, they would ask Stuart for a room or check into one of the motels along the freeway. Fortunately, Barnard was a large enough city, they could lose themselves in it. Sitting in the SUV around the corner from the hotel, Melanie called Stuart to discuss their next moves, only to find Stuart was already making his.

"What do you mean he went out of town?" Reg asked. "In the middle of all of this he decided to go fishing?"

"Not exactly," Melanie said. "Stuart said he was going to see Derek Thomason and Selma Baxter. He thinks we were right about Andy, and based on what Yvonne told us, Baxter and-or Thomason are the only ones who might know how to destroy this thing."

"What about Mike?"

"Mike's at home," Melanie said. "It's probably best if we keep him out of this as much as we can."

"Well, when is Stuart getting back?"

"Probably late. He's seeing Thomason this morning, not that it's likely to do any good, and he's scheduled a visit with Selma Baxter this afternoon."

"What did you mean about Thomason?" Reg asked.

"I read an article online when I was doing research. It said he hasn't spoken in nearly a year."

"That's newsworthy?"

"Well, when he was first apprehended, through the arraignment and for his first few months in prison, Thomason was acting like a movie star, sucking up all the attention he could get, making outrageous claims and joking with the press. He was quite the showman."

"Sounds like Mack," Reg said.

"Celebrity is the great equalizer," Melanie said. "Anyway, about a year ago, he went catatonic. Just shut down. I'm not sure of the details. For a while they hooked him up to machines because he wouldn't eat or drink on his own. According to the article, he's eating now, but uncommunicative."

"They think he's legit?" Reg asked. "I mean, any chance he's trying to get transferred to a hospital or someplace he might be able to slip out of?"

"Don't know," Melanie said. "I can't imagine him putting up that kind of act for an entire year. Something like that either works or it doesn't."

"At least he didn't find God," Reg said.

"Or if he did, he's not talking about it."

"So what now?" Reg asked.

"Stuart thinks we need to talk to that woman I met the other day."

"The Bolger lady?"

"Yes, Hannah Bolger. She's been contacting the other survivors. Stuart thinks we need to fill her in on our theory about Andy, then try and convince the others."

"I think I'd rather do the prison tour with Stuart," Reg said.

"Let's just hope he gets the information we need."

Melanie had braced herself for a second encounter with Hannah Bolger, but found her hesitance unwarranted. Hannah met her and Reg at the door with a warm, albeit small, smile—barely a curve at the corners of her mouth. She ushered them in and showed them to the kitchen where she had a pot of coffee waiting.

"I make awful coffee," Hannah said. "I'll apologize for that up front. It all tastes terrible to me, so I never know if I've gotten it right or not, but I made a pot, and I can offer you tea or a soda."

The woman's friendliness surprised Melanie, considering their first encounter, but she found herself accepting it easily, glad that whatever complaint Hannah had bore her now seemed to have moved on. Melanie and Reg decided to try the coffee and this seemed to please their hostess tremendously. But Hannah had been right. The coffee tasted bitter and chalky and ran down the back of Melanie's throat like acid. Over the years, she'd had a number of lousy cups of coffee. Hannah's brew easily made the top ten.

"I warned you," Hannah said with a laugh.

"Tastes fine to me," Reg said.

Everything tasted fine to Reg. Melanie couldn't once remember him complaining about a meal or a beverage since they'd been together, and sometimes she wondered if he was just too polite to say anything, or if his taste buds really were beyond discernment.

For herself, Hannah made a cup of mint tea and took the chair across the small table. "Now, Stuart tells me you have some information about my Ben."

"Well, yes and no," Melanie said uncomfortably. "We don't think that the apparition you've seen is actually your late husband."

"Really?" Hannah asked.

To Melanie the reaction seemed forced, too loud and sharp, like someone pretending to be surprised. "Yes," Melanie said. "We don't think it's a ghost at all, at least not as we understand ghosts."

Melanie explained what they'd found and went into as much detail as she could regarding the blank and malleable entity that Baxter and Thomason had molded and named Andy. She referenced Yvonne's description of the Hexekind, but did so quickly because Hannah's expression showed interest but not a hint of acceptance. When she finished, Melanie sipped coffee out of nervous reflex; she certainly wasn't enjoying the beverage.

"But that doesn't explain Ben," Hannah countered. "I know my own husband."

"No doubt," Reg said, "but Baxter and Thomason often questioned their victims, sometimes for hours, days even, and it was usually about very personal matters. They recorded all of these sessions on video, and they probably played them back a lot. It's very possible Andy is using those bits of information."

Hannah's brow knit and she looked toward the window. "Does Stuart believe all of this?"

"Yes," Melanie said.

"And how do you stop this…you called him Andy?"

"That was the name Baxter and Thomason gave him," Reg said. "And we don't know how to stop it. Stuart is visiting Derek Thomason this morning, hoping to get some answers. If that doesn't work, he'll be going to see Selma Baxter later."

"Right now, we think it's important to contact the other families of the victims," Melanie said. "I know you haven't experienced any threat from Ben, but there's enough evidence to suggest that others are in danger."

"I see," Hannah said. "Well, I have the list right here. It's rather short, and considering the circumstances, that's probably a good thing." She withdrew a folded sheet of copy paper from the pocket of her shirt. "I'm not sure exactly how wide to cast the net. I mean, many of these people had friends, but if they didn't attend my group, I couldn't give you names. At any rate, two of the victims—Blanche Parker and Victor Donicio—were pretty much loners. As you know, Blanche was a prostitute, and Victor was something less than stable in his residency. He drifted into town only a couple of days before meeting Selma Baxter.

Now, the Taylors still have two sons, but like my children, they no longer live in Barnard, and I assume we want to keep the search local for the time being?"

Hannah's voice had taken on a mellow lyricism, smooth and soothing. Melanie found herself drifting on the words. She shook her head to regain her focus and tried to smile. "Yes," she said. "I th-think so."

"Of course, there's Stuart, and Clarissa had a brother named Thumper, but he's a darling man, and I don't…"

"Thumper," Reg said. He chuckled and blinked, reaching for the mug of coffee before him.

"A nickname, of course," Hannah said. "His name is actually Philip, but he prefers Thumper." She shrugged and then continued with her list. "Chance Whiting's family moved away after his death, except for his father-in-law who recently died."

"We… we heard," Melanie said. Her tongue felt heavy and awkward, lying in her mouth like a dry roast.

"I imagine so," Hannah said, eyeing her with curiosity. "Regina's sisters are married and don't live in town, though one is only thirty minutes south in Austin, and her mother is in Houston with a sister. Delia couldn't even be bothered to drive back for Richard's funeral, which reminds me, I still need to fix something for the repast, but I hate the idea of bringing just another casserole, you know? Anyway, I don't think we have anything to worry about from Regina. Sadly, she didn't have many friends."

"Mike," Melanie said.

"Yes, Mike Addison. He and his mother are left now that Alan is gone."

"What about the father?"

"He lives in Dallas. He came back for Alan's funeral, but I believe he just drove in for the day. Would either of you like more coffee?"

"Please." Reg offered Hannah his mug. "I can't seem to wake up this morning."

"I'm fine," Melanie said, but it wasn't the truth.

She was anything but fine. It felt as if her head had been filled with water, thoughts drifting and turning on uneasy currents, head too heavy to hold up, and her vision feathered at the edges. The closest thing she could compare the sensation to was being drunk, but this had come on so fast. She took a deep breath but it filled her nose with a metallic, chemical scent reminiscent of the miserable coffee.

"Are you okay?" Hannah asked from behind her.

Melanie couldn't answer. She'd been drugged. Poisoned. Jesus Christ, the crazy old bitch had spiked the coffee.

"Melan…" Reg said. He leaned toward her.

A long narrow shape flew across the back of his head. There was a cracking sound, and Reg fell from his chair, collapsing to the floor. Melanie tried to get up to help him, but her legs felt like mud, dense and unwieldy and crumbling beneath her weight. She dropped on top of Reg and tried to roll over to protect herself, but her body refused her commands.

Hannah stood over them, holding a rolling pin, and someone was with her. It was a man with part of his cheek missing and long wounds on his torso. He looked old and very angry.

"Tie them up, beloved," the man said. "Then we'll call their partner."

Partner? Melanie wondered on the word until it sank beneath the padding of her drugged mind.

"And you'll stay with me?" Hannah asked. "If I do this thing you'll stay?"

"Forever," the man said. "Forever and forever and a little bit more."

38

Mike's mother called him down for breakfast, which was itself something of a shock. He couldn't remember the last time his mother had bothered to make toast, let alone pull out a pan and scramble eggs, but this morning, the scent of bacon filled the air and when he walked into the kitchen he saw his mother scrape eggs onto plates and deposit the dirty pan in the sink.

"I think there's some jam in the fridge," she said. "For your toast. If you want it."

"Thanks," Mike said guardedly. "I'm good."

He took the plate and carried it to the table, eyeing his mother and looking for some clue as to what had triggered this sudden bout of domesticity. Her hair and clothes were clean, and her eyes didn't have that distant, dreamy quality he'd come to accept as a permanent fixture of her expression. Lifting his fork, he noticed his hands were trembling, and he knew it stemmed from the conversation he'd had with Melanie, Stuart, and the others the previous day. The hate-filled spirit, Andy, used the people close to you for his violence. Mike remembered seeing a double of his granddad standing on the threshold of his house, slamming the door. He gripped the fork tighter.

"Shocking, isn't it?" his mother said.

"What?"

"That I still remember how to cook a meal," she explained.

"Oh, yeah," he said, forcing a smile. "Is it a holiday or something?"

She set her plate down and eased into her chair, but instead of lifting her own fork, she rested her elbow on the table and cupped her cheek with a palm. "I've been pretty fucked up," she said. "I don't need to tell you that, but it's good for you to know that I know it."

"It's okay," Mike told her. But his unease increased with every moment they spent together at the table. Conversation had rarely been a part of the family dynamic, seeing his mother focused and functional actually scared him, because it wasn't normal. He'd often wondered how she managed to keep her job.

"No, honey, it's not. I've been lost in my own little world, and that isn't fair to you. I mean, I've been popping these pills because the doctors told me to, and I kept telling myself that they're helping, but they really aren't. It's not like I'm coping with anything, or fixing anything, I'm just kind of drifting over the problems, staying high so I don't have to drop down and deal with them."

"You've been through a lot," Mike said.

"Yes, I have," she admitted, "but so have you."

"So, what changed your mind?" Mike asked.

"You'd think I was bananas if I told you," his mother said with a laugh. She shook her head in the cradle of her palm. "Let's just say it came to me in a dream."

"What do you mean?"

"You don't want to hear the ravings of your pill-popping mother."

"Yeah, I kind of do."

She appeared to think about it for a moment. Then she sat up straight and tried to smile, but the gesture looked awkward and she gave into the earnest frown that wanted to control her mouth. "Remember, these are just dreams. Okay? I don't want you to think I've gone crazy or anything."

"I know," Mike said.

"About a week ago, I dreamed that Dory was alive."

A knot formed in Mike's throat. He gripped the fork with such force his knuckles turned white. Could he use it on his mother if he had to? If she came after him, spouting Andy's gospel, could he actually defend himself against his mother?

"See," his mother said, pointing at him. "That expression is exactly why I didn't want to tell you about this."

"What did Dory want?"

"I'm not sure," his mother said. "In the dream, I was in bed and Dory climbed in with me, and I put my arm around her, but she felt soft—barely there at all. And she talked, but I don't remember what she said; I just remember holding her and wishing she didn't feel so… so insubstantial, like condensed fog or something. I can't really explain it. But it bothered me. We spoke for a long time, because I wanted her to know how much we missed her, and she interrupted a lot. Neither of us really seemed to be listening to the other. At any rate, I woke up the next morning and remembered the dream but almost none of the details. Then it happened again the next night. The same thing: Dory climbed into my bed; we talked; and then I woke up in the morning, remembering some of what happened but not really feeling anything about it.

"Last night was different," his mother continued. "Last night, Dory didn't come but your granddad did. I woke up, or thought I'd woken up, and Dad stood over the bed, staring down at me. He said some awful things, and I remember them because I knew he was wrong. I figured he was just having one of his spells, and I thought it was strange that his mental troubles should have followed him into death. But he kept talking, and finally he climbed into bed and put his arm around me, and I couldn't even feel it."

His mother paused and drank some orange juice. Tears formed in her eyes.

"And that's the thing," she told him. "I couldn't feel them. My daughter.

My father. Even though they were just dreams, I should have felt something, but there was nothing. When your sister was taken… after they found her… everything hurt so badly, I didn't think I'd be able to stand it, and thanks to my doctor and a variety of chemicals, I didn't have to. But I need to get off of them. I'm *going* to get off of them. I want to be able to feel again, even if it's just pain. They deserve that."

Mike knew he should say something but his thoughts and emotions conflicted; they collided like battling fish in his head. Andy had appeared to his mother, but he hadn't driven her to violence. Why?

"So, that's your mother at her craziest."

"I'm glad you told me, but are you sure you should just stop taking your pills?"

"I'll have to wean off of them, I imagine. I'm going to talk to my doctor today, but we'll get it worked out." She reached across the table and placed her hand on his, the same hand with which he still clutched the fork. "I love you, Mike, and I'm sorry I haven't been terribly available. That's going to change, I promise."

After Mike nodded, his mother pulled her hand away, and they shared breakfast. Despite his mother's story, her revelation, and her promise, he kept alert with the fork in his hand not knowing if his mother had set a trap in the hopes Mike would drop his guard. He knew it was paranoid; he believed everything his mother had said, but he also knew that nothing was what it seemed. Once breakfast was over and his mother left for work, Mike took his plate and the fork to the sink. Then he ran up to his room and retrieved his cell phone.

He had to let the others know what he'd found.

39

When he'd called to request a visitation with Derek Thomason, the soft-voiced man on the other end of the phone had suggested he not waste his time. True to the news reports, Derek Thomason, hadn't spoken a word in over a year and was unresponsive to both prison personnel and his fellow inmates. According to the voice on the phone, Thomason sat in his cell and stared at the wall. He didn't cry. Didn't pray. "You might as well visit a mannequin," the prison administrator told him.

Stuart had heard the reports about Thomason's catatonia, but thoroughness demanded he attempt speaking with the man, so he drove north and west toward the Stiers Correctional Facility. Fields of scrub grass and dry earth spread from the roadside to the opposing horizons. Amid this desolate, ugly landscape, Stuart found himself relaxing, at ease for the first time in days. No one could touch him here. He didn't have to look over his shoulders, wondering if the next friend he saw or the next colleague had been sent by Andy to cancel his life with a gun, a club, or a knife. This possibility had settled on him early this morning. Last night had been about grief, real grief, unhampered by soured emotions and bitter memories. He still regretted that the last handful of years of his marriage to Clarissa had been so stained by her insecurities, but he understood she'd felt the necessity to needle him and coax his temper. They should have talked about the problem long ago. Stuart hadn't even realized his behavior was a problem, because Clarissa had made an issue over every tiny thing, but never once pointed out the truthful source of her aggravation. Stuart wished he could apologize, wanted a few moments with Clarissa's real spirit, to let her know how sorry he was, but he didn't believe that would happen. An entity like Andy didn't prove the existence of ghosts, simply the existence of evil.

Upon waking, Stuart had begun to wonder who Andy would choose to hunt him. The obvious answer was Clarissa's brother, Thumper. According to the pattern Stuart had noted, Thumper and he were closer to Clarissa than anyone else. But this theory had faults. Roy Dermott hadn't been close to Chance Whiting at the end of his life, certainly not closer than his wife or children, but Wally Pepper had been coerced into attacking the man, and Carney's downstairs neighbors had no known connection to the Baxter-Thomason crimes at all, nor had Carney for that matter. She'd only rented the couple a house. So, Stuart decided it was best not to hang all of his security on the assumption of a distinct pattern. If Andy wanted him dead, the threat could come from Thumper or Harlan or any one of a dozen colleagues he saw at the station on a daily basis. All of this sufficiently worried him and made his day away from Barnard all the more welcome.

At Stiers he parked and worked his way through security checkpoints until he was led into a small waiting area where two other men stood. By the looks of them, the other two men were lawyers, and when a guard named Trevor came in to read through a list of instructions, both men rudely ignored the young guard. Though familiar with the rules, Stuart listened attentively and thanked Trevor when he finished. Then he waited.

Both lawyers were led out within twenty minutes of Trevor's closing remarks, but Stuart sat for an hour, and then another thirty minutes, before a square-jawed behemoth in a guard uniform stepped into the waiting area.

"Detective," he said, "I'm Officer Zeke. I've been instructed to take you to see Thomason, but I'm going to ask you to reconsider."

"I understand," Stuart said. "Thomason isn't likely to speak to me. That's fine. I'd still like to try."

"Right," Zeke replied, "as long as you know."

So, he followed officer Zeke through a series of corridors, three checkpoints, and one cellblock, where their presence caused hardly a stir among the inmate population. On the far side of the block, they reached another checkpoint, lorded over by a gruff guard with a shaved head.

"We got better things to do than waste time with this shit," the guard informed Stuart. "What the hell could you possibly need to ask him at this point anyway?"

Despite an overwhelming urge to berate the idiot and tell him to mind his own business, Stuart kept the exchange civil. "Doing my job," he said and left it at that.

The bald guard sneered and shook his head, then flipped a toggle that released the door lock. Zeke escorted Stuart into the hallway and led him around a corner into a longer corridor, where he faced a dozen metal doors. Every door had a window at face level, but locked steel plates covered all except one.

"That's Thomason's," Zeke said, pointing to the open window. "You can't go in, but you'll have enough privacy. Those doors are about as soundproof as you can get."

"Then how am I supposed to talk to him?"

"Detective, he isn't going to talk," Zeke reasserted. "You can lift that narrow hatch and say what you need to say, but don't hold your breath for a response."

Stuart noted the narrow mail-slot type hatch beneath the window and nodded.

"Look, I know why you're here," Zeke said. "I know what he did to your wife, Detective Lancaster, but you aren't going to get closure. Even if he could talk you wouldn't get it. You're better off just going home and getting on with your life."

"Thank you," Stuart said. "I appreciate your concern, but this isn't about closure. It's something else."

Zeke didn't appear convinced, but the guard didn't seem inclined to argue the point either. He stepped back and waited for Stuart to approach the cell.

Derek Thomason wore a red prison-issue jumpsuit and sat on a cot, his body turned slightly so that he faced the corner away from the open window. His chestnut-colored hair was long and unkempt, tangled, unlike the perfectly styled coif he'd worn when the cameras were on him. A low-watt light, likely recessed high in the ceiling of the cell, cast a grim yellowish glow on the scene. Looking at the man in the small enclosure brought a flare of sympathetic claustrophobia to Stuart's chest. He didn't know how people could survive in such a small environment and not lose their minds completely. Of course, the question was moot when applied to a lunatic like Thomason.

Stuart checked the mechanism for the latch and after two unsuccessful attempts managed to open it. "Derek?" he said. Thomason didn't move, not so much as a flinch at the ratcheting sound of the latch. "Derek, my name is Detective Stuart Lancaster, and I need to talk to you."

Thomason didn't move.

Stuart considered the situation and realized he could spend the rest of the morning and most of the afternoon babbling at the hole in the cell door and get nothing more from the prisoner than a fine impression of a statue. He was already cutting it close for his visit to see this psychopath's partner because he'd been made to wait nearly two hours before Zeke arrived to walk him through. He couldn't waste any more time.

"Andy is back," Stuart said. "I want to talk to you about Andy."

He looked with anticipation through the window, but Thomason remained motionless. Head turned, body slouched, knotted and oily hair hanging forward like a frayed curtain to hide the side of his face. There was no reason for Thomason to care about Andy or what he did; the man probably felt pride in the accomplishments of his adopted monster. This was getting Stuart nowhere.

He turned to leave, but a blur of motion stopped him. Gazing into the cell, he saw that Thomason still stared at the corner, but the man's arm was raised toward the window, the palm of his hand facing out. On the skin, he'd carved a symbol, like a figure eight on its side with a bar cutting diagonally through the center. Stuart recognized the symbol from the house on Ash Street; it had been on nearly every wall and door in the place when Thomason and Baxter were apprehended.

But Stuart couldn't get a word out of Thomason. He asked calmly what the symbol meant, and then he demanded an answer. He even resorted to bribery, telling Thomason he would pay for every word the inmate spoke, but the killer's silence could not be countered with greed. The symbol on his palm formed the only answer he intended to give.

Stuart had to hope Selma Baxter proved more forthcoming with information. He had to hurry if he intended to see her before the day was out.

Signs along the hallway read, *Wet Paint*, and the chemical stink of latex grazed Stuart's sinuses. Thick-paned windows ran on either side of him as he followed a stout Hispanic man toward a metal door at the end of the corridor. The guard was named Jorge, and he swaggered ahead of Stuart, looking casual, just another walk down the hall. Despite the fresh paint and the windows, Stuart was struck by the uniform dinginess of the prison—they were all like this. Even the administrative areas that few prisoners ever saw suffered a depressing atmosphere that couldn't help but suck the joy out of a person's soul, not that Stuart had much joy to feed the place.

At the door, Jorge paused. He turned to Stuart and said, "You know the drill, but you get no leeway here. Cop or not, you don't touch the prisoner. You don't hand her anything and you don't take anything from her. You don't leave your chair. I'll be here the whole time observing the visit, and any deviation from the rules will result in your removal from the room with the possibility of prosecution should your infraction warrant such action. Do you understand?"

"Yes," Stuart said.

"Cool," Jorge told him, lifting his arm in a wave to signal the control room sentry. A dull buzzing filled the corridor and the squat guard opened the door. "Ten minutes."

Stuart stepped forward and then stopped in his tracks.

Selma Baxter had already been brought into the room. He hadn't expected that, nor had he expected her to still appear so youthful and innocent. She sat on the other side of a broad rectangular table, hands folded neatly in her lap, a low drape of chain ran from the manacles on her wrists to a horseshoe bolt on her belt. Brown hair, washed and brushed smooth, hung in shimmering ribbons on either side of her soft oval face. The dichotomy of her fresh appearance and her gloomy surroundings struck him only moments before a jolt of anger tightened his jaw.

Selma, despite her prom queen facade, had been half of the duo who'd murdered his wife and ten other people. With her lover she had humiliated them, tortured them, cut them, burned them, strangled them. She was a monster and the mother of a monster—the thing they'd called Andy.

Selma smiled warmly at Stuart, gazing at him through her long eyelashes with an expression of serene flirtation. "I know you," she whispered.

"My name is Stuart Lancaster," he said. He tried to be casual yet confident as he crossed the room to his chair, but the joints in his knees and ankles felt as if they'd been replaced by pads of steel wool and each step proved an effort. He sat down and faced the dreamy-eyed killer. "Detective Stuart Lancaster," he said to exert his authority.

"Right," Selma purred. "I've seen you on the news. Some weird stuff. What's up?"

"You know what's going on in Barnard?" Stuart said.

"Not really," Selma said casually. She leaned back in the chair, causing the chain in her lap to rustle. "Everyone's being really mean. It's like I used to have all of these friends, but none of them call anymore and they won't let me email anyone. It's like being grounded, and it totally sucks."

Like being grounded, he thought. Could this animal really be that vapid?

"Mom and dad never visit, and they won't let Cassie come over, and Cassie was like my best friend, but she's blown me off. What a bitch."

"About Barnard," Stuart said, trying to keep the conversation on track.

"What about it? I told you; I'm like totally out of the loop."

"But you've seen the news."

"Yeah," Selma said, "fun, right?"

"Fun?"

"Everybody seeing ghosts," Selma said. "It's like crazy-bananas. Oooo, ghosts and spooks." She tried to lift her hands to wave them, but the manacles kept them at breast level. "All those nuts out there and they go and lock me up. Totally unfair."

"You killed eleven people, Selma."

A flash of hurt melted her features. "I didn't kill anyone. That was Derek. I couldn't do those things."

"I've seen the videos, Selma, so you can file that innocent bullshit right now. I'm not here on behalf of the courts or your lawyer or the police. Nothing that is said here is going to hurt or help your appeals."

"So what do you want?" Selma asked. "Are you one of those freaks who wants me to apologize?" She batted her eyes and leaned forward, her face etched with mock sympathy. "I'm very sorry about your wife, Detective Lancaster. If I could take back what Derek did, I would, and I know nothing I can say will ease your pain or suffering, but I'm ever so sorry."

His stomach rolled with disgust. Stuart clutched the edge of the table tightly, took a deep breath, struggled with his temper and the urge to lunge across the table and beat the beautiful face to a swollen mush.

"All better?" Selma asked, again batting her eyes. "Or do you want my apology on video? I know how much you like making movies."

Stuart flushed and then took a second to let the worst of his anger pass. Selma noticed his emotion and ran her tongue over her lips, gazing at Stuart with a half-lidded gaze that repulsed him.

"We could make a hot video," Selma persisted. "I'm already wet just thinking about it. I can make you feel so good, detective."

"I don't think so," Stuart replied coolly.

Her flirtation hadn't got the effect she'd wanted, and Selma dropped the dreamy-eyed façade. She slumped forward. "If you want an apology, go to Derek. He's the one that did everything. He's the freak."

"Derek isn't really taking visitors these days."

"Oh my god," Selma gushed as if she were hearing a piece of gossip she couldn't wait to expand upon. "I know! Weird, right? He's like all coma toast. What is *that* about?"

"I'm not here to talk about Derek."

"I bet he still looks hot," Selma said absently, pulling her lower lip between her teeth and clamping down. She released it and her tongue flicked out at the corner of her mouth as if to recover a fleck of spittle. "Yeah, he still looks hot. Nothing's ever going to change that. He should have been a model. I always told him we should bail Barnard and go to New York, and he'd be a model and I'd be an actress. It would have totally rocked. But no, not Derek. He had other plans—the lame-o. Now I'm here, and how much does that suck?"

"Tell me about Andy," Stuart said.

Selma Baxter reared back with an expression of dazed shock, and the excitement in her eyes was suddenly gone, as if twin hatches had just slammed shut.

"You remember Andy," Stuart said.

"Andy isn't real," she muttered, looking down at the chain in her lap.

"You talked to him like he was real," Stuart said. "On the tapes, he sounded very real. You even gave him a voice."

Selma visibly shuddered, then shook her head. "Just another one of Derek's fucked up games."

"It wasn't Derek. He was on screen while Andy was talking. You were both on screen, so who was making that voice?"

The atmosphere in the room changed, right along with Selma Baxter's expression. The bratty killer's anxiety melted away, leaving room for playful contempt, which she transmitted with a smirk. The air seemed to rush from the room then, leaving a weight in Stuart's chest. He waited for the woman to continue her game.

"You shouldn't have let it out," she said. Her voice was lighter now and vaguely humored. "He's really going to fuck things up. Seems like that's all he ever wanted to do."

"What is he?"

"A nothing."

"A nothing can't appear all over town; he can't convince people to kill each other."

"Whatever. I don't know what else to call him. It's not like we asked for him to hang with us. One day, we went downstairs and Andy was there."

"Derek didn't conjure him?"

Selma spluttered a machine gun of giggles. "Derek?" The idea seemed to be absurd to her. "He pretended he was all dark and magical, but he didn't know shit. I knew more about that junk than he did, and I don't know anything except what I've seen on TV. Andy came to *us*, and the longer he stayed, the more *Andy* he became."

"What does that mean?"

"I told you, he was a nothing at first. Just a boring shape. He didn't talk or do anything. He was just there, like a shadow the color of old hamburger, but he learned fast—totally fast. In a couple of days he was talking, but he had this high fucked up voice like a guy when his balls get smashed. I hated hearing him talk, even later when he impersonated other people's voices."

"What other people?"

"The ones Derek brought home."

"You mean your victims?"

"Derek's victims."

Stuart saw no benefit in arguing the point. He didn't have much time left with Selma, and he still didn't have enough information about Andy.

"So this thing could impersonate voices," he said. "And he could look like anyone he wanted to."

"Pretty much," Selma said. "But he never looked quite right because Andy was just mist and shit. When he first tried to impersonate a person it looked like some retard had knitted the guy, all loose and full of holes, but Andy got pretty good. Andy learned stuff fast, and Derek, who was thinking he was all Harry Potter, was convinced he'd summoned this thing and had to teach it shit."

"Like what?"

"Like everything," Selma said. She blushed at the edges of her smile and looked away. "Yeah, everything. But Andy got all bad ass there near the end. Total attitude. The fucking dweeb couldn't even do anything. Not really. If you gave him a knife or a rope, he could hold them, but he wasn't strong enough to make 'em work, so he got bitchy about it, like a guy who can't get his dick hard and blames you? He was telling us… telling Derek… how to cut people and kill them. It made him crazy and freaky and shit. Andy would scream like a fucking cat being ripped in half if he didn't get his way. Bastard."

That's because you wanted control, Stuart thought. *You wanted to tell Derek who to cut and how. Andy got that from you.*

"So how did you control him?" Stuart asked.

"More B.S.," Selma said. "Derek had a ring with this ugly symbol on it. He said it was a gold ring, but I totally doubt it. If it was, it was probably ten carat or something lame. Anyway, he told Andy that the symbol on that ring was magic, and Andy couldn't cross any boundary with that symbol on it. So if it was on a door, Andy couldn't walk through it. Totally weak, right? But it worked. Andy was like freaked by the symbol, so Derek started painting it and carving it all over the place. The weirder Andy got, the more symbols Derek made. Finally, he told Andy that the ring was all deadly and shit and if Andy ever touched it or was touched by it, he'd vaporize."

"And Andy believed him?"

Selma burst out laughing. "Hells yeah. Andy may have been a cruel M.F., but he was no genius. He believed everything we told him, and the ring thing totally messed with his head. It was such fairy tale bullshit. Oooooo. Bow to the ring. Fear *the ring*. It was epically lame, but it worked. After Derek told Andy what the ring could do, he totally disappeared. We never saw it again."

"Where did Andy go?"

"Don't have a clue," Selma said. "I think he was afraid and hiding."

"What happened to the ring?"

"It's just junk."

"Maybe, but do you know where it is?"

"I don't know. Gah, it's not like they told me what they did with all my stuff when I came in here."

The door behind Stuart opened and Jorge poked his head in the room. "That's time, Detective."

"One more question?" Stuart asked of the squat guard.

Jorge nodded and stepped back into the corridor, but he didn't close the door. Stuart turned his attention back to Selma, who seemed lost in a particularly unpleasant daydream. Uncertainty filled her eyes, and she chewed her lower lip.

"Why did you kill my wife?" Stuart asked.

"I didn't kill anyone. It was Derek."

"Then why did Derek kill her?"

Selma cast a glance at Stuart, looking put upon and annoyed. "It was just something to do," she said as if describing a minor act of vandalism or a harmless joyride.

He didn't respond. Stuart stood and walked toward Jorge who presented a look of disgust for the beautiful young Selma.

"Detective," she called. "Detective Lancaster."

"Yes?"

"I think we really pissed Andy off," Selma said. "You don't think he'll come here do you?"

Stuart thought about his reply. He turned back toward Jorge and the door, and said, "I couldn't be that lucky."

It was just something to do.

Stuart fumed over the phrase, driving out of the prison's lot. Boredom as motive struck him as wholly unlikely for the pair of privileged lunatics. The psychology went deeper, stemmed from something genetic or environmental that hadn't come up in the psych evaluations; it had to. This level of ice-cold cruelty didn't manifest randomly in a normal person. It couldn't just appear out of thin air. Human beings didn't start chopping each other up because there was nothing good on TV. Or at least, these were the things Stuart told himself. Another part of him thought that the behaviors of Selma Baxter and Derek Thomason were indicative of a time when entitlement and desensitization went hand in hand, and the pursuit of sensation—even a sensation as horrific as murder—was better than feeling nothing at all.

Alone neither one of them was a threat, but together they formed a third personality, a brutal, sociopathic killing persona.

Stuart considered the being they called Andy in light of Melanie's theory. Their doppelganger, their spirit, the hexekind had not imprinted on either Selma or Derek. It was this third personality, the violent one made of equal parts Selma Baxter and Derek Thomason—an unsympathetic and vicious personality, concerned only with power and pain—that had imprinted on Andy. He could have appeared in any other house on any other block and manifested as the double of a shy banker or sexually repressed shop clerk; he might have formed as the reflection of a florist whose only compulsion was model trains or internet porn; but Andy had either stumbled upon or been drawn to that basement, that house, that street. He'd soaked up the sickness of his two subjects and then allowed them to tutor him. But if Melanie was right, then Derek Thomason's ring would stop this being. It was a product of its creators, and Andy knew nothing beyond their instruction and decree; its entire existence and reality hinged on what it had been taught.

But where was the ring? Stuart had some ideas. He could check the evidence log back at the station. He would call Stiers and inquire about Thomason's possessions, those that had transferred with him from county. If the ring didn't appear in the prisoner manifest, if Thomason had hidden the thing, Stuart was in for some long days, tracking it down.

They had an answer, though, and it brought Stuart a glimmer of hope.

The monster was real, but there was a way to kill it.

He used the drive-thru at a fast food joint to pick up dinner before taking the ramp onto the highway. Night slowly fell. An unexceptional sunset greeted him as he rose onto the main stretch of interstate—no reds, no purples. The blue above the horizon appeared like a blank movie screen with black valances above and below, setting off the pale blue glow. Already anxious to find Thomason's ring, Stuart knew the drive back to Barnard, all three hours of it, would be frustrating as hell. It was too late to call Stiers; the administrative clerks wouldn't be able to run down Thomason's property until morning, which meant a long useless night.

Stuart thought about Hannah and Michael; Melanie and Reg. They'd be okay if they kept to themselves. The danger from Andy himself was nominal. Friends and family—those were the real threats. If Mike and Hannah stayed inside, and kept out of sight, they'd make it through. Of course there were other survivors, different loved ones of different victims, all of whom might become targets of Andy's attentions, but few of them remained in Barnard, and Stuart hoped Andy hadn't gotten around to them yet.

His cell phone rang and Stuart put down the lousy hamburger he'd been gnawing on before retrieving the device from the console. He checked the ID on the screen and saw with great unease that the call was from Harlan. Stomach kicking with guilt for having ignored his friend's messages for the last few days, Stuart accepted the call.

"So what's the fucking deal?" Harlan asked angrily, in lieu of saying hello. "We're not friends anymore or what?"

"Calm down, short round," Stuart said, thinking a bit of levity would defuse Harlan's temper.

Wrong.

"Fuck that shit," Harlan said. "You don't take my fucking calls. Don't return them. I'm taking shit from every front, and you decide to throw a heap on yourself. Are you really so backwater you'd trash twenty years of friendship over this? Calm down, my ass."

"Harlan, you know me better than that. There are things going on right now that I can't go into, and for that matter, I shouldn't have to fucking defend myself to you. If I haven't called it's because there's a damn good reason. It has nothing to do with the gay thing, okay?"

"Bullshit," Harlan replied.

"You saw the recording, Harlan. You know what's going on in town."

"What the hell does that have to do with anything?" Harlan roared. "You're a fucking cop. You're not a ghostbuster, and even if you were it doesn't explain the way you're freezing me out. What is it? Is it because I knew about that kiddie ring? You think I was part of that? A client? You think I'm sick enough to mess with kids?"

I don't know, Stuart thought. How else had Harlan come by such privileged information?

"That's what you think."

"No, Harlan…"

"Jesus fucking Mary and Joseph, you think I'm some kind of pedophile fuckwad like Taylor."

"Harlan," Stuart said.

"No. Fuck it. You figure I'm one kind of pervert, so I'm *all* kinds of pervert."

"I don't…"

"I expected better from you, Stuart," Harlan said. Then he hung up.

Stunned and uncertain what had just happened, Stuart kept the phone against his ear as if waiting for Harlan to reconnect, laughing about having just yanked Stuart's chain. *Got'ya*, Harlan would say. *Meet me for a beer at the Ox.* Harlan wasn't coming back on the line, though, Stuart knew. And even though he considered calling his friend, Stuart didn't. There were more important things to worry about right now than Harlan's temper tantrum. In a few days, once Andy had been dealt with, Stuart would call and take his friend to breakfast. They could hash through this bullshit without a ton of bricks hanging over their heads and maybe get their friendship back on track. Maybe. Stuart didn't believe Harlan had been one of Winston's clients, but he didn't *not* believe it either. The idea sickened him, and he wished he could be certain that his friend would never swim in such a foul moral pond, but he couldn't. Not yet.

Just don't go near him for now, Stuart thought. *Let him calm down or he's likely to rip your damn head off.*

In the wake of this thought, Stuart grew cold. What if Harlan's rant had been the preamble to a decidedly more physical and final confrontation? Harlan was being irrational. Was this the result of natural stress, or had Andy influenced him?

Christ, Stuart thought. *Not Harlan.*

In a straight up fistfight, Harlan could kick his ass. Stuart had no doubts about this. The man, despite his short stature and thick build, had proven superior in every fight Stuart had ever seen him in. And Harlan owned guns—everyone in fucking Barnard owned guns.

"Shit," Stuart whispered.

Harlan could get into his house, could meet him in front of the hotel, could stake out the station house—because half the force knew the man—patiently waiting to put a bullet in Stuart's head. No one knew Stuart better than Harlan Teague, which would have put the man at the top of Andy's list, and if Harlan succeeded, the others would be fish in a barrel.

40

Mike was beginning to get worried when Stuart called. He'd tried to reach Melanie and Reg all day but Melanie's phone kept sending him to voice mail. Unable to concentrate on anything real, he'd called Gwen but she'd sounded uncomfortable and offered little more than small talk; he'd tried to immerse himself in a video game, and then attempted to watch television—anything to fill the creeping time—but no distraction, regardless of its sensational imagery or audio bombast worked to alleviate his anxiety. He sat in the chair in the corner of his room, looking at the blank television screen with his stomach churning. Melanie should have answered her phone. She should have called him back.

Instead, Stuart Lancaster called and told him not to worry.

"I just got off the phone with Hannah," Stuart said. "Reg and Melanie were with her most of the day, going over names and making phone calls."

"Well, why didn't they call me back?" Mike asked.

"I don't know," Stuart said. "Everyone has to have one of these damn cell phones and then they don't use 'em when they should. I was heading over to the hotel to meet up with them, but Hannah told me they were interviewing the sister of one of the victims, so they'll be another hour or two yet."

"Oh, okay."

"Look, Mike," Stuart said, "I called because I've got some information, and I figure it's best not to keep it quiet."

He listened as Stuart told him about Derek Thomason's ring and the symbol at its center. Mike remembered the symbol from his visit to the house on Ash Street, but he wondered how a random symbol could hold so much power over this entity, how it could kill it, based on nothing more than Derek Thomason's claim. It hardly made sense, but then rational was a bit much to expect from a spirit that stole its appearance from the dead.

"The thing is, I don't know who to trust right now," Stuart said. "The more I think about this thing and what it's made people do, the more I'm convinced it has to have some influence over them, like the way you felt depressed and disoriented when Andy was near."

"Do you think it can make anyone it wants kill?"

"I don't know, but it doesn't seem to need much to motivate them. For now, I'd suggest you stay away from as many people as you can."

"That's helpful," Mike said. "You want me to lock myself in my room?"

"It's not a bad idea," Stuart told him. "If things go well, we'll be done with Andy in a day or two."

"And when have things ever gone well?" Mike asked. "You can't expect me to just sit around and see which one of my friends Andy sends to kill me."

"Then what do you want to do, Mike? You're not likely to be any safer with me or Melanie or Reg."

"At least I won't be alone."

"Okay," Stuart said, "but I have to make a stop at the station. I could be there awhile and I'd rather not have to explain you, especially since I'm technically on leave for the next two weeks."

"I'll figure something out. Should I meet you there?"

"No. There's a restaurant down the street called Lulu's. It stays open until ten, and I should be done by then. Meet me there."

"See ya," Mike said.

He shoved the cell phone in his pocket and headed for the door.

41

Pulse like a bass beat in her head. Pounding. Echoing. Aching. The painful rhythm galloped through her skull and down her neck to spread out in waves. Melanie floated as if suspended in thick syrup through which she somehow managed to breathe. Her fingertips tingled. Her legs were engulfed in stinging nettles and she couldn't feel her feet at all. Better to sleep. Waking up hurt too much…

"*No, Stuart. They just left…*"

Stuart, Melanie thought, and his face surfaced from the mire filling her head. Where was Stuart? His face remained with her for only a moment. Then thick waves of muck lapped at his cheeks and jerked his visage away to be replaced by ripples in the swampy contents of her head, pulsing to the miserable aching bass beat.

Better to sleep…

She had no idea how much time had passed, but the hammering in her head returned, then doubled, and Melanie struggled to open her eyes. Before her, Hannah Bolger spoke on a cell phone, fingering her hair and nodding enthusiastically. Why was Hannah there? Where…

"*Yes, of course. You're right. The interview will be far more effective if we do it at the house. And how many crewmembers will be with you? … Really?*"

Melanie remembered Reg falling to the floor of Hannah's kitchen. Not fell. Knocked. Reg had been knocked to the floor by the woman standing before her. Adrenaline washed away some of the disorienting paste clogging Melanie's thoughts, and the events leading to her sleep came clear. Hannah had drugged them. Sleeping pills or sedatives in that lousy coffee. Why? What was…?

"No, I just assumed you'd have a crew," Hannah said, her voice clear now. "Don't you need someone to run the camera...? Remote? How fascinating… Certainly. I'll see you there at eleven… No, I won't be late… Thank you."

The fog in Melanie's head dissipated sufficiently for her to understand the terrible situation they were in. Melanie tried to move; she wanted to lunge forward and tackle the insane woman, but her muscles were like damp bags of flour, and her arms and legs were tied to the frame of a kitchen chair. Her efforts didn't result in so much as a test of the binds. Attempting to open her mouth to scream, Melanie realized her mouth had been sealed shut with tape. Now more aware of her situation, she felt the tape circling her head, pasted tight over hair and skin.

Hannah threw an annoyed glance at her and hung up the phone. She put her hands on her hips and took a deep breath before walking around the table to stand before Melanie. A hard stinging slap high on Melanie's cheek sent her head sideways. The kitchen broke into half a dozen dislocated images laying one over the other.

"I don't like you," Hannah said. Then she stormed out of the kitchen.

Tears filled Melanie's eyes as fresh pain joined her already anguished body. *What the fuck did that old harpy slip us*? she wondered. Even before the slap, she felt as if she'd been used for a punching bag. She blinked away the tears and turned to find Reg.

He sat limply in the chair, ropes wrapped around his chest and tied at his wrists and ankles. His head bowed forward, and Melanie saw the ridge of blood on the collar at the back of his shirt. In that moment, Melanie convinced herself that Reg was dead; it hit her with a harsh, breathless certainty. Panicked and furious, she struggled against the cords securing her wrists, but they didn't give in the slightest. She attempted to rock her chair closer to his, but feared making too much noise. She looked at him, pleading for his chest to move, just move a little, so she'd know he wasn't dead.

Come on. One breath. Just enough to keep your heart beating.

The fabric of his shirt crinkled slightly then went slack. Melanie stared desperately at his chest, praying she hadn't imagined the motion, and then it came again. One more, she thought. One more.

Reg breathed in and his head swung a touch to the right.

Before Melanie could secure her relief, Hannah walked back into the kitchen, holding a pair of vicious looking garden sheers. She crossed to the small table and set the clippers on the picnic basket print cloth. Unhappy with their placement, Hannah nudged the handle until the curved blades angled toward Melanie. The woman walked to the sink and filled a glass with water, which she downed in a single gulp. At the far wall, she lifted a bright yellow apron with white blossoms from a hook and dropped it over her head. Securing the ties around her back, Hannah returned to the center of the room to face her prisoners.

"Ben had to go out," she said as if explaining her husband's absence to welcomed guests. "He's going to try and talk some sense into Stuart—for all of the good it will do. Stuart is just so stubborn. It's really no wonder Clarissa is furious with him. It must have been like living with a slab of concrete. But that's not my concern. Gossip is the candy of small minds, and I'll have none of it." Hannah crossed her arms and looked at Melanie, then shifted her attention to Reg. "I do not appreciate your intentions," she said. "Either of you."

Melanie tried to speak, but her voice was nothing more than a series of muffled vowel sounds.

"I *know* why you're here," Hannah snapped. "We've already had *that* conversation, but I'll be damned if I'm just going to sit back and let you send my

Ben away."

It's not Ben, Melanie mumbled against her secured lips.

"Do you have any idea what having him home means to me? Do you? Do you have any idea how lonely it's been without him? Do you even care? No. You want to make Ben into some monster, into this ridiculous Andy you keep talking about so you'll feel justified in killing him again. And I will not have it!"

Hannah reached out and retrieved the garden sheers, gripping the rubberized green handles tightly. She thumbed the side and the blades sprang open like the claw of a massive metallic crab.

"If you knew what I went through. All of the empty well wishes force fed by those idiots out there who didn't have a fucking clue. Every day was like having a searing blade drawn down my chest, and all I could think was to reach out to others who were going through what I was going through. I sat and listened for hours to their crying and their guilt and their sadness and their regret, and not once did they ask about me or my suffering. Oh, they had perfunctory questions and empty thanks and false remorse for someone who couldn't possibly be hurting as badly as they were. And then you people made your movie and turned Ben into some kind of amoral sleaze, and I had to sit back and bite my tongue."

Melanie trembled in the chair, feeling palpable waves of anger rolling off of the woman. Hannah brandished the sheers, waving them through the air as she spoke. Vulnerable and incapable of helping herself or Reg, panic slipped into Melanie's system, all but blotting out the physical aches.

"Maybe if you went through what I went through," Hannah said. "Maybe if I cut his throat and let you watch him die before your eyes, you'd have some modicum of understanding for what I have endured." In three quick steps, Hannah stood behind Reg. She shoved the claw-shaped blades under his chin and dug a point into his neck. Melanie screamed. "Is that what I should do?" Hannah asked.

Melanie shook her head furiously.

"Of course it's not," Hannah said. She withdrew the blades from Reg's throat and repositioned them at the side of his head. "Killing him will just make you feel sorry for yourself. You just need to think what your life would be like without him."

Hannah leaned forward and slid the sheers down, drawing an arc along Reg's head. Then she swung the claw upward catching Reg's ear in the joint of the blades. "You need to think about life without him," Hannah muttered.

She snapped the jaws closed, slicing through Reg's earlobe. The nub of flesh bounced from his shoulder to the floor. Blood spurted from the wound in gouts, covering his neck and collar. Splashing the chair and Hannah's festive apron.

Melanie screamed as the fury hardened in her veins, bringing back the bass beat to her temples.

42

Stuart drove through town, surprised by the teaming crowds near Brown Street and the traffic, which remained rush hour thick late into the evening. He navigated into the city center and slowed as he approached the police station's garage. Harlan Teague's silver Hummer idled at the curb between the garage entrance and the street entrance of the station. Under Andy's influence, the damn fool had brought the fight here? Within earshot of fifty cops? Though Stuart considered getting the confrontation over with, surprising Harlan where he sat with a gun to the back of his head and a command to surrender, Stuart couldn't bring himself to do it. None of this was Harlan's fault. He wasn't himself, and Stuart would never get his superiors to understand a thing like Andy. So Harlan would walk, knowing Stuart was on to him, or he'd end up in jail for whatever charges Stuart could make up between the sidewalk and the front desk.

Or he could kill you, Stuart thought.

Rather than pursue any of those options, Stuart braked hard and swerved into the alley running beside the parking garage. He followed it to the back of the building and parked his truck next to the prisoner transfer dock. Running inside, he flashed his badge at the confused rookie sitting behind a counter on the other side of the door. Three minutes later, Stuart was in his office with his computer booting up and his monitor slowly filling with icons.

Briefly he thought about Mike Addison who waited at a restaurant down the street. The poor kid seemed totally adrift, but that was to be expected. He'd lost a lot of family in the last three years. Stuart couldn't fathom how a father could just up and leave in the aftermath of losing a child, though he knew it happened all the time. Tragedies like the one that had befallen Dory Addison brought families together in the short term, but the adhesion seemed to eat away at some relationships. Blame and guilt. Remorse and anger. They gnawed at the family fabric, leaving it frayed and irreparable.

And it was all because of Selma Baxter and Derek Thomason. That spoiled, clueless woman and her catatonic boyfriend had triggered a chain reaction that still rained rubble down on Barnard. Even disposing of Andy, whatever that might mean, wouldn't end the damage, though it might slow it some.

He punched Baxter's and Thomason's names in and began to search the station's documentation, looking first for the chain of evidence, and then the locations of the different items that had been taken from the house on Ash Street. More than likely, Thomason's ring would have transferred with him to Stiers, or was still being held by the District Attorney's office amid a hundred bits of evidence relating to the case. Stuart read through the list of objects—knives, video equipment, power tools, kitchen gadgets, and the personal belongings of their victims—but found no mention of a ring. He performed a search of Thomason's personal items, the things taken off of the killer upon his arrest, but besides a wallet and twelve dollars in cash, Thomason had entered the system with nothing.

Could it still be at the house, he wondered? Could anything have remained hidden after his colleagues had torn that place apart?

They'd missed the DVDs, Stuart realized. The stack he'd waded through last night included a number of discs that had never made it into the hands of the Barnard Police Department. Yes, it was possible Carney had taken the copies long ago, before Alan had burned the place to the ground, but that struck Stuart as unlikely. What he knew about Pamela Carney was that she was a greedy woman, and she would have long ago found a way to make money from those recordings. Had Andy sent Pamela Carney to retrieve the recordings *and* the ring?

His spirits dipped deeper as he realized that if this were the case Carney had probably destroyed the jewelry at Andy's request, or at the very least disposed of it in a manner they would both consider irretrievable.

Checking the clock, he saw that he still had an hour before he needed to meet Mike at Lulu's. He read through the evidence list a third time, but nothing new was revealed.

He shut down the computer and pushed away from his desk. Pamela Carney sat in a cell on the floor below him. She wasn't likely to tell him a damn thing about the ring, but he had to try.

None of the officers on duty even questioned him when he requested access to the prisoner. Stuart had put in for leave. He wasn't suspended or otherwise on record for infractions, so his presence in the holding cells didn't even raise an eyebrow. One of the officers, a pretty young woman with jade green eyes and a determined jaw, asked, "You taking over on this one?" when he asked to see Carney. Stuart had responded non-commitaly, bringing a suspicious glint to the officer's eyes, but she didn't mention it again as she escorted him to the locked gate leading to the cells.

The brutality of Pamela Carney's crimes had earned her a private cell at the end of the corridor, but she wasn't the only person who'd succumbed to Andy's influence there.

"Hey, you," Tim Ohnegian said. "Hey."

Stuart looked at the emaciated young man, who'd put six slugs in Richard

Wolcroff. Ohnegian's eyes appeared dull and unfocused as if he were waking but still mostly engulfed in dream.

"Yeah?" Stuart asked.

"Have you heard from my dad yet?"

"No," Stuart said.

"Fuck," Ohnegian muttered. "Are you sure?"

Stuart didn't bother repeating himself. Instead, he continued to the end of the corridor, where he found Pamela Carney's body.

She was in a sitting position though her butt didn't touch the concrete floor. Her legs were splayed before her, arms folded into her lap. She'd twisted the sheet from her cot into a noose and looped it around one of the bars at her window, then she'd slid down the wall and gravity took care of the rest. She stared out at him with eyes, considerably more vacant than those of Tim Ohnegian. A purple-black nub of tongue parted her lips.

Stuart yelled for assistance, though he knew Carney was far beyond medical care at this point. Alarms sounded, gates crashed. The other prisoners started shouting. Some laughed. Boots and shoes clomped toward him along the corridor, but Stuart kept his eyes on the swollen face of the dead woman, even as he backed away to allow the officers on duty to enter the cell and cut the corpse free.

"Fucking bitch," Detective Brian Hall said next to Stuart.

He turned away from Carney and regarded the detective. The man sounded as if the woman's suicide were a personal affront.

Stuart said nothing, feeling the last thread of hope slipping from his fingers. Where did he look for the ring, now?

"I told them to put her on watch," Hall said. "Son of a bitch. Anyone who comes in that crazy has to be watched."

"It's not your fault," Stuart said. "If someone really wants to die; they're going to find a way to do it. You know that."

"Thanks for reciting the psych guide," Hall said. "Sorry. Sorry. I'm just so pissed off. I ordered the watch. That cot should have been stripped before they put her in the cell."

"How far gone was she?" Stuart asked. He didn't really care at this point, but he thought talking about it might help the younger detective work through his agitation.

"Raving about ghosts and shit," Hall said. "Sounded like a crazier version of Baxter or Thomason, and that is a sentence I never thought I'd speak. She went copycat, right? She kept talking about Andy, just like those two did. She even carved the A's in the bottoms of her victim's feet, but that was only the tip of the loony-burg."

"Yeah?" Stuart asked, humoring the detective. None of this was news.

None of it was going to help him stop Andy.

"Hell, the cavity search alone should have warranted restraints."

"The cavity search?"

Much of the time, entering the evidence room of the Barnard Police Department was no more difficult than flashing a badge, signing a sheet of paper, and saying "Hi" to Burbank, the heavyset disabled officer who monitored the section nights. Stuart had been in and out of the area a thousand times. He'd borrowed video evidence to copy at home for the collection he now found increasingly distasteful. Cameras rode on mechanized brackets in the corners, but they were monitored by colleagues who believed his business in and amongst the detritus of transgression was valid. Only if something went missing would they bother to read the logs, check the surveillance tapes, question him about his presence among the shelves, bins, and lockers.

Tonight was the same. He followed formality and showed Burbank his badge, causing the large officer to snuffle out a laugh. "Yeah, cause I ain't ever seen you before," he said. A familiar joke. Stuart was happy to hear it. It meant Burbank wouldn't give him any trouble.

Stuart signed the log and waited for Burbank to buzz him through. He casually asked where he could find the items taken from Carney and Burbank's face twisted up like he'd just tasted lemon.

During the cavity search, they'd found a balloon containing several pieces of jewelry stashed in Carney's vagina. Stuart could only assume that she'd grown more paranoid in Andy's presence, perhaps growing suspicious of the spirit. It was even possible that her greed outweighed Andy's control, and she had kept the ring in defiance of the thing—if in fact, she had kept the ring. Or she just went bat-fuck crazy.

"I don't care how many times they clean that stuff, I wouldn't touch it with three pairs of gloves on."

"Well, you don't have to. In fact, I'm hoping I don't have to touch any of it either. Just need to check something out."

"Bin A-12," Burbank said, pointing across the section to the back corner. "You need some light back there?"

"Please," Stuart said, setting off in the direction Burbank had sent him.

Lights clicked on above his head, burning away shadows, and Stuart found the locker marked A9-A12. After opening the door, he crouched down and reached for the bin handle, prayers running through his head as his fingers touched metal. He slid the drawer open. Three plastic containers were stacked in the drawer, and he removed the first. Through the plastic sides he noted neat layers of fabric—the clothes Carney had been wearing when she was processed. Stuart set this on the floor and lifted out the second container.

The items inside shifted, clattering and clanking against one another as they slid to the back of the bin. Stuart pulled off the lid, and his eyes fell on a ring, nestled amid three gold chains and a silver bracelet. The ring was masculine with a thick gold band and onyx field. And there in the middle of the black stone, a symbol like those decorating the house on Ash Street was drawn in a thin layer of gold.

Elation poured through him like amphetamines. He dropped the ring into his shirt pocket and sealed up the bin, then replaced the containers and slid the drawer closed before shutting the locker door. On his way out he waved to Burbank and thanked the officer.

"Find what you were looking for?" Burbank asked.

"Got it," Stuart called over his shoulder. He hurried through the reception room and into the hall, turning for the elevator.

Far down the hall bathed in a low watt light, Clarissa stood between the two elevator doors. She didn't move when he skidded to a stop in the corridor. She faced forward. Back straight. Shoulders thrown back. Her voice like air escaping a punctured tire hissed through the hallway. "How could you do this to me? How could you do this to me? How could…?"

The question ran in a terrible loop with no pauses for breath. It worked through Stuart's skin and muscle. Though he understood that what stood before him was not his late wife, not even a fraction of her spirit, Andy's perfectly crafted resemblance to Clarissa sufficiently intimidated Stuart. He reached up and placed his hand on the breast pocket of his shirt, feeling the lump of gold resting there, and he resumed walking toward the abomination dressed up as his wife. When he had cut the distance between them in half, he slid his fingers into the shirt pocket and touched the ring.

Andy-as-Clarissa faltered in the chant. The head ticked sideways.

Does it know? Stuart wondered.

Sensing he had only seconds to kill Clarissa's double, Stuart sprang forward. After two steps he was in a full run. Before him Clarissa's jaw fell away, leaving a gaping hole beneath her upper lip, and the skin and hair began to unravel. Stuart pulled the ring free and held it in front of him, charging the untying shape. But it was already a writhing thatch of frayed threads, whipping low to the floor and scurrying to the side. The stairwell door to his right burst open and the collection of fibers glided through it.

Stuart hit the door just as it was about to click shut, throwing it back against the wall with a deafening crash. He leapt up the stairs, but already there were no signs of Andy. Still he ran, step after step until he reached the ground level. He burst through the door, startling the officer behind the counter at the prisoner transfer exit and looked both ways hoping to see Andy in one of his many forms wandering over the tiled floor. But the lobby was empty except for Stuart and the guard.

"Shit," he said.

Where did it go?

He only had a second to think on this query when a face appeared beyond the mesh of the transfer door's window: Harlan. The man was yelling at him, pounding on the door. His face twisted with a desperate rage.

"Detective Lancaster," the officer said, "is everything all right?"

"No," Stuart said. He pointed at the door. "I want that man taken into custody. I'll explain everything later. For now, subdue him and get him in a cell."

"But it's Harlan?"

"Just do it," Stuart shouted.

He turned away from the guard, ignoring Harlan completely, and set off in a trot across the lobby toward the front of the building. Still, no sign of Andy. No signs of anyone. Behind him Harlan's voice called Stuart's name, but he didn't have time to deal with his old friend. Hopefully the effects of Andy's influence would wear off once the spirit was destroyed.

At the front door he pushed on the handle and walked onto the landing above the street. Harlan continued shouting at the top of his lungs. Stuart saw Mike Addison walking down the sidewalk toward him. Stuart lifted his hand to greet the kid and a gunshot sounded.

The bullet tore through Stuart's cheek, shattering teeth and tearing a divot across the top of his tongue before breaking another row of teeth and exiting in a spray of blood. The impact spun Stuart around, and he maintained a shaky footing for a moment. Then he dropped to the concrete. The world around him smeared into monstrous jostling shapes one piling atop another. Blood and fragments of teeth scraped the back of his throat and he coughed, sending bolts of pain through his body. What happened? How had… Another round of gagging coughs nearly made him black out.

He had to sit up or he'd drown in his own blood. Stuart crawled back against the low wall and propped himself against it. He lowered his chin, let the pooling blood drain from his mouth, and blinked to bring the muddy shapes before him into focus. One form emerged from the others, towering over him and aiming a gun at Stuart's chest.

"You tried to make her a whore," Thumper Tate said. Misery not anger covered his face and filled his eyes. The man dropped a DVD case on Stuart's chest. Stuart recognized it instantly. "You were going to sell your filthy movie so people could watch my sister. Why would you do that, Stuart? She loved you. Why would you stain her memory by making her a whore?"

Stuart couldn't reply. The pain was too great, and even if he could draw enough air to make his defense the damage to his jaw and tongue would never allow him to form the words. Besides, there was no reply. Nothing he said would defuse Thumper now. Andy had gone to him looking like Clarissa, manipulating the man's soft mind and using an old home movie as proof of Stuart's transgression.

I got it wrong, Stuart thought. *I'm sorry Harlan. I thought it was you.*

"She loved you," Thumper repeated.

I know, Stuart thought. *I know that now.*

Then Thumper shot him in the chest. The bullet pierced Stuart's heart, which stopped beating a second later.

43

The scene before Michael Addison took on a hallucinatory protraction with every movement stretching out, broad and fluid. There was Stuart lifting his hand to wave at Mike, and behind the detective a giant of a man with a neat beard and scraggly hair, wearing baggy blue jeans and a checked short sleeve shirt stepped away from the shadows at the side of the building. The man lifted a gun and fired it. So slowly. Then Stuart spun away, a spray of blood disappearing into the darkness beyond the light's touch. The gun's report seemed to come later, after Stuart had finished his turn, exploding in Mike's ears as the detective dropped to his butt on the concrete at the top of the stairs. The big man walked up to Stuart, holding the gun ahead of him. He threw something at Stuart, and it slid down his chest to his lap and then clicked and rattled when it fell to the concrete, and the big man fired again, but this time the explosion accompanied the flash of fire and the waft of smoke.

Mike cried out, some obscenity forgotten the moment it left his lips. Another man appeared in the doorway. This man was short and broad but moved with a speed and grace Mike wouldn't have expected, racing forward and launching himself at the giant with the gun. To Mike, it appeared the man hung in the air for far too long as if defying gravity. He hit the gunman like a cannonball and the two of them soared from the landing above, never touching the stairs but rather crashing to the sidewalk ten feet from where Mike stood. The giant tried to right himself, but the smaller man sprang to his feet and pivoted on his right foot, delivering a violent kick to the giant's head, sending him back to the concrete, moaning.

Above, voices filtered into the night, and Mike turned to see half a dozen men and women in blue uniforms gathered around Stuart. Two had crouched to their knees and were shouting into radios and the other four stood aiming their guns at the two men on the sidewalk.

Mike followed the barrels of their guns and watched as the shorter man kicked away the giant's gun. Once the weapon had clattered away into the street, he returned his attention to the giant, who still lay on his back.

"What the fuck?" the short man yelled. "What the fuck did you do? What did you do?"

The police officers shouted for the man to step away. One of them called him Harlan as if they were friends, coaxing the stout man rather than ordering him. The officers descended the stairs in a neat line, all of them sighting down their guns. Then, Harlan shot around them and ran back up the stairs, while the officers dealt with the unconscious giant.

"Where were you?" he roared at the two officers who now stood above Stuart's body. "I called five minutes ago. I told you that asshole was out here with a gun. I told you. Where the fuck were you? God damn it." Harlan sank to his knees at Stuart's side and said his name. "God damn it," he repeated miserably.

For a moment the scene froze and Mike's chest collapsed as he witnessed the picture of the short man, kneeling, head down, grieving beside the body with the two uniformed officers standing above. The sight struck Mike as somehow religious, reverent. Then the silence broke. More officers crashed out of the building, shouting curses and orders, gathering around the body of their fallen colleague and pushing Harlan away.

Mike stepped back himself, shocked by the fact of Stuart's murder. What was he supposed to do now? Where was he supposed to go? He continued to walk backwards on the sidewalk until a glint of light caught the corner of his eye.

There in the small patch of grass running between the building and the sidewalk he saw something metallic nestled in the blades just beyond a wedge of shadow. Whatever it was couldn't possibly matter, but as he turned away and the bit of metal moved to the corner of his eye, the scene froze again as if his brain were trying to make sense of things by breaking his perception into individual snapshots to be considered and processed before the moment could advance. He turned back to the glimmering object and walked across the grass.

He bent down and picked up the ring, eyeing it and dropping it in his pocket without understanding its importance until the act was completed. He then remembered Stuart telling him about the myth Baxter and Thomason had constructed, the myth that their monster Andy believed—the myth that defined its existence and its destruction.

"Hey, kid," a deep voice called from the stairs in front of the police station.

Mike looked up and saw the man one cop had called Harlan peering down at him. Tears cut shimmering lines from his eyes to his rounded jaw. Three police officers stood at his back, looking quizzically at Mike.

"You okay?" the stout man asked.

Mike turned and ran. Voices flew after him like ravens, demanding he stop, telling him to come back, assuring him it was okay, but Mike kept running.

44

Hannah hadn't returned to the kitchen since storming off after brutalizing Reg's ear, and though she was grateful the lunatic woman had left them alone, Melanie had spent the last sixty minutes in a state of emotional riot. The sick feeling in her stomach had hardened to a sharp-edged stone, and the aches in her body intensified from her strained muscles. Fighting the cords at her wrists and ankles had resulted in nothing but abrasions and cramps in her shoulders. Reg had blessedly passed out, his body forcing him to sleep through the agony. Melanie checked on him every minute, making sure his chest rose and fell. The wound at his ear had stopped gushing, but blood continued to ooze from the severed lobe, leaving a moist trail down his neck and saturating his collar. Occasionally he moaned against the tape covering his mouth, and the noise sent icy blades to Melanie's stomach, but he was alive, and for now, that was all she could hope for.

Eventually Stuart would figure out that they'd never left Hannah's. He was a detective. When Melanie and Reg didn't check in with him, Hannah's was the first place he'd look. How long would that take? Surely, he had to be back by now. Maybe he had some news, something they could use. Even if he didn't, he'd seek them out to share his conversation with Selma Baxter and plan the next steps. If Reg could hold on for another hour, maybe two, Stuart would show up. He'd cut them free and order an ambulance for Reg.

And that isn't going to happen, Melanie thought.

Hannah would have her story in place. Melanie and Reg had been unconscious most of the day, and a day was a long time to cover your ass. Hannah had probably already moved the SUV. God knows, she wouldn't just leave the vehicle out front for everyone to see. No, the woman was psychotic, which meant she had thought this through end to end. The SUV was likely ditched in a cul-de-sac several blocks away, someplace it wouldn't be noticed. Worse still, it could be miles from the city hidden in a wooded area and unlikely to be discovered for days or weeks.

Melanie glanced at the table and the bloodied blades of the garden sheers, and then checked on Reg again. If they were going to get out of this, Melanie had to make it happen. But how? None of her efforts had so much as loosened the binds. She could try to break the chair apart by tipping over, but the thing was sturdily constructed, didn't even squeak when Melanie threw her weight against the cords, so tipping the thing over would likely result in a quick reappearance of their disturbed hostess, and could mean further damage to Reg, or perhaps

Melanie would take the brunt of the punishment this time.

The desperation returned and Melanie clenched her jaw to keep from screaming. Sweat dripped into her eyes. She whipped her head from side to side to clear away the stinging perspiration and then tugged with all of her strength, resuming her futile attempt to slide her arms free.

Hannah appeared in a rush of motion, crossing the kitchen with a cell phone pressed to her ear and her free hand waving before her as if she were brushing aside invisible obstacles. "No," she said. "That's terrible…"

Melanie's heart skipped a beat. She thought Hannah was returning to the hook where she'd hung her apron after severing Reg's earlobe, believed the crazy woman was going to retrieve the garment to continue with her torture, but Hannah reached out and grabbed a small key ring from a hook beside the bloodstained apron. She pivoted on her heels and looked at Melanie. "I just can't believe Stuart's dead," Hannah said, false sorrow staining each word. She scowled at Melanie and continued through the kitchen and into the room beyond. "No, Mike, honey. I don't know where they are. I wouldn't be surprised if they left town. I mean none of this is really their concern. They probably got the footage for their little program and went home."

Hannah's voice became faint and then silenced completely. It hardly mattered; Melanie had heard enough. Stuart was dead. She didn't even know how to feel. Emotions came and went so quickly she could hold none of them long enough for identification and when they had passed, she was left empty and numb. There would be no rescue. She and Reg were now firmly and irrevocably in the hands of Hannah Bolger.

She looked at Reg and wished she could help him, but it was just a wish, and like all wishes it was devoid of any real hope.

"As for you two," Hannah announced, charging back into the kitchen, "Ben and I have some business with your partner. We'll be back shortly." She lifted the sheers from the table and waved them at Melanie. "If you make a mess in here or scratch my chairs, I'm taking your thumbs."

Hannah turned out the light as she left the room. Melanie closed her eyes. She couldn't even cry anymore. There was nothing left.

Melanie wasn't asleep, but her mind drifted through a grim trance, marked with dismal colors pulled from the spectrum of despair. She didn't know how long Hannah had been gone; time had become an irrelevancy. Buoyed by pain and hopelessness she traveled inside her head, searching for some peace, a sanctuary from meditating on the inevitable torment Hannah would offer upon her return.

The shattering of glass startled Melanie, and it did feel like she was being shaken from a deep sleep. Opening her eyes to the gloom of Hannah's kitchen, she couldn't immediately identify the source of the noise. She checked on Reg next to her and his head was turned toward the kitchen door. An arm snaked through the broken pane and slid up the door to the knob. Slender fingers twisted the push lock and then continued up to the deadbolt.

When she saw Mike Addison cautiously poking his head through the open door, she couldn't even muster relief. It was a trick. A sick game Andy and Hannah were playing with them. She damned the flicker of hope that was sparking in her chest. She refused to believe in this apparent miracle.

"Oh shit," Mike said, slapping at the wall until he found the light switch. When the overhead bulb came on, he upped his response to, "Fuck."

He wasted no time in cutting them loose. He pulled a long knife from a block by Hannah's sink, and then knelt beside Melanie so he could saw at the cords holding her arms in place. A rush of blood poured into her numb hands. The needles of pain came a moment later, but Melanie welcomed them, thanked them. Once she was free Mike appraised the tape wrapped around her head. "That's going to hurt," he told her. "You might lose some hair."

As if she cared about anything so trivial as her appearance at this point. Carefully, Mike slid the knife under the tape at her jaw line and slowly cut through. When he finished, Melanie grabbed the edge and ripped; it felt like the top layer of skin went with the adhesive, and instead of subsiding, the stinging sensation erupted into a burning agony, but she was free now. Because of Mike, she would live and so would Reg.

"I called," Mike said frantically, now sawing at the ropes holding Reg. "I saw your SUV outside but thought I should call before I knocked, and then Hannah said you weren't here, and I didn't believe her, but I didn't know for sure. I waited until she left and…"

"I'm glad you did," Melanie told him.

"But Stuart's dead," Mike said.

Through tears, the boy described the last seconds of Stuart Lancaster's life—something about a gun, something about a giant—but Melanie wasn't paying attention. Mourning the detective would have to be postponed. He wouldn't want her grief to interfere with what she had to do. She hurried to the phone to call 911. When the operator came on the line, Melanie demanded an ambulance.

"What is your location?" the operator asked.

"Trace the fucking call," Melanie yelled. "We need an ambulance now. Here. And you need to send the police to Ash Street."

"Miss if you'll just calm down."

"I will calm down when I hear sirens," Melanie told the woman. "My boyfriend has been injured badly and the woman who did it is either on her way to Ash Street or already there, and she intends to kill a man named Mack Durham. Her name is Hannah Bolger, and she held us prisoner in her house."

"Where on Ash Street?" the operator asked.

Melanie gave her the address. "And yes, I know it burned down, but that's where she was headed."

Melanie kept her eyes on Reg and Mike. The boy managed to loosen the cords around Reg's chest, and he collapsed to the side, held in place by the ties at his wrists. "Oh, baby," Melanie cried. She carried the phone with her and knelt down beside Reg. Gently she touched his cheek. His skin felt hot and it was slick with sweat.

That was good, wasn't it? He wasn't cold. That was something.

"He'll get away," Mike said.

Melanie was so distraught she misunderstood the boy. She'd thought he meant Reg, but as she puzzled over the oddity of the statement, she realized he was talking about Andy. She also realized he was right. But that didn't matter. Not right now. Reg needed to be in a hospital and maybe Mack could still be saved. It might not be too late.

Besides.

"He'll be back."

What followed struck Melanie as a near endless quiz show with some of the questions seeming so ludicrous she wanted to slap the individuals posing them. The paramedics started the process. *What did she use to drug you?* As if Hannah had given them a number of options to choose from. *How much did you ingest?* Because she'd managed to work up a toxicology report while tied to a chair. Eventually the first round of questions stopped. The police arrived as the paramedics began working on Reg in earnest and the quiz show started all over again. Melanie tried to be helpful but her concern for Reg made it so hard to focus. She couldn't take her eyes off of him even when answering the officers' questions. The EMTs applied a compress to Reg's ear and the back of his head, where Hannah had clubbed him into unconsciousness, and secured a neck brace before placing him on a gurney. One of the paramedics, a petite blonde who looked like she'd rather be on a beach, carefully retrieved the nub of Reg's earlobe and placed it in a baggie against an ice pack, which was laid beside Reg on the cart. Next to her a detective named Ballard, who looked like he might start crying at any moment read through a list of questions with no more enthusiasm than he would read through a shopping list of feminine hygiene products. Up to a point, the questions were rational enough; then he asked, "What did you do to provoke the attack?"

"Excuse me?" Melanie said.

"What did you do to provoke Ms. Bolger?" Ballard repeated, swiping the back of his hand across his eye. "Did she explain why she was holding you? Say anything at all about motive?"

"No," Melanie told him. She certainly wasn't going to get into the whole Andy affair with this man. She wouldn't even know where to start. She kept it simple. "We were interviewing her for our show. We host a…"

"I'm familiar with it," Ballard interrupted. "Could you have said anything Ms. Bolger might have taken as provocative?"

"I don't know," Melanie said. "But she had the coffee in our hands two minutes after we got here, so whatever her problem was, it started before we arrived. I certainly hope you're not suggesting we deserved this."

"No, ma'am," Ballard said. "We've just had a lot of random attacks lately, and after a while, you quit believing they're all that random."

"Let's move," the blond paramedic said, hoisting her end of the gurney.

"I'm sorry," Melanie told the detective. "Could I come to your office in the morning to finish this? I need to go with him to the hospital."

Ballard nodded slowly and closed his notebook. "I'll meet you at the hospital," he said, then turned away and left the kitchen.

She walked to the side of the gurney and took Reg's hand. He gazed up at her with unfocused eyes, giving her a weak smile.

In the living room, she saw Mike Addison being questioned by a uniformed police officer. Behind him, Detective Ballard hovered like a bodyguard. It occurred to her then that through all of the chaos of the rescue and the ensuing interrogations that she'd never thanked the boy.

"I'll be right out," Melanie told the paramedics. She crossed the room quickly and wrapped her arms around Mike's shoulders, startling the boy for a moment. His posture turned rigid, then he relaxed into the embrace and returned it. "Thank you," she told him. "I have to go, now. But we'll talk soon. Thank you for everything."

"No problem," Mike said.

Then she released her hold on him and hurried outside to the waiting ambulance. She climbed inside next to Reg, and they closed the doors behind her.

At the hospital, the questions started all over again. Climbing out of the ambulance, Melanie noted a number of uniformed officers milling around the entrance. Some smoked. Some cried. All looked miserable. She knew they were here for Stuart, and she shared their sadness, though she had no time to entertain it. Inside, the doctors asked about Reg's medical history, wanting as much detail as possible. Allergies? Chronic Illnesses? Drug use? Melanie answered as thoroughly as she could before they suggested she go up front to fill out the necessary paperwork. Here the questions were written down, but the quiz show continued.

Her system was exhausted but it refused to slow. Once she'd turned in the paperwork she walked outside. Though very late in the evening, the air still carried a comforting heat. The police presence had increased, but none of the uniformed men and women interested her. However, there was a man among them. He was short and stout with a graying Van Dyke and eyes that appeared swollen and bloodshot from crying. She recognized the man. The night she'd met Reg in the hotel lounge, he'd been sitting at the end of the bar, fidgeting and looking like he would jump out of his skin at any moment. The stout man looked at her. Maybe he saw kinship in his misery. He nodded to her as if they were acquainted, then he looked back at his feet while two policemen spoke and wrote down his statement on their notepads.

He's here because of Stuart, too, Melanie realized.

She allowed herself to think about the detective now. Reg was going to be okay, and there was so much relief, but no real joy at the news. Too many others had suffered. Stuart was dead. All of Andy's victims—those that had taken his pedagogy and those his lessons had killed—were only part of the sorrow. Like the victims of Baxter-Thomason families and friends endured the fallout of the core crimes, like waves of grief begun years ago by a couple of psychopathic kids, the ripples continued to spread.

And where was Hannah Bolger now? And Mack? Melanie hadn't heard from him, and the police had told her nothing of what they'd found on Ash Street. She'd called Mack's cell number four times in the brief ambulance ride, gripping Reg's hand tightly and praying the police had managed to interrupt any violence Hannah had planned for him.

When Melanie returned to the admitting area, she saw Detective Ballard sitting on one of the blue chairs, and next to him sat Mike Addison. She'd completely forgotten Ballard's comment about meeting her at the hospital until she saw him, and she didn't expect to find Mike in the detective's presence.

Ballard stood up when he noticed her and Mike did the same. A whole new kind of quiz show was about to begin.

45

Mike was glad to see Melanie. Though Detective Ballard hadn't been unfriendly to him, Mike felt intimidated in the man's presence. He didn't like the smell of the guy's cologne or the unreadable set of his features, and he particularly didn't like the fact the detective had insisted on questioning him about Stuart during the drive to the hospital. At Hannah Bolger's house when Ballard had first approached him, insisting Mike accompany him to a car, Mike had assumed he was being driven downtown, back to the police station. But they'd driven here instead, and then sat in Ballard's car for thirty minutes as the detective questioned him about Stuart's murder. There had been too many witnesses who'd clearly seen Mike at the scene, so he couldn't pull off ignorance of the killing. Instead he'd put it all down to a coincidence.

I was getting coffee at Lulus and walking home when it happened.

You always walk downtown for coffee?

I usually go to Porter's on Brown Street.

But not tonight?

The street's been swarmed since… you know… that thing they photographed.

You knew Detective Lancaster, didn't you?

Sure. We talked some after Dory was… after they found her.

And you know Hannah Bolger?

Some.

Just some? That's not really good enough is it? You were at her house less than an hour after Detective Lancaster was murdered? I mention it what with her having kidnapped and mutilated those two television people. And we got word that Ms. Bolger is implicated in another murder over at the Ash Street property, where it just so happens her husband and Stuart's wife were murdered a few years back. So you can see why all of this has me wondering exactly what the fuck is going on here.

I don't know.

That's not a very useful attitude.

On and on it had gone, always circling back to Ash Street. Mike knew the detective couldn't do anything to him, except maybe haul him in as a witness, but threat came off the guy as thick as his nasty cologne. Mike had been so relieved to leave that car and head into the hospital where a number of people stood by as comforting witnesses. Now Melanie was walking toward him and his strained muscles let loose a fraction of their tension.

"Hi, Mike," she said looking like she wanted to ask him a question.

"Hey."

"Detective Ballard," she said.

"How's your boyfriend?" he asked dryly.

"They think he'll be okay. Thank you for asking."

"I'd like to continue our discussion," Ballard said.

"Okay," Melanie told him. "Mike, why don't you grab a coke or something. We shouldn't be long."

"He's coming with us," Ballard said, putting his hand in the center of Mike's back.

Though surprised Mike didn't question the detective. He stepped away from Ballard's touch and walked beside Melanie and both followed the detective to a small patient lounge on the far side of the building. Chairs with bleached oak frames and mint green cushions ran along the lounge's walls beneath paintings of beach scenes. Mike sat next to Melanie and they both waited quietly for Detective Ballard to begin speaking. He didn't sit but rather took up a position against the far wall, leaning back with his arms crossed over his chest.

"We've had so many people killed in the last two weeks, I can't even keep track of them all. Those are tragedies. Senseless. But tonight my partner was murdered. And none of us are going home until I know why."

"But you caught the guy," Mike said. "The big guy with the beard."

"That's right, we have Philip Tate in custody. We have all of the suspects in all of these cases in custody or in the morgue, but that doesn't explain why it's happening."

From there Detective Ballard started with the attack on a man named Roy Dermott and worked his way through the murder of Stuart Lancaster, naming victims and culprits in each case. He talked about the victims on Ash Street and how all of these people were in one way or another connected to those unfortunate souls. He even mentioned the apparition of Regina Wolcroff. The detective had all of the pieces lined up in a nice row, but Mike knew Ballard was missing the connecting thread: Andy.

"Then tonight, we have you," Ballard said, pointing at Mike, "showing up the very minute Stuart gets gunned down and then racing from there to Hannah Bolger's where Ms. Bell and her boyfriend just happened to be held captive by a woman, who by all counts, was the epitome of a good citizen until about nine a.m. this morning."

"I already told you I was supposed to meet Melanie and Reg."

"Yes, you did," Ballard said, his voice as coarse as sandpaper on steel, "but why were you supposed to meet them, and how did you figure they were at Hannah Bolger's?"

"Detective," Melanie interrupted, "I can't see what you're looking for here, unless you think we're somehow involved. You already have the suspects in custody. You said so yourself. You can't possibly think that Reg or I, or Mike are accomplices in any of these crimes."

"Can't I?" he asked. "You and your boyfriend were at the scene of the Carney murders."

"That's right. We're the ones who caught her."

Mike watched the frustration burn to the surface of the detective's face, and he almost felt sorry for the guy. Ballard wasn't accusing them of anything; he just wanted to know what was happening, needed some kind of explanation for the apparent madness that had descended on his city. He wanted to know why his partner—his friend—was dead. The detective's jaw tightened, and he closed his eyes to express his complete aggravation with them both.

"Okay," Ballard said, "I need to step out for a minute, but I'd like you to wait for me here."

"I should really check on Reg," Melanie said.

"Just three minutes," Ballard said. "We're nearly done here."

They agreed to wait for the detective's return. Melanie grabbed Mike's hand when the door shut behind the man.

"We should just tell him," Mike said. "Even if he doesn't believe us."

"I was thinking the same thing," Melanie said. "He's almost put it together himself. Maybe he *has* put it together, and he's just waiting for us to confirm what he thinks."

"If he starts calling us crazy, we'll just shut up. He can't arrest us or anything. But don't tell him about this." Mike pulled Derek Thomason's ring from his pocket. "We don't want him taking it, especially if he doesn't believe us."

"What is that, Mike?"

"It's Derek Thomason's ring," he said. "Stuart thinks… well… Stuart thought it could stop Andy, maybe even kill him, so we can't lose it or let the police take it."

"We won't," Melanie said. "I'll go get him, and we'll get this over with."

Thank god, Mike thought.

46

Slipping out of the room, Melanie felt like a kid ditching class. A dull sense of guilt like she was doing something wrong covered her like a veil. She checked up and down the hall but didn't see Detective Ballard. He'd probably gone to the Men's Room or outside for some air. Melanie felt lost on this side of the hospital. She wasn't sure which direction took her to the main lobby and which would return her to the emergency room. Noticing a series of signs at the end of the hallway, Melanie set off toward them. She stepped into the intersection of two halls, and checked each corridor. What she saw on her left made her recoil and press against the wall, peering around the corner in disbelief.

Detective Ballard stood at the end of the hall, shaking his head and wringing his hands as Stuart Lancaster spoke to him. Melanie's stomach knotted when she saw the ragged hole in Stuart's cheek and the bib of crimson covering the front of his shirt. She couldn't hear what was being said, but she didn't need to.

Andy wasn't here to share good news.

Melanie ran back to the patient's lounge, bursting through the door and heading straight for Mike. "I need the ring," she told him.

"Andy?" Mike asked.

"He's talking to Detective Ballard," Melanie told him. Mike produced the ring and Melanie slid it into her front pant pocket. "Now, I want you to go back to the emergency room. See if any of those police officers are still there and send them, but whatever happens do not let Ballard get you alone. If he follows you outside, make a scene. Punch a cop if you have to. Whatever it takes."

"I should stay with you."

"No," Melanie said, "I'll be okay."

She guided him into the corridor, and seeing that it was empty save for a lone nurse crossing from one silent room to the next, she pointed down the hall and waited for Mike to go before she set off in the other direction.

So late at night, this part of the hospital felt desolate. Unlike the emergency room, which thrummed with noise and movement, this part of the hospital seemed little more than a dour labyrinth of the diseased. Grim lighting illuminated the institutional blandness of the walls and played off the broad tracks of linoleum, covering the floor. The nurse who had entered a room ahead, returned to the hall. She gave Melanie a curious, yet warm look, then passed her without a question. Melanie turned to watch the nurse, whose silence made Melanie uneasy, fearing that she might be yet another of Andy's forms, but the woman continued down the hall and entered yet another room.

"I thought I asked you to wait in the lounge."

Melanie spun to find Detective Ballard at her back. Behind him, Andy stood, still wearing the appearance of Stuart Lancaster and appraising her with an expression that was both serene and fascinated.

Melanie's mind locked up. She didn't know what to say to the detective. In fact, she imagined there was nothing to say. Andy had influenced the man; reason had fled the building.

Ballard didn't seem to need a response. He drew his gun, freeing the weapon but letting it hang at his side.

"I wanted you to tell me," Ballard said. "I wanted you to explain what was going on, to explain why so many people lashed out at the people they cared about. I wanted to understand, but you wouldn't tell me." He raised the gun, and Melanie felt her insides turn cold and liquid like a mountain stream. "Stuart told me," Ballard continued. "Except, I don't think it was Stuart."

Ballard turned and fired into the chest of the entity that looked like Stuart Lancaster. The bullet entered the bloodstained shirt, dimpling the fabric and then the entirety of the spirit. It passed through, leaving Stuart's form in a state of convulsion. A high-piercing shriek escaped from the mouth. It tore through Melanie's head and she clamped her palms over her ears to muffle the horrible sound.

Stuart's form frayed at the edges, thin tendrils whipped out like wisps of smoke, creating a shifting web of ragged lines. A moment later, the process reversed and the threads spilled toward the core, shifting colors as they ran. Then Andy didn't look like Stuart anymore. Now he had taken on the appearance of a little girl in a red shirt and blue jeans.

Mike's sister? Melanie wondered.

"You hurt me," Dory said, her lower lip pushed out in a child's endearing pout.

"Fuck me," Ballard whispered, taking a step back.

Melanie stepped around the officer, her hands out in front of her, palms up in an unthreatening gesture. Waves of hate fell over her as she approached the creature, making her scalp tighten and putting an aching clamp on her brain. Recognizing Andy's influence as it fell over her, Melanie focused on the little girl's face, refusing to think or to attribute the rage to any person lest it take hold. It was this child—this thing—that deserved her hate.

Hexekind, Melanie thought. Not human. Not deserving of compassion.

"That man hurt me," Dory whined.

"But you hurt a lot of people."

"It's different," Dory said.

"Why is it different?"

"Because when I do it, it's fun."

Dory sprang forward her body spreading into another net of colored threads. It enveloped Melanie like a spider's web, clinging to her body and hair, and a feeling of absolute hatred, unfocused and all-consuming worked through her skin and entered her bloodstream. She'd never felt an emotion this strong. It dominated every thought in her mind.

Die...They all deserve to die...Kill them...Every one of the fuckers...The world is full of victims...More are being born every day...Better than them...Better than all of them...They don't deserve to live...they deserve to suffer...to cry...to bleed...to die.

Far back in her mind, a place where the threads of loathing had yet to touch, spoke a series of names, some of them were people she'd never met—Regina, Chance, Clarissa, Alan, Ella, and more—but the others were—Stuart, Mike, Yvonne, and Reg. And she loved them. She loved them completely.

They all deserved to die.

No, only one thing deserved to die. It was a creation of man; a sick child tutored by two psychopaths wearing the faces of their victims.

Melanie slithered her hand into the front pocket of her jeans and felt the ring. It burned hot at her fingertips. She struggled to free it. The mesh of Andy wasn't strong, hardly there at all but her reflex action was to be repelled by its touch, complicating the simplest of movements. Finally she slipped her finger through the ring and yanked her hand free.

The symbol on its face grazed one of the confining threads, and the ear-piercing shriek sounded, only this time Melanie could not cover her ears. Even if she could it wouldn't have made any difference. The sound resonated in her head, played through her entire body. In this moment, Andy was part of her and she felt its agony as clearly as she'd felt its hate.

Then the confining web was off of her. Melanie fell back into the supporting hands of Detective Ballard, before her Andy continued to screech like a bandsaw cutting tin. The hexekind never regained a human form, but rather floated in the center of the hall, tendrils flailing like the shadowy counterpart to a Tesla globe. Melanie shook free of Detective Ballard's grip and walked forward, the ring pinched between her thumb and forefinger. Slender tentacles lashed out, striking harmlessly against her chest and face. When she reached the center of the writhing entity, she pressed the ring into the core, and the shrieking stopped. The whipping threads broke apart into a rain of static. And Andy was gone.

47

Clouds like steel wool covered the broad Texas sky. Rain pelted the sidewalks in sheets of gray static, and the uncommon morning heat added discomfort to the air. Melanie ducked low, racing from her SUV to the front of the building that housed the police station. When she reached the top of the stairs, she thought to pause, but instead ran faster. Mike had told her this was the sight of Stuart's death, and she didn't want to linger, certainly didn't want to picture Stuart in pain and bleeding all over the concrete landing.

Inside she ran her fingers through her hair to remove the worst of the rain. Then asked a passing patrolman where she might find the ladies room. Standing before the mirror, bathed in the unforgiving fluorescent light, Melanie scrubbed her head with paper towels, wiped her face and neck, and then decided she was just too soaked to do much else about it. She crossed through the building's lobby and entered the police station. At the front desk, she asked for Detective David Ballard. The sergeant she spoke to made a call, talked for a moment, and then pointed to a row of chrome chairs with dove gray upholstery and suggested Melanie wait.

Ten minutes passed, and Melanie had started to think that Ballard wouldn't show. Perhaps a new case demanded his attention, or he'd just changed his mind about seeing her. Regardless of his motivation, Melanie hoped he would show up soon. She hated being away from Reg, though the doctor had told her his condition was stable, and despite the severity of the blow to his head, mixed with a chemical cocktail that included Valium, Ambien, and Xanax, they suggested Reg wouldn't suffer any long term damage, but of course, they couldn't commit to this speculation. Melanie remained worried. Reg couldn't remember what had transpired in Hannah Bolger's kitchen, and his eyes were giving him trouble; he couldn't focus. The doctor pointed out the frequency of these particular complaints following a concussion, stating the symptoms "generally" didn't indicate irreparable harm to the brain.

Last night after finding Mike and waiting with him until his mother arrived to take him home, Melanie had sat down with Detective Ballard, and while she hadn't avoided the whole Andy conversation with him, she had taken great care to assure him he wasn't losing his mind. She'd been in a visitor's lounge this morning, waiting for an update on Reg's condition when Detective Ballard had called, insisting she meet him at the police station; he had something to show her.

She already knew Mack Durham was dead. Kee had left a very sad and uncommonly sincere voicemail message when he couldn't get her on the phone. Her feelings about this were incomprehensible. Too many horrific emotions had besieged her in the last forty-eight hours, and they rose in a din, like a discordant symphony playing multiple dirges—for Stuart, for Reg, for Mack, for Pamela Carney's victims—until none of the music made sense.

Finally Detective Ballard appeared, wearing a poorly-fitted linen jacket and a pair of brown slacks that appeared to have been purchased when Ballard was twenty pounds lighter. He saw her in the chair, and waved for her to follow as he turned back for the hallway.

Confused by Ballard's behavior, Melanie slowly stood and walked in the direction of the hallway, and when she reached it, she saw that he was already inside the elevator, holding the door open for her.

"Is something wrong?" Melanie asked, hurrying into the car.

"Plenty," the detective told her. "We had a team out at Stuart's last night after Phil Tate shot him. Nothing weird in that. Pretty standard in a murder investigation. But officers found a cache of DVDs, some regarding the Baxter-Thomason crimes and others that were totally random: robberies caught on store surveillance; witness testimonies; suspect interrogations. Shit Stuart shouldn't have. He borrowed most of the originals from the evidence room, but he had discs from the Baxter-Thomason case that we never saw. They didn't come through the proper channels, and internal affairs is going to be launching an investigation to see if Stuart had these recordings prior to the arrests of Baxter-Thomason."

A new emotional dirge began to play; it was fear played in a different key. Melanie knew which discs Detective Ballard meant, but she was afraid to tell him that they'd come from Pamela Carney's apartment—that she had stolen them from a crime scene and had made Yvonne ferry them to Stuart.

"It's a mess," Detective Ballard said. "Stuart was a good cop. Damn good. But all of this is going to throw a major shadow on his career, particularly in light of the disc Phil Tate dropped at the scene of Stuart's murder."

"What disc was that?" Melanie asked.

"It's very personal," Detective Ballard told her. "Unfortunately, it will probably be broadcast all over the news in the next few days, but I'd rather not discuss it."

"That's fine," Melanie replied, though intense curiosity suddenly needled her. "So why am I here?"

"I have something to show you. After what they found at Stuart's we have to move quickly. The department is cracking down on information leaks. You can't tell anyone what I'm going to show you. As it is, we may not get the chance to see it."

"To see what?"

"Your partner on the show, Mack?"

"Yes."

"He was conducting an interview with Hannah Bolger at the house on Ash Street, at least what was left of it. He recorded the whole thing, and we retrieved the tape."

Melanie bristled at the idea. "Detective Ballard, unless you need me to identify Mack, I'd rather not have to watch that."

"No, your producer already identified the body in lieu of next of kin. It's a positive ID. That's not why I wanted you to see this. In fact, the portion of the recording I want you to look at takes place after the murder."

Though she couldn't imagine what Ballard would show her, Melanie agreed, but she didn't want to see what Hannah had done to Mack. She insisted on this, and Ballard assured her the video was cued appropriately.

"Have you found her yet?" Melanie asked.

"Bolger?" Replied Ballard. "No. No sign of her." The elevator doors opened, and he led Melanie into a corridor between two fields of glassed-off cubicles. "We have bulletins out all over the state and surrounding region. We assume she saw the emergency vehicles at her house, then fled. It's unlikely she prepared for the likelihood of getting caught, so she should be easy enough to track down once she runs out of money. In here."

Detective Ballard opened a narrow door leading into a small office. Papers and file folders lay strewn on the desk, the filing cabinets and the floor.

"Take a seat in my chair," he told her, pointing to the far side of his desk. He closed the blinds over the window to the right of his door, then peered out quizzically before shutting the ones on the left. "I couldn't get the tape out of the station, but I don't want anyone to know I'm showing this to you." He looked through the glass pane in the center of the door, waved at someone in the far room, then lowered the blinds. Ballard walked around the desk and leaned over Melanie, reaching for the wireless mouse, sitting on a pad to her right.

He clicked on an icon at the bottom of the screen. A video window opened, and at first she saw nothing but gray lines on a black screen. It took her a few seconds to realize she was looking at the ruins of Ash Street; Mack had gone into the basement amid the charred timbers and wreckage to conduct Hannah Bolger's interview. The volume on the audio was low but audible. Something rustled and a terrible scratching sound skittered through the speakers. The image canted dramatically to the side, then righted as if the camera had been bumped, and Hannah appeared on the left, facing away from the monitor.

"Ben?" she whispered harshly. "Ben, where are you? We can't just leave him here. Goddamn it, you promised to stay with me." Tears had come into Hannah's voice, and from her posture and a series of rapid ducking gestures, Melanie knew the woman was searching the wreckage for the monster that had incited her to murder.

Then, Ben appeared. He rose up before the camera lens as if he'd been crouched before it the whole time. Melanie's stomach knotted at the sight of the man's dried wounds and the sickly pallor of his skin. She didn't want to watch this, not now.

"Ben," Hannah cried, still looking into the blackened ruins, unaware that the visage of her husband stood only feet behind her. "You promised."

Ben walked to Hannah's back and reached out a hand. He placed it on the top of her head and slowly stroked downward, his touch barely disturbing the strands. Hannah leapt with surprise and spun to him. A small, warm smile cut across her mouth.

"You didn't leave," she said, happily.

"But I will," Ben told her. "One more place to…"

"There," Detective Ballard said, lunging across Melanie and slapping at the mouse.

"Wait," Melanie said. "What… ?"

The video paused. In the foreground, Hannah looked tenderly at the monstrosity that wore her husband's façade, as if she were standing in a wedding chamber and not the blackened ruins of a crime scene. Detective Ballard pressed his index finger to the upper left side of the screen, indicating a place between a crosshatch of charred beams. Melanie looked at the point, and her heart tripped.

A face peered through the frame of burned wood, or at least Melanie thought it was a face, but the longer she looked at it, the less certain she became. A pale oval-shaped anomaly hovered there, with two distinct shadows where eyes would go. The form had the impression of ears and a dark smudge above the lip. Still, the longer she looked at it, the more it seemed to be just a trick of light, a bit of glare bouncing off of the camera lens.

"Just watch that point while I start this," Detective Ballard told her. He slid around behind the chair, jostling Melanie as he worked through the cramped space. Then he grabbed the mouse and started the recording again.

"…go," Ben said.

"There's always one more place to go," Hannah complained.

But Melanie was no longer interested in their conversation. The strange, pale anomaly had her attention. It floated there between the two beams, gently pulsing like a low-watt bulb, badly wired. Then the light surged, and for a split-second the features of a face became absolutely clear.

"Stuart?" she whispered in awe.

Detective Ballard clicked the mouse and reduced the window to an icon on his desktop.

"Good," he said. "You saw him, too."

"That's…" but Melanie didn't have the words.

"Last night, in the hospital, when Stuart—or whatever that was—appeared to me, I knew it wasn't him. Seeing him again hurt like a punch to the gut, but the way he spoke, the mannerisms, were all wrong. He wanted me to kill you and Mike Addison, and somehow he made it all sound very logical, but even beyond the idea that he'd returned from the dead, it hit me how completely wrong the whole scene was. I saw Stuart's face, but knew it wasn't Stuart."

Melanie wondered how Detective Ballard had eluded Andy's influence. Had others managed to escape his manipulation, and if so, what set them apart? She still didn't know, but she was grateful for it.

"But when I look at that," he said, pointing at the screen, "I see his face for just a few seconds, and I know without a single doubt that that *is* Stuart Lancaster, or at least a part of him. So, please, tell me what's going on, because I don't think I'm going to sleep again until I get my head around this."

Melanie considered what she would say. She leaned back in the chair and began, "I don't know all of the details, but I'll tell you what I know."

END

About the Author

Lee Thomas is the Bram Stoker Award and Lambda Literary Award-winning author of *The Dust of Wonderland*, *The German*, and *Torn*. Forthcoming titles include the short story collection *Like Light For Flies*. He lives in Austin, TX, where he is working on several projects. You can find him on the web at www.leethomasauthor.com

36027466R00160

Made in the USA
Lexington, KY
05 October 2014